WING COMMANDER

HEART OF THE TIGER

WILLIAM R. FORSTCHEN
ANDREW KEITH

BAEN

HEART OF THE TIGER

A Baen Books Original

Baen Publishing Enterprises
P.O. Box 1403
Riverdale, NY 10471

ISBN: 0-671-87653-8

First printing, April 1995

Distributed by Simon & Schuster
1230 Avenue of the Americas
New York, NY 10020

Printed in the United States of America

• PROLOGUE

Prince Thrakhath stood before the throne with head lowered.

"You failed me, grandson."

The Prince remained silent.

"When your new fleet left for Terra you promised that the war was at an end, that the humans would be finished. Now you return, half your fleet destroyed, a fleet that strained our resources to the utmost to build. Our coffers are empty, grandson. . . ." The Emperor paused.

"Empty!" His voice thundered in the audience hall.

Thrakhath looked back up.

"What now?" the Emperor roared. "Wait another half of eight years to build more carriers? And how will they be crewed? Too many firstborn sons of the nobles rode to their deaths aboard your fleet."

"They died gloriously for the Empire," Thrakhath replied calmly. "Their names shall be enshrined in the temples of their ancestors."

"Do you really expect them to believe that any more?" the Emperor gasped. "I am talking about our survival. After your defeat before Terra two assassination plots against me were barely thwarted. The other clans are poised on the edge of open rebellion."

Thrakhath looked at his grandfather in open amazement.

The Emperor nodded slowly.

"And if they had succeeded I daresay you would already be dead now as well."

The old warrior sighed and fell back into his chair.

"I want the new weapon unleashed," the Emperor finally said.

Thrakhath growled angrily. "That has never been our way. It is without the joy of the kill."

"I know, I know. But this war has changed beyond all our understanding, thanks to these humans. Let me make this plain to you. We can not sustain this war another year. It is not the humans. No, I believe the reports that they are crippled as well. We are two fighters who have battered each other into exhaustion. It will take but one more blow to finish them. The real threat now is what we fear lurks beyond our distant borders on the other side of the Empire."

"They are stirring?"

The Emperor nodded. "New reports came in while you were gone. They are still years, perhaps eights of years away, but they are coming in our direction again. When they arrive we must be ready, our other borders secured. All our resources must now be marshaled for that threat. For that reason alone I order that this war with the humans be finished, whether you like the methods or not. Secondly, and more immediate, is the clans. One more defeat like the last one and I fear the grasp of our family upon the imperial throne will be finished."

Thrakhath stood in silent rage at the mere suggestion that those beneath him could even dare to dream of overthrowing his clan's rightful claim to rule. The last baron who dreamed of it was now dead, and he had thought the infection of this alien thinking was gone with him.

"I demand that this new weapon be tested as soon as possible," the Emperor announced. "The humans are to be exterminated like the vermin that they are. Honor and the taste of blood are things of the past. Test this weapon, and if it works you are to kill them all, kill them all without warning."

The Emperor hesitated and then grinned, his teeth bared. "And once that is done, if any of the clans dare to resist me, we shall turn this new weapon on them as well."

• CHAPTER I

Shuttle Horatio Nelson
Torgo System

"ETA for TCS *Victory* now ten minutes . . . mark."
The soft computer-generated voice in his ear made
Colonel Christopher Blair shift uneasily in his seat. He
didn't like being a passenger aboard any small craft, even
a workhorse orbital shuttle like this one. For eighteen
years now Blair had been a fighter pilot in the Terran
Confederation Navy, and he had flown everything in
the Navy's arsenal short of a frigate. It was still difficult
to sit back and leave the controls to someone else,
especially when his monitor screens functioned
intermittently at best. Having a computer read canned
approach announcements just made matters worse. If
he had been in the cockpit with the control stick in his
hand, he would have read times and distances, thrusts
and vectors, with the instincts of a combat pilot, honed
in years of almost continuous warfare—and the ride might
even have been infinitesimally smoother.

Warfare . . . the war between the Kilrathi Empire and
the Terran Confederation started before Christopher
Blair was born. For nearly forty years now, the two sides
had hammered away at each other, and the Kilrathi
showed no signs of letting up. Sometimes Blair wondered
if he would live to see the war end. And sometimes he
was afraid he would.

4

With his monitor still not working, he switched his attention to the tiny newscreen clipped to one arm of his flight couch. Hesitantly, Blair tapped the green key at the bottom of the device. The logo of the Terran News Channel filled the screen for a moment before being replaced by a head-and-shoulder shot of the TNC's best-known anchorwoman, Barbara Miles. Her attractive features were almost too perfect, and Blair smiled fleetingly at the memory of a shipboard bull session a few years back where some of his shipmates claimed that the woman was actually a computer-generated simulation.

The recording was paused, of course, waiting for Blair to tap in his choice of news items from a menu in one corner of the screen. He selected war news, then listened as the anchorwoman summarized recent events in the struggle against the Kilrathi . . . the ones that had been declassified.

He had heard most of it already from previous TNC newsbriefs or official channels at the Confed HQ complex on Torgo III. News traveled slowly across interstellar distances, and the average lifetime of any particular report was apt to be long, especially from worlds along the more distant frontiers.

His attention snapped back to the screen as the report passed from news stories to a more general commentary.

"Despite recent losses in several densely populated sectors, Confederation spokes-people insist that humanity maintains the upper hand in its galactic struggle with the Kilrathi. However, our sources document a consistent under-reporting of Kilrathi incursions, especially against civilian and industrial bases."

The woman paused, looking directly into the camera, while conveying thoughtful, serious concern for her viewers. "There are even reports of Confed plans for a 'doomsday evacuation' of Earth to replant the seeds of humanity in a distant part of the galaxy. The question is . . . who would go? Who would be left behind? And, most importantly, *who* is making these decisions?"

Blair cut the newscreen off with a snort of disgust. Leave it to TNC to come up with that ancient evacuation rumor! That thing had been making the rounds of ships' wardrooms when Blair was a junior lieutenant. The sheer logistical nightmare of a wholesale evacuation from human space made the whole idea laughable. Anyway, it was a plain fact that any place mankind could reach, the Kilrathi could follow. There was no place for humanity to run.

Still, it was certainly true that the heavily-censored news released by the Confederation was slanted to hide the truth about this war. After forty years of warfare, that was not new. But Blair was afraid that some of the top brass were actually starting to believe their own propaganda mills, and that was a very bad sign indeed.

Admiral Tolwyn, for instance . . . there was a man who badly needed a reality check.

It was Admiral Geoffrey Tolwyn who had given Blair his new assignment. A vigorous man in his sixties who spoke in a clipped British accent and radiated the very essence of spit-and-polish military precision in everything he said and did, Tolwyn had earned quite a reputation over the years as the mastermind behind a pair of great Confederation victories, the raid on Kilrah and the Battle of Terra. But Blair had served under the man before, and he knew that a lot of the legend was little more than luck and PR hype.

Still, Tolwyn had been brimming with confidence and determination when Blair reported to his office. "Things are looking up, Colonel," he had said with a smile. "The Confederation has been making some very positive strides. The Kilrathi are on the run at Gardel and Morpheus. . . ."

True enough, except that the Terrans had lost three systems to new Kilrathi offensives at the same time, and in much more strategically vital sectors. And, of course, there was the loss of the *Concordia*.

Blair fought back a shudder. He'd been wing commander aboard the *Concordia* for three years, until the Battle of Earth. If he hadn't taken that Kilrathi missile which left him grounded for six long months, Blair would have been on board when *Concordia* fought the rearguard action over Vespus: fought and died. Blair had been part of the survey crew that had discovered the carrier's broken hull lying half-submerged in the waters off the Mistral Coast.

Concordia was gone, and so were the men and women who had served with Blair for so long, through so many battles. More casualties of the war. Statistics tallied up in news reports or concealed in the falsehoods of a Confed press release. But those people were more than mere statistics to Christopher Blair. They had been more than comrades, more than friends . . . a family, united by the strongest possible bonds of shared dangers and difficult service far from home and loved ones.

Blair closed his eyes, summoning up familiar faces. Iceman . . . Spirit . . . Knight . . . Bossman . . . the list kept growing, year after year. Shipmates went to the firing line and died, and a fresh crop of kids from the Academy came in to replace them . . . to die in their turn. Sometimes it seemed as if the war had lost all point or purpose. Now it was nothing more than good people giving their lives fighting for some chunk of rock that wouldn't have deserved a second look before the war.

Christopher Blair was tired: of fighting, of death, and of this endless war.

Fate had spared him while so many others died. Now Blair, certified to be ready to return to full active duty, had received his new assignment from Admiral Tolwyn's own hands. Wing commander once again . . . but wing commander aboard the *Victory*.

As if reacting to his bitter thoughts, the monitor finally lit up with an external view from the shuttle's nose camera. *Victory* rode in free fall less than half a click ahead. She was everything Blair expected (which wasn't much).

She was a light carrier left over from a bygone era, designed nearly half a century before the beginning of the Kilrathi War. With most of the newest carriers in the Confederation fleet either lost in action or held in the Terran Defense Fleet, ships like the old *Victory* were becoming more common on the front lines. Perhaps, Blair reflected, that was why the Kilrathi seemed to have the edge these days.

Even over this distance, it was plain she had seen better days. There were burn marks down one side of her hull, and deeper scars in her superstructure where battle damage had been crudely patched.

One thing was certain . . . she was no *Concordia*.

The monitor flickered off again. This shuttle was part of *Victory*'s complement of small craft, and it was clear that non-essential systems were getting short shrift when maintenance schedules were being drawn up. The interior of the vessel was distinctly shabby, with faded paint, fraying flight couches, and missing access plates which revealed jury-rigged repair work. It suggested the low standards in play aboard *Victory*, but Blair planned to see things change once he took charge of the flight wing. Perhaps the crew of the battered old carrier did not care enough to do more than go through the motions, but if Blair had his way, that attitude would soon change.

"Preparing for final docking approach," the computer voice announced quietly.

An outdated ship and a crew that apparently didn't give a damn any more. If *Concordia* hadn't been able to stand against the Kilrathi, how could *Victory* be expected to even put up a fight?

Blair had to ask himself, as the shuttle slowly maneuvered in toward the carrier's flight deck, what this assignment really meant. Did Tolwyn expect him to knock the ship and crew into some kind of battle-ready shape? Or did the High Command consider that Blair and *Victory* deserved each other, two old warhorses who had outlived their usefulness put out to pasture?

Flight Deck, TCS Victory
Torgo System

The boarding ramp made a grinding noise as it swung down to touch the deck. Blair winced at the sound. His first view of the interior of his new home made him wince again. It was even shabbier than he had imagined. There was a distinct smell in the air; an odor of sweat, lubricants, burned insulation, and other unidentified unpleasant scents. Apparently, the air circulation systems were not capable of keeping the atmosphere fresh and clean.

He slung his flight bag over his shoulder and started slowly down the ramp. Crewmen were drawn up in ranks in the huge open hangar area, most of them dressed in utility fatigues which had seen better days. Blair glanced at the end of the hangar where open space was visible beyond the faint glow of the force fields which kept the deck pressurized. He found himself hoping that they, at least, were maintained better than the rest of the ship. He pushed the thought away, trying to keep his feelings hidden from the crew.

A knot of senior officers awaited him at the foot of the ramp, dominated by a broad-shouldered black man with graying hair and the four stripes of a Line Captain prominently displayed on his sleeve. He didn't give Blair time to study his surroundings further, but stepped forward to meet him.

"Colonel Blair?" he said, smiling. "I'm William Eisen. Welcome aboard the *Victory*."

Blair snapped off a quick salute which Eisen returned gravely. Theoretically, they were of equal rank—a Colonel in the Confederation Space Force and a Captain of the Line—but aboard any ship in space, the commanding officer, regardless of rank, was always the senior officer (even if he was a mere lieutenant entertaining a visitor of higher rank).

The captain ended the salute by extending his hand. He had a firm grip that matched his proud bearing and an aura of quiet authority. "Allow me to present some of my senior officers, Colonel. This is Commander Ralgha *nar* Hhallas—"

"Hobbes!" Blair exclaimed, as Eisen moved aside to give Blair a clear view of the officers. Ralgha *nar* Hhallas would have stood out in any human crowd, for he was a Kilrathi nobleman. Tall and bulky, he was humanoid in form but distinctly alien in feature, with a head too large and flat for a man. His body and face were covered with thick fur, and his eyes, ears, and fangs gave him a distinctly cat-like appearance. The Kilrathi were not cats, of course, but they had sprung from carnivore hunter stock with many feline traits, and their ways of thinking were even more alien to humankind than those of Earthly cats.

Blair could hardly believe that more than ten years had passed since Lord Ralgha, a ship-captain of the Imperial Kilrathi fleet, defected to the Terran Confederation. TCS *Tiger's Claw* was in the squadron which helped him carry out his defection, and Blair (a junior lieutenant) had worn polish still fresh on his flight wings. Ralgha moved from supplying information to Terran Intelligence to serving in the Space Force, and he had remained in Blair's squadron for a time before new assignments took them down separate paths.

Many officers were reluctant to fly with a Kilrathi wingman, but Blair always found Ralgha cheerful, competent, and capable: a fine pilot and an excellent comrade. He was the one to bestow the nickname "Hobbes" on the renegade Kilrathi after encountering the name in an ancient piece of Terran folk art in a fellow pilot's collection.

"You know the Commander, then?" Eisen asked, raising an eyebrow.

"Not with that rank," Blair said. "Hobbes here is one of the best pilots who ever flew with the Flight Corps. What are you doing wearing that Line outfit? Getting too old to squeeze into a cockpit?"

Ralgha bowed slightly. "It warms my heart to see you again, Colonel," he said, his voice low and throaty with the odd intonation and slight accent Blair remembered well. "But I fear now is not the time to swap life stories."

Blair grinned. "Still the stickler, eh, Hobbes? Well, we'll talk later."

The Kilrathi bowed again.

Eisen introduced the department heads and senior staff officers. They were no more than a blur of unfamiliar names and faces to Blair . . . but still he felt heartened to know that at least one old friend would be with him on this cruise.

The captain concluded by introducing a fresh-faced young man wearing a lieutenant's insignia. "And this is Lieutenant Ted Rollins, Communications Officer."

"And general dogsbody," Rollins grinned. "Sir."

"I've assigned Mr. Rollins to extra duty, as your aide," Eisen continued, ignoring the lieutenant's interjection. "At least until you get settled in and make staff arrangements of your own. I hope that will be agreeable with you, Colonel."

Blair nodded. "That will be fine, sir. Thank you."

"The lieutenant will show you to your quarters and help you get the lay of the land. I would appreciate you joining me in my Ready Room at . . . shall we say sixteen hundred hours, ship's time? That will give you a few hours to get acclimated."

"Sixteen hundred hours," Blair repeated. He glanced around the hangar again. Would any length of time be enough to get acclimated to this old rustbucket of a ship? "I'll be there, sir."

"Very good. Dismissed." As Blair turned away, Eisen spoke again. "We're glad to have you aboard, Colonel."

Blair wished he could have returned the sentiment, but he knew it would come out sounding bitter and ironic.

Command Ready Room, TCS Victory Torgo System

"Come in, Colonel. Come in. Have a seat."

Blair glanced around the room, moving from the door to the chair Eisen gestured toward in front of the captain's desk. He noted that the tasteful if spartan decor and the well-kept atmosphere produced a startling contrast to most of what he had observed aboard the *Victory*.

"So, Colonel, I trust Mr. Rollins has been seeing to your needs." The Captain stood, crossing to a counter at one end of the room. "Will you have something to drink? We picked up a load of New Samarkand vodka a few months back that has a kick like a Gratha's blasters."

"Thank you, sir." Actually, Blair didn't particularly want a drink, but it was never wise to turn down a commanding officer's hospitality, especially not on the first day aboard.

Eisen returned with two glasses and handed one to Blair. "A toast, then, Colonel. To Victory!"

They touched their glasses and Blair took a cautious sip. "Is that the ship or the concept, sir?" he asked.

"Both," Eisen said, sitting down. Thoughtfully Eisen added, "We're going to win this war, Colonel, and I think this old ship will play a large part in it before the shooting's over."

Blair tried to keep his expression neutral. "I hope so, sir."

The captain regarded him with a penetrating look. "I'll admit, Blair, she's no *Concordia* . . ."

"Neither is the *Concordia* . . . any more." This time Blair didn't bother to hide his feelings.

"It was a terrible loss," Eisen said. "It's never easy to lose so much. You have my sympathies." He paused, looking into his glass. "Nevertheless, you're here now, and I expect nothing less than complete dedication and loyalty from every officer and rating on board this ship."

"You'll have mine, sir," Blair said quietly. "But if I may speak freely . . . ?"

"Always, Colonel."

"From what I've seen so far, you need a little less dedication and a lot more maintenance work from this crew."

Eisen leaned forward. "I'll admit she doesn't look like much, Blair," he said solemnly. "We're shorthanded in every department, and age and too damn many battles have taken their toll. The old girl was slated for retirement over a decade ago, but they put her back on the line instead. Maybe she doesn't look as good as the big ships you've served on in the past, but that doesn't mean she's not able to do her job. And it's the crew, the men and women who work overtime day after day just to keep her up and running, who are responsible for keeping us on the firing line. That dedication makes all the difference, Colonel, and even if it doesn't extend to slapping on a fresh coat of paint or making sure the food dispensers in the Rec Room have a full stock of chicken soup every day, it still means something to *me*."

Blair didn't answer right away. "I . . . take your point, sir," he said at last. "I'm sorry if I seem to be running down your command . . ."

Eisen smiled easily. "I'm used to it by now, Colonel, believe me. She *doesn't* look like much, I'll grant you that. But I was communications officer on *Victory*'s maiden voyage, my first assignment out of the Academy. I've been with her many times throughout my career, and I guess I'm just a little bit protective about the old girl after all."

"I can understand that, sir. You can get . . . attached to a ship, over time." He was thinking of the old *Tiger's Claw* . . . and *Concordia*. "I'll admit I wasn't looking forward to this assignment when Admiral Tolwyn told me about it. But I'm feeling much better about it now."

"My pep talk was that good?" Eisen asked with a grin.

"That . . . and finding out you have Ralgha *nar* Hhallas aboard. He's one of the best."

"Commander *nar* Hhallas? Yes, he's a good officer. He'll be my Exec this trip . . ."

"Sir . . . with all due respect, that's a real waste of talent. Hobbes is a natural-born fighter pilot. Putting him in a Line slot . . . I think it's a mistake."

"It was his own request, Colonel. I know his record, but . . ." Eisen trailed off, then shrugged. "Fact is, no one aboard will fly with a Kilrathi on his wing."

"Fifteen years of loyal service and a string of combat kills as long as my arm doesn't count for anything?"

The captain looked away. "Not with these people, Blair. Not after everything they've been through in this damned war. Anyway, *he* made the request for the good of the flight wing."

"Well, I'm in command of the wing now," Blair said. "And I want him restored to flight status immediately, for the good of the wing." He paused. "Not that I would try to tell you how to run your ship, of course . . ."

"Why not? Isn't that the accepted role of every wing commander in the fleet? You guys always felt the Line was nothing but a bunch of glorified taxi drivers." Eisen's smile faded quickly. "Look, Colonel, your loyalty is admirable, and I'll willingly transfer him back to flight, but the problem still remains—who would have a Kilrathi as a wingman?"

"I'll fly with him," Blair said coldly. "Even if none of the others will. He's the best damned wingman I ever flew with, and I have a feeling we're going to need him if we're heading into a combat zone."

"If you say so, Colonel," Eisen said, shrugging again. "But I think you're asking for trouble. Not that I'd tell you how to run your wing, of course . . ."

• CHAPTER II

Wing Commander's Office, TCS Victory
Torgo System

Blair's office was small, tucked between the Flight Control Center and one of the wing's four ready rooms. Aside from a desk with built-in computer links and a set of monitors, it was sparsely furnished. The only really noteworthy touch was the wall behind the desk: a single sheet of transplast revealing a view into the main hangar deck.

As Blair entered, Rollins looked up from one of the desktop monitors. "Just setting your schedule, Colonel," he said, rising to give Blair the chair. "So, I take it you got the full pep talk from the Old Man, eh?"

"Something like that," Blair said shortly. Rollins was young and eager to please, but there was an edge about him that made Blair uncomfortable. Rollins had a cynical air and a sharp tongue, and apparently felt free to say whatever he thought. Blair was a skeptic himself and often outspoken, but it seemed out of place coming from a kid fresh out of training.

"Well, take heart, Colonel. We've still got an ample supply of hot water to shower away all the bullshit."

Blair fixed him with a long, penetrating stare. "Captain Eisen seems to genuinely believe in his ship . . . and in his crew. That's a good attitude for morale."

"You haven't been monitoring the command traffic

the way I have, sir," Rollins said. "If the Old Man told the crew half of what he knows, they'd jump sector in half a nanosec and never come back!"

"Look, Lieutenant, I don't care what kind of paranoid fantasies you indulge in during your down-time," Blair told him harshly. "But I'd better not hear you sharing them with the rest of the crew. You read me, Mister?"

"Yes, sir," Rollins replied stiffly. "But I wouldn't just ignore what's going on out there, Colonel. Maybe it's not just paranoia, you know? If you change your mind and decide you want the straight dope, you just come to old Radio Rollins." He paused. "Might save your life someday."

"Yeah . . . and the Kilrathi might all become pacifist vegetarians overnight, too." Blair looked down at his desk. "I won't need you any more today, Rollins, so you can get back to your other duties. But on your way out, would you pass the word that I want to see Ralgha *nar* Hhallas? And whoever's my Exec, too, in that order. It's time I got this outfit properly frightened for the safety and comfort of their butts."

"Aye, aye, sir," Rollins said.

Blair's eyes followed the younger man as he left the office. It seemed ironic for Blair to be championing the establishment, given his own bitter feelings about the High Command and the state of the war in general, but he didn't have much choice. Private doubts were one thing, but doubts spread throughout the ship by someone in a position to leak classified information . . . that was an open invitation to disaster. One sour apple like Rollins could ruin the best of crews.

He put aside his concerns and turned to work; punching up the computer files on Flight Wing Thirty-Six. They had been assigned to *Victory* for over a year now with operations mostly in secondary theaters and rear echelons. There were four combat squadrons in the wing plus a support squadron which operated *Victory*'s contingent of shuttles, small boats, and other utility craft.

Four squadrons . . . forty fighters, interceptors, and fighter-bombers. Red Squadron flew Arrow-class point-defense fighters designed to fly close escort for the carrier and other capital ships. Though limited in range and endurance, they were well-armed for their size. In a close combat situation, they'd be worth their weight in platinum.

Blue Squadron flew space superiority fighters, Arrow-class interceptors. These had range, speed, and endurance for long patrol operations or sustained dogfights, but they were rather light when it came to arms and armor. Blair had flown Arrows before but never cared much for them. He liked a heavier ship, one with teeth, but still maneuverable enough to outfly as well as outfight an enemy.

Heavy fighter-bombers constituted the complement of the Green Squadron. Using the F/A-76 Longbow-class attack craft, the squadron gave *Victory* real striking power for offensive operations. The Longbow had a reputation for being underpowered and clumsy, but it had a good combat record nonetheless. Blair never considered himself a bomber pilot and had only flown an F/A-76 in simulations.

The Gold Squadron remained, based on the HF-66 Thunderbolt heavy fighter. Heavy fighters were used during offense and defense alike, with enough ordinance capacity to be pressed into service as bombers if the need arose. They still maintained the firepower and speed to be superb dogfighters. He was glad to see the Thunderbolts listed in the inventory. When the wing went into combat, Blair planned to be flying with Gold Squadron in the cockpit of one of those steady and reliable old fighters. He would have to reorganize the flight roster accordingly to accommodate Hobbes and himself. . . .

As if on cue, there was a knock at the door. "Enter," Blair said, and the computer picked up the order, opening the door. It was Hobbes.

Blair stood and met him halfway with one hand extended to grasp a large, stubby-fingered paw in a hearty handshake.

"It is good to see you, old friend," Hobbes said. "You are looking fine and fit. Does this war, then, agree with you so much?"

Blair chuckled. "Yeah, right, about as much as a pair of busted wing flaps on an atmospheric run." He stepped back, clasping the big Kilrathi renegade by the shoulders and looking him up and down. "Damn, it's good to see you, buddy. Nobody told me I'd find you aboard."

"Nor did we ever expect to see the likes of Maverick Blair on the *Victory*, my friend," Ralgha responded. "You must admit, it is quite a change from *Concordia* and her kind."

"Yeah . . . it is that." Blair said, looking away. "Come on, sit down. We've got some things to talk about."

"Old times?" the Kilrathi asked, lowering himself carefully into a seat that had never been built with a Kilrathi's bulk in mind.

"Nope. New ones. I've got good news for you, buddy. You're back on the flight roster, starting immediately, on the Gold Squadron—pushing a Thunderbolt."

Ralgha hesitated. "But I requested—"

"Yeah, Eisen told me. But just because you ran into a couple of bigots is no reason to sit on the sidelines now. We need you on the firing line, Hobbes. *I* need you. You'll be flying as my wingman, at least until I knock a few heads together and show these people the error of their ways."

"Colonel . . ." Ralgha trailed off. "There are many brave and noble pilots on this ship, my friend."

"When my ass is on the line, I want a wingman I can trust. And you're one of the damned few pilots I *do* trust, Hobbes. Like I said, I *need* you out there."

"Then I shall try not to disappoint you, old friend."

"I haven't had a chance to review the rosters yet," Blair said. "You rate as a Lieutenant Colonel in the Space Force. Do you know where that puts you in the chain of command?"

"Now that you are with us, I will be number two," Ralgha answered solemnly.

"My Exec?"

The Kilrathi nodded gravely, the human gesture seeming out of place. "I believe that was the principal reason for the opposition to my presence," he said. "Colonel Dulbrunin was the previous wing commander. He was killed in a battle just before I was transferred aboard, and I believe some of the other pilots were reluctant to serve with a Kilrathi as their commanding officer. Perhaps there will be fewer objections with you in command."

"I'll guarantee that much. Anyone with objections will keep them to themselves or I'll move them to another wing."

"Do not judge them too harshly. This has been a bitter conflict. It is difficult to avoid hatred between two such different species as yours and mine, and there are few who can learn to distinguish between allegiance and race when the differences are so plain to see."

"You're too damned noble, Hobbes. That's the only thing about you I still can't deal with. I keep expecting you to act like a human being and have a hidden dark side, but if you've got one it never shows."

"Humans, too, have hidden depths, for good or ill." Ralgha paused. "But there are better things to discuss than philosophy, such as old friends and comrades in arms. How is your mate, that fine pilot and comrade, Angel?"

Blair looked away again, his smile fading. He had been trying not to think about Angel. "I don't know, Hobbes," he said reluctantly. "I haven't heard from her in months. She's been assigned to some damn covert op, and even Paladin's keeping quiet about it."

"I . . . am sorry if I have stirred up bad feelings," Ralgha said. "But you know as well as I do that Angel can take care of herself. She will return to you in time, if the War God so wills it."

"Yeah." Blair nodded, but the sinking feeling in his stomach would not go away. Jeannette Devereaux (callsign Angel) began with Blair aboard the old *Tiger's Claw*, first as a fellow pilot, then a friend, and then . . . more, much more. But when Blair was offered the wing commander's slot aboard the *Concordia*, Angel transferred to Brigadier General James Taggart's Covert Operations Division. Blair never understood or accepted the decision, prompted, so she said, by her regard for Taggart (who had flown with them on the *Tiger's Claw* under the running name of Paladin). Covert Ops seemed such a complete departure for Angel, who was usually so cool and rational, so completely dedicated to the science rather than the emotions of warfare.

But she joined Taggart's outfit, and though Blair continued to see her (when possible), they had drifted apart. Finally, just after the Battle of Earth and Blair's long confinement in the military hospital, she simply vanished. Paladin admitted she was on a mission when Blair confronted him, but nothing more. Covert Ops drew the most difficult and dangerous assignments in the Confed fleet. By now, she might well be dead. . . .

Blair forced himself to put aside that bitter thought. "Look, Hobbes," he said slowly, "I don't want to cut this short. I'd like nothing better than to grab a couple of jugs of booze in the Rec Room and toast the old days with you, but I've got a pile of stuff to wade through before I can declare it quitting time."

"I understand, my friend," Ralgha said, rising slowly. He gave Blair a slight bow, the Kilrathi gesture of respect. "When the Captain makes my transfer official, perhaps I can take up some of the burden as your Exec."

"Tomorrow will do fine, Hobbes. And . . . thanks."

The Kilrathi pilot had not even reached the door when there was another knock. Ralgha ushered in the newcomer as he left, leaving Blair face-to-face with a familiar figure, another reminder of missions past.

The man had changed little over the years. He was a little heavier than Blair remembered him, and there was a touch of gray in his dark hair. But he still had the same air of brooding intensity and fire in his eyes.

"Maniac Marshall," Blair said slowly. "So you managed to stay alive somehow. Who'd have guessed it?"

"Colonel Blair." Major Todd Marshall looked anything but glad to see him, and the feeling was entirely mutual. Marshall was another of the old *Tiger's Claw* hands. In fact, he and Blair had a history together. As classmates in the Academy, they had been rivals in everything from the flight competitions in their final year as midshipmen to gaining the attentions of a particular young lady.

Marshall earned his running name in the Academy from his slapdash, hell-for-leather flying style. Always volatile and eager for glory, Maniac never fit in quite as well as Blair. He barely squeaked through graduation whereas Blair earned honors. While aboard *Tiger's Claw*, Marshall proved an unpopular wingman who was considered unreliable, even dangerous, by the rest of his squadron. He blamed Blair from the start for always managing to come out ahead in kills, awards, and promotions. Blair had been delighted when the two were posted in different ships after their tour aboard *Tiger's Claw*.

Now Marshall was a major, and Blair was a colonel, and the high command or some vengeful god of fate had thrown them together again.

"It's been a long time, Major." Blair didn't bother to stand, but gestured toward the chair Hobbes had vacated. "Sit down and tell me what I can do for you."

"Radio Rollins said you wanted to see your Exec," Marshall said as he took the chair. He smiled, but the expression held no warmth at all. "I guess that's me."

"That *was* you," Blair said bluntly. "But I've just asked the Captain to restore Hobbes to flight status, and he outranks you, I'm afraid. He'll be Exec and double as CO of Gold Squadron."

Marshall's face fell. "That damned kitty . . ." He stopped as he caught the look on Blair's face. "All right, all right. Can't go around maligning a fellow officer, and all that, right? But I never could understand what you saw in that cat, and that's the plain and simple truth."

"That's simple enough. He's a wingman I can trust."

Maniac gave a derisive snort. "Trust someone who'll kill his own kind? There's a great piece of command wisdom for you."

"At least I've never known Hobbes to break formation on me the way you did at Gimle. I need to know that I can count on a wingman to back me up, and not go hunting for glory, then yell for help when he gets in too deep . . ." Blair shrugged. He had gone over this same speech with Maniac time and again, but it had never done any good. He didn't imagine the man was going to change now. "When it comes right down to it, Major, I can choose whoever I want as my wingman. That's one of the privileges of rank, you know."

"Yeah," Marshall said, his tone hollow, bitter. "Yeah, those gold tracers on your collar look real sharp, Colonel Blair, sir. Bet you have to stay up pretty late at night to keep 'em polished so pretty."

"No, I don't," Blair said coldly. "I assign majors to do it for me."

"The difference in our rank, sir, is just a formality," Marshall said, standing up. "We both know who's the better man in the cockpit."

"That's right. We both do. And that's what has been eating at you ever since the Academy, isn't it, Major?"

Maniac's look was one of pure hatred. "Will there be anything else . . . *sir*? Or may I be dismissed?"

"That's all," Blair said, turning away to look through the window into the hangar. He waited until the door slid shut behind Marshall, then he wearily sat down.

Blair leaned back in his chair and closed his eyes, trying to calm himself after the angry confrontation. He had wanted to sit down with the wing XO to get an idea of the unit's strengths and weaknesses in equipment, personnel, and experience. But seeing Marshall after so many years had driven it all out of his mind, and he had let his personal feelings overcome his judgment. Maniac always had a talent for bringing out the worst in him.

Blair turned back to his desktop computer and called up the wing's personnel files on his screen. He picked Marshall's records first. Studying them, he began to understand the man's belligerence a little better.

He'd been the Exec under Colonel Dulbrunin with enough seniority to hope for a promotion to lieutenant colonel and to become *Victory*'s wing commander. No doubt the arrival of Hobbes had been a blow. Blair was sure now that Marshall was behind the ill feelings toward the Kilrathi renegade, since Hobbes had snatched his chance at commanding the wing.

Then Hobbes bowed out, and Blair arrived aboard to dash Marshall's hopes again. No wonder the man was feeling bitter. . . .

Another detail caught his eye. Marshall was also the CO of Gold Squadron. Blair had decided to have Hobbes take over that command, too. It was one more blow to Maniac's fragile ego.

He could reconsider the decision, of course, and let Marshall keep his squadron. But if Hobbes was going to be Blair's wingman, the two of them would have to fly with the same squadron, and Blair still felt more comfortable sticking with the heavy fighters in Gold Squadron. Should he reshuffle the roster to put Marshall in command of another squadron? Maniac certainly had the seniority, even if Blair doubted he had the temperament for squadron command.

But which squadron could Maniac handle best? He was not suited to command bombers, and point defense work required a leader who could subordinate himself totally to the needs of the fleet. Marshall would probably be happiest in command of the interceptors of Blue Squadron, but Blair shuddered at the thought of putting *Victory*'s crucial long-range strike fighters in Maniac's hands. Patrol duties would take Blue Squadron out of reach of higher authority, and it needed a man with a good head on his shoulders who knew when to fight, when to break away, and when to get word of a distant contact with the enemy back to the carrier. No, Major Marshall wasn't really suitable for any other squadrons. Colonel Dulbrunin probably made the same decision when making his original assignments. The kind of utility combat work which heavy fighters drew was the sort of operation Maniac was least likely to knock off course if he lost his head in a fight.

Well, that meant he would have to stay where he was, at least until Blair could see if age and experience had mellowed Maniac, at least in the cockpit if not in his dealings with others. The man would just have to accept flying under Blair and Hobbes.

But Blair knew it would make a tough job much more difficult for all of them.

Flight Wing Officer's Quarters, TCS Victory Torgo System

Blair was studying his predecessor's logs on the monitor above his bunk when he heard a knock. "Enter," he said, sitting up as the door opened to reveal Lieutenant Rollins.

"Sorry to bother you so late, Colonel," Rollins said, "but we're boosting to the jump point, and the Comm Shack's been buzzing with last-minute incoming traffic all evening. I just got off shift."

"We've got orders, then?"

Rollins nodded. "Orsini System. It's been pretty quiet up 'til now, but the scuttlebutt has it the cats have been moving in lately. Guess we're supposed to make 'em feel safe or something."

"Mmph." Blair stood up. "Okay, so we're jumping and you've been busy. Is there something you needed from me, Lieutenant?"

"I . . . wanted to make sure you got this. It came in with some of the other message traffic. Rerouted from Confed HQ, for you." He handed Blair a holo cassette. "Er . . . here it is, sir."

"You don't have to act so apologetic, man," Blair said, realizing the cause of his embarrassed manner. "Comm officers see a lot of personal messages. I'm not going to bite off your head for reading my mail, Lieutenant."

"Er . . . yes, sir. Thanks." Rollins left, still looking flustered.

Blair set the cassette on the small table beside the bunk and touched the message stud. Letters formed in the air above the device, spelling out a message. The block of code numbers dated it to more than six months earlier, before the Battle of Earth. That was typical enough for messages that had to chase their intended recipients through space from one planet or one ship to another.

PRIVATE CODED COMM RELAY TO:
Colonel Christopher Blair
Terran Confed Armed Forces
TCS *Concordia*
—REROUTED BY CONFED HQ TO—
TCS *Victory*

The words dissolved after a moment, and an image formed. It was Angel, still heart-stoppingly beautiful, looking out at him with the expression he remembered so well.

"Hello, *mon ami*," she began, flashing her brightest smile. "I hope the fight goes well for you and all the others aboard *Concordia*. I have been given new orders to head up a mission, so I'm afraid we must be apart a little longer. Always remember: *je t'aime, je t'aime* . . . I love you . . ."

Blair stabbed at the switch, cutting the hologram off while tears stung his eyes. "*Je t'aime*, Angel," he said softly. "I love you, wherever you are. . . ."

• CHAPTER III

Flight Control, TCS Victory
Orsini System

"Now hear this, now hear this," the shipboard tannoy blared. "Prepare for Flight Operations. Flight Deck personnel to launch stations."

Blair's stride was brisk and purposeful as he entered the Flight Control Center, his helmet under one arm. It was good to be back in his G suit again, even if the mission at hand was no more than a routine patrol. In his two weeks aboard the *Victory*, he had been unable to strap on a fighter once, but today he would finally get a chance to be free of a wing commander's console work and move among the stars where he truly belonged.

Chief Technician Rachel Coriolis looked up from a computer display with a grin. He had met her only once, in a general meeting of the flight wing's support personnel, without time to exchange more than a few words. That was Blair's problem ever since he took command of the wing: plenty of work, reports, plans, forms, and requisitions to be filled out, but precious little chance to know the rest of the crew.

Chief Coriolis was Gold Squadron's senior crew chief, and as such led the team of technical experts who maintained *Thunderbolt 300*, the fighter set aside for Blair's use. She was young—not yet thirty—and attractive, though her customary baggy coveralls and the inevitable

28

layer of dirt and grime streaking her clothes and face tended to obscure her beauty. According to her personnel file, she was a competent technician with an excellent service record. Blair hoped she would live up to those reports.

"Colonel," she said, straightening as he approached. "They say you're taking this patrol yourself. Your bird's just about ready."

"Good," Blair responded.

"Kinda strange seeing the big brass flying a routine patrol, though," she continued, apparently not affected by rank or seniority. "I don't think I ever saw Colonel Dulbrunin fly anything short of a full all-fighters magnum launch."

"I'm not Dulbrunin," Blair told her. "I like to get a few hours of flight time as often as possible, so don't be surprised if you discover that my bird needs more servicing than you planned."

She gave a nod in satisfaction. "Glad to hear it, skipper. Your predecessor knew how to fly a console well enough, a top-notch administrator. But I like pilots who fly the real thing. Know what I mean?" She cocked her head to one side. " Are you really taking on Hobbes as your wingman?"

"You got a problem with that, Chief?" Blair growled.

"No, sir," the technician said, shaking her head. "I say it's about jolly well time. That cat's one hell of a good pilot, and I'm glad to see him back on the roster."

Blair studied her for a long moment, then gave an approving nod. "Glad to hear it, Chief," he said, warming to her. At least there was someone on the flight deck who appreciated Ralgha *nar* Hhallas. Her praise sounded sincere. Rachel Coriolis struck him as the kind of tech who judged a pilot on how he handled his fighter, not on superficial things like species or background. "So . . . give me a status report on my bird."

Using a remote, she switched on a set of viewscreens filled with data readouts on the fighter. "Here she is, one Thunderbolt; prepped, primed, locked, and loaded . . . and ready to kick some serious ass out there."

Blair studied the data display for a few moments then gave an approving nod. "Looks good, Chief," he finally said. "What about the ordinance?"

"All taken care of, skipper. The Captain downloaded the mission specs while you boys were finishing your briefing. I doped out the weapons requirements and loaded her. You're all set for this one."

Blair frowned. "Better let me review the load, Chief," he said slowly.

"Typical," she said, calling up the ordinance display on one of the monitors. "You flyboys just don't think anybody else knows what you're going to need out there."

He checked the weapons mix, then reluctantly nodded. "Looks good enough," he admitted.

"Maybe next time you'll trust your Auntie Rachel with the loadout, huh, skipper?" She gave him a quick smile. "I promise you, Colonel, I'll never disappoint you."

"I'll bet you won't," he said. Blair took a last look at the fighter stats then turned toward the door. It was time to launch.

"Good luck, skipper," the technician said, "and Godspeed."

He left Flight Control and took the elevator to the next level down, emerging on the main hangar deck in the midst of a confusion of people and machines engaged in the familiar purposeful chaos of pre-launch operations. Hobbes was already there, with his helmet on but his faceplate open. "Fighters up, Colonel," he said seriously. "Ready to fly."

"Then let's get out there," Blair responded, lifting his own helmet and settling it over his head carefully. His flight suit and gauntlets made the motion awkward, but

Hobbes helped him get seated and dogged down. A pair of technicians bustled around guiding them toward the fighters resting side by side in their launch cradles.

Blair climbed into the cockpit, his stomach churning the way it always did in anticipation of a launch, as techs supervised the final preparations, checked the seals on the cockpit canopy, removed external power and fuel feeds, studied readouts, and compared them with the incoming data from Flight Control. Blair ran through his own checklist.

When all the lights on his panel glowed green, he nodded his head and lowered his faceplate into place. He switched his radio to the command channel. "Thunderbolt three-double-zero," he said. "Ready for launch."

"*Flight Control*," Rachel's voice sounded in his ear. "*Confirming, Thunderbolt three zero zero ready for launch.*"

Blair's faceplate came alive with a Heads Up Display of the fighter's major systems. Seconds ticked away on a countdown clock in the lower left-hand corner of the HUD readout. The time seemed to drag into an eternity, but at last the readout flashed through the final few seconds. Blair took a firm grip on the steering yoke with one hand while the other rested on the engine throttles. *Three . . . two . . . one . . .*

Blair rammed the throttles forward and felt the engines engage. "Thunderbolt three-double-zero, under power," he reported. Then he was free of the carrier, climbing outward into the star-studded depths of open space.

A moment later Hobbes came on the line, his voice slightly distorted by the computer reconstruction of his encoded transmission. "*Thunderbolt three-zero-one, under power.*"

"*Roger that, three hundred, three-o-one,*" the voice of Lieutenant Rollins rang loudly in his headphones.

"*Your mission designation is Snoop Flight, repeating Snoop Flight.*"

"Confirming," Blair replied. "Snoop Leader, establishing flight coordinates now." As Hobbes added his own response, Blair tapped a key to check the autopilot's flight plan on the navcomp. A flight from Blue Squadron had detected signs of possible enemy activity on long-range sensors around three different coordinate points, but pursuant to standing orders had not investigated closely. Instead, they brought their information back to the *Victory*. Now Eisen wanted those potential trouble spots checked more thoroughly, with Gold Squadron's heavier Thunderbolts doing the scouting in case they ran into opposition.

A routine patrol . . . except that Blair had long since learned that no mission was ever entirely routine.

The two fighters flew in close formation, side by side, with a minimum of conversation passing back and forth between them or the carrier. The first of the three target areas were free of enemy ships, although some random space debris did show up on sensors to suggest what the first flight had detected. They remained in the area long enough to double-check all their sensor readings, then set course for the second navigation point on the flight plan.

"*Range to navpoint, eight thousand kilometers,*" Hobbes reported finally. "*Switching to full-spectrum sensor sweep . . . now.*"

"Confirmed," Blair replied tersely, activating his own sensor array. What seemed like extremely long seconds passed as the computer began to process the information pouring through the system. The tracking screen in the center of his control console lit up with a trio of red lights.

"*Fighters, fighters, fighters,*" Hobbes chanted over the tactical channel. "*I read three fighters, bearing three-four-six by zero-one-one, range two thousand, closing.*"

Blair checked his own target readouts. "Confirmed. Three bad guys, two of us. But I'll bet you they're only a little bit nervous at the odds!" He paused for a moment, studying the sensor data. "I read them as Dralthi-class, probably type fours."

"Then they should offer only a mild challenge," Hobbes said. The Dralthi IV was a good craft, but classed as a medium fighter with less weaponry and lighter armor than the Terran Thunderbolt. *"May I have the honor of the first engagement, Colonel?"*

Blair frowned. His instincts were at odds with what he could see on the screen. Something wasn't quite right. . . . "Wait, Hobbes," he said. "I want to finish the scan."

The sensors covered the whole volume around the Terran fighters to their extreme limits, but the computer was still crunching numbers and trying to extrapolate detailed information from their readings. There was a single, massive asteroid near the same bearing as the enemy fighters, yet closer and several degrees to port. An asteroid that size could hold a Kilrathi depot or advanced base, perhaps armed. . . .

"Steer clear of that rock, Hobbes," he said, still frowning. "I don't like the looks of it. Let's keep in supporting distance until we see which way those boys are going to break."

"Acknowledged," Ralgha responded. Blair thought he could detect a note of disappointment in the alien's voice.

"Going to afterburners," Blair said, pushing the throttles into the red zone and feeling the press of acceleration on his chest. Hobbes stayed close, matching his course and speed.

"They see us, Colonel," Ralgha reported a moment later.

On Blair's targeting screen, he could see the three fighters breaking formation. It looked as if they were getting ready for a typical Kilrathi attack pattern, with individual ships hurling themselves into action in succession rather than attempting a coordinated assault. That was the legacy of their carnivore forebears: the instinct to fight as individual hunters and warriors rather than group together in a mass effort. Blair knew Hobbes was feeling the pull of that same age-old instinct, but he also knew his friend's rigid sense of duty and self-control, which would hold him in formation until he was released.

The first Dralthi accelerated toward them, driving at maximum thrust. Over the open radio channel the enemy pilot screamed a challenge. "*Die, hairless apes!*" translated the communications computer. "*Die as you live, without honor or value!*"

"*I am no ape,*" Hobbes replied. "*I am Ralgha nar Hhallas, and my honor is not to be questioned by a* Kilra'hra *like you!*" Blair's wingman rolled left, opening fire on the Dralthi with blasters and a pair of anti-ship missiles.

The lead Kilrathi fighter dodged and juked, eluding one of the missiles and increasing thrust as it turned onto a new heading angling away from Hobbes. The other missile scored a hit on shields already weakened by blaster fire, raising a cloud of debris amidships as the blast ripped into armor plating.

Blair started to follow his comrade's course, ready to maintain a close formation and keep enemies off Ralgha's back. But he spotted motion on his sensor grid, and swore softly. "Damn it, the other two aren't sticking around to fight," he said.

"*Pursue them if you wish, my friend,*" Hobbes replied grimly. "*I wish to finish this one.*"

He hesitated a moment. Blair was a firm believer in the value of formation fighting and mutual support between wingmen, but the mission profile called for the

Terran fighters to eliminate as many opponents as possible once an engagement began. The idea was to sweep each of the suspect areas clean and not to allow escaping Kilrathi to regroup or summon reinforcements to redeem an initial defeat. If those two broke off, there was no telling how many of their friends they would contact.

Blair changed his vector to follow the two ships as they veered toward the shelter of the asteroid he had noted earlier. On their present heading, they would not pass close enough to pose any particular danger to either pursued or pursuer. If they could put the irregular lump of rock and ore between their ships and Blair's Thunderbolt, they might be able to confuse his sensors long enough to make their escape.

On their present course they were opening the range separating them from the first Dralthi, which was running in the opposite direction with Hobbes close on the enemy fighter's tail. That was one less thing to worry about. Apparently the Kilrathi had no great interest in rescuing their comrade.

Blair kept one eye on his fuel gauge and the other on the enemy ships. High-thrust operations burned fuel at a terrible rate, and the last thing he needed now was to use so much of his reserve that he wouldn't be able to make it home. Judging from the heat outputs of the two Dralthi, they were not using their full thrusters. They were probably already low on fuel, nearing the end of an extended patrol. That meant he could still close the gap and engage them. . . .

Then the enemy exhaust plumes started burning hotter. The two craft suddenly began to swing around, their symbols changing quickly on his sensor readouts. They were turning, but not to run. This time they planned to attack.

In the same moment, three more targets appeared on Blair's screens, closing from starboard.

These, too, were Dralthi. Blair cursed. The new arrivals had been lurking in the lee of that asteroid, dangerously close to the huge rock. Evidently the Kilrathi picked up the first patrol flight and realized there would be a follow-up mission, so they organized an ambush. With Hobbes distracted by his one-on-one fight with the original attacker, the enemy squadron could concentrate on knocking Blair out of action while he was still unsupported.

"Hobbes," he said urgently. "Talk to me, buddy. I've got five bandits surrounding me with damn little running room. Break off whatever you're doing and give me an assist."

Blair was already reversing course as one of the Dralthi broke and plunged toward him. His fingers danced over the autopilot keyboard as he programmed the computer to begin random bursts of thrust at odd vectors to keep his opponent from getting a firm lock on the Thunderbolt. Then there was nothing more he could do except wait, jaw clenched, as he watched the Dralthi slowly close in. Soon the enemy pilot would be able to match his vector, and when that happened . . .

He fired his maneuvering jets to execute a tumbling turn just as the Dralthi settled on the Terran fighter's tail. Suddenly, the Kilrathi ship filled his forward viewport, and Blair opened fire with his blasters in a quick succession of shots that burned power too quickly for the weapons generators to respond. His last shot was with a Dart unguided missile, the type pilots referred to as "dumb-fires." But even without a homing system, the missile wasn't likely to miss at this range.

The missile barely left his ship before Blair's fighter was twisting again. He didn't see the missile punch through the weakened shields and detonate over the weakest armor, around the Dralthi's cockpit. But his sensors registered the blast, and Blair felt a momentary thrill as he realized he had scored a kill.

But that still left four-to-one odds.

He did not waste time. The other Kilrathi fighters were still out of range even though they were closing in fast. Blair reignited his afterburners and tried to put some distance between his fighter and the pursuers, but this time it was Blair who was concerned about his fuel supply. The four Dralthi were running flat out, apparently unconcerned about their reserves.

"Talk to me, Hobbes," he said again. "Where the hell are you . . . ?"

His answer was a blood-curdling, triumphant snarl that the computer translator utterly failed to interpret, and for an instant, Blair thought it was Ralgha's opponent proclaiming a triumph. Then he realized it was Hobbes, giving way to his instincts and emotions in the heat of battle and forgetting, for the moment, the thin veneer of Confederation culture that lay over his Kilrathi heritage.

Then his rigid control seemed to clamp down again. "*I have dispatched my opponent*," he said stiffly, as if the earlier Kilrathi war-call had come from someone else entirely. "*I am coming to your support now, my friend.*"

"Make it soon, tall, dark, and furry," Blair said. "These guys want to put me in a trophy room."

Another Dralthi was approaching, and once again Blair knew he must steer a fine line if he was going to fight. Every time he let himself be drawn into a dogfight, the other Kilrathi ships tightened the range a little bit more. At that rate, he would never be able to win. And sooner or later the odds would tell against him.

This time he didn't wait for the other ship to get so close. Instead, he threw the Thunderbolt into a tight, high-G turn and opened fire as soon as his weapons came to bear. The Dralthi returned fire with a full spread of blaster bolts and missiles, and for all of Blair's attempts at dodging, they racked up three solid hits, scoring away more than half the armor on his port wing.

Blair rolled away from the oncoming fighter, trying to keep his starboard side facing the Dralthi, but the Kilrathi pilot was a veteran who knew how to efficiently maneuver his craft. More blaster shots struck his weakened side in rapid succession, sapping his shields.

But the attack carried the Dralthi past Blair's Thunderbolt, and for a few seconds the advantage went to the Terran. He slapped his weapon selector switch and called up a Javelin heat-seeker. Blair's fingers tightened around his steering yoke as he tried to line up the targeting reticule over the Kilrathi fighter on his HUD display. It was close . . . very close.

The target indicator glowed red, and Blair fired blasters before releasing the missile. The Javelin locked onto the heat emissions from the Dralthi's engines and leapt outward. Seeing his danger, the Kilrathi pilot made a fast turn, attempting to get under the missile's sensor cone to confuse its on-board tracking system. Blair cursed as his board showed the missile losing its lock.

His energy readout showed his guns hadn't finished recycling yet, but Blair took a calculated risk and switched power from the shields to the weaponry systems. Then, determined to keep his fighter in line with the rear of the Dralthi despite its twisting, turning maneuvers, the Terran opened fire again. The blasters tore through the weakened shields, the armor, and the entire rear section of the Dralthi, which erupted in gouts of flame and spinning metal. "Scratch two!" Blair called.

Then Hobbes was beside Blair, firing a warning shot at long range to let the other three Kilrathi craft know the odds had changed. Almost immediately they veered away, charting new vectors, as if deciding against pressing the battle.

"They are withdrawing," Hobbes said. *"Do we pursue?"*

"I'm showing some pretty bad damage on the starboard side, and I'm down to one missile," Blair replied grimly. "What about you?"

"*The first foe put up a valiant struggle,*" the Kilrathi replied. "*I fear my own missiles are exhausted, and I have forward and port-side armor damage.*"

"Those guys are fresh," Blair said. "I don't know why they're giving up so easily, but I figure we'd better just count our blessings and head for home before they spring any more little surprises on us."

"*The Captain will not be pleased, I fear. It seems we have not carried out our mission.*"

Blair didn't answer his wingman's comment directly. "Let's get these crates moving, buddy. Set course for home base, standard thrust."

• CHAPTER IV

Thunderbolt 300
Orsini System

Of all the evolutions carried out by a fighter on deep space service, a carrier landing was the most difficult and dangerous maneuver. Bringing a fighter in with battle damage was that much worse, especially when shipboard diagnostics could not pinpoint the full extent of the harm done by the enemy hits. Blair studied his readouts as he drifted in his assigned holding pattern, waiting for Hobbes to land. Half a dozen amber lights were vying for his attention in port-side systems, including thrusters, weapons mountings, and landing gear. Any one of them could fail if put under too much strain, and the results would be catastrophic not only for the fighter, but possibly for the carrier as well.

Therefore, Hobbes was going in first. Once Rollins established the fact that Blair was uninjured and in no immediate danger, the communications officer waved him off. If Blair crashed and burned coming in, it wouldn't leave Hobbes stranded with a damaged flight deck and empty fuel tanks.

So Blair waited—gloomy and brooding. His first trip off the carrier deck ended in defeat. He should have considered the possibility of more Kilrathi ships hiding near that asteroid, kept a tighter rein on Hobbes . . .

Right now he was mostly surprised by their survival.

The cats had surprised him twice today; once by springing the ambush, then by backing off when he and Hobbes were ripe for the picking. That seemed to be the only reason Blair and Hobbes were still alive, and that grim thought worried him. Was he finally losing his edge?

He had witnessed this during years of war. A veteran pilot with an exemplary record would find his skills slipping away and his judgment calls evolving into errors. Such flyers would get sloppy and careless, and they did not live very long.

Ever since the Battle of Earth, and especially after *Concordia*'s loss, Blair found himself growing increasingly uncertain about the war and his role in it. Were his doubts starting to sap his cockpit performance? If that was true, maybe it was time to rethink his whole position. He could retreat into the purely administrative side of his job, as his predecessor had apparently done . . . or he could request a new assignment, even resign his commission and leave the war for a younger generation who still knew what they were fighting for and had the sharpened skills needed to carry on that fight.

It was a tempting thought. But how could Blair drop out now? Wouldn't that be a betrayal of all his comrades who hadn't been so lucky? He wished he could talk to Angel. She always knew how to put everything into perspective.

"*Snoop Leader, you are clear for approach,*" Rollins said over his bitter reflections.

"Roger," he acknowledged. Blair brought his full attention back to the problems of landing. Fighter and carrier had matched vectors and velocities precisely, and they were drifting less than a kilometer apart. Using minimum thruster power, Blair steered closer, lining up the flight deck with a practiced eye while watching the damage readouts for any sign of a sudden failure in a critical subsystem. A pilot like Maniac Marshall would have made a more dramatic approach, coming in under power and killing all his velocity in one last, well-timed braking thrust, but Blair wasn't taking any chances this time.

The most critical moment of any carrier landing came at the end. Blair had to steer the Thunderbolt directly into the narrow tractor beam that would snag the fighter and guide it down to the flight deck and into the hangar area. A tiny error in judgment could cause him to miss the beam and plow into the ship's superstructure. Or he could hit the beam with the fighter in the wrong attitude and damage both Thunderbolt and flight deck.

As the range in meters dropped steadily on the readout in the corner of his faceplate HUD, Blair held his breath and activated the landing gear control. A few seconds went by, and the amber damage light flickered, blinked . . . then went out. A green light nearby declared the wheels down and locked, but Blair raised a video view from the carrier deck and zoomed in for a close-up of the fighter's undercarriage, just to be sure. The blast burns and pockmarked hull plating made him wince, but the gear had deployed and the fighter looked as ready for a landing as it ever would be.

He killed almost all of his momentum then, and the range countdown slowed. Then, abruptly, the fighter shuddered as the tractor beams took hold. Blair kept his hands poised over the throttles and the steering yoke, ready to apply thrust quickly in case the tractors failed and he had to abort. Slowly, carefully, painfully the fighter closed in, and the carrier's superstructure loomed large in the cockpit viewport.

The wheels touched down evenly, and the fighter rolled freely along the deck, still pulled along by the tractor beams that held the Thunderbolt despite the absence of gravity. The force field at the end of the hangar deck cut off and the fighter glided smoothly into the depressurized compartment. A moment later Blair's craft rolled to a complete stop, and Blair gratefully relaxed and started the powering-down process.

It took several minutes to repressurize the hangar deck. Blair was still running through his shutdown checklist when the overhead lights flashed red, signaling that the atmosphere was safe to breathe and that artificial gravity was about to be restored. Outside he saw technicians bracing themselves. Then the welcome sensation of weight gripped him again, gradually rising until the gravity was set at Earth-normal. Techs, some fully suited and others in shirtsleeves, swarmed on the deck around the fighter.

The cockpit swung open. Blair unstrapped himself and stood slowly, stiff yet glad for the chance to move around again. After a moment, he clambered down the ladder built into the side of the Thunderbolt. "It's all yours, boys and girls," he told the technicians.

Rachel Coriolis was there, her face creased in a frown. "Looks like you were nearly cat food, skipper," she commented. "You'd take a lot better care of 'em if you were the one that had to fix 'em up!"

He shrugged, not really feeling up to a snappy comeback. "And maybe mechanics wouldn't grumble so much if they had to be on the firing line."

"What, and give up all this glamour?" Her grin faded. "Captain wants you and Hobbes in his ready room for debriefing. And I don't think he's handing out any medals today. Know what I mean?"

Captain's Ready Room, TCS Victory Orsini System

"If this mission was any indication of your abilities, Colonel, then I must say that I wonder how you earned such a good reputation."

Blair and Ralgha stood at rigid attention in front of the captain's desk, listening to Eisen's angry appraisal of their patrol mission. *Victory's* captain was plainly agitated, unable to sit still. He prowled the confines of the ready room like a caged beast, pausing from time to time to drive a point home to the two pilots. Neither of them had ventured a response to Eisen, and Blair for one agreed with most of what he had to say. The mission had been mishandled from start to finish, and as senior officer Blair bore the full blame for everything that had gone wrong.

Eisen leaned heavily on his desk. "I expected better of both of you," he said, more quietly this time. "Especially you, Colonel. But maybe I'm just expecting too damned much. Maybe the Confed has just pulled off too many miracles in the past, and the miracles are starting to run out now." He looked up. "Well? Do either of you have anything to say?"

"I screwed up, sir," Blair said softly. "Underestimated the Kilrathi and let the situation get out of hand instead of keeping a grip on . . . things." He looked at Hobbes. "I allowed myself to get separated from my wingman, and soaked up unacceptable damage in the process. That made it impossible to press the fight when we were able to hook up again, even though the enemy seemed unwilling to stand and fight."

"And you, Ralgha?" Eisen asked. "Anything to add?"

The Kilrathi renegade shook his head. "No, Captain, save that the Colonel fought with skill and honor."

"Honor doesn't matter to me nearly as much as winning," Eisen commented, straightening up slowly, "but at least you both got back in one piece." He mustered a faint smile. "The Confederation needs every pilot it can muster, even a couple of senile old screw-ups like you."

"Next time out, sir, I guarantee things will be different," Blair told him. "You can count on it."

"I'll hold you to it," the captain said. "All right, let's move on. I want a heavier patrol dispatched as soon as possible. Draw up a flight plan for my approval. I suggest a minimum of four fighters this time, and maybe a backstop of four more in case the first team runs into trouble. We'll smoke the bastards out one way or another."

"I'll get on it, sir," Blair said. "Hobbes and I will lead 'em . . ."

Eisen shook his head. "You know the regs. Except on magnum ops, you stick to the flight rotation schedule. You're the wing commander, Colonel, and you can't start trying to jump on board every op. That will burn you out, and that's the last thing we need right now."

Reluctantly, Blair nodded in acceptance. "As you wish, Captain," he said slowly.

"All right, then. You're both dismissed."

Outside the ready room, Ralgha reached out and halted Blair with one massive paw. "I am very sorry, my friend," he said gravely. "I let you down out there today. And yet you were willing to accept the blame from Captain Eisen that should have been directed at me."

Blair shook his head. "Sure as hell wasn't all your fault," he told the Kilrathi. "I should have been ready for the bastards."

"Nevertheless, I failed you. That insolent peasant and his challenge . . . I should never have allowed myself to be drawn into fighting him, leaving you to face the others alone." Ralgha paused. "Did it seem to you, my friend, that the enemy behavior was out of character?"

"How so?" Blair asked. He, too, had wondered about the way the trap unfolded, but he was especially interested in whatever observations Hobbes might share. After all, Ralgha *nar* Hhallas was the closest thing to a genuine expert on Kilrathi psychology aboard the *Victory*.

"In the beginning, it seemed to me they were intending to fly a traditional attack plan. There was no good reason to launch that first attack if their aim was to draw us into an ambush. It was only after I was engaged that the others broke off and attempted to draw you into their trap. Could it be that the Empire has a particular interest in you?"

"In me? How—"

"You can be assured that the Empire has sources of information within the Confederation, agents who could have identified your new assignment to this ship. Spies are remarkably easy to plant, particularly when the Empire has many human slaves to recruit."

"You really think a human would spy for the Kilrathi?" Blair asked. "And that the Empire would rely on a human slave to work in the Imperial interest out of reach of the nerve lash?"

"There are always a few who betray willingly, my friend. Their honor is less strong than their ambition or greed. And Imperial Intelligence does have techniques for guaranteeing cooperation from even the unwilling: personality overlays, deep conditioning . . . many things. There are surely spies reporting to Kilrah. And with your record and reputation, it is possible that the Emperor or his grandson has singled you out as a human leader to be terminated. War is far more personal with my people than with yours, and it would be a great triumph to eliminate a wing commander of your stature in battle."

"So you think the ambush was planned? That would mean there is an agent aboard this ship . . ."

"Not necessarily," Ralgha said slowly. "We know the Empire can monitor some of our ship-to-ship transmissions. I used your rank several times during radio messages, and if that information was joined with knowledge of your assignment to the *Victory* and of Confed troop movements. . . . I merely feel you should consider the possibility. The trap may well have been prepared in hopes of your arrival, but it was not set in motion until the battle had already begun."

Blair shrugged. "Maybe you're right. But on the other hand, if I had been in command of that Kilrathi flight, I would have done my best to divide and conquer, just the way they did; no matter who blundered into the trap." He paused. "Fact is, it looked more to me like they were damned interested in you."

"In me? It was only that first *kilra'hra* who dared challenge me."

"That's my point," Blair said. "He charged in looking for hairless apes, and it was only when you identified yourself that all hell started breaking loose. And when you finished the first guy off and hooked back up with me, the other guys got pretty shy all of a sudden."

"Are you coming to doubt me, my friend?" Ralgha asked.

"You know better than that. I'm just curious, that's all." Blair studied his friend's alien features. "Maybe it's you they are afraid of. Your reputation has to be at least as big as mine, after all these years. Maybe bigger where the Empire's concerned. A renegade noble turned Confed fighter pilot . . . I could see a few Kilrathi getting nervous if they ran into you during a fight."

The Kilrathi gave a rumbling chuckle. "That, my friend, sounds unlikely. I am a disgrace among my people. I am nothing. It is only to a good friend like you that my poor life means anything at all." Ralgha looked away for a moment, a surprisingly human mannerism. "Although I must say, it certainly felt good to be out there again. My gratitude for your trust and support of me is endless."

"Forget it, buddy," Blair told him. "You're back where you belong now."

Flight Wing Rec Room, TCS Victory Orsini System

The victory party was in full swing when the lift deposited Blair outside the recreation hall set aside for use by the flight wing. He paused in the corridor, reluctant to go inside. After all, they were celebrating a successful op that had made good the mistakes he and Hobbes made the first time out, and Blair didn't much care to be reminded of that fact tonight. But as wing commander, he had a duty to his outfit, and part of that duty was to show his support for them in success and failure alike, even when it left a bitter taste in his mouth.

He squared his shoulders and opened the rec room door.

The noise was almost overpowering at first, with the blare of music competing for dominance with the babble of conversation, laughs, and cheers coming from a cluster of men and women around the flight simulator in one corner of the compartment. Blair stopped just inside, scanning the room. Gradually some of the noise died away as pilots became aware of his presence.

"See, the conquering hero comes!" Maniac Marshall proclaimed loudly. The half-empty glass in his hand and the slur in his voice made it clear he was well under way with his own celebration of the successful afternoon's battle. The major had a female crew member with comm department shoulder tabs backed into a corner, but as he turned toward Blair, she quickly slipped away to join the spectators by the flight simulators, looking relieved.

"So," Marshall went on. "Come to join the victory party, is it, Colonel? Guess you have to find 'em wherever you can, huh? When you can't manage to earn one, that is."

That provoked a few nervous laughs. Luckily, one of the pilots approached Maniac with a pitcher of beer, offering him a refill. Marshall held out his glass unsteadily and let her fill it for him. In the comparative quiet that followed, Blair took a step forward and cleared his throat. "I just wanted to drop by and congratulate Gold Squadron for a job well done today," he said loudly. "I'm sure there's nobody as proud of you people tonight as I am."

"Damn straight," Maniac interrupted. "Not just ten Kilrathi fighters—two of 'em killed by yours truly—but also a cap ship. And a supply depot hidden inside that asteroid. All cleared out courtesy of Maniac Marshall and the Gold Squadron . . . with an able assist by those two brilliant scouts, Wrong-Way Blair and the King of the Kitty Litter! What would we do without 'em, huh?"

Blair fought down a flash of anger. Marshall was drunk and offensive, but he was entitled to a little boasting. The major had led three other fighters to probe the same region where Blair and Hobbes had run into trouble, and flushed out a nest of Kilrathi fighters and a light cruiser that had moved in after the first battle. According to all reports, Marshall had done a decent job of keeping his command together while awaiting the back-up flight's arrival. They accounted for ten Dralthi and managed to knock out the capital ship as well. Although some of the Thunderbolts were heavily damaged, none had been destroyed. All in all it had been an excellent job.

"Captain Eisen asked me to let you know that the drinks tonight are being charged to the shipboard recreation fund," Blair went on as if Marshall hadn't spoken. Usually, drinks were paid for by the individual officers and crewmen, with their cost charged against shipboard pay accounts. But this was a special occasion—the first triumph of *Victory's* new tour of duty. "So enjoy yourselves while you can. You'll be back on the flight line soon enough!"

That brought cheers from everyone. Most of the flight wing's personnel were in the rec room for the party, except for pilots and technicians who had duty tonight or first thing in the morning. There were also a fair number of people from other carrier departments. Blair saw Lieutenant Rollins at the bar, deep in conversation with a pretty redhead from Blue Squadron.

He looked around the room again and noticed a woman

sitting alone at one of the tables, her eyes resting on him with a coldly intense expression. He recognized her from the Wing's personnel files: Lieutenant Laurel Buckley (callsign Cobra), a member of Gold Squadron. That was all he knew about her since her family and background records were sketchy. She consistently received high marks in Colonel Dulbrunin's quarterly evaluations in her file, but beyond that she was a mystery.

The door opened behind Blair. He glanced over his shoulder and smiled at Ralgha, receiving a slight bow in response before the Kilrathi moved on toward the bar.

"Hey, Hobbes," a new voice cut over the chatter that filled the room. "How 'bout going a round with me, huh? Bet you a week's pay on one hand."

The Kilrathi shook his head gravely. "Thank you, no," he said, turning to the bartender to order a drink.

Blair studied the man who had hailed his friend. He was seated nearby, a Chinese flight lieutenant who looked about thirty standard years old until you saw the age in his eyes. The man caught Blair's look and flashed him a lazy grin, holding up a deck of cards in one hand.

"What about you, Colonel?" he asked, riffling the cards expertly. "Want to play a hand? Since you're the new boy in town, I'll let you call the game."

"I think I'll keep my money if it's all the same to you," Blair said, sitting down. The man was another pilot from Gold Squadron, and from all appearances didn't have any problem serving with Hobbes. That recommended him to Blair right away. "I learned a long, long time ago never to play cards with the shipboard shark."

"Well, it's a free Confed." The lieutenant put down the cards and stuck out a hand. "I'm Vagabond. A belated welcome aboard's in order, I guess. Or would condolences for your little scrap this morning be more appropriate?"

"Not much for protocol, are you?" Blair said, taking

the proffered hand in his. "Do you always go by your callsign or do you just have something against the name Winston Chang?"

He shrugged. "Formalities tend to be forgotten when you spend most of your time just trying to survive, wouldn't you say?" He smiled, lifted his drink, and took a sip. "What little spare time we have should not be wasted on practicing salutes and mastering the intricacies of military make-work."

Blair looked him over, liking the man despite Chang's irreverent manner, or maybe because of it. "With that attitude, I'm surprised you've been able to adapt to the military life at all."

Vagabond shrugged again. "I've always felt that the military should learn how to adapt to me, Colonel," he said with another grin. "After all, I'm a genuine high-flying hero type, with pilot's wings and everything!"

Blair was about to make a sarcastic reply when his attention was drawn to Hobbes. The Kilrathi had finished his drink in silence and turned from the bar, heading for the door again, probably uncomfortable in the crowd of humans. Ralgha, a Kilrathi noble before his defection, never relinquished his aversion to large groups and noisy surroundings, especially when they involved non-Kilrathi gatherings. It was one of the reasons people found him so aloof and seemingly unfriendly, but it was nearly as much a matter of carnivore instinct as of aristocratic breeding.

As he approached the exit he brushed against the woman Blair had seen watching him earlier, Lieutenant Buckley. She reached the door just before Hobbes and stopped to listen to someone. Hobbes barely touched her, but she spun quickly to confront him with an angry expression which marred her attractive features. "Don't touch me!" she grated. "Don't *ever* touch me, you goddamned furball!"

Ralgha recoiled from her as if stricken, started to speak, then seemed to think better of it. Instead he gave one of his bows and circled cautiously around her. She glared at him until the door closed behind him.

"Excuse me, Lieutenant," Blair said, suppressing the anger welling inside him. "I have . . . a matter that needs to be attended."

Chang looked from Blair to Buckley and back again, his smile gone. "I understand," he said with a nod. "But I hope you'll keep something in mind, Colonel. We've got a lot of good people on this ship. Even the ones who may not fit in with your idea of . . . decorum."

Blair stood up and crossed to the door. Buckley was still standing nearby, flushed and angry. He took her elbow and pointed toward the door. "Time we had a little talk, Lieutenant," he said quietly. "Outside."

She let him lead her into the corridor. When the door closed and the party sounds were no longer heard, they faced each other for a long moment in silence.

"Want to tell me what that little outburst was all about, Lieutenant?" Blair asked.

Buckley fixed him with an angry stare. "Ain't much to say, Colonel," she said, managing to make the rank sound more like a swear word. "You insisted on flying with *it*, and even after it let you down you'll probably still take its part. Doesn't leave much scope for conversation, does it?"

"Lieutenant Colonel Ralgha *nar* Hhallas is a superior officer, Lieutenant," Blair said sharply. "You will refer to *him* with respect. I will not have one of my officers treating another member of the wing with such blatant bigotry and hatred. Some day you might have to fly on his wing, and when that happens . . ."

"That won't happen, Colonel," she said stiffly. "I can't fly with . . . *him*, and if you order it, I will resign my commission on the spot. That's all there is to it."

"I should take you up on that resignation right now, Lieutenant," Blair said. "But you're a good pilot, and we need all the good pilots we can get. I'd rather work this thing out. If you'd just give Hobbes a chance—"

"You don't want me flying with him, sir," she said. "Because I won't defend him in a fight. Better we go our separate ways . . . one way or another."

"Why? What's he ever done to you?"

"He's Kilrathi," she said harshly. "That's enough. And there's nothing you can do to change the way I feel."

"I . . . see." Blair studied her face. It was a bad idea to let something like this simmer inside the wing, but he wasn't willing to force a confrontation. Not yet, at least. "I'll try to keep the two of you apart for the moment, Lieutenant, but I expect you to behave like a Confed officer and not a spoiled brat. Do you understand me?"

"I wasn't asking for special favors, sir," she said, shrugging. "Just thought you should know how things stand."

"Just so you know where *you* stand, Lieutenant," he said softly. "If I have to pick between the two of you, I'll pick Hobbes every time. I'd trust him with my life."

She gave him a chilly smile. "That, Colonel, is *your* mistake to make."

• CHAPTER V

Flight Wing Rec Room, TCS Victory Orsini System

The rec room was much quieter tonight than the night of the party and considerably less crowded. Blair finished another long shift of poring over reports and requisitions. He decided that a quick drink and a few moments of simply sitting alone, perhaps watching the stars through the compartment's viewport, would help him get over the feeling of confinement and constriction which plagued him more and more lately. As he walked briskly through the door, he was hoping for some solitude. He wanted to forget, just for a few minutes, that he had anything to do with *Victory*, or the flight wing . . . or the war.

But the impulse for solitude left him when he spotted Rachel Coriolis at a table near the bar, viewing a holocassette that seemed to be displaying schematics of a fighter Blair didn't immediately recognize. The chief tech was one of the few people on board he felt comfortable around, and he was certain she would know more than what information appeared in his official files: real stories of some of his pilots and their backgrounds. After the incident with Cobra Buckley the week before, Blair was still in the dark about the woman's attitudes, and so far he hadn't been able to find any answers.

He stopped at the bar and ordered a glass of Tamayoan fire wine, then walked over to Rachel's table. She looked up as he approached, giving him a welcoming smile. "Hello, Colonel, slumming with the troops today? Pull up a chair, if you don't mind being seen with one of us lowly techie types."

"Thanks, Chief," he said. He sat down across the table from her and studied the holographic schematics for a moment. "Don't think I recognize that design."

"One of the new Excaliburs," she said, her voice tinged with excitement. "Isn't she a beauty? Heavy fighter with more guns and armor than a Thunderbolt, but increased maneuverability to go with it. And I've heard a rumor they're going to be mounted with a sensor cloak, so the little darlings can sneak right past a Kilrathi defensive perimeter and nail the hairballs at close range!"

"Don't they classify that stuff any more?" Blair asked with a smile.

She gave an unladylike snort. "Get real, skipper. Maybe you flyboys don't hear anything 'til it gets declassified, but the techs have a network that reaches damn near everywhere. We know what's coming off the line before the brass does . . . and usually have all the design flaws spotted up front, too."

Blair chuckled. "Well, I hope your techs don't decide to turn on the rest of us. I doubt we'd last long if you did. You like your job, don't you, Chief?"

She switched off the hologram. "Yeah. I always liked working with machines and computers. An engine part either works or it doesn't. No gray areas. No doubletalk."

"Machines don't lie," Blair said, nodding.

"Not the way people do. And even when something's wrong with a machine, you always know just where the problem is."

Blair didn't say anything for a few minutes. Finally he looked her in the eye. "I've got a people problem right now, Chief. I was wondering if you could help me with it."

"It ain't what I'm paid for," she told him, "and my free advice is worth everything you spend for it. But I'll take a shot if you want."

"Lieutenant Buckley. What can you tell me about her? The straight dope, not the official file."

She looked down at the table. "I heard about her little blowup with Hobbes last week. Can't say anybody was surprised, though. She's never made any big secret out of the way she feels about the Kilrathi."

"What I want to know is *why*? I've been in the Navy for better than fifteen years, Chief. I've been in all kinds of crews, seen all kinds of shipmates and their hangups. But I never met anybody so single-minded about the Kilrathi before. I mean, Maniac's got good reason to resent Hobbes personally . . . but with Cobra, we're talking blind hatred. She won't even give him a chance."

"Yeah. Look, I don't know the whole story, so don't take this as gospel." The tech leaned closer over the table and lowered her voice. "Right after she came on board a buddy of mine from the old *Hermes* pointed her out to me. She served there a year before she transferred here . . . her first assignment."

"I was curious about that in her file," Blair commented. "She seems older than that. I'd have put her at thirty or so . . ."

"That's about right," Rachel told him. "She got a late start. My friend told me that the story on Cobra was that she'd been a Kilrathi slave for ten years before the Marines rescued her from a labor camp. She spent some more time in reeducation, then joined up. She won top honors piloting, and just cut through everything with this single-minded determination. I think sometimes that the only thing holding Cobra's life together is the hate she has for the Kilrathi. And I can't really say I blame her."

Blair nodded slowly. "Maybe I can't, either," he said

slowly. "I can't even begin to imagine what it would be like to grow up a Kilrathi slave. She must have been taken as a kid, raised to think of her own race as animals . . ."

"So it's no wonder she can't stomach Hobbes," the tech said bluntly. "You and I know he's okay, but to her he just represents everything she grew up hating and fearing." Rachel took a sip from her drink. "So cut her some slack, Colonel. If you really want to fix the problem, that is."

"I do," he said quietly. "But there are limits, you know. I sympathize with her, but sometimes you just can't bend things far enough in the Service to make all the square pegs fit."

"That's why I'd rather work with machines," she told him. "Sooner or later, people just screw up the works."

"Maybe you're being too hard on people," he said. "Some of us are okay when you get to know us."

She looked him up and down with a slow smile. "They need to pass inspection, same as anything else." She stood up, collected the holocassette, then tucked it into a pocket of her baggy coveralls. "I got certain hours for that kind of quality control work, of course."

Blair returned her smile, warming to her. "You keep that schedule posted somewhere, Chief?"

"Only for a select few, Colonel," she told him. "The ones with the best schematics."

Ready Room, TCS Victory
Tamayo System

"I hope you're not expecting anything too exciting, Blair. This is probably just another milk run, from the looks of it. At least that's what we're hoping for."

Blair studied Eisen's face, trying to locate a hint of sarcasm in his expression. Since Gold Squadron's triumph

over the Kilrathi cruiser and its escort, enemy activity
in the Orsini system had virtually disappeared, and *Victory*
had jumped to the Tamayo system, where they had been
carrying out a seemingly endless string of routine patrols.
Blair and Hobbes took their turn on the duty schedule
along with the rest of the wing, but so far there was no
further combat. The only excitement since the first big
clash came when a pair of interceptors from Blue
Squadron tangled with four light Kilrathi fighters, sending
them running in short order.

Eisen was right about the missions to date being milk
runs, but was there something more behind his comment?
Meaning that was all Blair could handle, perhaps? His
impassive face gave away nothing as he called up a
holographic mission plan for Blair and Ralgha to study.

"The cats—" Eisen broke off, shooting a look at
Hobbes. "The Kilrathi have been steering clear of the
Victory, but they sent a couple of squadrons of raiders
to work the edges of the system, near the jump point to
Locanda. In the past week, they've picked off three
transports outbound for the Locanda colony while we've
come up empty."

Blair frowned. "I was posted in that system once, a
few years back. There's not a hell of a lot there. I'm
surprised we *sent* three transports that way in one week."

The captain didn't reply right away. Finally he gave a
shrug. "Some of our intelligence sources in the Empire
received word that the enemy is planning a move against
the Locanda System. Confed's been pumping resources
that way to try to catch them unprepared. Apparently
the main reason they are hanging around is to harass
our supply lines." He looked from Blair to Hobbes, then
back to Blair again. "Needless to say, that information
stays in this room."

"Yes, sir," Blair said. Ralgha nodded assent.

"Right, then. Another transport is set to make a run

today, but this time we're sending an escort. We want to see if we can break this little blockade of theirs once and for all, then open the pipeline into Locanda again. Your job is to provide the escort and be ready for trouble. Like I said, with luck, they will miss this one. But if the bad guys return, we want that transport covered. Understood?"

"Aye, aye, sir," Blair replied formally.

"Good. Let's cover the details . . ."

It took a good ten minutes to go over the specifics of the mission, establishing rendezvous coordinates and other details. When it was all over, Blair and Hobbes stood. "We're ready, Captain," Blair said. "Come on, Hobbes, let's get saddled up."

"A moment more, Colonel, if you please," Eisen said, holding up a hand. He shot Ralgha a look. "In private."

"I will see you on the flight deck, Colonel," Hobbes said. The Kilrathi seemed calm and imperturbable as ever, but Blair thought he could detect a note of concern in his friend's tone.

Blair sat back down as the Kilrathi left the room. "What can I do for you, sir?"

"Colonel, I'd like to discuss your attitude," Eisen said as soon as the door had closed behind Hobbes. He sounded angry. "Seems to me you're under the impression that you're too good to mix with the rest of the pilots."

"I'm not sure I understand, Captain," Blair said slowly. "I've been getting to know them . . ."

"But in three weeks aboard this tub, the only wingman you've flown with is Hobbes." Eisen cut his attempted protest off. "I know he's your friend, and I know there's still some bad feelings among some of the others about working with him, but it isn't helping morale by you refusing to pair with anybody else. I know Chang would fly with him, and probably one or two of the others as well, so you could at least trade off now and then."

"Sir, with all due respect, that isn't your decision to make," Blair told him quietly. "You are CO of this ship, but the flight wing is my bailiwick. Mine alone. I run the wing my way. A pilot has to be able to trust his wingman, feeling complete total confidence in him, which is exactly the way I feel about Hobbes. I choose to fly with him."

"Even though he let you down your first time out?"

"Sir?" Blair had been careful to keep the details of the first patrol ambiguous in his official report.

"Come on, Colonel, you know the networks. Even the CO hears some things, no matter how much everybody works to cover them. Hobbes hared off after an enemy fighter and left you in the lurch when they jumped you."

"I don't blame him, sir. The whole situation just sort of . . . developed."

"Well, it's pretty difficult to see how you can continue to have confidence in Hobbes after that mess, no matter how much you close your eyes to it. And there's another point here, Blair. By saying how much you trust Hobbes, you're implying that you *don't* have any faith in the others. I don't like that. It's bad for morale—not just in your precious flight wing, but involving the entire ship. I won't stand for anything that hampers the performance of *Victory* or her crew." Eisen studied him for a few seconds. "*Do* you have a problem with the rest of the wing?"

"Sir, I just don't know them well enough yet," Blair said. "The only one I do know is Marshall, and quite frankly I wouldn't fly with him if he was the only pilot on this ship. He's a menace who should have had his wings taken away a long time ago."

Eisen looked thoughtful, but didn't speak.

"As for the others," Blair went on. "Lieutenant Buckley has a good record, but I'm not sure her head's screwed on straight. Chang seems like a nice guy, but undisciplined and unpredictable. The others . . . I'm still finding out about them. They are accustomed to each other, and they're already paired into some pretty good teams. I don't think it is wise to rock the boat until I've got a better handle on how they perform."

"How will you find anything out about them if you don't fly with them?"

"Every time they go out the launch tubes, I follow the mission from Flight Control, Captain. Believe me, I'm starting to get a pretty good idea of how they fly . . . and how they think. I'll start rotating the roster when I'm ready . . . and not before then."

"Well, I strongly suggest you speed up the process a bit, Colonel," Eisen said. "Get to know them and start flying with them. If you don't, I think you're going to have a serious morale problem. Is that clear?"

"As a bell, sir."

"Then you're dismissed." Eisen hesitated a moment. "And . . . good luck out there today, Colonel."

"Thank you, sir." Blair stood and gave Eisen a quick salute, then left the ready room. As he rode down the elevator to the Flight Deck, he reviewed in his mind everything the captain said. By the time the doors slid open, he was seething inside.

Someone plainly ran to Eisen behind his back, carrying tales, and hinting that Blair was unfit. Blair was sure he knew just who it was.

Wing Commander's Office, TCS Victory Tamayo System

A knock on the door made Blair look up from his computer terminal. "Enter," he said.

"You wanted to see me, Colonel?" It was Maniac Marshall, wearing a flight suit and carrying his colorfully painted helmet under one arm. "I'm up for a patrol in fifteen minutes, so this'd better be quick."

"It will be, Marshall," Blair said coldly.

The major started to sit, but Blair fixed him with an angry stare. "I didn't give you permission to make yourself at home, Mister," he told the pilot. "You're at attention."

Marshall hesitated a moment, then straightened up. "Yes, *sir*, Colonel, *sir*," he responded.

"I have a little job for you, Major," Blair said, his voice low and dangerous. "This morning, before my escort run with Hobbes, Captain Eisen chatted with me about this unit's morale. He seemed to feel that I was not inspiring confidence and good feeling among my people here."

Marshall didn't respond. There was a long silence before Blair continued. "From some of the things he said, I suspect that someone in the wing has been going behind my back to him, carrying all sorts of complaints about the way I choose to run things. Needless to say, Major, I regard this as a very serious breach of protocol. Members of a flight wing *do not* go outside the chain of command with their petty jealousies and personal problems, and I intend to have no repetitions of this little incident. Therefore, Major, I'm putting you in charge of reporting any further violations of military procedure in the wing to me. If it comes to my attention that there have been additional incidents of wing personnel going outside the chain of command this way, I'll hold *you* responsible. Do I make myself clear, Major?"

"Crystal clear," Marshall said, enunciating each syllable precisely. After a long pause he added, "Sir."

"Very good, Major," Blair said. "I won't keep you from your patrol any longer. You're dismissed."

He leaned back in his chair as Marshall left the office, feeling some of the anger and tension draining from him. Blair was convinced from the very beginning that

Marshall was the one who had been complaining to Eisen, but of course he had no proof. This put Maniac on notice without requiring any actual accusations.

The confrontation alleviated some of the frustrations of the morning operation. He and Hobbes had escorted the transport to the jump point without any sign of an enemy fighter. The return trip proved equally peaceful. That was good, in one sense, but it was beginning to seem as if he would never get a chance to compensate for their first unsuccessful mission. It was even more unnerving to discover that raiders had hit another ship leaving the Locanda System at the same jump point just an hour after Blair and Hobbes returned to the *Victory*.

The whole situation gave him pause for thought. He could not help mulling over the conversation with Hobbes after their first battle and the Kilrathi's speculations about the possibility of an intelligence breach. *Could* someone be feeding details of Confed ship movements to the enemy? And, if so, was there some specific reason why he and Hobbes might be singled out for special attention? Blair was still struck by the fact that the Kilrathi had seemed to want to avoid engaging Hobbes. . . .

He remembered old Cultural Intelligence briefings about Kilrathi social customs. Perhaps there was a high-ranking Imperial noble assigned to the Orsini System who had declared a formal state of feud with Ralgha *nar* Hhallas. That might make other pilots wary of getting involved, leading them to avoid action against Hobbes.

It sounded like a good working theory . . . but it still suggested that the Kilrathi knew much more about Confed operations than they should. Were they simply keeping close track of Terran communications or might there be spies in the fleet, even here aboard the *Victory*?

Did Cobra, the ex-slave, have any place in all this? Or was it all just an unfortunate but suspicious coincidence?

Blair hoped that was the case. He did not want to

face the reality that someone in his flight wing was actually
a Kilrathi spy.

Flight Control, TCS Victory
Tamayo System

"Sir?"

Blair turned his chair to face the door to the Flight
Control Center. It was nearly midnight, ship's time, but
he had decided to spend some extra hours tonight going
over flight plans for the Wing's projected operations for
the next day. He hoped to extend patrols to cover the
Locanda jump point more effectively so that future losses
in that volume of space might be avoided. If he couldn't
find a better way to keep the Kilrathi raiders under
control, he would talk Eisen into actually moving the
carrier closer to the jump point for a more constant watch.

He was glad of the interruption. It was difficult and
tedious work at best. After working for hours, any break
in the routine was welcome.

Blair studied the slender, slightly-built young woman
standing in the open doorway. She was another of Gold
Squadron's pilots, Lieutenant Robin Peters, but so far
he had not spoken with her. Nonetheless, Blair was
impressed by both her combat record and her patrol
performance since he had joined the ship. She was most
frequently teamed with Chang as wingman. The two
made a competent team. "They call you Flint, right?"
he asked.

She nodded. "Glad to see you've at least looked over
the flight roster, sir," she said with a faint smile.

"I've given it a glance," Blair responded.

"Then maybe you've noticed, sir, that there are other
pilots on board, aside from Colonel Ralgha."

"People on this ship sure as hell do take a lot of
interest in my choice of partners," Blair said. "Wingman

assignments were still my prerogative, last time I checked."

"Sir," the lieutenant began, sounding tentative. "I come from a long line of fighter pilots. My brother, my father, his father before him . . . I guess you could say flying's in my blood."

"Your point being . . . ?"

"I know your record, and I would expect you to at least look over ours. We have racked up our share of kills. We're not scrubs out here, sir."

"Nobody said you were," Blair told her.

"No, sir, nobody ever *said* anything. But you've made it pretty clear you don't think the rest of us are worth flying with." She looked away. "If you don't give us a try, how are you ever going to decide if we're up to your standards?"

"Oh, I've made a few decisions already, Lieutenant," Blair said. "Believe it or not, I do know something about how a flight wing works. I've only been serving in the damned things for my entire adult life." He paused for a moment. "So you feel I should be flying with other wingmen, not just Hobbes. You have any specific recommendations?"

She looked back at him with a hint of a smile. "Oh, I would never presume to do your job for you, sir. After all, choice of wingmen is your prerogative, isn't that right? I just work here . . ."

"Well, consider your message delivered, Lieutenant." He smiled, coming to a decision about the woman. "And tomorrow afternoon, when you take that fourth shift patrol you're scheduled for . . ."

"Yes, sir?"

"I hope you'll be willing to break in a new wingman. He's an old-timer, but not a scrub . . . at least I hope not."

"I'll be looking forward to it, sir."

• CHAPTER VI

Thunderbolt 300
Tamayo System

"Well, looks like we came up dry again," Blair said over the comm channel, not bothering to hide his disgust. "Shall we head for home, Lieutenant?"

"*Sounds good to me, sir,*" Flint responded.

The patrol was routine, like so many others the *Victory's* pilots encountered these past few weeks. It seemed that changing wingmen had not brought any corresponding change in Blair's luck.

"*Watchdog Leader, this is Kennel. Do you copy, over?*" The voice belonged to Lieutenant Rollins. *Victory's* Communications Officer sounded keyed up.

"This is Watchdog Leader," Blair said. "What've you got, Kennel?"

"*Long-range sensors are picking up a large flight of incoming bogies, Colonel,*" Rollins said. "*And they ain't friendly, by the looks of things. They're coming from quadrant Delta . . . looks like a full-scale attack force, not just a patrol. Captain requests you RTB immediately.*"

"Roger that, Kennel," Blair said. "We will Return To Base immediately." He was visualizing the tactical situation in his mind's eye. Relative to the carrier's position, ships coming out of Delta Quadrant would be almost exactly opposite the point he and Flint were covering on their patrol, and if the enemy appeared on the long-range sensors, they would be located within the same range of the ship as the two Thunderbolts. Blair could expect to get back to *Victory* at approximately the same time as the enemy, presuming they were planning to press home the attack.

Suddenly he wished that he had not complained about the lack of action quite so much. . . .

"Kennel, this is Watchdog Leader," Blair went on after a moment's pause. "Order Red and Gold Squadrons on a full magnum launch, all fighters up. Colonel Ralgha to take operational command until I arrive. And call in all Blue Squadron patrols as well. I want them to rendezvous with me at coordinates Beta-Ten-Niner."

"*Rendezvous . . . Beta-Ten-Zero-Nine*," the lieutenant repeated. "*Understood.*"

"Have Chief Coriolis put up a refueling shuttle to meet us at those coordinates. Launch ASAP . . . before the furballs get close enough to interfere."

"*A fuel shuttle, Colonel?*" Rollins sounded uncertain.

"You heard me, Lieutenant," Blair said. "All of the patrol flights are near the end of their cycles out here. I was about to head for home, but I don't plan on any of us hitting an all-out donnybrook with dry tanks, so we'll do some in-flight refueling before we join the party. Any problems with that on your end?"

"*Ah . . . wait one, Watchdog*," Rollins said. Blair could picture the man, in the silence that followed, passing on the gist of his orders to Eisen for confirmation.

While he waited for a confirmation from *Victory*, Blair called up his navigation display and entered the rendezvous coordinates into the autopilot. "Flint, you copy all that?"

"*Yeah, Colonel*," she responded, sounding excited. "*Looks like we get a little party after all.*"

"*Watchdog, this is Kennel*," Rollins said before he had a chance to respond to Peters. "*Your instructions are*

*being carried out. Captain says not to stop for any
sightseeing along the way."*

"Tell him the cavalry's on the way," Blair said, smiling.
"Okay, Flint, you heard the man. Punch it!"

The computer took over the controls, steering the fighter
toward the rendezvous point while Blair concentrated
on monitoring the comm channels to keep track of the
unfolding operation. It appeared things were going
smoothly on the ship. Fighters were routinely kept on
standby, prepped for a magnum launch on fifteen minute's
notice or less. If Blair was right about Chief Coriolis, it
would definitely be "or less" today. He had faith in her
department . . . as well as in her.

What worried him more was the wing itself. Hobbes
would have to take charge until Blair was close enough
to do more than hurl advice, and with the previous bad
feelings about the Kilrathi renegade, there could be
trouble on the firing line. If a hot-head like Maniac or
Cobra decided not to accept Ralgha's orders, the whole
situation could degenerate into a disaster in minutes.
Hobbes knew all the right moves, but did he have a
sufficiently forceful personality to make a collection of
Confed pilots, a notoriously independent breed at the
best of times, carry out those moves the way they were
supposed to?

"Rendezvous coordinates coming up, sir," Flint
reported, jerking Blair out of his reverie. "The shuttle's
on my scope now."

He checked his own monitor. "Confirmed. Looks like
we're first." That made sense. The long-range interceptors
on patrol in Alpha and Gamma Quadrants were further
from the ship when he issued the recall order, probing
ahead of the *Victory*. He and Flint took the rear patrol,
covering both Beta and Delta in the carrier's wake. "All
right, Flint, belly up to the bar and get your fighter a
drink."

"Roger," was her laconic reply.

After a few minutes, she reported her tanks full and cast off from the shuttle, making room for Blair's fighter. He lined up the boxy little craft with practiced ease, letting the shuttle's tractor beams snag the Thunderbolt and pull it in slowly. When they were bare meters apart, a refueling hose extended from the belly of the shuttle to plug into the tank mounted amidships. "Contact," he announced as the green light showed on his status board. Fuel began to flow from shuttle to fighter.

When it was finally over, Blair released the hose and watched it reel into the shuttle before applying reverse thrusters to edge the Thunderbolt away. "Watchdog Leader to Shuttle *Hardy*. Thanks for a wonderful time. But I'm not always this easy on a first date, y'know?"

The shuttle's pilot chuckled. "You mean you're not going to stick around and cuddle? You flyboys are all alike." There was a pause. "Nail a couple of kitty-cats for us, Colonel, since we can't be in the shooting."

"They also serve who only stand and pump fuel, *Hardy*," Blair misquoted. "You just keep our people flying."

Hunt Leader
Tamayo System

Flight Commander Arrak could feel the battle lust surging through his veins. For better than eight days, his squadron operated in this human-held system, yet with orders not to press a full-scale battle with the enemy. Ambushes of enemy transport ships and clashes with Terran fighter patrols were reported by other squadrons off the carrier *Sar'hrai*, but all strictly limited to the point where pilots were beginning to complain of the stain on their honor.

Now that was changed. Operation Unseen Death was

beginning, and *Sar'hrai* now was ordered to damage or destroy the Terran carrier stationed in this system, to further isolate the main target of the Kilrathi strike, the nearby system the humans called Locanda. Warriors of the Empire need not hold back any longer. . . .

"*Hunt Flight, Hunt Flight, this is Sar'hrai Command.*" The voice belonged to *Khantahr* Baron Vurrig *nar* Tsahl, the carrier's commanding officer. "*Remember standing orders. Engage all enemy craft encountered . . . but if you identify the fighter belonging to the renegade Ralgha, he is not to be attacked. Repeat, on positive identification of the Terran pilot called Ralgha, or Hobbes, break off action and do not press the attack.*"

The order made Arrak want to snarl in defiance. Didn't the High Command realize what a problem it was distinguishing Terran fighters in combat? The orders had been issued since the arrival of the Terran ship. They had already deprived Arrak of the chance to score a kill against the renegade the day before, his one chance of real action to date. Kilrathi ships monitored Terran communications closely to track the movements of the renegade, and a pilot in the Talon Squadron was executed by the *Khantahr* for protesting those orders in the name of a feud between his clan and the renegade.

Clearly the orders came from very high up indeed, if they overrode a clan feud. Arrak heard a rumor that the order originated within the Imperial Palace, which meant Crown Prince Thrakhath must have taken a personal interest in the matter. But it would not be easy, in the heat of a major battle, to carry out those instructions.

The renegade was better dead anyway. Years ago he had defected, carrying an entire capital ship and enough vital secrets to set back the Imperial war effort by a decade. Since that time, the scum (once a Lord of the Empire but now nothing more than an outcast) actually dared fly human fighters against his own kind.

Well, the confusion of battle made it difficult to know when orders were violated accidentally . . . or deliberately. And given any chance at all, Arrak knew he would not turn from destroying the traitor Ralgha if the chance presented itself.

"Hunt Flight," he said, exulting at the approach of battle. "Prepare to engage!"

Thunderbolt 300
Tamayo System

"Here they come!"

"Maintain formation. Meet the enemy with overwhelming force, and he will be ours."

"Look sharp, people . . ."

The voices on the radio were growing more and more excited, except for the rigidly controlled growl from Hobbes. Blair could feel his own adrenaline pumping as if he was already on the firing line beside the other pilots. He fought to keep from adding encouraging comments of his own to the radio traffic that was already out there.

He checked his autopilot display again. ETA four minutes . . .

Blair was torn between waiting for the outlying patrol ships to assemble and refuel so the entire force could strike at once, and plunging straight into the fray as quickly as he and Flint could to reach the vicinity of the Victory. Eisen had urged them not to lose any time, but a larger relief force would certainly have been worth a few extra minutes.

In the end, though, Blair had decided that he and Flint needed to join the others as quickly as possible. The question of how well Hobbes could control the wing loomed over him in addition to the potential ill effects on morale if Blair missed the second large-scale fight mounted by his flight wing. So he left instructions for the two interceptor patrols to form a single relief flight, but he and Flint were already on their way into battle.

He was glad of the decision now. It would be four minutes before the two Thunderbolts could join their comrades, and in combat, four minutes could be an eternity.

"They're breaking formation," a voice announced. Blair thought it was Lieutenant Chang. *"Starting their attack runs . . . now!"*

"I've got the first hairball," Maniac Marshall announced. *"Watch my tail, Sandman."*

"Do not lose contact with your wingmen," Ralgha's voice urged. *"And do not let them draw you away from the carrier."*

From the chatter, Blair could picture the unfolding battle even before Rollins fed him tactical information on his monitors. They counted at least thirty incoming Kilrathi ships, a mix of Dralthi and lighter Darket, ranged against eighteen Confed fighters and the larger but less responsive hull-mounted defensive batteries aboard *Victory*. From the sound of things, Hobbes was trying to keep the Terran craft in a rough defensive line, with paired wingmen watching over one another. But hotheads like Marshall were likely to let themselves be distracted by individual opponents and drawn into dogfights, forgetting the big picture.

The Kilrathi had ships to spare. They would still be able to hurl a powerful force against the Terran carrier after all the screening fighters were accounted for.

"I've got the next one." That voice, cold and deadly, belonged to Lieutenant Buckley. Another pilot easily drawn by the enemy, if she took her attitude into the cockpit with her. *"See how you like this, kitty!"*

"I always heard about target-rich environments!" Blair recognized the voice as belonging to Captain Max "Mad

Max" Lewis, another Gold Squadron pilot. *"C'mon, Vaquero, let's show 'em a thing or two!"*

"Scratch one! Scratch one! We have achieved kitty litter!" Marshall's cry was triumphant.

"Make that two," Cobra chimed in a moment later. Despite the depth of her hatred, she sounded as tightly controlled as Hobbes, as if the wild passion were translated into a cold, deadly intensity.

Blair checked his autopilot. Two minutes . . .

"Flint, go to afterburners," he ordered. "Full power. Let's get up there!" He shoved his throttles fully into the red zone, feeling the extra G-force press him against his seat.

"Maniac! Maniac! I've got two on my tail! Give me a hand, Maniac!" That was Marshall's wingman, Lieutenant Alex Sanders, running name Sandman. After a pause, he went on, voice rising with excitement . . . or panic. *"For God's sake, Maniac, give me a hand!"*

"Break left on my signal, Sandman," Ralgha's voice cut him off. *"Steady . . . steady . . . break!"*

The tactical sensors were picking up details of the battle now, and Blair watched as the symbols representing Hobbes and Vagabond moved together to support the beleaguered Sanders. Maniac Marshall was far away now, almost at the limit of the scans, hotly engaged with a Dralthi and paying little attention to the other Confed pilots.

One of the Kilrathi ships pursuing Sandman disappeared under the onslaught of Ralgha's sudden attack, while Chang dove in toward the second and forced it to break off.

"Thanks, Hobbes," Sanders said, a little breathless now. *"I . . . thanks."*

"I'm hit! Front armor's gone . . . my shields . . ." Mad Max Lewis was almost incoherent. *"He's coming in for another pass . . . Noooooo!!"*

The symbol representing the Terran Thunderbolt faded

from Blair's tactical screen. The rest of the fighters were jumbled together, a mad, chaotic dance played on the screen while Blair clenched his hands around his steering yoke in frustration. Gold Squadron was fully engaged now, while the lighter craft of Red Squadron operated on the fringes of the battle, surrounding any Kilrathi ships that penetrated the defensive line. But the sheer weight of numbers began to play a major role as more and more Kilrathi pilots jumped into the fray. Even though they flew as individuals, they were still a team determinedly pressing their Terran opponents.

"*Enemy coming into range, Colonel!*" Flint warned. "*What's your pleasure?*"

"Stick close, Flint," he said, powering up his weapons and locking his targeting array on the nearest Dralthi. "And watch my back. Things are going to get pretty damned rough out here in a second or two!"

His target chased a Thunderbolt, the two fighters circling each other, attempting to find some type of advantage. Now, as Blair and Flint appeared, the Dralthi broke off and rolled left, dodging and juking as it tried to gain some distance.

"Not this time, fuzzball," Blair said, lining up the crosshairs and opening fire with his blasters. The energy bolts raked along the top of the enemy fighter, hitting directly behind the cockpit, between two large, forward-sweeping bat-wings. The Kilrathi fighter seemed to stagger and wrenched away to port as the pilot tried to evade. Blair used his thrusters to spin his ship in flight and lined up on the Dralthi again before the Kilrathi could finish his turn.

His fingers tightened over the firing stud, and the blasters tore through the weakened shields and armor. The fighter disappeared in a ball of flame and spinning debris. "Got him!" Blair said. He checked his sensor monitor for a fresh target.

"Thanks for the assist, Colonel," said the pilot of the fighter he had rescued. It was Lieutenant Mitchell Lopez, Vaquero, who had been Mad Max's wingman.

"Welcome to the battle, my friend," Ralgha said. *"Will you take over the command?"*

"I relieve you, Hobbes," Blair told him. "Gold Squadron, from Blair. Reform on me! You're getting too damned spread out. Repeat, reform skirmish line around me. Hobbes, what's the story?"

"One Thunderbolt and two Hellcats destroyed, Colonel," Ralgha said formally. *"And Lieutenant Jaeger's Thunderbolt is severely damaged."*

"Right. Jaeger, disengage. If you think you can make a safe landing, get back to the carrier. Otherwise pull back and we'll help you in later. Who's your wingman?"

"Cobra, sir," Helmut "Beast" Jaeger responded.

"Okay. Vaquero, Cobra, you're teamed now. Cover Beast's withdrawal and then get back in formation. Got me?"

"Understood," Vaquero replied.

There was a pause before Cobra spoke up. The tactical display showed she was still engaged with a Darket, but her opponent suddenly vanished from the screen. *"I'm on it, Colonel,"* Lieutenant Buckley said at last. *"Let's do it, Vaquero, so we can get back in there and kill us some cats!"*

The three Thunderbolts peeled off, while the rest of the Terran craft began to take their positions around Blair and Flint . . . all except one.

"Marshall!" Blair rasped. "Maniac, if you don't get your tail back here I'll open fire on you myself!"

"Coming, Mother," Maniac responded, unabashed.

The fighting was still going on, and Blair restrained himself from flinging himself into the action as he issued orders and studied the tactical situation. By now the battle had moved close enough to the *Victory* for the carrier's big guns to join in the defense, and that was forcing the Kilrathi force to be cautious. Their casualties were heavier than the Terrans', but they still outnumbered Blair's command slightly, and more of their ships were comparatively fresh and undamaged. The odds still didn't look too good.

Blair's mind raced, grappling with the tactical picture on his screen. Somehow the Terrans had to take the initiative, force the Kilrathi to battle under conditions favoring the defenders. *Victory*'s guns would go a long way toward redressing the balance. So would the four interceptors, but they were still at least six minutes away, and after the initial surprise of their arrival they could not sustain a long-term advantage under these circumstances. What they needed was a way to maximize *all* of the Terran assets in one thrust, something the Kilrathi would not see coming.

He found himself smiling grimly under his helmet. There was one maneuver that just might work . . .

"Kennel, Kennel, this is Watchdog Leader," he said urgently. "Come in, Kennel."

"*Reading you, Colonel*," Rollins replied.

"Go to tight-beam and scramble," he ordered, switching the circuits on his comm system. A moment later a green light shimmered under the comm screen, indicating that Rollins had set up a tight laser-link between the carrier and his fighter. The system was excellent for secure communications between large ships or between the carrier and an individual fighter, but it was inefficient for ship-to-ship transmissions between fighters due to their smaller size, higher speeds, and unpredictable maneuvering.

But what Blair wanted to do now must be kept secret until his trap was sprung.

"I want you to pass the word to each fighter, Lieutenant," Blair said without preamble. "New orders for all ships. On my mark . . ."

Hunt Leader
Tamayo System

Flight Commander Arrak gave a snarl of triumph as he listened to the computer translation of the Terran command frequency radio broadcasts.

"*We can't take any more of this!*" the human commander was saying. "*All ships, break off and withdraw! Break off while you still can!*"

That was what Arrak had been waiting to hear. The Terrans put up a good fight, but they were outnumbered and outgunned, and he knew they would be stretched too thin sooner or later. This was his chance.

"They are beginning to withdraw," he said, the battle madness singing inside him. "Concentrate fire on the carrier. We will deal with the apes once the capital ship is destroyed!"

On his tactical screen, the Terran fighters were breaking off to flee past the covering bulk of the carrier. Arrak showed his fangs and pushed his throttles forward. He sensed a moment's regret that he was unable to corner the ship he had identified as the renegade's, but his duty now was clear.

The renegade would still be out there, and helpless, once the carrier was destroyed.

"Talons of the Emperor!" he called, the old battle cry making him tremble with anticipation of glory. "Attack! Attack! Attack!"

• CHAPTER VII

Thunderbolt 300
Tamayo System

"They're heading in," Blair said. "Look sharp, people."

On his screen, he saw the blips representing the Kilrathi attack force gathering speed as they advanced toward the *Victory*. With the Terran fighters withdrawing from the battle, the Kilrathi could begin high-speed attack runs on the carrier, using maneuverability and velocity to evade the beams from the capital ship's defensive batteries. It was exactly the kind of situation every pilot hoped for: a big, clumsy carrier stripped of its defensive fighters and lying almost helpless against a massed bombing run.

Only this time, the carrier wouldn't be quite as helpless as she appeared . . .

"Captain says any time you're ready, Colonel," Rollins said, a note of worry creeping into his voice.

He didn't let the lieutenant's fears push him into acting too soon. Blair checked his sensors again, saw the four interceptors beginning their swing to bring them squarely behind the attackers. His own fighters had started this maneuver feigning panic and disorder, but now they were beginning to reform into four distinct groups.

The time was almost right . . .

"Execute!" He almost shouted the order as he wrenched the steering yoke fiercely and advanced the throttles into the afterburner red zone again. By the time this counterthrust was over he would be nearly dry again, but hopefully none of the Confed fighters would need any fuel reserves after this. "Execute turn and attack at will!"

Inevitably, someone—it sounded like Maniac—gave a whoop and shouted *"Who's Will?"* Blair ignored it and concentrated on the enemy ships clustered ahead.

The carrier opened fire with a barrage from her main batteries. One of the attackers flew straight into the beams. It came apart, looking like a spectacular fireball that seemed to herald the beginning of the new phase of this savage fight.

Blair hoped it would be the final phase.

Hunt Leader
Tamayo System

"It is a trap! The apes have set a trap!"
Arrak somehow refrained from cursing or snarling, but despite his control he still thought longingly of sinking his fangs into the neck of the pilot, whoever he was, who filled the comm channel with his inspired revelations of the obvious. Yes, the apes had set a trap, drawn his fighters in closer to the Terran carrier where they would be caught between the capital ship's big guns and four . . . no, make it *five* converging groups of fighters. There were more Confederation craft out there now, a whole new group that had not been in the fight until now. It was a masterful trap, worthy of a Kilrathi hunter.

"Break off!" he snarled. "Break off the action against the carrier and regroup. It seems we have to give the hairless apes another lesson before we can finish this."

Then he had no more time for talk. A pair of heavy Terran fighters suddenly appeared out of nowhere and were trying to lock onto him from the rear. Arrak needed all his skill and concentration to keep the enemy from winning that decisive advantage. He pulled a tight, high-G turn to starboard, using his attitude thruster to make the Dralthi swing around even faster, and opened fire with all guns at once. The Terran fighter's shields absorbed most of the damage, but his sensors registered a hit against the underlying armor as well.

"*You fly well,*" the Terran pilot commented, using the standard Imperial tactical band. "*Are you worth fighting? Declare yourself if you wish the honor of battle with Ralgha* nar *Hhallas.*"

Arrak showed his fangs under his flight helmet. The renegade! He couldn't reply, lest he reveal to his superiors his disobedience of standing orders, but he could defend himself against the enemy attack . . .

The Kilrathi passed mere meters from the Terran fighter, close enough to see the bulky spacesuited shape of his adversary through the viewport.

It would be a battle to remember.

Thunderbolt 300
Tamayo System

"*A hit! A hit! That'll show the kitty who's the boss!*"

"Rein it in, Maniac, and do your job," Blair snapped. He lined up a shot and launched a heat-seeker at the nearest Darket, his eyes already searching the sensor screen for a fresh target. He hardly needed to look to know when the lighter Kilrathi ship blew up. He had encountered these fighters often enough over the years to know just about what level of punishment they could take, and he was rarely wrong.

Close by, Flint was heavily engaged with a Dralthi, the two fighters weaving a complex pattern as they circled and dodged, looking for a moment's advantage to administer a lethal strike.

"You need an assist, Flint?" Blair asked, steering toward the dogfighters.

The Thunderbolt delivered a sustained burst of energy beams at the Dralthi and dived in hard and fast. *"Find your own party, Colonel,"* Flint said. *"This furball is all mine!"*

A pair of missiles streaked from the underside of her wings and struck home just above the Dralthi's engine mountings. An expanding ball of superheated gas and whirling debris consumed the Kilrathi ship, and Peters drove her Thunderbolt straight through the fireball with a triumphant shout, *"Yes! That's another one for you, Davie!"*

Blair wondered who she was talking about or to, but only for a moment. His attention returned to the monitor, showing the Terran trap closing perfectly. By having Rollins pass his orders by tight-beam communications links, he was able to prime the entire Terran force to fall back on his broadcast command. It looked and sounded like a panic-stricken withdrawal, but in fact everyone knew their precise jobs and prepared for a counterattack as soon as he gave the signal. Now the carrier was laying down a withering barrage, and the four refueled interceptors from Blue Squadron appeared to join the Hellcats and Thunderbolts in closing off the enemy escape route.

Now the Terran fighters were spread in a rough hemispherical formation, trying to keep the Kilrathi from escaping the trap. Even if they did, the Kilrathi took heavy losses in the counterthrust. They knew they were in a fight, that much was certain.

"Hobbes, can you help me out?" That was Vagabond, his breathing sharp and rapid. *"I got two of these guys all over my tail! I need help here . . ."*

"I cannot assist," Ralgha replied. *"My opponent is pressing me very hard."*

Blair checked his screen, noted the two fighters. They weren't far away. "Flint, you back up Chang," he ordered. "I'll backstop Hobbes. Got it?"

"*Got it,*" Flint confirmed. "*Vagabond, you just keep the little bastards busy. I'm on the way!*"

Ralgha and his opponent were well-matched, though the heavier Thunderbolt should have given Hobbes an edge. That was probably offset by the fact that the Dralthi was more maneuverable, at least in the hands of a good pilot, and from the looks of things this one was little short of brilliant. Before Blair could get into effective range, the enemy ship executed a perfect fishhook maneuver, angling away from the Thunderbolt until just the right moment, then suddenly turning back on itself and driving in fast with guns blazing. Somehow Ralgha managed to evade the worst of the fire and loop around to settle on the other pilot's tail as he shot past, but a moment later the Dralthi applied full braking thrusters and Hobbes shot past him. Now their roles were reversed, with the enemy pilot tailing Ralgha.

The targeting reticule on Blair's HUD flashed red, the signal for a target lock. Blair opened fire, concentrating on a weakened spot in the Kilrathi's shields. The enemy ship took a hit, then rolled out of the line of fire and accelerated off at an unexpected angle.

"Damn," Blair muttered. "This guy's good."

"*Agreed,*" Ralgha said gravely. "*But not, I think, good enough to fight us both, my friend. He withdraws now.*"

His sensor screen confirmed Ralgha's comment. The enemy pilot was still accelerating away from the two Terrans, evidently content to leave them alone for the time being.

Hunt Leader
Tamayo System

Flight Commander Arrak felt his blood lust begin to fade. For a few moments he nearly lost himself to the battle madness, until the second Terran fighter appeared and launched, its devastating attack. Although he managed to evade the worst of it, the enemy fire shorted out his weapons systems and left Arrak without armaments, unable to carry on the dogfight.

Some Kilrathi pilots might have continued in the battle anyway, seeking one good chance to ram an opponent and die with his claws figuratively at the enemy's throat. That was the stuff of battle songs and the Warrior's Path. But Arrak was a flight commander, and he owed duty to his warriors as well as to his Clan and his honor. Right now it was Arrak's duty to extricate as many of his pilots from this debacle as possible. There was no way that throwing himself into a collision with the renegade or another Terran ship would help to accomplish what needed to be done.

He studied his tactical display with a sinking feeling that was only partial regret for failing to finish the fight. Only one fighter in four of his original force of four eights was still flying, and most of those were damaged. Still, they broke clear of the Terran defensive line while the Confederation fighters engaged their less fortunate comrades. Now it was the Imperial force that was outnumbered and outgunned, and there was little hope of achieving any sort of dramatic success now. They might take out a few of the Terrans, but at an even heavier price than they had paid already.

"All ships return to *Sar'hrai*," Arrak ordered reluctantly. "Withdraw and return to *Sar'hrai* immediately."

"*Flight Commander, not all of our comrades have disengaged,*" a pilot argued, snarling anger. "*If we withdraw they will fall to the fangs and claws of the apes . . .*"

"Then stay and die with them!" Arrak snapped. "And your Clan will know the dishonor of owning a warrior who disobeys a direct order in the face of battle!"

He didn't wait for a reply. At full acceleration, the

Dralthi turned away from the disastrous battle and drove through the empty dark, seeking the security of home.

Flight Deck, TCS Victory
Tamayo System

Blair's fighter was last to return after the battle, and it took several minutes for the backed-up traffic handlers on the flight deck to get to him. By the time his Thunderbolt rolled to a stop in its repair bay, the deck was fully pressurized and the gravity was restored to Earth-normal. All three shifts of technicians were assembled to handle the returning fighters, and there was a lot of activity on the deck when Blair finally climbed out of his cockpit and started toward the entrance to Flight Control.

A welcoming committee met him, not just technicians and some of his pilots but crewmen from every department of the ship, surging into the expanse of the flight deck, cheering loudly. Eisen was at the head of the pack, with Lieutenant Rollins close behind him. Rachel Coriolis stood to one side with a grin on her face, flashing him a thumbs-up sign.

"Good job, Colonel," Eisen said. "A credit to the ship. You did the old girl proud today."

"Outstanding!" Rollins added. "You really outfoxed those kitties today!"

Blair returned their smiles, but inside he was feeling anything but triumphant. They had barely beaten off the Kilrathi attack; a few more enemy fighters would have turned the tide against the Terrans. Then there was the inevitable butcher's bill: Mad Max Lewis was dead, along with five pilots from Red Squadron and one from Blue. Seven dead out of twenty-four pilots engaged . . . steep losses indeed. And some of the ones who made it back suffered serious damage in the fighting. They could easily have lost twice as many ships if the Kilrathi had only been a little luckier or a little better armed.

Everyone else saw it as a great victory, but for Blair it was just one more battle. One more chance for good men to die staving off defeat for a little while longer without accomplishing anything significant in the process. That had been the story of the war for as long as he could remember now: meaningless victories, defeats that drove the Confederation further and further down, and always death. Death was the only constant through it all.

He left the cheering throng behind and pushed through to the steps that led up to Flight Control. Maybe the others could celebrate, but all Blair felt like doing now was mourning the dead.

Flight Wing Rec Room, TCS Victory Tamayo System

There was another victory party scheduled for the evening, and it promised to be even bigger and more boisterous than the earlier one. Blair knew he would have to put in an appearance, but he decided to drop by the rec room early to get a drink or two under his belt before things got too far out of hand.

When he arrived, he thought for a moment that he was already too late. He opened the door to a blast of raucous music just as he had at the previous celebration. But this time there were only a handful of people clustered around the bar.

An officer was sitting at the terminal controlling the sound system, one hand making tiny adjustments to the board while the other tapped to the rhythm of the music. The man slumped in his chair, his eyes closed, completely mesmerized by the sound. Blair recognized his aquiline profile. He was Lieutenant Mitchell Lopez, callsign

Vaquero, the man he had assigned as wingman for Cobra in the middle of the battle.

He stood behind the man and waited for a long while, wincing a little at the loud music. When it was clear that Lopez wasn't planning to come up for air any time soon, he finally tapped the pilot on the shoulder.

"Hey, man, can't you have the decency to wait for the piece to end?" Vaquero said without opening his eyes.

"Lieutenant . . ." Blair said the word blandly, but Lopez recognized his voice at once. He was out of his chair and standing at attention in one quick movement. Blair had to fight to keep from smiling at the man's reaction.

"Uh, sorry, sir," Lopez said, stammering a little. "Didn't expect you here until the party, sir."

"At ease, Lieutenant," Blair said, smiling.

Vaquero relaxed. He caught the look Blair gave in the direction of the speakers and hastened to turn down the volume. "Just getting the system set for tonight, sir," he explained.

"Aren't there technical people who're supposed to do that?" Blair asked. He gestured to the seat Vaquero had vacated, and when the lieutenant was sitting, Blair took another chair nearby.

"The last guy who did this job had a tin ear and ten thumbs," Lopez said with a grin. "And his musical taste left a lot to be desired, too. So I just kind of took over."

"Musical taste," Blair repeated.

"Yes, sir. You know, music really does set the mood. Playing something with nothing but minor chords makes you want to run a suicide mission. But this is different." He waved a hand toward the board. "*Rockero* from the Celeste System. It's bright, it heats your blood, it makes you want to live a long life."

Blair gave him a sour look. "It makes me want to put on a flight helmet to filter out some of the noise," he said, smiling briefly to take the sting out of the comment. "I like something a little more soothing . . . like a bagpipe duet or a couple of cats in heat."

The Argentine pilot laughed. "I guess *my* musical taste isn't for everyone. But I've had no complaints so far . . . until you, that is."

"I'm not complaining, Lieutenant. Just pleading for a little moderation." Blair signalled a waiter. "Can I buy you something to drink?"

"Tequila," Vaquero said. The waiter nodded, taking Blair's order for a scotch as he left. "That was quite a fight today, wasn't it, Colonel?"

Blair nodded. "I'll say. We were damned lucky."

"Yes, sir. Uh . . . thanks again for the way you bailed me out. Thought I'd played my last tune for sure."

"Are you a pilot or a musician, Lopez?"

"Oh, I'm a pilot, sir. Pretty good one, too. Check my kills; you'll see." He looked down at the table. "But my family, they made guitars for many generations. I've got one that's almost two hundred years old. The sound just gets richer as it gets older, you know?"

Blair nodded, but didn't speak. There was something in the man's eyes that made him unwilling to break his mood.

"I'm the first one from my family to go into space," Lopez went on a moment later. He sounded wistful. "The first to be a fighter instead of a craftsman or a musician. But some day I'm going to open a cantina and bring in the best to play that guitar. We need a place for old fighter jockeys like you and me, Colonel, where we can get together and swap lies about our battles and tell each other how much different things are without the war . . ."

Blair looked away. It was a pleasant dream, but he wondered if Lopez would ever really get his wish. The war had existed longer than either of them had been alive, and it didn't look like humanity was likely to end it soon. He was afraid that the only way the war would end in his lifetime was in a Kilrathi victory. More likely it would claim them all, and drag on to claim another generation's hopes and dreams. "Hope there's enough of us to keep you in business, Vaquero," he said quietly.

"Don't you worry, sir. We'll make it through. And you and I can sit at a quiet table, watch the beautiful women and listen to the music of that guitar . . ."

"You still don't sound much like a pilot, Vaquero," Blair told him.

"Don't get me wrong, sir. I do my job, whatever it takes. But some of the others, they actually like the killing. Me, I do it because I have to, but I take no pleasure from it. And when it's over, I will walk away with no regrets."

Command Hall, KIS Hvar'kann
Locanda System

"My Prince, the shuttle from the *Sar'hrai* has arrived. With Baron Vurrig and the prisoner."

Thrakhath, Crown Prince of the Empire of Kilrah, showed his teeth. "Bring them, Melek," he said, not bothering to hide the contempt in his voice. His talons twitched reflexively in their sheaths.

A pair of Imperial Guardsmen ushered two newcomers before the lonely throne at the end of the Command Audience Hall. Here, by long tradition, the noble commander of a ship in space dispensed justice to the warriors under his command. Today Thrakhath upheld that tradition yet again.

"My Lord Prince." *Khantahr* Baron Vurrig *nar* Tsahl dropped to one knee. The other officer, hands in manacles, sank awkwardly to both knees beside the noble. "*Sar'hrai* is at your command, as ever."

"Indeed?" Thrakhath fixed the Baron with an icy stare. "I wanted the jump point from Orsini cut, and the Terran carrier damaged beyond capability to interfere with Operation Unseen Death. But the blockade was only partially effective and the attack on the carrier was repulsed without touching the ape ship. Is that a fair assessment of your performance?"

"Lord Prince . . ." Vurrig quailed under his stare. "Lord Prince, there were many . . . complications, especially due to the renegade. We could not press home attacks against ships he escorted without risking a breach of your orders . . ."

"This one did, or so your report claimed."

"Yes, Lord Prince. This is Flight Commander Arrak. He engaged the traitor in battle despite my specific orders to the contrary."

"But Ralgha was not harmed?"

"No, Lord Prince."

"So, Arrak, you are inept as well as insubordinate, is that it?"

Arrak met Thrakhath's stare with unexpected spirit. "In battle, Lord Prince, it is not always so easy to set conditions," he said defiantly.

Thrakhath felt a stir of admiration. The flight commander knew he was doomed for his disobedience, so he met his fate with a warrior's pride. Baron Vurrig, on the other hand, danced and dodged like prey on the run from the hunter.

"Let Arrak have a warrior's death. He may fight any champion or champions who wish the honor of dispatching him." Thrakhath noted Arrak's nod. He was proud to the bitter end. "As for you, Baron . . . because of you we must push back the timetable for Operation Unseen Death. We must await additional ships so that we may ensure the Terrans not intervening when we launch our strike. You will be relieved as commander of *Sar'hrai* . . . and suffer the penalty for your incompetence. Death . . . by isolation. The coward's end, alone, ignored, cut off until you die from thirst, starvation, or madness. See to it, Melek."

"Lord Prince—" Vurrig began. He was grabbed by the guardsmen and dragged away, his appeals for mercy echoing hollowly in the chamber.

"I regret the failure, Lord Prince," Melek said quietly, "but at least the renegade came to no harm."

"We must hope that the War God continues to smile on us, Melek," Thrakhath said coldly. "The time is not yet ripe to deal with Lord Ralgha . . . but it is coming. As is the day of our final victory."

• CHAPTER VIII

Captain's Ready Room, TCS Victory Tamayo System

"According to Chief Coriolis, the last of the battle damage should be repaired by this afternoon," Blair concluded. "So the wing will be up and running . . . except for the ships we lost."

"Good job, Colonel," Eisen said. "I'd say three days is a pretty good turn-around time, considering the way your fighters looked when they touched down. Give my compliments to the Chief for a job well done by her techs."

"Yes, sir. They did a fine job." Blair paused, then cleared his throat. "About the losses . . ."

"We've already taken care of the situation," Eisen told him. "Mr. Rollins?"

The Communications Officer consulted his portable computer terminal. "No problem at all on the Hellcats, sir," he said. "The CO at Tamayo Base called for volunteers from the point defense squadron stationed there. They'll be aboard first thing tomorrow."

"Fast work, Lieutenant," Blair commented.

"The commander was pleased with the support he's been getting from the Navy. He was eager to help." Rollins frowned. "I'm not so sure about Mad Max's replacement."

"What's the problem, Lieutenant?" Eisen asked.

"There's a home defense squadron on Tamayo that flies Thunderbolts, sir," Rollins said slowly. "Strictly reservists, mostly rich kids who figured it was a good dodge to avoid active military service and still get to wear a pretty uniform and boast about being hot fighter pilots. The squadron was activated into Confed service when the cats moved into the system."

"Well, we've had green pilots before," Eisen said. "I dare say the Colonel can break in one of these kids fast enough. Or are they being sticky about transferring someone?"

"Oh, they're willing to give us a pilot and his fighter, sir," Rollins said. "A little too willing, the way I see it. I think they're planning on handing us one of their discipline problems."

Eisen shrugged. "Hardly unusual. We'll just have to ride him until he snaps to attention. Right, Colonel?"

"Or ground him and find another qualified pilot," Blair said, nodding. "What makes you think he's going to be a problem, Lieutenant?"

"Hey, I told you, Colonel," he responded with a grin. "Radio Rollins always has his ear to the ground. One of my . . . sources at Tamayo Base was warned by the Home Defense boys that they were looking for a place to dump this guy. I just gotta wonder though, what kind of a screwup gets thrown out of an HD squadron? Know what I mean?"

"As long as he can fly and he's got a Thunderbolt, I can use him in Gold Squadron," Blair said. "He can't be any more difficult to handle than Maniac Marshall."

"I hope you and Major Marshall can work out your little . . . problem, Colonel," Eisen said quietly. "I don't like to have this kind of conflict between two senior officers. Marshall's record is impressive, even if it's not quite as outstanding as yours. I'm not sure I understand why the two of you have such difficulties with each other."

"Part of it's purely personal, Captain," Blair said. "We've been competing against each other since the day we met. At least he's been competing with me." He smiled. "I, of course, am blameless in the whole thing."

"Of course," Eisen said blandly. Rollins chuckled.

"But I do my best to keep the personal problems and the cockpit apart, Captain," Blair went on seriously. "I mean, you don't have to *like* a guy to serve with him. But Marshall's flying style . . . it scares me, sir, and just about everybody else who flies with him. You saw the tactical tapes on the battle?"

Eisen nodded. "Yeah. Marshall got heavily involved out there a couple of times."

"He chased anything he could see," Blair told him. "Hobbes saved Sandman because Marshall was too busy playing the personal glory game to support his own wingman. He gets kills, sir, but he does it by ignoring the team. You of all people should know that the team must always come first."

"Sounds like you don't want him on your team at all," Eisen said. "I'd rather not try to transfer him . . ."

"I'm not asking you to, sir," Blair told him. "Look, Maniac is not my idea of the ideal wingman, but he's better than when we were on the old *Tiger's Claw* together. And despite his lack of discipline, he's a good pilot who knows how to score kills. Right now we need everyone like that we can find." He paused. "I know you're concerned about having us clash, but I guarantee that when the Kilrathi come into range we're on the same side. If there's one thing we agree on, it's our duty."

"Glad to hear it, Colonel," the captain said. "I think things are about to get a lot rougher for us, so I want to be sure we're all up to it."

"Rougher, sir?" Blair asked.

Eisen nodded. "That's the reason for the big scramble to get the wing up to full strength again. We've been given new orders, Colonel. Seems the situation in the Locanda System is getting tense. There has been a sharp uptick in Kilrathi activity there, even a couple of sightings that could be the *Hvar'kann*, Crown Prince Thrakhath's new flagship. And we know for a fact the carrier that launched the attack on us, the *Sar'hrai*, withdrew through the Locanda jump point shortly after the battle. It seems that a major installation of troops will arrive on Locanda, so the High Command wants us to reinforce them."

"Seems a damned strange place for a push," Blair commented. He remembered the Locanda System: a struggling colony world with a few scattered outposts, all of which had seen better days. "Twenty years back, maybe, it would have made sense, but they've tapped out most of the really valuable mineral resources. When I was stationed there, they were in the middle of an economic depression because a couple of their biggest industries decided to relocate out-system. I don't see the attraction for the Empire's attention . . . certainly not the Prince himself."

"Yeah," Eisen grunted. "Intelligence hasn't been able to come up with anything yet. But ours is not to reason why."

Rollins looked like he was about to say something, but he didn't. After a moment's silence, Blair spoke up. "When do we jump?"

"Two days. Time enough to get our rookies settled and take on fresh stores. Then we're out of here."

"And smack in the middle of trouble," Rollins muttered. Blair doubted that Eisen heard the comment.

"The flight wing'll be ready, sir," he said formally.

"Good. If it's true the cats are building around Locanda, we'll have to be ready for anything." Eisen looked from Blair to Rollins. "That's all for now. Dismissed."

Outside the ready room door, Blair touched the comm officer's sleeve. "A moment, Lieutenant," he said.

"Sir?"

"I had the feeling you knew something more about this Locanda op. Am I imagining things, or have you been listening to more of your . . . sources?"

Rollins met his eyes with a steady gaze. "You sure you want another dose of paranoia, Colonel?"

"Cut the crap, Lieutenant. If you know something about this operation . . ."

"It's nothing definite, Colonel," Rollins said reluctantly. "Not even from the official channels. Captain doesn't know anything about it."

"Well?"

"I know a guy on General Taggart's staff in Covert Ops. He said Thrakhath was reportedly working on some new terror weapon which was just about ready for testing. I don't know if this has anything to do with that, but if Thrakhath's really in Locanda then this could be the test. It makes sense, when you think about it."

"How so?"

"Well, like you said, Locanda's past its prime. It's of no real strategic value, depleted of all valuable resources. The Kilrathi could raid it for slaves, but they can get slaves anywhere. If they really do have some new weapon, something big enough that it will cause mass destruction, Locanda Four would be a pretty good place to try it. Whether it works or not, the cats don't take out anything they want . . . but if it did work, it would be a pretty damn good demonstration."

"Any idea what this wonder weapon is?"

"My guy didn't say. But I've got my suspicions that Intelligence knows more than they're telling us about the whole mess." Rollins lowered his voice. "You know those transports we've been trying to pump through the jump point to Locanda? They've all been medical ships; like the High Command was getting ready for a lot of casualties."

"Bioweapons," Blair said, feeling sick.

"That's my take," the Communications Officer agreed. "Think about it. Thrakhath would love to get his hands on the Confed infrastructure. Except for a small stock of slaves, the Kilrathi don't want humans around to compete with them. Seeding choice colony worlds with some new kind of plague would be the perfect way to kill us with a minimum of damage to technology or resources. If the weapon tests well, you can bet the Kilrathi will be hitting someplace important the next time around: Earth."

"Yeah . . . maybe. We certainly showed 'em the way, back when the *Tarawa* made the raid on Kilrah a couple of years ago. If they've got an effective biological agent and a reliable delivery system, a handful of raiders could wipe us out." Blair fixed Rollins with a stern look. "Still, this is all just speculation, Lieutenant, based on your leak over at Covert Ops and a lot of guesswork."

"Theory fits the facts, sir . . ."

"Maybe so. But it's still just a theory until you get genuine proof. Don't spread this around, Rollins. There's no point in getting everybody in an uproar over a possibility. You read me?"

The lieutenant nodded slowly. "Yes, sir. I'll keep it to myself. But you mark my words, Colonel, this is going to be one hell of a nasty fight this time."

Flight Control, TCS Victory
Tamayo System

Flight Control was fully crewed with a dozen techs and specialists monitoring the activity going on around the carrier and on the flight deck. This morning, Blair decided to preside over operations himself. He took his place on the raised platform which dominated the center of the compartment at a horseshoe-shaped console that could tap into all aspects of wing activities.

"Last of the new Hellcats is down and safe, Colonel," a tech reported from a nearby work station. "Deck will be clear for the Thunderbolt in two minutes."

"Two minutes," Blair repeated. "Well, Major, what do you think? Will they do?"

Major Daniel Whittaker, Red Squadron's CO, watched over Blair's shoulder while the new arrivals were coming in. He was old for his rank and position, with iron-gray hair and an air of cautious deliberation. His callsign was Warlock, and Blair had to admit he could have passed for a high-tech sorcerer.

"They fly well enough," Whittaker said quietly. "I've seen better carrier landings, but these boys and girls have been rotting away in a planetside base where you don't get much chance to practice carrier ops. We'll whip them into shape quick enough, I'd say."

"We'll have to, Major. If the bad guys are out in force around Locanda, point defense will get a real workout."

"*Thunderbolt HD Seven-zero-two, you are cleared for approach,*" a speaker announced. "*Feeding approach vectors to your navcomp . . . now.*"

Blair turned his attention back to the external camera view. The computer enhanced the image so he could see the Thunderbolt clearly against the backdrop of brilliant stars. As he watched, he could see the flare of the fighter's engines as the pilot maneuvered his ship onto its approach path.

"What the hell is that idiot doing?" someone demanded. "He's ignoring the approach vectors we're feeding him!"

"*HD Seven-zero-two, you are deviating from flight plan,*" the comm tech said. "*Recheck approach vectors and assume designated course.*"

The image on Blair's screen swelled as the fighter stooped in toward the carrier, still gathering speed. Blair punched up a computer course projection and was relieved to see that the projected flight path would cause the ship to steer clear of the carrier, but it would be a near miss. If the idiot deviated from his path now, he could easily dive right into the deck. "Belay that transmission," he snapped, "and have the flight deck emergency crews on standby."

An alarm, low but insistent, rang across the flight deck, and Blair could see technicians scrambling to their emergency stations.

The Thunderbolt streaked over the flight deck with bare meters to spare, executing a roll-over as it passed. Then it looped away, killing its speed with a sharp braking thrust and dropping effortlessly into the original approach path. Blair let out a sigh of relief.

"He's on target," someone announced laconically.

"He does that again and he'll *be* a target," someone else said. Blair shared the sentiment. Rollins had warned Blair that the new pilot was likely to be a problem, but he'd never imagined the man would pull a stupid stunt even before he reported aboard. Fancy victory rolls looked good in holomovies and stunt flying by elite fighter show teams, but they were strictly prohibited in normal carrier operations.

The new pilot had a lot to learn.

The Thunderbolt performed perfectly, hitting the tractor beams precisely and touching the deck in a landing maneuver that could have been used in an Academy training film. Moments later, the fighter rolled to a stop inside the hangar deck. Gravity and pressure were quickly restored as the technicians secured from their emergency preparations.

Blair, seething, was on his way to the deck before the gravity hit one-half G.

The pilot climbed down the ladder from his cockpit and paused to remove his helmet, an ornately decorated rig which carried the word FLASH in bright letters, presumably his running name. He was a young man, under thirty from his appearance, but his flight suit carried a major's insignia. He glanced around the hangar with an easy grin, stopped to wipe away a speck on the underside of the Thunderbolt's wing, then sauntered casually toward the exit. He seemed completely oblivious to Blair.

"Hold it right there, Mister," Blair snapped.

The man gave him a quick look that turned into a double-take as he caught sight of the bird insignia on Blair's collar tabs. He drew himself erect in something that approximated attention and rendered a casual salute. "Didn't expect a high-ranking welcoming committee, sir," he said. His tones were lazy, relaxed. "Major Jace Dillon, Tamayo Home Defense Airspace Command. I'm your replacement pilot."

"That remains to be seen," Blair said. "What's the idea of pulling that damned stunt on your approach, Dillon?"

"Stunt, sir? Oh, the flyby. Hell, Colonel, it was just a little bit of showmanship. They don't call me Flash for nothing, you know." Dillon paused, seeming to realize the depth of Blair's anger for the first time. "Look, I'm sorry if I did something wrong. I just thought I had to show you Regular boys that Home Defense isn't a bunch of no-talent weekend warriors, like everybody thinks. Figured if you saw I knew how to handle my bird then you'd know I could pull my weight, that's all."

Blair didn't answer right away. He could almost understand the man's thinking. Home Defense units had a poor reputation with the regular Navy, often entirely undeserved. There had been a time, back when Blair was this kid's age, that he might have pulled the same kind of stunt to make a point with a new command.

"All right, Dillon, you can fly. You proved that much. Next time I see you in that bird of yours you better show me you know how to obey regs, too. You hear me?"

"Yes, sir," Dillon replied.

"Your Home Defense unit . . . does it use standard Confed ranks?"

"Yes, Colonel."

"And you're a major . . ."

Dillon flushed. "Yes, sir, I am."

"I find that a little difficult to believe, Dillon. A major is usually more seasoned."

"The rank's legitimate, sir," Dillon said, sounding defensive. "Rank earned in Home Defense units is automatically granted in the Confed Regulars upon activation of the unit."

"Of course." Blair studied him for a moment. "So you hold a major's commission in the Home Defense. Let me guess . . . your father's either the unit commander or a prominent local backer who helped fund the unit, and you were bumped through the ranks to Major in consequence, right?"

"Sir, I'm fully qualified as a pilot . . ."

"We established that, Major. I'm interested in your rank qualifications. Is my assessment correct?"

Dillon nodded reluctantly. "My father donated some funds when the unit was put together," he admitted. "But the rank is legitimate, sir. I was a test pilot with Camelot Industries before I signed on with the HDS, and I've been with my squadron for two years now."

"Two years," Blair repeated. "Any combat action?"

"Er . . . no, sir."

He sighed. "Well, Dillon, you're a major in the Confed Navy Flight Branch now, heaven help you . . . and the rest of us. Try to conduct yourself as a responsible officer of this ship and this flight wing. Do I make myself clear?"

"Yes, Colonel."

"Then . . . welcome aboard, Major Dillon. Report to Lieutenant Colonel Ralgha for indoctrination and assignments. You're dismissed."

He watched the young man leave the hangar, not quite

as cocky or relaxed any longer. It seemed that the Home Defense squadron had truly dumped a hard-shelled case on the Navy. Dillon was an inexperienced kid who carried a major's rank and the powerful protection of a wealthy family to boot. Dillon would soon learn that neither benefit would mean much when the wing went into action. It was ironic, in a way. His father had probably put him into the HDS to get him out of the dangerous job of test pilot.

Blair found himself hoping the kid would not have to learn his lesson the hard way. Not that he particularly cared what happened to this young showoff . . . but if he turned out to be the weak link in the wing, he could take better men and women down with him before it was all over.

Wing Commander's Office, TCS Victory Locanda System

The ship completed the jump to the Locanda System and began normal operations immediately. Blair spent a long day in Flight Control, supervising the first patrols dispatched to scout the region of space around the jump point and trying to get a feel for the new pilots in his command. As Whittaker had predicted, the new additions to Red Squadron seemed to be settling in well, but Flash was another matter. It still bothered Blair to have an inexperienced combat pilot with such a high rank, and the problem had caused him a sleepless night before he finally decided how to handle it.

He needed to team Dillon with a wingman who outranked him, that much was evident. Let Flash be the ranking officer on some patrol mission which ran into trouble and the result would be disaster. Blair knew he would have to match Dillon with either himself, Hobbes, or Maniac Marshall—the only three pilots in

Gold Squadron with the rank to keep Dillon under tight control.

Blair was sorely tempted to assign Flash as Maniac's wingman. The two deserved each other, and it might have been a valuable lesson for Marshall to see what it was like to fly with someone unreliable on his wing. But that would have been a risky choice at best. If Maniac *didn't* rise to the challenge, Blair would end up with two dead pilots. Even unreliable fighter jocks were assets not to be squandered so carelessly.

So the choice remained between himself and Hobbes. He hesitated over it for a long time before finally putting Flash on Ralgha's wing. Blair was concerned that he was letting his personal distaste for the younger man cloud his judgment, but in the end, he decided that the Kilrathi renegade's calm, tightly-controlled manner was the right counterbalance to Dillon's inexperience and enthusiasm.

Flash accepted the match-up with equanimity. Apparently he harbored no special feelings against the Kilrathi, and seemed content to fly with Hobbes. The two left on patrol soon after the jump and the patrol was successful, without incident.

But Blair found himself resenting the necessity which forced him to assign Hobbes and Flash together. He missed flying with Ralgha on his wing. Flint had done a competent job, and he had flown a couple of patrols with Vaquero that went well, but it wasn't the same. He still didn't know the others in the squadron the way he knew Hobbes, and he couldn't count on them to know his mind the way the Kilrathi always did.

Blair wearily straightened in his desk chair. Sometimes it seemed as if he would never get a handle on the assignment to *Victory*. He had always found it easy to meld into a new ship's company, but this time was different. He came on board determined to remain distant from the others. Blair needed to avoid getting too close,

as he had done with his comrades on the *Concordia*.
Blair doubted he could handle losing another shipload
of friends . . . but he was finding it difficult to deal with
day-to-day life among people who were still essentially
strangers. Perhaps he had made the wrong decision from
the start.

He slowly rose. The day's work was done and his bunk
was waiting for him.

All that really seemed to matter anymore was getting
through one more day, performing his duties, and
somehow staying sane in the face of a war that seemed
more insane every day. It was a far cry from the dreams
of glory that had once beckoned Christopher Blair into
the life of a fighter pilot, but duty—simple and
straightforward—was all that remained for him.

• CHAPTER IX

Flight Wing Rec Room, TCS Victory *Locanda System*

At first glance, there were no customers in the Rec Room when Blair entered, only the grizzled old petty officer who ran the bar. He was a member of the crew from the old *Leningrad* years ago; one of the handful of survivors who managed to escape the Kilrathi attack that destroyed her. The wounds he suffered in the escape were enough to have him invalided out of active duty, but Dmitri Rostov loved the Service too much to really retire. So he tended bar and swapped stories about the old days, never complaining about the arm and the eye sacrificed in the service of the Confederation.

Ironically, *Leningrad* was destroyed by the Imperial cruiser *Ras Nik'hra*, under the command of Ralgha *nar* Hhallas before his decision to defect. Blair had been pleasantly surprised to learn that Rostov didn't seem to hold a grudge against the Kilrathi, indeed he rather seemed to enjoy talking to the renegade when Hobbes came in to drink.

It was a pity some of the people who served with the Kilrathi pilot could not bury the hatchet the same way.

"Hey, Rosty, how's it going?" Blair gave him a friendly wave. "Don't tell me none of my drunks are hanging out here tonight."

Rostov shrugged and grunted as Blair approached the

bar, gesturing toward the observation window on the far side of the compartment. One lonely figure stood framed against the star field, staring out at the void. It was Flint.

"A slow night tonight, Comrade Colonel," Rostov agreed. He ventured a heavy smile. "Perhaps you work them too hard, tire them out too much. Even when I get a customer, it is to look, not to drink."

"I'll take a scotch," Blair said. He waited while the one-armed bartender programmed the order then handed him the glass, using his thumbprint to charge the drink to his account. "Thanks, Bear."

He crossed to the window where Flint stood, but didn't speak. Part of him wanted to respect her privacy, but another part wanted to draw her out, discover something about the woman behind the barriers she put around herself. She was his wingman, and Blair needed to know more about her, even if she was reluctant to be open with others.

The lieutenant seemed totally absorbed in her own thoughts, and Blair doubted she even noticed him. But after a moment she glanced at him. "Sir," she said quietly. That one word carried a range of emotion; sadness, and loneliness mixed with a hint of stubborn pride, exposing a glimpse into Flint's soul.

"I didn't mean to disturb you, Lieutenant," Blair said. "I was just wondering what it was about the view that had you so . . . involved."

"Just . . . thinking," she said reluctantly.

"I flew here once," Blair went on. "A lot of places to hide in this system, with the moons and the asteroids. Your first time?"

Flint shook her head ruefully. "This is my home system, sir," she told him. "My father commanded a Home Defense squadron after we settled here from Earth. Taught me everything he knew about flying."

"A family tradition, then," Blair commented.

She looked away. "He planned to pass it on to my brother David, but . . . the Kilrathi had their own plans."

"I'm sorry," Blair said, knowing the inadequacy of words. He should never have questioned her, dredging up the past this way.

"Everyone's lost someone, I guess," Flint said with a little shrug. "They don't give you medals for it. But coming back like this . . . it brings back a lot of memories, is all. A lot of stuff I haven't thought about since I went away to the Academy."

"You haven't been back since then?"

She shook her head. "Not much point. My mother took Davie's death hard. She just . . . gave up. He died when I was fifteen. My Dad was killed in the cockpit, fighting the cats when they raided here the year after I left. He scored twenty-one kills over the years after Davie was killed. He said each one of them was dedicated to Davie's memory, so he'd have a proper escort of cats to join him in the afterlife. They said . . . they said he died trying to nail number twenty-two, which would have matched Davie's age, but Dad didn't make it." Her voice was flat, level, but Blair could see a hint of tears in her eyes. "I've made eighteen kills since I left the Academy. Four more for Davie, and then I start racking them up for Dad. Maybe I won't score fifty-seven for him, but I'm damned well going to try."

Blair didn't say anything for a long time. He wasn't sure what bothered him most, the woman's preoccupation with vengeance or the cold, matter-of-fact way she talked about it. It was almost as if she was so wrapped up in her quest that she had lost touch with the emotions that set her on the path in the first place.

Finally he changed the subject, gesturing toward the viewport. "Which one was home?"

She pointed to a distant gleam of blue-green, barely

showing a disk. "Locanda Four. The main colony world." She paused. "It's a pretty world . . . or it was. Dark purple nights, with bright moons that chased each other across the sky. The insects would sing . . . different serenades, depending on the closeness of the moons. Davie and I would sit up late together, just listening . . ."

"I could try to get you some planet leave, while we're here," Blair offered. "You must have some family left? Or friends, at least?"

"Just my uncle's family," she said. "I haven't been in touch with any of them for years." Flint hesitated, still staring at the distant point of light that had been her home. "No, thanks, Colonel. I appreciate the offer, I really do, but I've got too much I need to do here with the rest of the wing. I can't be on the sidelines if the cats are really planning a fight. Not here of all places. I need to be a part of whatever comes down."

Blair studied her with a penetratingly probing gaze. "Look, Flint," he said at last, "I know something about the way you feel. Lord knows I've lost many people who were important to me over the years. But when we climb into our cockpits and get out there in space, I'm not sure I can afford to be with both you *and* your brother on my wing. I need you fighting for yourself, for the Wing, for the ship . . . not for a memory, not for vengeance. It cost your father his life. I don't want you to have to pay the same price."

She looked at him, the tears in her eyes catching the light. "I just can't give up now, Colonel," she told him. "It's too much a part of who I am and what I've become. You've seen me fly; seen me fight. You know I can get the job done. Don't take it away from me. Please . . ."

Blair took a long time to answer, sipping his drink to give himself more time to think. "All right," he said at last. "I guess you're not carrying around any more baggage than the rest of us. Maniac's still trying to prove he's the best, Hobbes is trying to live down being from the wrong damned species, and Cobra just . . . hates cats. You're in pretty good company, all things considered."

"What about you, Colonel? What baggage is Maverick Blair carrying around after a whole lifetime spent fighting in the war?" Flint's eyes held a glint of interest that made her whole face seem more alive.

He thought about *Concordia* . . . and about Angel, still out there somewhere on her secret mission. "Classified information, Lieutenant," he said, trying to muster a smile. "One of the privileges of being a colonel is never having to let the troops know you're human."

"And are you?" she asked.

He let out a sigh. "All too human, Lieutenant. Believe me, I am all too human."

They stood side by side and watched the stars for a long time in silence.

Flight Wing Briefing Room, TCS *Victory* Locanda System

"Okay, people, let's get down to business," Blair said. "I'd like to conclude this briefing sometime *before* peace is signed, if you don't mind."

A few scattered chuckles greeted his sally, and the ready room quieted. Blair glanced at the faces grouped around the table: the squadron commanders, deputies from each of the four squadrons, and representatives from the Wing's technical and maintenance staff and from *Victory's* Intelligence Office. Rollins was there as well, still functioning as Blair's aide and liaison between the flight wing and the bridge crew.

"Okay," Blair went on. "Here's the drill. For those of you who don't pay attention to the daily shipboard news, we've jumped into the Locanda System. It's been on or near the front lines for years now, and subjected to repeated raids by the Kilrathi Empire." He pushed a stray thought of Flint and her family from his mind and continued. "Until sometime early last month, there was an Imperial base deep in the asteroid belt on a fairly large rock designated Felix on our charts."

He activated a holographic projector to display the star system. "But three weeks ago, a patrol out of Locanda Four discovered that the Empire was no longer maintaining perimeter patrols around Felix, so a well-equipped force was sent to check it out: a destroyer, a heavy fighter escort, and a transport carrying a company of Marines. They met no resistance, and they discovered that the Kilrathi base was completely abandoned. Everything had been cleaned out. That base supported at least three squadrons of fighters and a depot large enough for a carrier to do a field refit. But they gave it up—lock, stock, and fighter bay."

"But I heard there was supposed to be all this activity here." That was Denise Mbuto, callsign Amazon, the major commanding the interceptors of Blue Squadron. "Everybody said there was going to be some kind of big push."

Blair nodded. "Yeah. Felix was abandoned while reports were received concerning *increased* Kilrathi ship activities in these parts, such as several capital ships, including three carriers. One was the *Sar'hrai*, which launched that strike on us at Tamayo. There was also a report placing Crown Prince Thrakhath's brand-new flagship here. Certainly there have been a lot of little dustups involving Kilrathi fighter patrols and a few light cap ships, destroyers and such."

"It would make little sense to abandon a well-defended base while building up the fleet presence," Ralgha said slowly. "Thrakhath is many things—arrogant, ambitious, ruthless—but I have never considered him to be a fool. There is something here which we cannot see as yet."

"Maybe the local boys are just seeing things," Marshall

said. "One carrier passes through on the way to hit us at Tamayo, and it turns into a whole damned fleet with the head kitty-cat in person commanding."

Blair shook his head. "No. Most of the reports are too well supported by evidence. We have tracking and sensor data that bears out the notion of three carriers and maybe eight smaller capital ships. That's a pretty fair sized force to be hanging around a backwater like Locanda. And Hobbes is right. The asteroid base would have been a useful adjunct to operations . . . too useful to be abandoned casually."

"Perhaps the fleet was sent to cover the withdrawal of the base contingent," Warlock Whittaker suggested. "It would take a lot of transports to dismantle a base that size, and if they thought we had enough ships to interfere with them, they would have a powerful escort in place."

"They might even be moving the base," Major Luigi Berterelli, commander of Green Squadron, added. "If they were looking to expand their facilities, or if they just thought our patrols had learned too much about the post on Felix, they might have decided to set up something bigger and better elsewhere. That would require an escort, too, while the new base was still getting up and operating . . . and if they *had* a new base, it could be supporting whatever else the cats have planned for that flotilla of theirs." Berterelli had an anticipatory gleam in his eyes, as if he could already see this new base lined up in his bombsights. Green Squadron had not seen much active service lately, but a Kilrathi base would give the bombers a chance to show what they could do.

"Those are possibilities," Blair agreed, "but by no means the only ones." He nodded toward Commander Thomas Fairfax, *Victory*'s senior intelligence officer. "Commander?"

"Headquarters has been monitoring Kilrathi radio

transmissions regarding Locanda for several weeks now, trying to discover just what their intentions are with regard to the system. A courier in from Torgo this morning brought a summary of the most recent findings." Fairfax paused, consulting a portable computer terminal. "First of all, it is believed that their original timetable for whatever is happening at Locanda has been rendered inoperative, possibly due to problems which have arisen in related missions elsewhere."

"Tamayo, maybe?" Mbuto suggested with a savage smile.

"Uncertain," Fairfax said seriously. "At any rate, we believe them to be behind schedule already, which means the action could get heavy any time now."

"The real question is, what action?" Major Ellen Pierce, Whittaker's Exec, put in.

"Linguistics are relating trouble with certain intercepted Kilrathi broadcasts." The Intelligence Officer plunged ahead as if she hadn't spoken. "One message in particular definitely refers to Kilrathi intentions for the Locanda System . . . it uses a word we've never seen before. *Trav'hra'nigath*."

"Bless you," Maniac said with a grin.

Blair glared at him. "Hobbes . . . does that mean anything to you?"

Ralgha was giving the Kilrathi equivalent of a frown. "The nearest English translation, my friend, would be literally *to grant the prize without struggle*." He paused. "Surrender? That is not a concept my people embrace. Struggle is the one constant in life."

"They are planning to surrender the system?" Blair asked. "That doesn't explain the buildup, though it would at least account for abandoning the base."

"The implications of the messages we've intercepted suggest that the Empire intends some gesture at Locanda," Fairfax said. "A demonstration of power . . .

or of intentions. Again, we're not entirely sure about the exact meaning of all that we've intercepted."

Whittaker was nodding. "I could see that. Even if they're starting to think in terms of giving up real estate, the cats aren't likely to just quietly turn tail and run. That wouldn't fit into their system of honor, would it, Colonel?" He was looking at Hobbes.

"Ceasing to struggle for a prize one deems worthwhile is not honorable at all," Hobbes said slowly. "A tactical retreat, yes, especially if there is duty to one's followers involved, but the ultimate object is never abandoned."

"Well, I say they feel the need for a parting shot," Whittaker insisted. "Something to salve their pride when they withdraw. Three carriers could deliver a real punch and flatten the colony facilities before anybody knew what hit them. Then they sail away toward their real target."

"Perhaps," Fairfax said. He looked down at his terminal again. "The only other possibility Intelligence can release to us right now is what appears to be a code name for the Kilrathi operation here. *Krahnakh Ghayeer* . . ."

"Unseen Death," Ralgha said.

Blair exchanged a quick glance with Rollins. Nobody spoke for a many moments.

"Unseen Death," Maniac repeated at last. He sounded unusually thoughtful. "I don't like the sound of that. It reminds me of something I heard back at Torgo . . ." He trailed off, frowning. "Yeah, that was it. I remember a guy telling me about some backwater system the Kilrathi raided a few months back. Only instead of just dropping in for a quick loot'n'scoot, they cleaned the place with some kind of new bioweapon. Pandemic, he called it."

"I heard about that, too," Pierce said with a nod. "Rumor has it that Confed HQ slapped a blackout on the whole thing and quarantined the system."

Rollins was about to speak until he caught the look

in Blair's eye. "The war's bad enough without listening to all the rumors flying around," Blair said sharply. "If the cats have a bioweapon, we'll locate it soon enough, you can count on that. In the meantime, we have to concentrate on what we *do* know—and on learning what we *don't know*. Isn't that right, Commander Fairfax?"

The intelligence officer nodded, looking unhappy.

"Right, then," Blair went on. "For the moment the name of the game is recon. We know there's a Kilrathi squadron in these parts, and we think they're planning something nasty. If Major Berterelli is right, we need to look for signs of a new base. At the very least, we need to pinpoint areas of enemy activity and try to estimate both their intentions and their exact strength."

"So it's back to patrols, then," Amazon Mbuto said.

"Unless one of you has a crystal ball that can show us where they're hiding," Blair said. "We're drawing up a full schedule of recon ops. I'm doubling the shifts by putting more fighters out at any given time, so I'm afraid we'll all be contracting extra duty for a while. Major Berterelli, I would like an assessment from you on whether we can adapt Green Squadron to take over point defense work. That would give us the Hellcats for other patrol ops."

"Range would be pretty short on Hellcats," Whittaker said. "They were never meant for long-duration patrol work."

"After our little scrap back at Tamayo, I started thinking about in-flight refueling," Blair told him. "A refueling shuttle with an escort of Thunderbolts could allow your whole squadron to operate over a normal patrol route." He shrugged. "We'd better see if the bombers can replace them before we talk about it further. At any rate, people, we've got to find out everything we can about the Empire's plans before they spring them. So make sure your pilots are sharp and ready for anything. When this thing goes down, whatever it is, we'll need to be ready. Dismissed."

Command Hall, KIS Hvar'kann
Locanda System

Thrakhath lounged in his chair, his thoughts far away. The war was entering its final stage now, and soon the Terrans would be brought down like prey caught in an open field. That would be his doing, Thrakhath, Crown Prince, victor over the Terran prey, hero of Kilrah . . .

And some day soon his grandfather would be dead, and Thrakhath's claws would grasp the Empire with a grip that would draw blood.

"Lord Prince . . ." It was Melek, his closest retainer, bowing as he approached the throne.

"Your report, Melek," he said mildly.

"Lord Prince, the Terran carrier has been identified as the *Victory*. As you predicted . . . the ship that carries the renegade."

"The ship *Sar'hrai* failed to neutralize," Thrakhath added, showing his fangs. "It is of small consequence. The forces we are mustering now will guarantee the success of Unseen Death, no matter what attempts the apes make to intervene. But be sure to emphasize that all pilots must avoid contact with the renegade. I want no repetitions of the incident with Arrak."

"Understood, my liege," Melek said with a bow. "Lord Prince . . . we know that the new weapon will work. The field tests revealed that. Why do we not simply mount a raid on Earth now? It need not be a full-scale attack. All that is necessary is a single ship, a single missile, and the Terran homeworld is infected and wiped clean. That would shatter the apes, making them helpless prey under our talons."

"Not quite, Melek," Thrakhath said quietly. "Do not

forget, we have attacked their homeworld before, to devastating effect, and yet done them only minor harm in the greater scheme of things. Our agents claim they have powerful new weapons in preparation now, weapons capable of destroying entire planets . . . even golden Kilrah itself. These weapons are not deployed around Terra, so a strike on their homeworld will only trigger massive retaliation. We cannot allow that to happen. I will not trade one homeworld for another, Melek. That would be disaster."

"But the loss of Terra . . ."

"Would mean less to the apes than the loss of Kilrah would to us," Thrakhath said, leaning forward. "You have not studied the humans as I have. You do not grasp their nature. If Kilrah was lost to us, we would suffer great harm. The Emperor, the heads of the great Clans, the ancient landholds and monuments of our people . . . these are what tie our race together, separate us from the animals. Take those things away and the Empire withers. But the apes are savages. Terrans would mourn the loss of their home, but it would not destroy them. They would continue to swarm in their multitudes, disorganized but still determined."

"Then can we truly win this war?" Melek asked. "If we are so much more vulnerable than they, do we have any choice but a glorious death?"

Thrakhath smiled. "We know only a little of their doomsday weapon, this . . . Behemoth, as they call it. Our agents say it is untested, but they have not been able to penetrate its secrets as of yet. We must draw out the apes; force them to commit their new weapon before it is fully ready, in a way we can control and manipulate. Unseen Death will be the first stage. By demonstrating our bioweapon and proving our willingness to use it, we will leave the Terrans no choice but to deploy the Behemoth."

"Against . . . against Kilrah?" Melek's look was one of horror and fear, but Thrakhath didn't reprimand him for his shameful display.

"Not at once," the Prince told him. "They will test it first. We will learn where the weapon is to be tested, and we will discover its weaknesses. For this purpose we keep the Heart of the Tiger in readiness. And when we have destroyed their one hope of retaliation, leaving their Navy demoralized and confused . . ."

"Then Terra dies," Melek said softly.

"Then Terra dies," Thrakhath agreed. "The first of many human worlds . . . until their race is gone forever."

• CHAPTER X

Thunderbolt 300
Locanda System

It felt strange to be in the cockpit of a fighter and yet drifting free, without acceleration or preprogrammed destination. Blair had never thought of flying a Thunderbolt as a claustrophobic experience, not with all of space in full glory around him . . . but he was ready to admit that it could be cramped, constricted, and more than a little bit boring.

They had been in the Locanda System now for three days, operating frequent recon flights in search of some sign of the Kilrathi fleet. Today was the first time they had put up the Hellcats in a recon role, and Blair had elected to fly escort on the refueling shuttle with Flint rather than assign the job to one of the other Gold Squadron teams. The entire force, four Hellcats, the two Thunderbolts, and the shuttle, had flown together to this prearranged rendezvous point at the edge of the point defense fighters' maximum range. They topped off their tanks and set out in two patrols to sweep a wide arc before they returned. Then they would refuel and make the return trip to the *Victory* together.

Everything went like clockwork. Blair hoped their luck would continue to hold.

The worst part of being alone in deep space for long amounts of time was the scope it provided for brooding.

The lack of specific information on Kilrathi intentions and dispositions made for a game of hide and seek extending over an entire solar system, and it was a game where the Kilrathi had all the advantages. The idea that they might be planning a biological attack on Locanda bothered Blair more than he cared to admit. It suggested that the Empire was upping the ante by introducing the prospect of mass slaughter, possibly escalating to an all-out genocide. Blair had felt that, before, both sides had agreed on what "winning" meant. And now the Kilrathi might be trying to change that definition. If the Kilrathi turned to weapons of mass destruction on any major scale . . . the Confederation would have no choice but to answer them in kind.

But something else troubled Blair; something he hadn't shared with anyone, not even Hobbes. Given that the Kilrathi had this new weapon, and given the rumors that it had already been tested elsewhere, why Locanda? The system was practically worthless in any strategic or material sense, although its long-time position on the front lines gave it a certain sentimental and media prominence the place hardly merited. It was as if the Kilrathi had picked a place to wield their terror weapon which was most likely to attract Confed attention. It would be much more difficult for the High Command to seal off the system and black out the news, because Locanda was so well known to the Confederation at large.

A bioweapon attack here would be like a gauntlet thrown at the feet of the High Command; a challenge . . . but why hadn't the Empire chosen some system where they would win more than just a propaganda stroke? Tamayo, with its high population and important shipyard facilities, or the Sector HQ at Torgo, or any of a dozen other systems nearby would have made far more logical choices than Locanda. There had to be something more behind the Kilrathi campaign, but Blair couldn't fathom it.

He wasn't even sure that he was working from anything more than rumor, speculation, and fear.

"Hey, Colonel, tell me again how we're contributing to the success of the mission," Flint's voice crackled on the radio channel. She sounded bored.

"They can't all be free-for-alls, Flint," he told her, glad of the interruption. He didn't like the depressing turn his thoughts were following.

"You really think this latest sighting's going to pan out? I'll lay you ten to one that freighter captain was drunk when he logged that sensor echo."

The current reconnaissance effort had started after a report from a tramp space freighter of multiple sensor readings at the edge of his scan range two days back. It wasn't much to go on, but it was the only solid lead they had just now.

"No bet, Flint," Blair said, checking his sensor screen as he spoke. "I know better than to believe in elves, goblins, or reliable tramp skippers."

"You want to know what I think, sir?" Flint said. *"I think some Kilrathi cap ships might've shown themselves to that freighter just to get us away from the colony. Know what I mean?"*

"Any special reason, or are you just getting good at reading Kilrathi minds? I can get you a cushy job with Intelligence if you can tell what the cats are thinking." Blair caught a flash on his sensor screen. "Hold on . . . I'm reading contacts at two o'clock, low, outer ring. Check me."

There was a pause before Flint responded. *"Yeah, I got 'em. Three . . . no, four bogies, inbound. And I don't think they're our buddies from Red Squadron."*

"Shuttle, power up and get the hell out of here," Blair ordered, "we'll cover your withdrawal. But keep in mind our guys will need a drink when they get back here, so don't go too far unless the bad guys break through us."

"*Roger that,*" the shuttle pilot replied. Blair saw the twin flares as the boxy little craft accelerated away, gathering speed. "*We'll relay word to* Victory, *too.*"

"Okay, Flint, let's welcome our guests," Blair said, bringing the fighter around and firing up the engines. "Keep close formation as long as possible, but remember the top priority is to screen the shuttle. You see somebody breaking past and heading his way, you nail the bastard, and don't stop to ask for permission."

"*Don't worry, Colonel,*" she replied. "*I hardly ever ask permission anyway.*"

Bloodhawk Leader
Locanda System

"*I read three targets, two fighters, the other . . . a utility vessel of some kind. It is moving off. The other two are turning our way.*"

Flight Lieutenant Kavark nodded inside his bulky helmet. The report matched what his own sensors detected. His patrol, four Darket off the Imperial carrier *Ras Nakhar,* was near the end of its scheduled pattern when the targets suddenly appeared at the edge of their sensor range. He promptly ordered a course change to investigate.

"This confirms my readings," he said. "Target computer says the combatants are Thunderbolt class: heavy fighters. We have the advantage of numbers even though they are better armored than us."

"*Then the greater glory accrues to us for fighting them!*" Flight Lieutenant Droghar responded eagerly. Kavark felt a surge of pride. The pilots in his section were warriors, one and all, and it only enhanced his honor to command them today . . . even if it was a hopeless fight. "*What of the other vessel?*"

"It is an unarmed shuttle, of no importance. We may

safely deal with it after the escort is defeated . . . if anyone feels the need for target practice."

There were harsh laughs from the other three pilots. Kavark showed his fangs under his flight helmet, wondering briefly if any of them ever doubted their place in this war. "Ghairahn, you may have the honor of the first challenge, if you wish."

"*Yes, Leader*," Ghairahn replied. He was a young pilot, newly assigned to the section, but a distant member of Kavark's Clan. This would be his chance to earn his first blood in combat. "*Thank you, Leader*."

"Remember the instructions. If the renegade is detected, we break off the action. There will be no arguments, no loss of honor." Kavark paused. He knew they faced almost certain destruction by engaging, but honor demanded they fight. He would go through the motions, do all that was expected of him . . . embrace death with talons unsheathed, if that was what Sivar, the War God, demanded. "Now . . . for the glory of the Empire and the honor of Kilrah . . . attack!"

He forced himself to bare his fangs again in a savage smile as Ghairahn's Darket fighter broke formation and accelerated toward the enemy.

Thunderbolt 300
Locanda System

"*Here they come!*"

The first Darket was at maximum thrust, bare seconds away from the Thunderbolt's weapon range. A second fighter supported close behind, but the other two, true to Kilrathi practice, had not yet broken their formation to join the battle. This gave the Terran pilots a brief advantage, since a Darket was no match for a Thunderbolt in a stand-up, one-on-one fight.

They made use of this advantage quickly. To cripple

or destroy the first two fighters before the other Kilrathi ships joined the fray was the plan. If the enemy started swarming around either Terran ship with superior numbers, the odds could quickly turn against Blair and Flint.

Energy weapons blazing, the lead Darket dived directly toward Blair, not even trying to use evasive tactics. The pilot was either very confident or very inexperienced, Blair thought. He held off returning fire. Instead, he kept a target lock on the Darket while allowing it to approach so he could achieve the maximum effect from his weaponry.

"*For the honor of my noble race,*" a computer-generated voice translated the Kilrathi pilot's radio call. "*My claws shall grasp your throat today, human.*"

Blair didn't respond. He watched the Darket streak in, keeping one eye on the shield readouts. His forward screen took the full brunt of the Kilrathi attack, and the power level was dropping fast . . . maybe too fast. He rolled sideways, killing his forward speed with a hard reverse thrust that wrenched his gut. As the fighter slowed, he used his maneuvering thrusters to put the fighter into a fast spin just as the Darket, surprised by the maneuver, darted past with weapons now probing uselessly into space.

For a few brief moments, the Kilrathi's vulnerable stern was visible in Blair's sights. Smiling grimly, he powered up his engines again and opened fire with full blasters, adding a heat-seeking missile for good measure. "Curl your claws around this, furball," he said.

The volley cracked the Imperial fighter's rear shields, and the missile flew right up the tailpipe. It exploded, and the fighter came apart in a spectacular ball of raw energy.

"*You really nailed him, Colonel,*" Flint said. "*Now it's my turn . . .*"

She drove her Thunderbolt right into the guns of the second Darket, ignoring the withering fire her opponent was laying down. A moment later she spoke again. *"Bye, bye, kitty,"* she said. Missiles and beams leapt from her fighter's underbelly, and the Darket went up in a second brilliant fireball that momentarily dimmed the stars. *"Never mess with a gal on her home turf! That makes nineteen, Davie . . . and more to follow!"*

Bloodhawk Leader
Locanda System

Kavark watched the destruction of Ghairahn's fighter with a curious lack of emotion, showing neither anger nor blood lust, nor even pride in the warrior's sacrifice. The second Darket's loss was the same; just another statistic in the long fight against the ape-spawn humans.

Sometimes it seemed that the conflict would go on forever. Once it seemed a great thing, a glorious thing, to venture forth in battle for the glory of Empire and Emperor and Clan. But the fighting continued endlessly, and though the Kilrathi had the advantage of numbers and sheer combat firepower, somehow the apes always managed to move from the brink of defeat to rally and overcome the Emperor's forces. The Terran spirit embodied a refusal to give in despite overwhelming odds. And their warriors, though outnumbered and outgunned, were superb fighters.

"We must attack, Leader," urged his surviving pilot, Kurthag. He never doubted. He saw everything in black and white, honor against dishonor, victory against death.

"No, Kurthag," Kavark said. "One of us must report to the Fleet. They must know where the Terrans are operating."

"I will fight, Leader, while you withdraw . . ."

"Sharvath!" Kavark snarled. "Would you have me

abandon honor? I command here. Mine is the honor of battle!"

There was a long pause. *"Yes . . . Leader,"* Kurthag said at last. *"I obey . . . despite the dishonor."*

" 'The warrior who obeys can never be dishonored,' " Kavark told him, quoting from the famous words of the Emperor Joor'ath. "Now, go. And . . . tell my mate my last battle song will be of her."

He cut the channel and changed course to place his fighter between the Terrans and Kurthag's craft.

Sometimes the only way to deal with doubts was to face them . . . no matter what the price.

Thunderbolt 300
Locanda System

"They're splitting up," Blair said, studying his sensor screen. "One of them is making a run for it. Why is this other idiot sticking around? Doesn't he know he's no match for *two* heavy fighters?"

"Who knows what a cat's thinking?" Flint said, sounding distracted. *"Let's get him before he changes his mind!"*

"On my wing, Lieutenant. We'll take down this baby by the book . . ." Blair continued to study the screen as he spoke. If that Kilrathi fighter was heading for home, maybe he'd be able to lead the Terrans to the missing Imperial fleet. Assuming they could track him somehow . . .

"I can get the one who's running, Colonel," Flint announced suddenly. *"Going to afterburners. I'll be back before you finish toasting the dumb one."*

She suited actions to words before he could respond, her fighter streaking away at maximum thrust. Blair wanted to call her back, but at that moment the remaining Darket opened fire and accelerated toward him. There was no time to remonstrate with his headstrong wingman now.

He looped into a reciprocal course, trying to keep his sights framed on the Kilrathi, but this pilot was no hotheaded amateur. His maneuvers were unpredictable, and he knew just how to get the most out of his fighter.

The combination was dangerous, even in an uneven matchup like this one. Before Blair could line up a shot, the Darket pulled a tight turn and passed directly under his port wing, blasters firing. None of the hits pierced the shield, but they weakened it. Then the Darket turned away to avoid the arc of the Thunderbolt's rear turret.

Blair turned again at maximum thrust, the G-force pressing him firmly into his seat. The enemy ship appeared on his HUD again, and he tried to center the targeting reticule on the fighter despite the Kilrathi pilot's evasive action. But the other pilot seemed to anticipate his every move, weaving in under him a second time, unloading a full volley of beams and missiles against the same weakened spot.

A red light flashed on his console. *"Burn-through, port shield. Armor damage. Structural fatigue at ten percent."* The computer's flat, unemotional report was incongruous, and Blair didn't know if he wanted to scream or laugh.

The Kilrathi fighter spun in a tight turn and started another run. "Not this time, my friend," Blair muttered under his breath.

The weakness on the port side of the Thunderbolt would be a real danger now; another good hit in the same area could seriously damage the fighter. Ironically, it gave Blair an opportunity. There was little doubt as to what the Kilrathi pilot would do this time. He would be drawn to repeat that same attack a third time . . .

Blair initiated a turn before the attack developed, letting his nose swing down and left. The enemy pilot opened fire, but the shots caught the forward shields, not the port side. Simultaneously, Blair triggered his own weapons, and the Kilrathi ship flew right into the firing arc. A pair of missile launches exhausted Blair's stocks, but they were sufficient.

The pilot had time for one last transmission before the end. *"There must be . . . something more . . . than Death without end . . ."*

And then the fighter was gone.

Flight Deck, TCS Victory Locanda System

Blair scrambled from the cockpit as soon as the environmental systems in the hangar were restored, brushing past the technicians and ignoring Rachel's grinning "Looks like you took a real pounding out there" comment. Seething, he crossed to Flint's fighter and waited for the woman to come down.

By the time he'd dealt with the Darket, Flint had already engaged the fleeing ship. She had dealt with it quickly and competently, taking none of the damage Blair had suffered in his engagement. Her target had turned into expanding gases in a matter of seconds.

Before Blair could read her the riot act, though, the shuttle had returned, and the sensors registered the approach of the four Hellcats on the return leg of their patrol. He refused to dress down another pilot over an open channel. But all the way back, his anger had been building. Flint had blown their best chance to track the enemy.

She let go of the ladder halfway down and dropped to the deck beside him, pulling off her flight helmet to reveal a grin. "Score's twenty now, Colonel," she said. "Davie'll have his escort soon enough."

"Only if you're flying, Lieutenant," he said, his voice

low but harsh. "And I'm not sure how long that's going to be, after what I saw out there today."

"But—"

"You talk when I say you can talk, Lieutenant," he cut her off. "First you listen. I gave you a direct order to stay on my wing when I engaged that second Darket. Instead, you went charging after the other one. I expect that kind of attitude from Maniac or even a rookie like Flash but not from the pilot I pick as my wingman."

"But, Colonel, you didn't need me to deal with a Darket," she protested, looking stricken, "and I was able to make it a clean sweep."

"A clean sweep," he repeated. "That's what it was, all right. Of course, if there had been one survivor running for cover we *might* have been able to lie back at extreme sensor range and track him back to his mother ship. Maybe we'd find the whole damned Kilrathi fleet. But a clean sweep . . . that's certainly worth passing up a result like that for, isn't it?"

She took a step back. "Oh, God . . . Colonel, I never thought . . ."

"No, you didn't," he said. "You never thought. Well, Lieutenant, think about *this*. Intelligence thinks the cats are planning an all-out attack on Locanda Four, not just a raid but something big and nasty. And if we don't find their fleet and pinpoint it pretty damned soon they will have a clear shot. So when your pretty purple skies are filled with Kilrathi missiles, you *think* about whether we could have nailed them today if *you* had just obeyed orders instead of playing your little revenge game."

She looked down. "I . . . I don't know what to say, sir," she said slowly. "I'm sorry. Were you serious . . . about yanking my flight status, I mean?"

He didn't answer right away. "I don't want to," Blair finally told her. "You're a damned good pilot, Flint, and you know how to make that Thunderbolt dance. But I told you before that I need a wingman I can trust." He paused. "Consider this a final warning. You screw up again, Flint, and I'll have your wings. You get me?"

"Yes, sir." She met his angry eyes. "And . . . thanks, Colonel, for giving me a second chance."

As she turned and walked slowly away, Blair hoped he wouldn't regret the decision later.

• CHAPTER XI

Flight Wing Rec Room, TCS Victory Locanda System

Blair paused at the entrance to the rec room and glanced around. This evening the lounge was fairly busy, the Gold Squadron particularly well represented. Vagabond, Maniac, Beast Jaeger, and Blue Squadron's Amazon Mbuto were playing cards. Judging from the stack of chips in front of Lieutenant Chang, he was ahead. Vaquero was alone at another table with headphones over his ears, his eyes closed, and his hands tapping out a beat as he blissed out on his *rockero* music. Hobbes and Flash were talking earnestly at a table by the viewport, and Sandman was sharing drinks with a blonde from the carrier's weaponry division.

Lieutenant Buckley, alone at the bar with a drink in her hand and a half-empty bottle on the counter in front of her, looked up at Blair. She stood with exaggerated care and walked over to him.

"I hear you're down on Flint," she said, the words slurring a little. "What's the matter, Colonel, you only like pilots who've got *fur*?"

He looked at her coldly. "You've had too much to drink, Lieutenant," he said. "I think you'd better head back to your quarters and get some rest."

"Or what? You'll ground me? Like you threatened Flint?" She jabbed a finger at him. "You save your high-

and-mighty Colonel act for the flight deck or the firing line. I'm on down-time now . . ."

He grabbed her shoulder as she staggered, steering her back to the bar. "I don't know what set you off, Lieutenant, but . . ."

"What set me off? I'll tell you what set me off, Colonel, sir. Flint's one of the best damned pilots on this tub, and you treat her like dirt. Just like you treat all the pilots, 'cept your furball buddy over there. After she came off the flight deck this afternoon, she was ready to find an airlock and cycle herself into space. I spent the whole damned afternoon trying to straighten out the damage *you* created, chewing her out that way."

"She screwed up," Blair said softly. "And we can't afford any mistakes."

"Can't you let her be human once in a while? Do you have any idea what kind of strain Flint's under? This is her home system, you know . . . and everybody's talkin' about the cats planning to use bioweapons here."

"There have been stories about bioweapons," he said guardedly. Inwardly he wondered who had been talking. Probably not Rollins; he'd sounded sincere when he promised not to spread the story. But everyone at the squadron commanders' briefing knew about the rumors now, and some of them—Maniac, for example—wouldn't think twice before sharing the stories with the rest of the crew. "Right now they're just that: stories. Whoever's been circulating them probably wouldn't know a bioweapon from a biosphere."

"Oh, come off it, Colonel," Cobra said. "The cats've been working on these kinds of weapons for years. They use human test subjects from their slave camps. They've tried their bugs out on other human planets already. It's only a matter of time before they start using them routinely. If the grapevine says it'll be here, I wouldn't argue with it."

"You know a hell of a lot about what the Kilrathi are doing, Lieutenant," Blair said. "Maybe you should spend more of your time talking to Intell, and a little less on telling me how to run my Wing."

"Intell! I've had enough of Intell people and their questions!" She shook her head. "Anyway, you're just trying to change the subject. The simple fact is, *Colonel*, that there are some damn fine people on this ship who deserve better than what you're givin' 'em. Flint's jus' the worst case. But if I was *you*, I'd start treating people *right*, or you just might find out what friendly fire's all about sometime—" She broke off and started to stagger to another seat but ended up sitting down heavily where she was and putting her head down on the bar next to her bottle.

"Should I call Security to give her an escort to her quarters, sir?" Rostov asked from behind the bar. Blair wasn't sure how long he'd been there.

He shook his head. "Let's keep this in the family," he said, looking around. He caught Flash's eye and summoned him with a wave. "Major, I need a favor. Could you help Lieutenant Buckley back to her quarters, please? She's had a little too much to drink . . ."

"Sure, Colonel," Flash said with a grin. "I was starting to wonder how much booze she was going to be able to put away before she pulled a crash-and-burn." He helped Cobra to her feet, wrapped one of her arms around his shoulders. "Come on, Cobra, let's get you home."

Blair watched them leave, then let out a sigh. "Give me a drink, Rosty," he said, feeling suddenly weary. "A double anything. It's been that kind of a day."

He took the glass from the one-armed bartender, but didn't drink it right away. Instead he stared into the amber liquid, his mind a whirl of conflicting emotions. From the very start he was an outsider here, unable to pass the barriers his pilots held against him. Sometimes it felt as if he was flailing the air. Most of these pilots had been through a lot together and felt the same type of comradeship he had shared with the men and women of the *Concordia*. They resented him, resisted him, and everything Blair did only seemed to make things worse.

At least there were a few people he could still trust. Blair picked up the glass and took a sip, then walked to the table where Ralgha was still sitting, alone now. "Mind if I join you, Hobbes?" he asked.

"Please, my friend," the Kilrathi said, gesturing courteously toward the chair Flash had relinquished. "It would be good to spend some time with someone who . . . truly understands what this war is about."

"I take it you and Flash don't see eye to eye?" Blair sat down across from his old comrade.

"That cub!" Ralgha was uncharacteristically vehement. "He sees everything through the eyes of youth. No judgment. No experience. No concept of the truth of war."

"When he gets to be our age, he'll know better," Blair said. "If he lives that long. But I know what you mean. Things sure have changed since the old days."

Ralgha gave him a very human smile. "Maybe not so much," he said. "I can recall times when I thought I was immortal . . . and when you would get drunk and tell off a superior officer."

Blair shot him a look. "You heard all that?"

"My race has better hearing than yours," Hobbes reminded him. "And the lieutenant was not exactly concerned with keeping her voice low. Alcohol may cause some people to speak and act in very strange ways, my friend. I do not think there was any serious intent behind her words."

"*In vino veritas*," Blair said.

"I am not familiar with those words," the Kilrathi said, looking puzzled.

"It's Latin. A dead Terran language. It means 'there is truth in wine.' "

"I do not think Cobra would actually fire on you," Ralgha said. "Perhaps me, given the intensity of her dislike. But despite her anger tonight, I believe she respects you as a pilot . . . and even as a leader. Unfortunately, she also has a high regard for Lieutenant Peters, who saved her life in the last battle before the ship refitted at Torgo. And you should understand what it means to defend a friend from what you see as unjustified persecution."

"Yeah, I understand. I just wish there was a way to get through to her . . . to all of them."

"Perhaps you should consider unbending somewhat," Hobbes said slowly. "You have seemed . . . aloof . . . on this mission. That contributes to the trouble."

"I know that, too," Blair admitted. "But . . . I don't know, Hobbes. I just keep thinking about all the other times aboard the *Tiger's Claw* and the *Concordia*. It seems like every time I make friends and start to share something with good people, they end up dead. When I first arrived, I thought I would be better off keeping my distance. I thought maybe it wouldn't hurt as much, if it happened again. But that isn't the answer, either, because even if I can't call them my friends, I still feel responsible for these people. I respect them. And I'll still mourn them, if they buy it out there."

"I doubt it could be any other way, my friend," Hobbes said gravely. "Not as long as you are . . . yourself."

"Maybe so." Blair drained his glass. "Well, who knows? Maybe we're into the last game, after all, like all the Confed press releases claim. Maybe the Kilrathi Empire is about to give up the whole thing as a bad idea, and we'll have peace and harmony and all that sweetness and light."

Ralgha shook his head slowly. "It is a time for strange

ideas," he said. "My people have invented a word for surrender, a concept I can still barely grasp after years among your kind." He gestured toward the viewport. "I used to raid these worlds with my brethren. Now I defend them . . . and my people talk of giving themselves up without further struggle."

The Kilrathi paused, and for a moment Blair thought he looked lost. "I cannot guess at what my one-time comrades might do next. But I do not believe that the Imperial family can change so totally. If there is peace, it will be because the Emperor and Thrakhath are overthrown, and their supporters broken. That will not happen without a major change in the way this war progresses."

Flight Wing Officer's Quarters, TCS Victory Locanda System

Angel was with him, looking just as she had the day she left *Concordia* with her kit bag slung over one arm and the open ramp to the shuttle yawning behind her like a black, toothless maw.

"Farewell, *mon ami*," she said. "Look after the others for me, all our comrades. I will come back when Paladin does not need me . . ."

"Don't go, Angel," Blair heard himself saying the words as if from some great distance. "Stay here. If you go, everything will fall apart . . . everything . . ."

The words were wrong. He knew it, even as a shrill screech rang in his ear and brought him out of the dream. The words were all wrong . . .

He had let her go that day without a protest. He told Angel that he understood, told her that he would wait for her. But she hadn't come back to the *Concordia*. And he wasn't sure she'd ever come back to him. *Angel* . . .

The noise didn't go away even after he had sat up,

his eyes wide open, staring at the bare walls of his quarters. It took Blair quite a while to realize the noise was the shrilling sound of the General Quarters alarm. He started to rise when a computer voice joined the cacophony. "Now, General Quarters, General Quarters. All hands to Combat Stations. This is not a drill. General Quarters, General Quarters . . ."

A moment later the computer voice was replaced by Rollins, sounding excited. "Colonel Blair, to the Captain's Ready Room, please. Colonel Blair to Captain's Ready Room!"

As he finished tugging on his uniform, Blair glanced at the watch implanted in his wrist. It read 0135 hours, ship time. With a muttered curse, he grabbed his boots and started wrestling them onto his feet.

He wasn't sure which was worse: the dream of his loss or the reality of the war.

Dressed and almost awake, Blair forced himself to move through the corridors at a brisk yet measured pace. *Never let your people see you run, laddie,* Paladin had told him once back in the days they served on *Tiger's Claw* together. *Even when the whole bloody universe is falling around your ears, walk like you haven't a care in the world, and the other lads'll take heart and fight the better for it.*

It took all his willpower to remember the old warrior's lesson this time. The incessant alarm and the crewmen hastening to their combat stations set every nerve on edge. He knew long before he reached the ready room that this mission was the one which they had been awaiting—and dreading—for so long.

"Blair!" Eisen's voice boomed out as he entered the compartment. "Thought I was going to have to send somebody to roust you out of bed, man! We've spotted the bad guys, and we haven't got a second to lose."

He joined the captain, Rollins, and Hobbes at the big

table, watched as Eisen manipulated a terminal, activating a holographic chart in the air above the smooth surface.

"Leyland and Svensson spotted two carriers and five destroyers *here* eighteen minutes ago," Eisen said, indicating a set of coordinates approximately ten million kilometers ahead of the carrier's present position. "They made a positive ID on both of the carriers. One is the *Sar'hrai*, our friend from Tamayo. The other is definitely the *Hvar'kann*."

"So Thrakhath is here, just like the reports indicated." Blair fought himself to suppress a betraying tremor in his voice. "I wonder how much of the rest of it's true?"

"Most of it, Colonel," Eisen said levelly, meeting his eyes with a bland stare. "Intell sent us an update last night. The Kilrathi are carrying missiles armed with biological warheads, and they are going to attempt to use them against Locanda IV. The missiles are a new type, designated *Skipper*. They're too big to carry aboard fighters, so they'll be launched from capital ships."

"They had to wait until now to confirm it?" Blair asked bitterly. "They couldn't give us time to get ready?"

"The confirmation only came in from outsystem yesterday. One of General Taggart's resources finally gave us the full specs on the weapon . . . for what it's worth."

"You haven't heard the really bad news, either," Rollins put in. "These Skipper missiles carry cloaking devices, so they'll be damned hard to track. And as for the warheads . . . well, we might as well not have the specs at all. There's no counter for those bugs. Nothing."

Eisen gave Rollins a quick, angry look. "Once the pandemic is introduced into a Terrestroid ecosystem, it'll spread very quickly," he said. "And Mr. Rollins is correct. Even the Kilrathi don't have a cure for it."

Blair's nod was sober. "So we can't let them get any missiles through to the planet," he said. He looked from Eisen to Rollins. "But how do we stop cloaked missiles?

Hell, I didn't think the targeting system on a missile could handle cloaked flight. Everything I ever saw said you need a pilot to handle a bird when it's under cloak."

"According to the specs, the Skipper doesn't stay under cloak all the time," Eisen said. "It drops out of cloak every few seconds to update its flight profile. So they *can* be tracked . . . but only intermittently."

"Lovely. Any more good news?"

"Leyland was able to get an accurate scan of the Kilrathi. From the looks of things, both carriers had an absolute minimum of fighters deployed." Eisen's eyes studied him through the hologram. "They have the escorts doing most of their recon and CAP work. You know what that means as well as I do."

"Yeah." Blair nodded again. "They're prepping the fighters for a magnum launch. Right, Hobbes?"

The Kilrathi renegade sounded grave. "I fear that is the only likely explanation, my friend," he agreed.

"They're still pretty far out for a strike," Blair said. "Range is extreme for a run against Four."

"I agree," Eisen said. "But if I was about to make an all-out strike on a well-defended target, I'd prep early and keep my people ready. That way I could launch the moment I knew the enemy had discovered my ships. They may not be planning the strike right away, but they'll be good to go at any time."

"Where does that leave us?" Blair asked. "No criticism intended for the *Victory* and her crew, sir, but I'm not wild about the idea of us tackling the whole Kilrathi force alone. We might get in some hits, but some of the bastards will escape . . . and then where would we be?"

"Agreed," Eisen said. He looked at Blair. "Even I'm not so proud of the old girl that I think she'd survive a stand-up fight with seven cap ships. And our battle group isn't strong enough to even up the odds, either."

That prompted nods around the table. Three destroyers,

Coventry, *Sheffield*, and *Ajax*, had joined the carrier at Tamayo as escorts, but two of them were as old and outdated as *Victory* herself. Only *Coventry* carried her own half-wing of fighters. All in all, they weren't much when set against the Kilrathi force.

"Do *you* have any recommendations, Colonel?" Eisen went on.

Blair studied the chart. "Yeah," he said slowly. He allowed himself a wolfish grin. "Hit 'em now . . . and hit them hard."

Eisen looked doubtful. "It'll be a mismatch," he said. "Can you do anything against those odds?"

"Yes, sir, I can," Blair said, although a part of him didn't share the confidence he tried to project. "We won't be going in to take on the whole Kilrathi fleet. My notion is to threaten them with an attack and make them launch their missiles early. That's what I'd do, if I wasn't sure what was hitting me. So we stir them up, make 'em commit. And then we go after those missiles with everything we've got. *Victory* won't be in any danger, because I don't see how they could mount a counterstrike in the middle of their attack op. The risk falls entirely to the Wing."

"I was hoping you'd come up with something better, Colonel," Eisen said, sounding weary, "because that was the only plan I was able to rough out, too. And I'm afraid your pilots are going to be in for one hell of a fight."

"Yeah," Blair said. "I know. But I don't see anything else we can do without throwing away the one advantage we have right now."

"Advantage? We have an advantage?" Rollins looked and sounded incredulous.

"Surprise, Mr. Rollins," Blair told him with a slow smile. "Fact is, nobody would be crazy enough to do what we're talking about doing."

• CHAPTER XII

Flight Control, TCS Victory
Locanda System

"Battle Alert! Battle Alert!" the computer announced. *"Now, scramble! Scramble! Scramble! All Flight Wing personnel to magnum launch stations. Scramble!"*

A monitor showed the view as the ready rooms erupted in a sudden outburst of activity. For a few seconds it was a scene of utter chaos, with pilots running for the Hangar Deck. Some were still zipping up flight suits or dogging down helmets as they moved, but there was an underlying sense of order beneath all the confusion. These people were professionals who knew their jobs.

Blair glanced around Flight Control Center, nodding in satisfaction. The room was fully crewed, with Captain Ted "Marker" Markham, *Victory's* Flight Boss, presiding over the technicians with his usual autocratic flair. Ignoring the others, Blair focused his attention on Maniac Marshall, who was with Rachel Coriolis near the door. The major seemed to be debating his fighter's combat loadout with the technician, waving his hands in the air and talking with an excited intensity.

He waited until the discussion was over before crossing to Maniac. "We don't have any room for grandstanding today, Major," he said quietly. "This mission has to be flown perfectly. Otherwise . . . scratch a whole colony world and everyone on it. You read me, mister?"

139

Marshall met his eyes defiantly. "I know my duty, damn it. And I've never let *my* end down."

"Just remember what's at stake. You don't have to like me, major, any more than I have to like you. But today you'll *follow my orders*, or I'll have your head."

"I'll do my job," Maniac told him. "You just do yours."

Thunderbolt 300
Locanda System

Blair and Flint launched last, joining the other fighters already on station around the carrier. All four squadrons were up, thirty-three fighters in all. Leyland and Svensson had two of Blue Squadron's interceptors in position closer to the enemy flight, and the techs had down-checked five fighters—two Arrows, two Hellcats, and a Longbow—as unable to fly the mission.

He was glad Gold Squadron hadn't suffered any down-checks. At least all ten Thunderbolts would be going in today.

"All squadrons, this is Wing Commander," he announced as he settled his fighter into formation between Flint and Hobbes. "We've gone over the drill often enough, so I expect you all know your jobs by now. Warlock, I wish you were with us on this one, but in-flight refueling would complicate things too much. Keep your guard up, and make sure the old rust-bucket's still here for us when we get home."

"*Godspeed, Colonel,*" Whittaker replied.

"The rest of us have a fleet to catch," Blair continued. "Amazon, take the lead. Green Squadron to follow, Gold in the rear. Let's punch it, boys and girls!" He rammed his throttles forward as if to punctuate the order, felt the engines surging to full power and the G-force pressing him down. "Engage autopilots," he said. "Anybody who thinks he can sleep, this is your last chance for a catnap before things start getting hot!"

He doubted if anyone actually slept, though with the autopilots set it would have been possible—assuming adrenaline and anticipation left any room for any of them to relax. It was a forty-five minute flight at maximum thrust, and Blair spent the time reviewing his plans and trying to spot ways to improve their chances of success. He saw precious little hope of shortening the daunting odds against them. Everything depended on luck, now.

Blair was surprised when the computer alarm sounded the warning. They were close to their navigation checkpoint now, and the autopilots were disengaging automatically. He checked his scanners, saw the blips representing the two watchdog interceptors trailing the Kilrathi fleet ahead. The enemy showed up on long-range sensors, which showed the presence of large vessels, but so far his monitor showed nothing in range of the more accurate but less powerful short-range scan.

That was exactly as it should be. So far, so good . . .

"Shepherd to flock," he said, breaking radio silence. "Commence your run . . . NOW!"

Flag Bridge, KIS Hvar'kann
Locanda System

"Lord Prince!"

Thrakhath looked up from his computer display. The Tactical Officer sounded frightened, but whether it was due to something on his scanners or the danger of bothering Thrakhath was difficult to tell. "Lord Prince, I have multiple targets on close-range sensors. Small . . . a cluster of fighter-class targets. At least four eights of them!"

"Position?" Thrakhath rasped.

"Bearing to port and low, range five thousand *octomak* and closing." The officer paused. "They are Terran by their signatures, Lord Prince . . ."

"Of course they are Terran, fool!" Thrakhath raged. "Who else would send fighters against us? But how . . . ?"

"The Terran carrier," Melek said. "*Victory*."

"*Victory*," Thrakhath repeated, his claws twitching in and out of their sheaths with the violence of his emotion. "The Terrans must not be allowed to stop Unseen Death. Order all *Vrag'chath* missiles fired immediately, and launch fighters. Do it now!"

"We could deploy the Red Fang squadron to engage them, Lord Prince—"

"No! Red Fang has its own role to play. They will adhere to the battle plan!"

"As you wish, Lord Prince. But I am afraid that the Terrans might have more surprises planned for us." Melek's words were grim as he turned to carry out Thrakhath's orders.

The Prince summoned up a holographic tactical chart in the air in front of his command seat. He glared into it as if the very anger in his eyes was a weapon to destroy the Terran with. "It is they who will be surprised, I think," he said quietly.

Melek glanced up from his console. "The renegade will be among these pilots, Lord Prince," he pointed out. "Do the orders regarding him stand?"

Thrakhath didn't answer right away. If only *Sar'hrai* had carried out the job of crippling the Terran carrier at Tamayo, none of these complications would be around to plague him now. Carrier and renegade would be safely ensconced in some Confederation shipyard, waiting for the moment when they would join in the intricate dance of Thrakhath's grand design. He hoped *Sar'hrai*'s late captain was suffering on the unending barren plains of the Kilrathi netherworld for his failure. "If detected, the renegade must be avoided," the Prince said at last. "It is not yet time for Ralgha to realize his destiny . . ."

Thunderbolt 300
Locanda System

"The big boys are launching missiles, skipper." The voice in Blair's headphones had been scrambled, decoded, and computer-reconstructed, but he recognized Vagabond's smooth, laid-back tones. *"Big suckers . . . must be those Skippers you warned us about."*

"Time to give them something else to think about," Blair said. "Green Squadron, execute Plan Hammer. Amazon, give 'em cover . . ."

"Acknowledged," Major Berterelli said, his tone bland and professional.

"On it, Colonel," Mbuto chimed in a moment later. *"Come on, Blue Squadron, let's give the cats something they can really chew on!"*

The Longbows and Arrows peeled away, headed toward Thrakhath's command carrier. Blair had been forced to improvise an attack plan quickly once the Kilrathi fleet had been spotted, and Plan Hammer was a modification of a standing tactical operation he hoped would do the job.

The main vulnerability of the Kilrathi was their reliance on a highly organized leader cult at all levels of their society. From the Emperor down to the most ordinary noncom, leaders were looked to for virtually all decisions, even minor tactical choices a human would automatically make on his own initiative. The chain of command in the Empire allowed for a certain amount of flexibility, but an Imperial force without a leader grew rapidly unstable.

And Kilrathi leaders were well aware of this. They fought honorably in battle, like any of their race, but they were also all too conscious of the need for protection.

A threat to Thrakhath's flagship, then, might just get the full attention of the Kilrathi prince, at least for a time. He would almost certainly concentrate his capital ships to meet the danger, and that might just give Blair and Gold Squadron the time they needed to do something about the Kilrathi missiles that were already accelerating away from the enemy fleet. If the Kilrathi concentrated on defending themselves, their missiles might just be vulnerable.

"Gold Squadron, stay with me," he went on. "Let's give the heavy stuff a wide berth if we can."

"I'm for that!" Vaquero said. *"The wider, the better."*

Still at full thrust, the Thunderbolts raced in pursuit of the Kilrathi fighters, but despite Blair's preference their course led them directly past one of the enemy destroyers. For a moment he debated steering clear of the ship, but that would give the Kilrathi strike force too much lead time. Blair decided their only choice was to risk the capitol ship's defensive fire. . . .

"Check your shields, people," he ordered. "And hold your fire. Our targets are the fighters."

"Goddamn," Maniac said, almost too soft to hear. *"We could nail this bastard if we wanted to. . . ."*

"Stick to the program, Maniac," Blair warned.

"I know, I know," Marshall said. *"But you can't blame a guy for dreaming, can you?"*

The destroyer opened fire, massive energy discharges crackling from each of her turret batteries. One shot grazed Blair's starboard shields, and his status board lit up red as the computer assessed the power loss. It wouldn't take too many such hits to overwhelm the shielding and start sloughing off armor.

The biggest problem, though, was just gripping the steering yoke and trying to stay on course. Every nerve and muscle within him wanted to take action, any kind of action, but Blair forced himself to maintain his course and press on. He hoped the others would follow his lead.

"*I'm hit! I'm hit!*" That was Beast Jaeger. "*Direct hit on bow shielding. The generator's overloaded—*"

"*Hold on, partner,*" Cobra said. She was flying as his wingman again today. "*Ease off a bit. I'll slide in ahead of you.*" Blair glanced at his tactical display and saw that the lieutenant was suiting actions to words, bringing her Thunderbolt in directly ahead of Jaeger's. She could soak up at least some of the energy that came his way now . . . but it was a dangerous move, keeping such a tight formation.

"What's your status, Beast?" he asked.

"*Bow shield generator's off-line, Colonel,*" Jaeger reported, calmer now. "*But I'm re-routing the system now. It'll be makeshift, but I'll get the shields back up.*"

"You could abort . . ."

"*No way, Colonel. I'm in it for the long haul.*"

"*Bastard's still firing,*" Maniac commented. "*Damn near singed my wings. I still wish I could take him down.*"

"Maniac, if we take out those missiles, I personally guarantee you we'll come back and toast this cat's whiskers," Blair told him. "Any other damage?"

There was none. They had cleared the destroyer's primary kill zone now, though a few stray shots might still find them even here. But the worst was over. . . .

Except, of course, for stopping those missiles.

Flag Bridge, KIS Hvar'kann Locanda System

"The stalker is loose among the meat-herd, Lord Prince. Their bombers have damaged the forward shields and knocked out our primary missile launcher."

"The Terrans are prey, not predators," Thrakhath snarled. He didn't like the way Melek was beginning to regard the enemy. Respect or admiration was an accolade to be accorded only to predators, and the Terrans certainly didn't qualify for that status no matter how hard they fought to stay clear of the Imperial claws and fangs.

"Perhaps not," Melek said, almost mildly. "But at the moment that prey is dangerous. The threat to the flagship cannot be ignored, Lord Prince. And it is not the only problem—"

"The Terran success will not last," Thrakhath told him. "They are too badly outnumbered to deal with all our ships. Particularly once the fighters are fully deployed."

"The attacks on the flagship may be no more than a diversion, Lord Prince. The Terrans feint and threaten, but do not press home their thrusts. Nor are they eager to engage our fighters. We have destroyed two medium interceptors and a bomber, and others are damaged. But one of their squadrons is pursuing the missile flight. If they can intercept the missiles, the whole plan will be lost. We should consider diverting additional fighters to cover the missile strike."

"No, Melek," he said at last. "No, the Red Fangs will be sufficient for that task. The other fighters will remain here, to support the fleet. And to threaten the Terran carrier, once they break off their attacks here."

"As you command, Lord Prince," Melek acknowledged. But Thrakhath thought he could detect an undercurrent of dispute in his retainer's tone. That would have to be dealt with, at some point, lest it grow into open rebellion.

A pity, really, if Thrakhath ultimately was forced to do away with him. Melek was too useful a subordinate to dispose of casually.

Thunderbolt 300
Locanda System

"Stay on 'em," Blair said through tight-clenched teeth. "Stay on them . . ."

A cluster of Kilrathi missiles glowed bright on his short-range scanner, almost within weapons range now as the Terrans continued their pursuit. Then they were gone again, cloaked, equally invisible to electronic scanning and the naked eye. It made the chase a frustrating one, never knowing just when the targets might be visible or where their essentially random course changes might put them next. But patience and a little bit of luck would still be enough to stop the Kilrathi warheads . . . provided the Terrans kept on top of the Skippers. If any of them got past the Confederation fighters, picking up their trail again later would be well-nigh impossible.

"Hobbes, you and Flash get to play tag with these boys," Blair announced on the tactical channel. "Stick with it until you clean them up, and try to let us know if any of them get past you. Save your missiles if you can . . . there might be some tougher opponents for you to go after later on." He paused. "The rest of you stay with me. We'll track down that next batch while Hobbes has his fun here. Fire at any target of opportunity, beams only . . . and don't deviate from your flight paths. Let's do it!"

Red Fang Leader
Locanda System

Flight Captain Graldak *nar* Sutaghi accelerated his *Strakha* fighter to full power and studied the tell-tales flickering on his sensor screen. The Terrans were among the missiles now, beginning to fire as the *Vrag'chath* popped in and out of view to allow their computers to make course corrections in flight. It was time for Graldak's warriors to make their presence known.

He outnumbered the Terrans, with two eights of fighters in his command against eight-and-two of the Terran Thunderbolts. But it wasn't much of a margin of superiority. If only Prince Thrakhath had provided

additional fighter support for the missiles! But instead
he had chosen to hold back the bulk of the Imperial
fighters to defend his flagship, even though a half-blind
churnah could see that the Terran attack had been a
mere feint to hold Imperial assets in place around the
fleet while they tried to stop the missiles.

It would be fitting if Thrakhath's flagship *was* blown
away, Graldak thought. The Prince and his half-senile
grandfather had done nothing right since the war with
the Terrans had first begun. There was a stirring
throughout the Empire these days, the first scent of
change on the wind. If only the Imperial family's iron
talons could be pried loose for a time, the Clans would
rise and sweep them aside. Then the Empire could end
this fruitless war with the humans, come to terms with
them as predators rather than continuing to view them,
as Thrakhath did, as prey.

But meantime the War went on, and Graldak had duty
and honor to maintain.

"Red Fang Leader to Gleaming Talon Squadron,"
Graldak said aloud. "Drop out of cloak and engage the
Terrans. The honor of battle is yours."

Gleaming Talon's fighters were a good match for the
Terran Thunderbolts, especially with the element of
surprise on their side. They would tie the Terrans up
for a few critical minutes, at least, and that would give
the other flights of missiles time to get further away.
Once they were more than a few thousand *octomaks*
from the Terran fighters, they would be even harder to
detect.

And, meanwhile, Red Fang squadron would remain
clear of the fighting, until Graldak could decide how
best to intervene. After all, it wasn't just missiles that
could hide behind a cloak.

• CHAPTER XIII

Thunderbolt 300
Locanda System

"*We got us some company, Colonel. I count eight on an intercept course, bearing zero-one-six by three-five-eight.*"

The target reticule flashed on his HUD, and Blair glanced down at the targeting data display to his right even as Flint's words were registering. Targets . . . ? Where had *they* come from?

The answer made a cold lump in his stomach as the computer displayed a diagram of the nearest target, asymmetrical, with projecting horns that gave it a menacing, alien shape. Even before he saw the name Blair recognized the design and cursed under his breath. He should have realized what he was up against immediately.

Strakha fighters.

They were comparatively rare in the Kilrathi arsenal as yet, an advanced-technology space fighter on the cutting edge of Kilrathi science. Intelligence had nicknamed them "Stealth Cats" before they'd ever actually been encountered in combat, and they lived up to the name. They were designed for sneaking, pure and simple, with sensor-distorting materials incorporated into the hull and a shape that tended to confuse most scanning systems. Worst of all, though, they mounted a cloaking

149

device that could actually obscure the craft from any detection whatsoever, at least for short periods of time. But unlike the Skipper missiles, they could *stay* hidden, without having to drop the cloak to make navigation checks.

The new Excaliburs Rachel Coriolis had been drooling over a few weeks back had been designed to incorporate a Terran knock-off of a captured Kilrathi cloak, but the Excaliburs weren't in production yet. Strakha were. And they were here, in the Locanda system, right now.

"I see them, Flint," Blair acknowledged his wingman's call. "Escorts, to take our minds off the missiles."

"Hard to ignore 'em," Flint said. *"When they want to meet us so bad and all . . ."*

He didn't answer her. "Maniac, Cobra, engage the escort fighters. Wingmen, stay with your leaders. The rest of you, stay on course and only engage if you have to."

"Ready to rock'n'roll!" Marshall responded. *"C'mon, Sandy, let's teach these kitties a few new flying tricks!"*

"We're on it," Cobra added a moment later.

Four Thunderbolts broke formation, Maniac and Sandman rolling left, Cobra and Beast to the right as they spread out to meet the oncoming Kilrathi craft. He hoped his people could deal with two-to-one odds.

That left four Terran fighters to pursue the Imperial missiles. And if even one of them got through . . .

Blair forced the thought from his mind. He couldn't afford doubts now.

"Here, kitty, kitty," Maniac was taunting. *"Get ready to become cat chow!"*

The Thunderbolts maintained formation as they drove through the enemy squadron. Blair's target computer selected the closest fighter and locked on, and as the crosshairs glowed on his HUD Blair triggered his blasters. Energy beams raked the Kilrathi ship, not quite enough to penetrate the shields. But a moment later Flint was firing. The target ship tried to dodge out of range, but too late. Flint's blaster tore through shields, armor, and hull, and the Strakha blew.

"*Twenty-one!*" Flint called. She sounded excited, eager. "*Thanks for laying him open for me, Colonel!*"

"Any time, Lieutenant," Blair told her. "Just remember to keep your wits about you. Keep it frosty."

Another explosion flared to port, where Vagabond had scored a hit. Hobbes and Flash, meantime, had broken formation to pursue the flight of missiles. The four remaining Thunderbolts in Blair's dwindling force raced on, past another Skipper that Vaquero and Blair each managed to tag. It didn't blow, but Blair's targeting computer reported extensive damage to the guidance systems and steering jets. That made it virtually certain to miss its target.

They didn't have to destroy their targets, just disable them. Another advantage, however slight . . .

They still needed every advantage they could muster.

Thunderbolt 308
Locanda System

"Look out, Beast, you've got one on your tail!" Lieutenant Laurel Buckley bit off a curse as she brought her fighter around to support Jaeger. Almost from the moment they'd come into weapons range the Kilrathi had been pressing their attack hard, their fighters swarming like angry hornets around the outnumbered Terrans. Strakha were dangerous foes when the odds were even. When they had numbers on their side as well they were deadly.

But the four Thunderbolts could keep them busy for a while, and that might give Blair the time he needed. Cobra found herself wondering, briefly, if the colonel's decision to order her and Maniac to deal with the escorts was Blair's way of getting rid of the pilots he trusted least. Everyone in the Wing knew how he felt about Marshall . . . and she suspected he had the same opinion of her, after their clashes over Ralgha and Flint.

And Jaeger had the only fighter damaged by the destroyer's fire. Was he being left as a diversion because he, too, was considered expendable?

On the other hand, he'd kept Dillon paired with his precious Kilrathi friend, and nobody figured Flash as anything but deadwood.

No, Blair didn't strike her as the kind to let personal feelings dictate his tactical choices. He probably figured that she and Maniac would be better at this kind of free-for-all dogfighting than they were likely to be pursuing and attacking the strike craft. Four Thunderbolts against eight Strakha—no, six, now, after Flint and Maniac had each managed to take one out—called for aggressive flying, and that was one thing Cobra Buckley was good at.

"Hold her steady, Beast," she said, lining up on the fighter behind Jaeger. "Steady . . . turn port! Port!" She squeezed the trigger on her blasters as she shouted.

Jaeger cut sharply to the left, then broke right again as he applied braking thrust. The Strakha, pounded by Cobra's beams, shot past Beast's Thunderbolt, and Jaeger opened fire on the exposed tail where the shields were still shimmering from the fury of Buckley's attack.

For a moment nothing happened. Then the shields collapsed and Jaeger's blasters tore through armor. A shot penetrated to the power plant, and the Strakha exploded.

"Nice shooting, partner!" Cobra called, grinning.

"*You set it up,*" Jaeger said. "*Only five more to go!*"

"*Four!*" Maniac cut in. "*I've already nailed two of the bastards. Come on, you two, join the party! Plenty of little kitty asses for everybody!*"

"Two more coming in, Cobra," Jaeger reported. *"Up ahead . . . shit! My shield generator's fritzing on me again!"*

"Back off, Beast, let me handle—"

The two Strakha dived straight in, concentrating their fire on Jaeger's Thunderbolt. Shot after shot raked the fighter. He was trying to turn away, but Buckley could see he was too late. The bow shield was failing . . .

Then it was over. The fireball consumed Jaeger's fighter, so bright her computer cut in the polarizers for an instant to protect her eyes. When she could see again, nothing remained of Helmut Jaeger's craft but a rapidly-expanding cloud of twisted, scorched metal fragments.

She could hardly believe it had happened so suddenly. One instant Jaeger had been out there . . . now, nothing. It took her back to the horrors of the Kilrathi labor camp, to guards who would strike down a slave without warning and to people she knew who vanished in the night. The cats were always the same, always killing without warning and without mercy, taking joy from death and fear and pain . . .

"Bastards!" she screamed, hitting her afterburners to dive toward the nearest Strakha as she opened fire with all her energy weapons at once. *"Damn cat bastards! I'll see you all in hell!"*

Strike Leader
Locanda System

Graldak *nar* Sutaghi bared his fangs as four Terran fighters accelerated away from the developing battle. *So, the Terran strike leader knows how to hunt,* he thought grimly. Prince Thrakhath had bestowed a name upon their Flight Wing commander: The Heart of the Tiger. Today the human was living up to the honor of that name, clinging to his mission despite all the barriers the Empire raised in his path.

Did Thrakhath realize what kind of warrior this ape was? The Prince wasn't known for esteeming his Terran foes, even those who received a Kilrathi vendetta-name.

No matter, now. The only thing that counted at the moment was victory, and that was very nearly under Graldak's claws. The Terrans had managed to destroy two of the four flights of missiles, and they had almost reached the third. But they would get no further.

"Red Fang squadron," he said aloud, feeling the battle-lust surging through his veins. "Decloak and engage at will!"

Thunderbolt 300
Locanda System

"Keep them off me! Keep them off me!" Vaquero's voice was urgent in Blair's headphones. *"Where the hell are you, Vagabond?"*

"Just hang in there a little longer," the Chinese pilot responded. *"The cavalry's coming."*

Blair wrenched his attention back to his HUD as a Strakha dived toward him, guns blazing. This last batch of enemy fighters had come at them out of nowhere, eight against his four, and the Terrans were fighting for their lives. Even as he flipped the Thunderbolt into a tight, high-G evasive turn a part of his mind was on another part of the battle entirely . . . and on the clock. Each second ticking away took the final flight of Kilrathi missiles further from the Terran fighters, letting them spread out. Soon it would be all but impossible to detect them even when they weren't cloaked.

He tracked the Strakha in, holding his fire and waiting for an opening. Then Flint swept past, her blasters searing, battering at the other ship's shields. Blair joined the barrage, and the Strakha came apart.

"Twenty-two, Lieutenant," he remarked dryly.

"No, sir, that one was yours. I just softened him up." Flint sounded as tired as he felt.

"We'll debate it when we get back to Old *Vic*," he said, trying to sound encouraging. Flint had done yeoman duty on his wing today, keeping formation, supporting him constantly, never forgetting herself or yielding to temptation. Since that first hit she hadn't scored a clean kill, but she didn't seem to be concerned at missing her chance to rack up more points in her quest for revenge. After this, he wouldn't doubt her again, he told himself as he turned his attention back to his sensor readouts. "Scanning for new targets."

There were four more Strakha ahead.

"Everybody up to another dogfight?" he asked. "Targets at eleven o'clock, low. Let's nail them!"

The four Thunderbolts closed up into tight formation and drove for the newest targets. The Strakha broke formation promptly, not waiting for the usual round of individual sorties that usually marked a fight with the Kilrathi. *Their CO must be one hell of a leader*, Blair thought.

"Vaquero, Vagabond, you guys dance with these four," Blair called. "I want to try for the rest of the missiles. You with me, Flint?"

"On your wing, Colonel," she told him.

He broke to port and increased thrust, with Flint's fighter sticking close by. The other two Thunderbolts drove straight toward the Strakha, but these Kilrathi pilots didn't rise to the bait of close combat. Blair saw the images on his scanner flicker and go out as the Strakha engaged their cloaks again. He muttered a curse under his breath.

"Keep a sharp eye out, people," he said over the comm channel. "They'll be back. Bet on it."

And suddenly they were back, two of them, at least. The pair of Kilrathi fighters materialized right on his tail, releasing missiles and then fading out of sight once again. Blair dumped a decoy missile and banked sharply, feeling the familiar rush of adrenaline in his blood. One of the enemy missiles picked up the decoy and homed in on it, but the second wasn't fooled by the electronic signature and continued to hurtle after the Thunderbolt. Blair altered course sharply again, veering back toward the decoy's flight path. The timing would have to be damned tight. . . .

His fighter flashed past the two missiles just seconds before the Kilrathi warhead detonated. The blast that erupted behind him was like a false dawn. His shield indicators registered a noticeable power loss, but nothing close to what he would have suffered if the full force of the blast had been absorbed by the shields themselves. After a moment he checked his screens, a let out a sigh. The explosion had caught the second enemy missile.

Then another Strakha was in sight, firing on him with beams and missiles from dead ahead. Blair returned fire, and seconds later Flint joined the fray with all her guns blazing. Just as Blair's forward shield was registering zero, the Strakha went up in a magnificent fireball. Blair heard Flint cheering. A moment later Vaquero and Vagabond were joining in, proclaiming another kill.

"*The other two boys are running!*" Vaquero shouted, all trace of the peaceful musician submerged now. "*Looks like we've taught 'em a real lesson this time!*"

"*Permission to pursue, sir?*" Flint added a moment later.

"Negative," he snapped. "Negative! We've still got missiles to track down! Get on your scanners, people. Now!"

But it was too late. His sensors turned up nothing but debris and open space, out to their maximum limit. The remaining Skipper missiles, five at least, were gone.

Blair stared at the empty screens, unable to accept what they were telling him. They'd come so damned close.

Flag Bridge, KIS Hvar'kann
Locanda System

"A report, Lord Prince."

"What have you got, Melek?" Thrakhath leaned forward in his chair to study the bulky figure of the retainer.

"The Strakha have eluded the Terran Thunderbolts, Lord Prince." Melek paused. "The surviving missiles are well on their way, and interception by the Terrans now is most unlikely. The colony will not survive."

Thrakhath bared his fangs. "Good. Then we have done what we came here to do. This will surely spur the Terrans into a rash attempt at retaliation." He could barely contain the pleasure that burned inside him. This was the first step to ending the long war. "The fleet will disengage and set course to the jump point to the Ariel system. Let us leave the Terrans to their . . . possession. Let them decide if they are pleased at the price they have paid to drive us away from their colony."

"Lord Prince . . . many of the fighters are damaged and low on fuel. The Strakha are at the very limit of their range. Should we not move to pick them up first?" Melek's look was almost challenging.

"The Terran reaction will be unpredictable, Melek. They could decide to launch a retaliatory strike, once they realize that all they have left is vengeance. We must not delay too long. Any fighters that can rendezvous with us may do so, but we will not wait for stragglers." Thrakhath paused. "You may order tankers to refuel them, if you wish. Carry out my orders . . . now."

Thunderbolt 300
Locanda System

"Good God, Colonel, what do we do now?" Flint's voice was ragged, with fatigue or shock or disappointment. Blair wasn't sure which. *"They're . . . gone."*

"We do whatever we still can," he said, hard-pressed to keep the despair out of his own voice. "And we pray the in-system defenses spot those bastards before they do any damage to the colony . . ."

"I counted five of them all told, Colonel," Vaquero said. *"Can't we blanket the approaches and pick them up before they reach the planet?"*

"We can try," Blair said.

"So . . . we head for home, skipper?" Vaquero asked.

"But . . . the colony," Flint said. *"We can't just turn back now. We have to try to stop those missiles!"*

"We'll do what we can, Lieutenant," Blair told her. "Spread out and keep hunting, and call for refueling from *Victory*. The Home Guard and whatever other ships are closer in to Four can search, too. But we can't track what we can't see. And I don't hold out much hope at this point."

• CHAPTER XIV

Thunderbolt 300
Locanda System

"The last word we received put the Kilrathi concentrating around the jump point to Ariel. Looks like they're pulling out. Not even bothering to gather in all their fighters, either. Could be we can round up a few more of the bastards before the whole thing's over."

Blair wasn't particularly interested in the Kilrathi, not any more. He had other concerns. "Any word on the situation on Four, Lieutenant?"

"It doesn't look good, sir," Rollins said heavily. *"The reports from the colony indicate at least five missiles got through. They were set for high airbursts, so the ground defenses never had a chance to fire at them. We won't know for a while if the pandemic is as bad as everybody claims, but . . . well, like I said, it doesn't look good."*

"Acknowledged, *Victory*. Leader clear." Blair nodded slowly. The report was about what he expected, but that didn't make it any easier to swallow. Five Kilrathi biowarheads exploding high above the surface of the colony world . . . that would ensure a fast spread of the tailored disease they carried. It would not be long before the effects of the attack became visible.

Locanda IV was as good as dead already, and Maverick Blair, the great pilot and war hero, was the man to blame for it all. The man who failed. . . .

He forced the thought aside and concentrated on his fighter's controls. Blair's Thunderbolt came through the long fight with only light damage, but he had trouble with the port-side maneuvering thrusters, and the computer was unable to reroute the circuits through a more dependable network.

They were near the original coordinates of the Kilrathi fleet, which thankfully was moving away at full speed toward a nearby jump point. Blue and Green Squadrons, after maintaining a prolonged diversionary action against Thrakhath's flagship, had returned to *Victory*. Gold Squadron remained out, however, searching for a lost sheep.

Incredibly, only Beast Jaeger's fighter was confirmed as destroyed in battle, though several of the others were in terrible shape. How Hobbes still flew at all was a mystery, and Vaquero's weapons systems finally overloaded in the last fight against the Strakha. But one of the Thunderbolts remained missing, and Blair ordered Gold Squadron to spread out and search for the missing man . . . or some sign of his fate.

Lieutenant Alexander Sanders, callsign Sandman . . . Blair never really knew him. He had served as Maniac's wingman throughout the current deployment and spent most of his off-duty hours hanging with Marshall. Although he always struck Blair as a complete opposite to Maniac—steady, dependable, loyal, reliable—Sanders and Marshall were good friends as well as wingmates. Neither Blair nor the lieutenant were very comfortable with each other as a result of the ongoing feud dividing the colonel from the major.

Now it looked as if Blair would never get a chance to know the man. Maniac had allowed himself to be separated from his wingman in the battle with the Kilrathi escort squadron while Cobra covered herself after Jaeger's death, so no one saw Sandman fighting. He might have been destroyed, or simply damaged and left adrift . . . or he might have ejected from his fighter. Until they were sure, they had to look.

A refueling shuttle arrived from *Victory* to rendezvous with the squadron and top off their tanks, and now the eight remaining fighters were to form a broad search pattern, hunting for some signs of the lost pilot. They were barely within sensor range of each other, and the comm channels were mostly quiet. Everyone knew the mission had failed. Everyone was exhausted by hours of continuous stress and tension punctuated by more fighting than any of them had seen in a long, long time.

"*Bad news, Colonel,*" Cobra broke into his reverie. "*I've got a debris field here. Material analysis reads consistent with a Thunderbolt's hull armor . . . It's gotta be Sandy's.*"

"You're sure it isn't part of Jaeger's ship?"

"*No way, sir. Too far from where Beast caught it.*"

"Start a close scan, Cobra. If there's an escape pod around there, find it."

"*I'll try, sir, but you know the cats. If they spot a pilot after he ejects, they'll either blast him where they find him or tractor him in for interrogation and a sporting death entertaining a ship's nobles.*"

"Check it out, anyway, Lieutenant. If there's any chance Sandman's still alive, I want to find him." Blair paused. "All fighters, from Leader. Converge on Cobra's beacon and concentrate your search there."

Bringing the fighter around, he increased his thrust. Cobra was right, of course. The odds against finding Sanders alive were too high a bet for anyone but a blind optimist, but he had to try.

It was a pitiful gesture set against his failure defending the colony, but it was all he could do right now.

Bridge, TCS Victory
Locanda System

"Approaching Gold Squadron's search grid now, sir."

"Very good, Mr. DuBois," Eisen acknowledged the helmsman's report. "Go to station-keeping. Sensors to full sweep. Let's help the Colonel look for his man. Any word, Lieutenant Rollins?"

"Nothing from Gold Squadron, sir." Rollins turned in his chair to face the captain. "*Coventry's* broadcasting updates on the Kilrathi fleet. Several of their ships have jumped, but it looks like *Sar'hrai* is delaying. Probably to pick up stragglers from the cat fighter strike. If we teamed up with the cruiser, sir, we might get a few licks in . . ."

"This is a carrier, not a dreadnought, Lieutenant," Eisen told him. "A carrier with a fighter wing that isn't likely to be able to pull a strike mission for quite a while. And that close to a jump point you always run the risk of something popping in when you least expect it."

"Yes, sir," Rollins said. He sounded disappointed.

"Look, I know how everybody feels. The cats broke through, and the colony's probably . . . in trouble. You want to hit back. So do I, believe me. But there's no sense in compounding one tragedy with another. ConFleet can't afford to throw away ships on meaningless gestures, and that's what it would be if we tried to take *Sar'hrai*."

They were the right words, Eisen told himself. But he didn't like them at all.

"Captain?" That was Tanaka, the Sensor Officer. "Sir, I'm only reading seven fighters in the search grid. There ought to be eight . . ."

"What the devil?" Eisen demanded. "Find that other fighter. And Rollins . . . get on the line and tell Blair it's time he took roll call!"

Thunderbolt 300
Locanda System

"Sensors confirm it, Colonel. Lieutenant Peters didn't respond to your orders to tighten the search grid. Instead she's vectored off toward the Ariel jump point."

"Goddamn . . ." Blair didn't finish the curse. "She must've been listening on the comm channel when you filled me in on enemy movements. Decided to even some scores with the Kilrathi fighters you said were likely to get left behind."

He should have watched Flint more closely, he told himself, angry and bitter. She had been a model wingman throughout the battle, but it must have been dreadful for her to see those last few fighters escape to launch their deadly missiles at the colony.

At her homeworld . . .

All she needed was one more kill to fill the score to avenge her brother, with nearly sixty more for her father. But how many more Kilrathi would Flint have to kill to avenge the population of an entire world?

"Colonel," Eisen broke onto the channel. *"There's still a Kilrathi carrier near the jump point. Possibly some undamaged fighters as well. Your Lieutenant Peters is heading right into a slaughterhouse, and she's not acknowledging our return-to-ship orders. Can you do anything to stop her?"* The captain paused for several seconds. *"It's your call, Blair."*

He stared at Eisen's image on his comm screen, his mind racing. Flint had a huge head start, and by the time he mounted any sort of rescue mission she might be dead. Gold Squadron was battered, exhausted, with missile stocks low and battle damage plaguing every one of the Thunderbolts. Common sense dictated that they cut their losses now and let Flint have her final, suicidal gesture. No matter how upset she might be,

Robin Peters was no fool. She just wanted to go down fighting.

But there was another part of Blair that couldn't just give up on her. The same part that prolonged the search for Sandman. Good pilots don't give up on their own, especially not on their wingmen.

"I'll go after her, sir," he said at last. "See if there's anything I can do."

Eisen didn't respond right away. *"Understood, Colonel,"* he said at last. *"And . . . Godspeed."*

"This is Leader," Blair said, more crisp than before. "If Sanders had managed to eject, we would have found him by now. Pack it in, people. Hobbes, get 'em down to the deck. I'm going after Flint."

"My friend, you cannot go alone—" Hobbes protested.

"I'm with you, Colonel," Cobra overrode Ralgha's soft voice. *"Let's move!"*

"I'm alone on this one," Blair said firmly. "That's a direct order. All fighters return to *Victory*. One rogue pilot in a day is enough."

"But—" Cobra sounded ready to start another war.

"A direct order, I said." Blair paused. "But . . . Cobra, you and Vagabond have the least damage, after me. Get down on the deck, let the techs patch anything essential that's damaged, and then rearm and refuel. Prep another fuel shuttle and escort it toward the Ariel jump point. Flint and I will be needing fuel before we get back."

"If you get back," Ralgha said. *"I do not understand why you are doing this, my friend. You are putting yourself in danger for no good purpose . . ."*

"She's my wingman, Hobbes. I have to go. Now carry out your orders." He cut the channel with a savage stab at the comm button, then switched on the navigation computer to plot a course after Flint.

Blair's only hope was that he wasn't making the same empty gesture as she was.

Thunderbolt 305
Locanda System

Flint glanced mechanically from her sensor board to the weapon status display, hardly aware of what she was doing any more. Somehow the shock of what had happened was dull and distant, as though she was watching someone else react in her place. The emotion that nearly overpowered her as she had realized her planet was under a slow, savage death sentence faded away now, replaced by grim determination.

It felt the same way when Davie died . . . and when the news came in to the Academy about her father. The grief and pain were there, but they were suppressed by the overwhelming need to *act*, to do *something*.

She must do something, even though she knew it was hopeless. If she didn't die on the firing line, her career would probably be over anyway by the time Blair got through with her. She had disobeyed orders and let her vengeance get in the way of the mission once again, even after the Colonel gave her a second chance. This was the last time she would be in the cockpit, facing the Kilrathi, one way or another.

Robin Peters intended to make this last time count.

Her navigational computer signaled that she was fast approaching the Ariel jump point. Her autopilot cut out instantaneously, and Flint forced herself to relax and let her combat training take over.

The sensor board came alive with targets.

Thunderbolt 300
Locanda System

"Blair to Peters. Blair to Peters. Respond, please." Blair closed his eyes for a moment, caught somewhere between anger and concern and fear. "For God's sake,

Flint, answer me. Break off and head for home before it's too late."

But his autopilot told him it probably was too late already. With her head start, she would have reached the jump point zone eight minutes ago, and eight minutes could be an eternity in a dogfight. By his best estimate, Blair's Thunderbolt was still two minutes from contact.

He ran a quick inventory of his weaponry. There was still one fire-and-forget missile slung under his wing, and both his gun turrets were fully charged. If there was any real opposition waiting ahead, it would be all too inadequate, but he didn't plan to remain for a long dogfight. Blair wanted to find Flint in one piece, then persuade her to withdraw in a hurry. Hopefully, the Kilrathi would be too concerned with getting their fighters back to *Sar'hrai* so she could jump to worry about chasing two foolhardy Terrans . . .

If not . . . well, it wasn't likely to be a long battle in any event.

The computer beeped a warning and cut the autopilot, and Blair focused on the sensor board as it began to register targets. The view before him wasn't encouraging.

The Kilrathi carrier dominated the scene, huge and menacing, hovering near the jump point. There was a great deal of activity around the big ship, and for a moment, Blair feared that Flint had driven straight in to attack the capital ship, a brave but utterly futile gesture indeed. But the blips he was registering were all Kilrathi, and after a moment, he realized that the bulk of the targets were keeping close to the carrier to protect incoming fighters attempting to land on *Sar'hrai*'s flight deck.

Then he picked up Flint. She had not pursued the carrier after all, but she was heavily involved with a trio of Vaktoth fighters which locked her in a classic wheel attack: circling her fighter and pounding at her shields without mercy. Flint handled her Thunderbolt impressively, managing somehow to dodge and turn out of the line of fire again and again, but inevitably some of those enemy beams penetrated her defenses. It was only a matter of time before her shields finally failed, leaving her fighter exposed to the full fury of the Kilrathi attack.

Blair took in the scene in an instant and cut in his afterburners. The Thunderbolt surged forward as if eager for battle, and in mere seconds his targeting computer locked on to one of the heavy fighters ahead. He would have to make this fast before any of the other Imperial fighters decided to intervene.

His blasters caught the Vaktoth at its weakest point, in the rear section just above the engines. There was a flaw in the shield pattern there, making the fighter vulnerable to a concentrated attack, but even the weak spot on a Vaktoth was formidable by anyone's standards. Blasters could punch through the shields, perhaps even damage armor underneath, but they didn't cycle fast enough to allow the Thunderbolt to exploit a successful hit. The usual tactic was to add a missile to the mix, preferably a heat-seeker that could fly right up the enemy's main thruster outlet while the shields were off-line . . . or, lacking missiles, to rely on a wingman to finish the attack.

Blair couldn't count on his wingman, not until she snapped out of her crazy urge for vengeance. He must use his last missile.

It was over in an instant. The Vaktoth came apart in a blinding fireball. The other two Kilrathi pilots broke the wheel and turned away, but Blair knew they weren't ready to run yet. They just wanted to regroup, assess the new threat.

And perhaps call in reinforcements.

"Flint!" he called. "This is the only chance we're going to get. Break off *now!*"

"*Break off . . . Colonel? What are you doing? You're supposed to be back at the ship . . .*"

"So are you," he snapped. "I decided you needed a personal invitation." On his screen he saw the two Vaktoth making slow, wide, outer loops to launch a converging attack from two directions. There was no sign that others planned to join them, but it would only be a matter of time. Sooner or later more fighters would reinforce these two, unless the two Terrans abandoned the battle.

"*Leave me here, Colonel. I'll cover your retreat.*"

"Forget it, Lieutenant," he told her. "I don't abandon my wingmen . . . not even when they abandon me. Either we both go back to the ship or neither one of us does."

"*I . . . yes, sir.*" Her voice was like lead.

"Those two are coming in fast," he said, still studying the sensor board. "We'll have to fight our way out. Follow my lead, Flint. I'm counting on you."

He banked left, accelerating, driving toward one of the two widely-separated Vaktoth. Flint stuck close to his wing, trailing a little but evidently obeying him.

Blair locked on his targeting computer, but held his fire. The Vaktoth grew in his crosshairs, looming closer. It opened fire, and blaster shots slammed into the Thunderbolt's shields where the earlier fighting had already weakened his defenses. There was precious little armor left under those intangible barriers of energy, and if they failed now it would be the end.

He pulled his steering yoke up hard at the last possible second, sliding over the top of the Kilrathi ship with only meters to spare. Blair spun the Thunderbolt around using maneuvering jets, praying the damaged one wouldn't let him down this time. Then, applying full thrust, he tried to kill his velocity while opening fire with his blasters at point-blank range. Shot after shot pounded the rear shields of the Vaktoth until the blasters exhausted their energy banks.

Blair spun the fighter around again and accelerated before the Kilrathi pilot reacted. Moments later Flint was there, unleashing her own beams in a furious attack on the weakened Vaktoth. The enemy ship began bringing its weapons to bear, but too late. Flint's blaster fire penetrated the hull and set off a chain reaction of explosions in the fighter's fuel and ammo stores.

For the first time since he'd flown with her, Blair didn't hear Flint counting her score.

"Let's get going, Lieutenant. Before the rest of the welcoming committee catches us."

The last Vaktoth came into weapon range, firing a few random shots just to measure the distance. On his screen, Blair could see four more ships detaching themselves from the force watching over the carrier.

If they got too involved with this one, they'd soon be facing those reinforcements, and Blair doubted he could manage another stand-up fight.

"*Your hull looks pretty bad, Colonel,*" Flint said, echoing his thoughts. "*I'll drop back and hold them.*"

"You'll follow my lead, like I said before." More shots probed after them, and Blair could feel the sweat starting to run down his forehead under the flight helmet despite the carefully-maintained environment of the cockpit. He wasn't sure he could pull another rabbit out of his hat this time.

"*Colonel! Targets! Targets ahead!*" Flint's voice was more alive as she called the warning.

Four blips appeared ahead, blocking their escape route back to *Victory*. With pursuers behind and this new force ahead, they couldn't evade another battle for long. Blair knew they couldn't last once engaged.

Suddenly the four new blips changed from amber, the color-code for an unidentified bogie, to green. Friendlies . . . Confed fighters. Blair could hardly keep himself from whooping in sheer joy at the sight.

"*This is Flight Captain Piet DeWitt of the destroyer* Coventry," a cheerful Terran voice announced. "*Captain Bondarevsky tells me you carrier hot-shots need a little assist. We're here to escort you home, Colonel. Fall in ahead of our formation, and leave the bad guys to us.*"

"We're in your hands, Captain," Blair said, breathing out a long, soft sigh. Already the nearest Vaktoth broke off at the sight of the four Arrow interceptors, and the rest of the Kilrathi pursuit was slowing noticeably as they studied the newcomers and tried to assess what the Terrans would do next. "We thank you all."

"*Compliments of Captain Bondarevsky, Colonel. He told me to tell you this makes up for that time off New Sydney.*"

Blair felt the relief flowing through him, and with it another sensation . . . fatigue. Now that the pressure was gone, it took the full force of his will to program the autopilot to take the Thunderbolt home.

Then, at last, he slumped in his acceleration couch, exhausted. He didn't win any victories today, but he survived, and Flint with him. And maybe that was enough.

• CHAPTER XV

Flight Deck, TCS Victory
Locanda System

Blair stepped to the makeshift podium reluctantly, and bowed his head for a moment before speaking. There were many aspects of a wing commander's duties he didn't like, but this morning's duty was the worst of them all.

He raised his head and studied the ranks of officers and crewmen gathered on the flight deck, assembled in orderly rows, and wearing their dress uniforms to mark the solemn occasion. Pilots from the four combat squadrons were prominent in the front of the formation. Even Maniac Marshall looked solemn today as he mourned the loss of his best friend on board.

Commander Thomas White, *Victory's* chaplain, gave Blair an almost imperceptible nod.

"We're here to say good-bye to the men and women of the flight wing who gave their lives in battle yesterday," Blair began slowly. "Nine pilots were killed fighting the Kilrathi, dedicated warriors whose places will be as difficult to fill in our hearts as they will be to replace on our roster. I haven't served on this ship very long, and I didn't know any of them all that well, but I know they died heroes."

He paused for a long time before continuing, fighting back a wave of emotion. These nine officers would hardly be noticed in comparison to the population of the colony on Locanda IV, but their deaths were much more immediate and vivid to Blair. They died trying to carry out his orders in a failed mission, and as wing commander he carried the full burden of responsibility for their deaths—and for the colonists they were unable to protect—squarely on his own inadequate shoulders.

"I wish I knew the right words to say about each and every one of these lost comrades," he went on at last. "But the only accolade I can give them now is this: each of them died serving in the best traditions of the Service, and they will be sorely missed."

He stepped back from the podium and gave a signal. Behind him, the first of nine sealed coffins rolled forward. Only one of them actually held a body, since Captain Marina Ulyanova was the only pilot who managed to eject before her ship was destroyed during the fighting around the Kilrathi flagship. She died from her wounds a few hours later. The other coffins were empty except for plaques identifying the pilots they commemorated.

"Present . . . ARMS!" the Confed Marine commanding the seven-man honor guard barked. The first coffin stopped moving for a moment, ready for launch.

From his place in line, Hobbes looked up and spoke in slow, measured tones. "Lieutenant Helmut Jaeger," he said.

Up in Flight Control a technician activated the launch sequence. The coffin hurtled into space on fiery boosters, and the second one rolled in to replace it.

"Lieutenant Alexander Sanders," Hobbes went on. Beside him Maniac bowed his head, his lips moving silently. In prayer? Or just saying good-bye? Blair didn't know.

When the third coffin was in place Amazon Mbuto took over the roll call. "Captain Marina Ulyanova," she said. Then, "Lieutenant Gustav Svensson."

The grim muster went on until all nine coffins were ejected. When the task was completed, the honor guard raised their weapons and fired three low-power laser pulses through the force field at the end of the hangar deck, then stepped back, standing at attention. Chaplain White stepped forward. "We commit these men and women to the empty depths of interstellar space," he said slowly. "Watch over them, Lord, that they may find peace who died in the fires of war. In the name of Jesus . . . Amen."

Wing Commander's Office, TCS Victory Locanda System

"You wanted to see me, Colonel?"

Blair was hard-pressed to speak. Instead he nodded and gestured toward the chair near his desk. This was one interview he didn't want to conduct.

Lieutenant Robin Peters sat down. "I guess I know what this is about," she said, almost too softly to be heard. "You might have died out there, chasing after me."

He found his voice. "I might have."

"The captain ordered you . . . ?"

"No." Blair shook his head. "It was my call to make."

"Well . . . I suppose you had your reasons. In your shoes, I would have stayed put. Let the stupid bitch get what she deserved." She looked away. "Sorry, Colonel. I've never been very good at saying thanks."

"You're welcome," he told her dryly.

"I want you to understand, sir—"

"Understand? There's nothing *to* understand, Flint. You lost it out there. Maybe you had good reason. Lord knows what it's like to have your homeworld . . . infected, like that. All at once, and despite everything we could do." Blair paused. He didn't want to go on, but he knew he must. Even though he understood Flint's feelings, he couldn't simply ignore her actions. "We don't just decide to fly off on a suicide mission because we're hurting. You have to fly with your head, Flint, not with your heart."

"You've never done that, sir? Flown with your heart?"

He fixed her with a steady stare. "The day you see me do that, Lieutenant, you can shoot me out of space yourself." A part of him, though, was well aware that he might have done the same thing himself. No pilot was an automaton, able to ignore his feelings at will. "We already talked once about this, Flint. And I told you what would happen if you let your heart get in the way of your duty. You haven't left me a hell of a lot of choices."

"I know, sir," she said, dropping her gaze. "I guess I was kind of hoping you'd let me off easy, let me keep flying. But you can't."

"No, I can't," Blair said, voice level and cold. "We can't afford to let every pilot pursue some private little war. That's a sure way to let the Kilrathi win. Until further notice, Lieutenant, your flight status is suspended. You're grounded."

Now it was Blair who couldn't meet her eyes. Something left them both, and only the expression of hopelessness and death remained.

"Dismissed," he added, and turned back to his computer terminal. He waited until she left the office before sagging into his chair, feeling as though he had just taken on an entire Kilrathi squadron on his own.

Captain's Ready Room, TCS Victory Blackmane System

"Sit down, Colonel. I'll only be a minute."

"Take your time, sir," Blair said, settling wearily into a chair while Eisen turned his attention back to a computer terminal.

Victory's captain looked even more tired than Blair felt, with the haggard expression of a man who had gone too many nights without enough sleep. Everyone had been working overtime in the five days since the battle off Locanda IV. Yesterday they had jumped from Locanda to the Blackmane System, leaving behind a world already in the grip of spreading panic and plague.

Eisen finished whatever he was working on and turned his chair to face Blair. "Well, Colonel. How's the work going with the flight wing?"

"About what you'd expect, sir. The techs have most of the fighters up and running again. There was some battle damage we couldn't fully repair, but we're getting back on track. I hope we can get some replacement birds from Blackmane Base . . . and some pilots to fill the roster out, while we're at it."

Eisen frowned. "That won't be so easy, but I'll see what I can do."

"Sir?"

"Word just came in. With Locanda Four gone and the whole system quarantined, HQ's decided to consolidate our resources in this sector. That means Blackmane Base is being shut down. Everything's shifting to Vespus and Torgo. Anybody who can herd a boat will be needed to fly ships for the evacuation. I might be able to snag some fighters. They'll probably be glad to unload a few from their reserve stocks and save space for other outgoing cargo."

Blair felt a sinking sensation in his gut. "Evacuate the base? Isn't that a pretty extreme move? What about the colonists in this system?"

The captain shook his head, frowning. "Doesn't look good. Confed's just getting stretched too damn thin. If the Kilrathi are going to start using these bioweapons routinely, we can't mount an effective defense in every system. So the orders are to concentrate on defending the ones that are really vital. For the rest . . . I guess they get to rely on the good old-fashioned cross-your-fingers defense initiative."

"If the Confederation can't protect its own civilian population anymore, we're in worse shape than I thought," Blair said quietly. "Things can't go on like this."

Eisen nodded agreement. "According to our resident rumor mill, Rollins, they won't. There's supposed to be some kind of big plan circulating back at Torgo to end the war once and for all. Tolwyn and Taggart are both supposed to be involved somehow, and if you believe Rollins and his sources it will be something pretty damned spectacular."

"Great," Blair said without enthusiasm. "We're stretched to the limit, and HQ is going to unveil another one of their master plans."

"All we can do is hope it works," Eisen said. He studied Blair from dark, narrowed eyes. "Have you had a medical evaluation lately, Colonel?"

"No, sir." Blair frowned, uncertain at the sudden change in the direction of the conversation. "Why?"

"You look like hell, for one thing."

"Right back at you, Captain. I don't think there's a man on this boat who looks too good now . . . except maybe Flash. I've never seen him looking anything but perfect."

"I'm serious, Blair. We've all been working hard, but I've had reports on you. You're pulling double shifts every day. You're not eating enough, and you're certainly not getting enough sleep. You haven't been, since before the fight at Locanda." Eisen hesitated. "And, frankly, I have to wonder if it hasn't been screwing up your judgment."

"My combat judgment, you mean," Blair amplified the thought for him.

The captain met his look. "You came on board with a

hot reputation, Colonel. And I'd stack your wing up against any in the Fleet. But it wasn't enough to turn the cats back at Locanda Four. There are some people who claim you had just . . . come back from your medical leave a little too early, that your judgment was impaired and the mission suffered as a consequence."

"Captain, I never claimed the reputation everyone insists hanging on me," Blair said slowly. He was angry, not just at Eisen's words, but at the fact that deep down he had been trying not to think the same things himself. "Fact is, we were just plain outmatched. There were too damn many of them, and yet we still came within a few minutes of nailing the bastards. If it hadn't been for those damned Strakha . . ." He took a breath. "My people did everything humanly possible, and I think I did as well. But if you want me to apply for a transfer, let someone better qualified take over—"

Eisen held up a hand. "I wasn't suggesting any such thing, Colonel. All I'm saying is that you're human, too, just like the rest of us. And if you drive yourself too hard, something's going to give eventually. Find some balance, man . . . before you really *do* screw up a mission."

"It's easier said than done, sir," Blair said. "You should know it, if anyone does. You have to hold this old rustbucket together, come what may."

"Oh, I understand what you're going through, all right," the captain told him. "More than you might imagine. There've been a few ops I've been on where I didn't live up to the reputation I'd racked up, and then I'd work twice as hard trying to recapture what I thought I'd lost. Usually I only got half as much done in the process. Take my advice, Blair. Don't dwell on the past too much. Even if you've made mistakes, don't let them become more important than the here and now. And don't take out your frustrations on other people. Like Lieutenant Peters, for instance."

Blair looked at him. "Are you overriding me on Flint, sir? Putting her back on flight status?"

The captain shook his head. "I don't get involved in flight wing assignments unless I have to. You grounded her. You'll have to be the one to decide to reinstate her." He paused. "But I should tell you. She applied this morning for a transfer to Blackmane Base. She needs to fly again, one way or another. I turned her down. With the base shutting down, nobody needs the complications a transfer would involve. But something'll have to be done on that front sooner or later, Colonel. She's a pilot, and a damn good one . . . when her head is screwed on straight. Weren't you the one griping about wasting good pilots, back when you found Hobbes off the roster?"

"Hobbes never pulled a stunt like Flint's, sir," Blair shot back. "And he's from a race that raised the vendetta to an art form."

Eisen nodded reluctantly. "As long as you're aware, Colonel. I agree she needs to get her act together. But too much time on the sidelines could ruin her."

"I know, Captain. I know."

Blair left the ready room more uncertain than ever.

Wing Commander's Quarters, TCS *Victory* Blackmane System

Vespus . . . he was back on Vespus again, and Angel was with him. They walked hand in hand along the top of a bluff overlooking the glittering sea, with a light breeze blowing off the water to stir her auburn hair.

Blair knew it was a dream, but the knowledge didn't change the intensity of the illusion. He was really with her, on Vespus, the week they'd taken leave together. It was a time when neither of them had imagined ever being apart again.

The view from the clifftop was beautiful: the setting sun, one of the three great moons hanging low above the horizon, sea and sky red with the gathering twilight. But Blair turned away from the spectacular vista to look into Angel's eyes, to drink in *her* beauty. They kissed, and in the dream that kiss seemed to last for an eternity.

Now they were sitting side by side, lost in each other, oblivious to their surroundings. Another kiss, and a long, lingering embrace. Their hands explored each other's bodies eagerly as passion stirred.

"Is this forever, *mon ami*?" Angel asked, looking deep into his eyes, almost into his soul.

"Forever's not long enough," he told her. They came together . . .

The dream changed. Vespus again, where sea and shore came together, but stark, bleak, with storm clouds gathering on the horizon. Blair stood with General Taggart, this time, looking down at the broken spine of the hulk that been *Concordia.* He stirred, but he couldn't awaken, couldn't recapture the other dream . . .

Now he stood on the flight deck, near the podium, as a line of coffins rolled past. The general was with him again, reading out the names of the dead in deep, sonorous tones. "Colonel Jeannette Devereaux . . ."

Blair snapped awake, stifling a cry. His hands groped on his bedside table until they wrapped around the holocube she had sent him. For a moment he fumbled with it, and then her image appeared, lips moving soundlessly with the volume turned down.

He stared at the ghostly figure and tried to control his breathing. Blair was never a superstitious man, but the nightmare was like an omen, a vision. Angel was gone, and he was afraid that he would never get her back.

Flight Wing Rec Room, TCS Victory
Blackmane System

Another evening, another day of seemingly endless work. Blair was looking forward to a tall glass and a chance to unwind, and although he wasn't eager for company, the rec room was preferable to his quarters. He spent too many nights lately staring at those four walls, awakened from sleep by the recurring nightmare. At least Angel couldn't haunt him here.

There was a cluster of officers at the bar, Lieutenant Rollins right in the middle. They were grouped around a newspad, watching the latest Terran News Channel update just beamed in from Blackmane. Barbara Miles, perfect as ever, looked out of the screen with an expression of mingled concern and reassurance as she spoke.

"Despite denials from official Confederation channels, TNC now has independent confirmation that the Locanda star system has been placed under absolute quarantine in the wake of an outbreak of a virulent plague said to be the result of a Kilrathi biological weapons attack. There are unconfirmed rumors that this is not the first time such weapons have been used against human colonies. It is now generally believed that the colony on Locanda Four has already suffered heavy losses, and may be all but wiped out as the disease runs its course."

She paused significantly. "In other news from the front, TNC has learned that a strategic withdrawal of Confed forces is underway in several outlying sectors. While government and military spokesmen officially deny any such actions, unofficially several sources have suggested that these withdrawals have been ordered as a means of consolidating the front lines by surrendering unimportant territory in the hope that the Kilrathi will spread themselves too thin and thus be exposed to a significant counterstroke.

But independent military analysts retained by TNC have labeled this suggestion as spurious, and believe the 'consolidation' is merely an improvised response to the advances of the enemy.

"This is Barbara Miles reporting, with another TNC Infoburst . . ."

"Shut it off, Radio," a lieutenant Blair recognized as one of the carrier's shuttle pilots growled. "Always the same old line from those cat symps."

Rollins blanked the screen. "Hey, Trent, where've you been? We were *at* Locanda . . . and they're breaking down Blackmane Base right now. I hear tell there's been talk of sending a peace envoy to Kilrah . . . that we're as good as ready to surrender. So how can you keep buying the fantasy that we're actually winning this war?"

"What I want to know, Rollins," Blair said, placing a hand on the lieutenant's shoulder, "is why you're so all-fired eager to tell us how bad everything's going?"

"Ah, c'mon, Colonel," Rollins said. "You'd have to be blind to miss the facts. Things are bad . . . and they're getting worse. Fact: we haven't had a real shore leave in months. Fact: they keep shuttling this old bucket around from one trouble spot to another, as if one battered carrier and one fighter wing was all they could spare to cover half the sector. Fact: we've been on one defensive op after another, and we always seem to end up pulling back when it's over. Seems pretty damned clear to me, Colonel. This war's winding down, all right. But we're not on the winning side."

Blair looked from Rollins to the others grouped around him. Most of them were nodding their heads in agreement, though a few, like Lieutenant Trent, were frowning at his words. "You want facts, Lieutenant? I'll give you a few to chew on. Fact: the grunts on the front lines, even the ones with lots of well-placed sources, never see the whole picture in a war. Fact:

the fastest way to lose a war is to allow morale to be sapped by half-assed young officers with big ears, bigger mouths, and no common sense at all. And fact: I know a communications officer with too much time on his hands who is letting his love for gossip jeopardize the morale of this ship."

"With all due respect, sir, I'm entitled to my opinion," Rollins said stubbornly.

"Indeed you are. But if I hear any more of this defeatist talk, you'll be reassigned to Waste Recycling, where your crap belongs. Get my drift?"

"Telling him to shut up won't make the truth go away, sir," one of the others spoke up.

"If it is the truth, wailing about it isn't going to change a damned thing," Blair said. "We'll just have to play the cards we're dealt. But like I said, the grunts at the front hardly ever know what's really happening. Hell, maybe it's worse than old Gloom and Doom here thinks. But maybe it's a lot better. Point is, if we decide everything's lost anyway, and give up, we might end up letting down some folks who need us to turn things around." He paused. "I'm not telling anyone what to think. Or even saying you can't shoot the bull over a few drinks. But spreading the worst possible rumors—that's crossing the line. I've heard my share of rumors that were a lot less nasty, and I'm sure Rollins here has heard them too . . . but those don't get much play, because they're not spicy enough."

Rollins gave him a long look, then shrugged. "Maybe you're right, sir," he said. "Maybe I do like to shoot my mouth off."

"Well, as of now, consider the safety on." Blair forced a smile. "Anyway, aren't there better things to talk about than this damned war? The girl you left behind . . . or the shore leave you'll never live down?" He turned to the bartender. "Rosty . . . a round on my account. But only to the ones who have something pleasant to talk about, okay?"

That boosted some spirits, and the others were laughing and chattering happily as Blair moved to an empty table by the viewport. He sat there staring into the darkness.

He could have been quoting from a manual on keeping up morale when he'd spoken to them. The trouble was, he didn't believe a word of it himself.

CHAPTER XVI

Captain's Ready Room, TCS Victory
Blackmane System

Blair paused at the entrance to the captain's ready room, reluctant to touch the buzzer. *Victory* was astir with fresh rumors today, speculations rising from the arrival of a courier ship from Sector HQ at Torgo. No one knew what word the ship brought to Eisen, but everyone was sure it heralded a change of orders, perhaps fresh action. Blair wasn't looking forward to learning what was in store for them now. He didn't feel ready to go back into action again so soon, not with the failure at Locanda still hanging over him. It wasn't something he could admit to anyone, either, not without requesting a transfer to some rear-echelon outfit, off the firing line.

As tempting as that idea might be, Christopher Blair refused to give in to it. There was no way he could let others fight the war while he sought safety. He owed it to all his comrades who had stayed and fought.

With an effort of will, he forced himself to compose his features and hit the buzzer.

"Enter," Eisen's voice came, and the door slid open.

"Reporting as ordered, sir," Blair said.

"Ah, Colonel, good." Eisen stood up, and the officer in crisp whites opposite him did likewise. "This is Major Kevin Tolwyn, from sector HQ."

"Hey, Lone Wolf," Blair said, genuinely pleased to

see the younger man. He advanced to clasp Tolwyn's hand, smiling broadly. "It's been a long time, kid."

"Another old acquaintance, Colonel?" Eisen asked.

"Yes, sir," Blair responded. "We served together on the *Tarawa* a few years back." He looked Tolwyn over. Short, baby-faced, the nephew of Admiral Geoff Tolwyn didn't look old enough to shave, much less to be a Confed officer. "Major, now, is it? That's a pretty good bump. You were only Lieutenant Tolwyn last time I heard . . ."

Tolwyn blushed. "Brevet rank, Colonel. I made Flight Captain after the Battle of Terra, the brevet came through after I got wounded during the mop-up after Vespus." He hesitated. "I guess one fighter too many cooked off underneath me and my uncle pulled me into a staff job for awhile, he said I'd already cashed all my lucky chips in and he wasn't going to take a chance on next time."

"Staff slot, huh. I'm sorry to hear it. You should be on the flight line, kid, where you belong."

"Don't I know it," Tolwyn said. "But . . . I didn't have any say in the matter. The admiral wouldn't take no for an answer, and here I am."

Blair nodded in understanding. He'd heard stories of Admiral Tolwyn's open displays of emotion, first when he had feared Kevin missing or dead, then later when the younger man was recovered and returned to the fleet. Maybe the staff job was a real effort to keep Kevin Tolwyn out of harm's way. He was, after all, the admiral's closest surviving kin and had done more than his share of fighting while serving on the *Tarawa*. The Medal of Honor on his chest was more than enough proof of that.

"If I can interrupt the reunion, Colonel, I think we'd better get down to business." Eisen gestured to the chairs by his desk. As they sat down, he continued. "Major Tolwyn brings us fresh orders from HQ. It looks like the war's heating up, at least as far as we're concerned. Major?"

"The attack on Locanda Four was a real wake-up call," Tolwyn said. "We knew the cats were working on a number of strategic weapons projects, but we didn't expect them to bring them into play as long as their fleet was still able to hold its own. It's against everything in the Kilrathi philosophy to resort to this kind of blatant genocide. They're supposed to like their fights up close and personal, and this is a complete departure from everything we thought we knew about them."

"Do we have any evidence they're going to use bioweapons elsewhere?" Blair asked. "Or was this some kind of . . . special case?"

"We don't know," Tolwyn said. "And that has the High Command doing some serious nail-biting, let me tell you. All we know is that the cats have escalated the war, and if we don't match the ante we might as well just fold now."

"Match the ante . . . how?" Blair asked.

"The Confederation's been working on its share of doomsday weapons, too," Tolwyn told them. "The Battle of Terra scared the hell out of all of us. The big Kilrathi offensive caught everyone off guard. I don't think I need to tell you that we're on the ropes. One more attack like that and the game's over. Remember, they managed to drop over twenty standard warheads on Earth in the last attack. If only one of them had been a bio the home-world would be a lifeless desert today. There's no way around it, this one's to the death and we have a couple of counter punches almost ready to go."

Blair said nothing. The idea of matching the Kilrathi atrocity at Locanda with a Terran retaliation against civilians appalled him, but he tried to keep his reaction from showing in his voice or expression.

Tolwyn fixed Blair with his gaze. "One of the projects is being pushed by General Taggart and the folks at Covert Ops, and the other's my uncle's pet project. That's why he got pulled from *Concordia* just before it went down."

Eisen cleared his throat. "If you don't mind, Major, I'd appreciate it if you'd stick to the briefing."

"Sorry, sir," Tolwyn said. "Both projects actually stem from the same basic research. It seems some of our survey work off Kilrah during *Tarawa*'s little end run raid there a few years back has yielded some unexpected results. Kilrah is much less stable, in planetological terms, than Terra. Subject to seismic problems, quakes, volcanoes, the whole bit. Apparently there are some severe tidal stresses at work on Kilrah that render the planet extremely vulnerable to widescale seismic activity." He paused. "Given a big enough shaking, Kilrah would literally come apart."

"And HQ has a weapon that could do it?"

"More than one, Colonel. I've not been briefed on the Covert Ops project, except for generalities. But Project Behemoth, my uncle's preference, uses high-intensity energy beams on a massive scale to trigger seismic shocks. Aimed and fired properly, the Behemoth weapon could trigger the destruction of Kilrah."

"And the loss of the homeworld would cut the foundation from under the whole Empire," Eisen said slowly, with a slight smile. "It certainly is ambitious, I'll say that."

"It's genocide," Blair said quietly. "How many civilians would we be killing?"

"How many died on Locanda Four?" Tolwyn demanded. "How many more will die if they unleash their pandemic again? Look Blair, our intel people are telling us the Empire is tottering on the edge of civil war. The various clans are fed up, especially after the failure of the attack on Earth. That's why they didn't immediately launch a second attack when we had nothing left to stop them. The Emperor had to regroup—build back his fleet and keep enough forces close at home to counteract any threatened coups. It's given us the breathing room to get our new weapons on-line. If we wait any longer, though, the Kilrathi might be the ones to strike first and then its us that are finished."

Blair shook his head. "The end justifies the means? That wasn't what they taught back at the Academy. I thought the Confederation stood for something better than that."

Tolwyn looked away. "Yeah . . . yeah, you're right. It does." He paused. "Well, anyway, we're hoping we don't have to actually attack Kilrah. That was the deciding factor when it came down to choosing Behemoth over the Covert Ops concept. Apparently whatever they've hatched is a one-shot deal. But Behemoth is a weapon that can be used several times, and the idea is to try a few very public tests on Kilrathi military bases. Let the cats draw their own conclusions about what we could do to Kilrah with the same weaponry. That's the operational plan, at least. Our hope is a good demonstration might actually push the clans into a palace coup. The Emperor and his grandson are overthrown and the other clans sue for peace."

"I guess that's better than blasting Kilrah out of existence," Blair said. "I mean, the Empire's the enemy and we have to do whatever it takes to win. But there are a lot of innocent Kilrathi out there who have nothing to do with the Emperor or Thrakhath or the whole damned war effort. Some of them are dissidents, like Hobbes was before he defected. I wouldn't want to be party to killing them all."

"Well, we'll hope it doesn't come to that," Eisen said. "I agree, it would be a nasty choice to have to make. But if we can convince them we mean business . . ."

"So what's our part in all of this?" Blair asked.

"Right now, we're still putting the finishing touches on the weapon," Tolwyn said. "It won't be ready to deploy for a few more weeks. But in the meantime, we're starting to prospect the sector for a likely-looking first target. We need to conduct some extensive recon work, checking defenses, and surveying possible target planets to make sure the Behemoth will be effective against them. It wouldn't do to cruise in, open fire, and then find out the place was so tectonically dead we couldn't even cause a good earthquake."

"Recon work," Blair repeated. "That'll be quite a change, after what we've been doing."

"It'll be difficult and dangerous," Tolwyn said. "We can't afford to send large forces in anywhere, for fear of putting the cats on guard. We've got a handful of carriers going out individually into the selected target systems. *Victory's* drawn Ariel, where we're fairly certain we've got a very suitable Kilrathi base to test."

"Ariel's a pretty tough nut," Blair commented. "I hope you're not expecting us to take them on single-handed."

"The system is inside the Caliban Nebula," Eisen said. "Dust and gas and energy discharges will play hell with shipboard sensors . . . on *both* sides. We can sneak in, gather as much information as possible, and sneak out again and probably never tip the cats off that we were there. Maybe even pull off a few ambushes along the way."

Tolwyn nodded. "You'll actually have it better than some of the other carriers on this duty," he said. "And when you get back, the admiral's already decided that *Victory* will get the real plum job. Flagship for the Behemoth Squadron . . . so you'll be in on the kill, as it were."

"Flagship? Us?" Blair raised his eyebrows. "Your uncle must have developed a sudden taste for slumming, if he's not going to go out in one of the big boys."

"*Victory* has its . . . compensations, Colonel," Tolwyn told him. "Like a genuine expert on Kilrathi psychology, your buddy Hobbes. You also have a one-time Intelligence source with specialized knowledge of cat behavior, too. I think the name is Lieutenant Buckley. In fact, the admiral had this in mind when he assigned you here as wing commander."

"That was before Locanda," Blair said, "before things escalated. You mean Tolwyn planned to use this Behemoth thing even before the cats started with the bioweaponry?"

"Some of the data we later decoded from that deep intel probe *Tarawa* had on board, leading into the discovery of the Kilrathi super-carriers, contained information about the bio program. That's why we've been running the race to get the new weapons on line, and why *Behemoth* sails now, ready or not. Locanda was a horrible tragedy, but thank God it wasn't one of the inner worlds or Earth—and believe me, that will be their next target."

Blair held up his hand. "Never mind, Kevin," he said. "Don't try to explain. I know your uncle well enough to know what he had in mind. And why."

"Just what are you getting at, Blair?" Eisen asked.

He shrugged. "It's just that the admiral has always been . . . zealous, sir. I've served with him a few times, and he's always been the same. *He* wants to win the war . . . Admiral Geoff Tolwyn, himself. He'd love it if he could lead the ConFleet to victory, sign the papers that ended the war in orbit over Kilrah . . . whatever. And if Behemoth can make it possible, he'll use it . . . and the devil take moral questions and anything else that stands in the way."

Eisen's frown deepened. "I don't think it's a good idea to pursue this, Colonel," he said slowly. "It's coming dangerously close to libeling a superior officer."

"Maybe so, Captain," Blair said, shrugging again. "But it isn't libel when you're telling the truth." He shot the younger Tolwyn a look. "Sorry, Kevin. I know he's family, but . . . well, you know how I've always felt."

"You haven't said anything I haven't thought a dozen times over, Colonel," Tolwyn said. "But, like the Captain says, we'd better stick to the briefing."

"Agreed. What else do we need to know about?"

"Captain Eisen's been bruising a lot of ears back at HQ about the flight wing's shortages. I've brought out authorization for you to requisition fighters, munitions, parts, and stores from Blackmane Base before the last load goes out next week. They've got all types of fighters in mothballs there already, so that won't be a problem."

"The real shortage is in pilots," Blair said. "We have nine empty slots to fill."

"You won't get all of them, I'll tell you that much up front," Tolwyn said. "I've already spoken to the base commandant. You'll get four or five, no more. Sorry I couldn't do better." Tolwyn looked wistful. "I'd volunteer for a slot myself, but the admiral would never approve it."

"I wish you could," Blair told him. "Well, four or five is better than none at all. Major Mbuto lost five ships at Locanda Four, so she'll get first call on any pilots we do get. I just hope to God it's enough."

"It has to be, Colonel," Eisen said. "Now that we finally have a ray of hope that we might see the end of this damned war, it has to be enough."

Flight Deck, TCS Victory
Blackmane System

"Okay, skipper, this one checks out too. Looks like those no-talent bums at Blackmane Base actually sent us some real fighters, and not just junk off the scrap line."

Blair checked off the last of the new fighters on his

portable computer pad and nodded. "I'll breathe a little easier now, Chief," he told Rachel Coriolis. "I was starting to think we'd never get the replacement fighters aboard."

Four days had passed since Kevin Tolwyn was whisked aboard his courier ship to report to his uncle, and in that time, Blair's life became nothing but a string of petty frustrations. The worst problem was expediting the requisitions Tolwyn issued to Blackmane Base in the midst of the chaos and confusion which reigned during the last days of the base's closing process. But after many shouting matches over the comm channel, Blair finally got results. Now he possessed a full contingent of fighters in *Victory*'s hangar deck, storerooms bulging with spare parts and stores of all kinds, and three new pilots to assign to Mbuto's interceptor squadron. It was progress, of a sort. But it had been slow going for a time, and Blair was worn out with the constant strain of it all.

A tractor towed the fighter, a Longbow looking as if it had never been flown, toward a storage bay. The flight deck was bustling with activity, but for the moment Blair and Rachel were out of problems. It was a rare yet pleasant feeling.

"Uh . . . skipper?" Rachel spoke with none of her accustomed brashness. "Can we chat? Off the record . . . ?"

"Isn't that the way we usually do it?" Blair asked her.

"Yeah," the chief admitted. "That's one of the things I like about you." She hesitated. "And the fact that I *do* like you is why I want to say this . . ."

"Spit it out, Chief," he said as she paused again.

"You've got this . . . look in your eyes that I've seen before," she said slowly. "I had this guy, see? A pilot. One day he saw his wingman get fried, and he came in blaming himself for it. Didn't matter what I said, what anybody said, he was convinced he let old Shooter down."

"And?" Blair prompted.

"A few days later . . . he took an Arrow out and just

kept on going. Hit a jump point just as the Kilrathi were coming through. There were a lot of fireworks . . ." She trailed off, her eyes focused on someplace far away. "They never found him . . . not even a debris field. He might still be out there, for all I know."

"I'm . . . sorry," Blair said quietly. "But . . . why tell me about it?"

"That look in your eye, it's like the one he had before he cracked, skipper." She paused again. "You want to talk? I may be a lowly techie, but I've got a sympathetic ear."

Blair didn't answer for a long time. "I had . . . have . . . someone, too. I don't know which it is, any more. She got caught up in some hush-hush mission, and nobody's heard from her for months. Maybe she's managed to sidestep the whole war—ditched in neutral territory somewhere. But I keep having these nightmares about her . . ." He looked away. "I keep thinking, one way or the other, I would hear . . . only I haven't heard, and I'm afraid . . . you know."

Rachel nodded. "I know. Maybe your gal and my guy found each other out there."

He forced a smile. "Yeah . . . maybe so. At least they'd both be alive, then . . ."

"Yeah, but on the other hand if I found out he'd been making time with some hot-shot lady pilot, I'd have to kill him myself when he finally got back." She managed a laugh.

After a moment, Blair joined in. It felt good to laugh.

Flight Wing Rec Room, TCS Victory Blackmane System

"Scotch," Blair said, perching on a stool at the bar. "Preferably something that's at least been in the same *sector* as Scotland, this time."

Rostov grinned at him. "There's a war on, Colonel. You gotta take whatever they hand you, *da*?"

Maniac Marshall was sitting further down the bar, studying a holomagazine and sipping at a tall glass of beer. He looked up as if only just noticing Blair's arrival. "Well, well, honoring the peasants with another visit, eh, Colonel? Shall I kiss your ring, or will a reverential bow be enough?" He mimicked the slight bow Hobbes often made.

"Can't we have a truce, at least for tonight, Maniac?" Blair said wearily. "I'm not in the mood for sniping."

"Hah! You looked like you were in a pretty good mood down there in the hangar deck today," Marshall said. "What's the matter, loverboy? You put the moves on everybody's favorite grease monkey and get yourself shot down?"

Blair frowned. "I didn't 'put the moves' on her . . ."

"Hey, man, it's all right, really it is," Maniac told him with a grin. "I mean, even a high flyer like you has to have an off day now and then. Of course, I doubt it'd take a whole hell of a lot of high-risk maneuvering to get into *her* pants, but maybe you're just out of practice . . ."

"So what's your excuse, then, Maniac?" Blair asked. "You must have tried out your usual wit and charm on the lady. Did you crash and burn?"

"Yeah, right," Marshall said, looking away. "As if I'd waste my time on some punked-out little techie. Of course, you never did have any taste. First that snotty French bitch . . . now. . . . Wise up, Blaze-Away. There's a lot better to choose from on this tub than that cheap slut . . ."

Blair was out of his seat and beside Marshall in a single quick move. He grabbed the front of Maniac's uniform and hauled him to his feet. "Get this, Marshall, and get it good," he hissed. "You can talk about me any way you want to. But I won't tolerate you running down anyone in this wing, man, woman . . . or cat. And if you want to keep using that nose to breathe through, you won't *ever* insult Angel again . . . or Rachel Coriolis either, for that matter. You getting any of this, mister?"

Maniac pulled back, freeing himself from Blair's grip and holding up both hands. "Whoa! Back off, man." He studied Blair for a moment. "Looks like you've got a real case, after all. Question is, which one's the lucky girl?"

Blair took another step forward. "I told you to lay off, Major," he said slowly.

"Okay, okay, I'm sorry. It was supposed to be a joke, man. I'm sorry." Maniac turned to leave, then faced Blair one more time. "But listen to me, Colonel, sir. If you don't start loosening up pretty damn quick, you're cruising for a psych hearing. You're tighter than a vacuum seal, and I wouldn't like to be around when everything blows out."

"Mind your own business, Maniac, and let me worry about mine," Blair told him. "And in the meantime, just stay out of my way."

• CHAPTER XVII

TCS Victory
Ariel System

In due course, *Victory* entered the Ariel System, traveling by way of a jump point in the Delius Belt. Deep in the heart of the Caliban Nebula, the system had only one planet of any notable size, though there were many other smaller worldlets, asteroids, and similar junk in the system as well. Ariel I was never judged worthwhile as a potential colony, but Confederation Intelligence sources had long identified it as a major headquarters for Kilrathi raiders. Previous Terran attempts to deal with the base met with little success, thanks to the strength of the ground-based defenses on the planet and the difficulties of mounting operations within the nebula. Long-range sensors were virtually useless, and even short-range scans required more time, more power, and more computer interpolation than usual, which made for many extra problems.

But the conditions also helped hide *Victory* from detection, as Eisen had explained during the original briefing. The Kilrathi maintained a network of detection buoys around the planet and near most of the jump points, but away from those the Terran carrier was able to avoid contact from everything except an extremely close pass by enemy ships. It was almost as good, Eisen maintained, as mounting a cloaking device aboard the ship.

On the other hand, the sensor limitations cut both ways. Blair was forced to double patrols again just to sweep nearby space for Kilrathi shipping. It required some skillful flying to penetrate the web of detection buoys to put fighters close enough to Ariel I to conduct the surveys Headquarters needed. Over the course of nearly two weeks, the flight wing operated at peak capacity, almost without let-up, and the strain inevitably took its toll on people and equipment alike.

Blair could only hope that ship and crew were up to the job.

Flight Control, TCS Victory
Ariel System

Blair came out of the elevator next to Flight Control and nearly ran into Rachel Coriolis. She was clutching a personal data pad in one hand and a half-disassembled control module in the other, walking briskly with an air of distracted urgency. As she caught sight of Blair she made a face.

"Can't talk now, skipper," she said, hardly slowing her pace at all. "All you fighter jocks were so damned eager to draw recon work. Well, now you got it, and that means us common techies have to bust our asses to keep you flying."

"Okay, okay, Chief," he said, holding up one hand. "On behalf of the entire wing, I apologize. Next time HQ gives us an assignment, I'll tell 'em to clear it with you first."

She grinned as she dodged past him and into the lift. "Maybe if us techs had a say in things you hot-shots wouldn't always be getting in so much trouble."

The doors snapped shut, and Blair turned back to the entrance to Flight Control.

There were only routine patrols out now, no survey

missions, so the chamber was manned at minimal levels. The relative calm in the room was a stark contrast to the scene visible through the windows overlooking the hangar deck, where technicians and fighter crews were hard at work on maintenance, repairs, and mission prep for the next batch of launches, scheduled to begin shortly. The bustle of activity would have been a scene of utter confusion to the uninitiated, but Blair recognized the order and purpose underlying the chaos. It was the dance of the deck, the almost rhythmic cycle that made any pilot's heart beat just a little bit faster.

He became aware of another figure standing by the windows, intently watching. It was Cobra, wearing her flight suit and carrying a helmet under one arm. Blair was surprised to note her smile. It transformed her entirely, changing her customary bitter moodiness into a genuine look of enthusiasm and anticipation.

"About time," he heard her say softly, as if to herself. "About time we showed 'em."

"Lieutenant," he said quietly.

She looked at him. "Sir?"

"I don't recall ever seeing that before," he said. When she looked confused he continued with a grin. "That smile on your face. It looks good. Suits you."

The wolfish smile reappeared. "It's good to be in their back yard for a change. I can almost smell 'em, Colonel. And with any kind of luck, I'll get a couple of them in my sights sometime soon . . ."

He raised an eyebrow. "Well, being on the offensive seems to have helped bring you out of your shell, I'd say."

"Scuttlebutt says we're here to scout the cats out for a real attack. That HQ has a weapon that'll blast them to hell, where they belong. I want to be here for the kill. I didn't become a pilot just to baby-sit bases and such."

Blair frowned. He supposed the spread of rumors about the Behemoth project was almost inevitable. Nothing stayed secret on a ship in space for very long it seemed, despite the best efforts of Confed security. He wondered if Rollins had been leaking information, or if this story started somewhere else.

At any rate, at least this rumor was having a more positive effect on morale than some of the earlier ones.

"Look, Cobra, I'm glad to see that smile, I really am," Blair told her. "But you've got to be pumped on every mission, not just the ones you like."

"Point taken, Colonel," she said slowly. The smile had faded now. "Well, I guess I'd better get down to the launch bay. I'm up in fifteen . . ."

After she left, Blair frowned at his own reflection in the window. For some reason he could never find the right things to say when talking to Lieutenant Buckley. Why couldn't he have allowed her to enjoy her new-found enthusiasm for *Victory*'s current operation? Instead, he'd managed to deflate her just when it seemed she was ready to start letting down the barriers which kept her apart from the rest of the wing.

Sometimes he wondered if he would ever really get a handle on his job.

Flight Wing Rec Room, TCS Victory Ariel System

"Pull up a chair, Colonel, and join me. I'll stand you to the first round."

Acknowledging Vagabond's greeting with a nod and a smile, Blair took the chair opposite him. Lieutenant Chang played with the inevitable deck of cards in front of him, and if the continual cycle of missions was getting to him it didn't show in his grinning face. The pilot might have been fresh from leave instead of unwinding after flying a survey sweep with Hobbes only a few hours earlier.

"You must be getting pretty lonely if you want to buy your CO a drink," Blair commented. "What's the matter? You already clean everybody else out?"

"Unfortunately, it doesn't take too long to get a reputation, if you know what I mean. And even the new chums from Blackmane caught on to me after a few days. Gets pretty tough to get up a game when everyone's afraid to take you on. Know what I mean?" Chang held up the deck. "C'mon, Colonel. Why don't you try your luck?" Without waiting for an answer, he started dealing.

"Whoa, there, sharpie," Blair said, holding up a hand. "Don't I at least get to cut the deck?"

Vagabond laughed and gathered in the cards again. "You'd be surprised how many rookies just ante up and look surprised when they lose the first pot."

"Well, they deserve what they get, then." He took the cards from Vagabond and shuffled the deck with practiced ease, getting a reluctant nod of admiration from the Chinese pilot. "Me, I've been around. And early on I discovered the two things you never leave to somebody else: shuffling the cards and checking your ordinance."

Chang accepted the deck from Blair and started to deal again. Though he was still smiling, there was a troubled look in his eyes. "This mission . . . you know there are stories going around about some superweapon. That's why we're supposed to be running recon."

"You know, Lieutenant, that if the info wasn't officially released then I can't comment on it one way or the other," Blair said quietly. "Rumors are just that—rumors. Even if I knew anything, I couldn't talk about it."

"Yeah, I know." Vagabond looked at his hand for a moment, then laid it on the table. "Look, Colonel, I know you can't spill any secrets, but the stuff I've been hearing . . . it really bugs me."

"How so?" Blair asked. He laid his own cards aside and met Chang's level gaze.

"Word is this weapon, whatever it is, will scorch a whole damned planet. A strategic weapon, I guess the brass would call it. And I'm not sure I want to be part of something like that."

"Conscience bothering you, Lieutenant?"

"Yeah, it is, Colonel. I didn't sign on to be part of something that kills civilians, whether they're people or cats or something slimy living under the rocks on Alphacent." Vagabond looked down at the table. "Some folks take the war real personal, like Cobra and Flint. But that's not me. When I wax somebody out on the firing line, I like to think it's a fair fight. That he's got an equal chance to nail me. Pretty stupid, I guess, but that's the way it is."

Blair nodded, understanding. He shared Vagabond's doubts. "Fact is, I understand you a lot better than I'll ever understand Cobra or Flint. The last thing you need in the cockpit with you is hate. And I think you really have to hate before you could go along with something as horrible as wasting an entire planet, civilians and all." He hesitated. "Look, secrets aside . . . if you've heard the rumors right, we're scouting for this new weapon, right?"

Vagabond nodded.

"All right, then, we're surveying a planet we know has nothing but a military installation on it. No colony. No civilians, or at least none who aren't involved in base operations somehow. Seems to me if there is a superweapon, HQ must figure on aiming at a military target."

"Maybe so," Chang said, nodding but still looking uncharacteristically serious. "Maybe so." He paused. "Still, it bothers me a little. I mean, maybe they'd start with a base like this. But where does it end? HQ's got a real bad habit of labeling every target a military installation, even when they're not. So, what if we cross the line later?"

Blair looked away, uncomfortable. He was thinking of Kevin Tolwyn's comments about Kilrah, and about the Covert Ops plan that apparently could only be used against the enemy homeworld. If the Kilrathi didn't comply with the threat posed by the Behemoth, where would HQ draw the line?

And, more importantly, where would he stand if the next target did include large numbers of civilians? Just how badly did he want this war to end?

He looked back at Vagabond. "Hey, we're the good guys, remember?" he said, forcing a smile. "We don't kill the innocents. That's supposed to be the difference between us and them, you know?" Inwardly he felt like a hypocrite, but he couldn't admit his own doubts to Chang without confirming the stories about the mission.

The Chinese pilot touched the deck with one slender finger. "Well, Colonel, the way I figure it, it's a lot like cards. A lot of people never think to cut the deck before they see what they're getting dealt."

Wing Commander's Quarters, TCS Victory Ariel System

"Colonel Blair to Flight Control! Colonel Blair to Flight Control! Urgent!"

Blair flung down the PDP he was studying and swung his feet out of the bunk. This was not a General Quarters alarm, but the voice on the intercom—Flint's voice—sounded worried. A sinking feeling gripped his stomach. Vaquero and Flash were on survey duty tonight.

With the Wing already short-handed and Flint still grounded, Blair had been forced to rotate wingman assignments frequently since the Ariel operation began. That meant he couldn't always keep Flash under the watchful eyes of Hobbes or himself any more. And Vaquero, experienced as he might have been, was what pilots referred to as an "RV," a Recon Virgin, someone who had never conducted behind-the-lines reconnaissance missions. The combination was potentially explosive, but Blair had simply run out of options.

He forgot his usual rule about not running and raced down the corridor to the lift, hoping he was wrong. If Flash and Vaquero had run into trouble out there, it would be his fault for letting the two of them team up. . . .

Flight Control was fully manned, and the tense atmosphere that met Blair as the doors slid open for him did nothing to calm his fears. Flint had the duty as Officer of the Watch, her suspended flight status leaving her plenty of time to serve in such shipboard wing duties.

"What have you got?" he asked crisply, joining her at the Duty Officer's command console.

"Trouble, sir," Flint said. "Flash and Vaquero were on their way back in when they read a bogie on their short-range scanners, and Major Dillon decided they should check it out. He ordered Vaquero to back him up before we could countermand the orders from here, and since they were already right on top of the Kilrathi . . ."

"Any idea what they're up against?"

"At least six Dralthi, Colonel," Flint told him. "But Vaquero reported he was getting some other readings that might have been something bigger, a whole lot bigger."

"Christ," Blair muttered. "Probably a transport . . . but it might be a cap ship under fighter escort. How're they doing so far?"

"Holding their own, but they haven't been able to obey recall and break away. The Dralthi keep swarming them." Flint looked apologetic. "We didn't want to commit the ready alert birds without your say-so, Colonel. The standing orders are to avoid a fight."

"Yeah, I know. I helped draft 'em, remember?" Blair realized his tone had been sharper than he'd intended. "You did well, Lieutenant. Okay, who's on ready alert?"

"Maniac and Vagabond," Flint said. "They're in their fighters and ready to launch."

"Good. Launch immediately, then. But tell the flight crew to get two more Thunderbolts ready for launch."

"Who's on deck, Colonel?" There was a faint light of hope in her eyes.

"I'll take one. Call Hobbes to fly wingman with me." He saw her face fall, disappointed. "I know you want back on the roster, Flint, but I don't have time to discuss it tonight. Call out Hobbes. I'll be in the ready room suiting up. Put through a call to the captain and route it to me there. He'll have to know what we're getting into."

"Aye, aye, sir," she said, voice flat.

He had his flight suit on and was wrestling with his boots when a vid screen came to life on one wall of the Gold Squadron ready room. Eisen looked like he'd been asleep. "They tell me you have a situation, Colonel," he said.

"We certainly do, sir," Blair told him. "Two of my pilots ran into a Kilrathi flight and have become heavily engaged. I've got two more on the way to back them up, and Hobbes and I are joining the party as soon as our fighters are prepped." Hobbes came into the ready room as he spoke and crossed to his locker.

"That's a pretty strong response, Colonel," Eisen said quietly. "Just how many Kilrathi did your people run into out there, anyway?"

"That's not clear yet, sir," Blair said. "That's why I'm flying the extra cover. There could be a cap ship involved, too. We're not sure yet."

"Damned sensor clutter," Eisen said, nodding. "Well, I guess all good things must come to an end. After all this, the furballs won't be letting us sneak around any more. We'll have to hope we've got all the data HQ wants, because I'm ordering a withdrawal to the jump point ASAP."

"Agreed, sir," Blair said, "though I'd appreciate it if you'd hold off until we're back. I wouldn't want to misplace the *Victory* in the middle of this mess."

Eisen chuckled. "Oh, I think we can wait for you, Colonel. Just don't keep us waiting too long, okay?" He cut the intercom without waiting for an answer.

"Another flight together, my friend," Hobbes commented. "I am glad. It has been too long since you were on my wing."

"Yeah, I'll say." Blair picked up his helmet and looked at the renegade Kilrathi pilot for a long moment. "Do you ever find yourself wishing for the old days, Hobbes? Back when we were junior pilots, flying for the sheer hell of it all? Sometimes I'd give everything I've got to be back on the old *Tiger's Claw* with you, and Angel, and Paladin, and the rest of the old gang. No decisions to make, nothing to worry about but flying . . ."

Hobbes shook his head. "I do not think about that time often, I fear," he said. "It was a period of great stress for me, as you may remember. Trying to prove myself to you all." Ralgha's expression became bleak. "But sometimes, in my dreams, I find myself yearning for the days before I left the Empire. Once, long ago, I did not have doubts about my own kind. I knew my place in the universe, and I was proud of it. Those are the days I find myself remembering." He picked up his helmet and fell in beside Blair. "But the past is gone, my friend. All we have now is the present."

"And the future?" Blair asked.

Hobbes shook his head. "For many years I have known that I have no real future. In peace or in war, my own kind reject me and your kind, with only a few exceptions, shun me. What future do I have, save to fight and die in the cockpit of my fighter? Sometimes I feel that I am somehow bound up in the whole outcome of this war, that I might play a key part in victory or defeat before I die. But that is not a future. That is my fate, hovering over me . . ." He looked at Blair. "It is not a concept easily grasped by non-Kilrathi. But it is all I understand."

"Come on, Hobbes," Blair said, troubled by the glimpse Ralgha had given into his alien soul. "Let's get down to the flight line. That's all the future either of us can afford to worry about for now."

Command Hall, KIS Hvar'kann
Ariel System

"Lord Prince, we have a report of enemy activity in the system. A convoy is under attack by Terran fighters."

Thrakhath leaned forward in his chair to study Melek in the dull red light of the audience chamber. "They dare attack us here, in our space? Perhaps they did not learn their lesson at Locanda."

Melek bowed acknowledgement. "You did say you expected them to respond, Lord Prince," he pointed out. "Intercepted radio traffic indicates that the Terran ships may be from the *Victory*."

"So . . ." Thrakhath turned the report over in his mind. "This . . . complicates our response. I had not looked for them to be ready for further operations for some time to come. We must drive them out . . . and we must discourage them from looking toward this system any further. It would be an embarrassment if they were to plan to demonstrate their new weapon here before the fleet was fully assembled."

"Yes, Lord Prince," Melek said, "though it would be a worthy irony if they brought their weapon here and fell into your trap."

Thrakhath gestured negation. "No. No, I do not want to stage a major battle here. Not when the nebula effects make detection so difficult. When the Terrans reveal their doomsday weapon, and we learn its secrets, I want no chance of mistakes when it comes time to destroy it. We must . . . urge them to take an interest in some other system, not this one." He paused. "So we must threaten their ship, but ultimately allow it to escape with sufficient evidence that they should leave us alone here. Order the fleet to cover the jump points to Locanda, Delius, and Caliban. And have all squadrons prepare to initiate the Masking Effect."

Melek bowed again. "As you direct, Lord Prince."

Thrakhath watched him leave. When he was alone, he allowed his fangs to show for an instant. It was unfortunate that the Terrans must be allowed to win free in the end. He would have relished the destruction of that carrier . . . but it carried the key to ultimate victory for the Empire, and nothing could be allowed to interfere with that now.

• CHAPTER XVIII

Thunderbolt 300
Ariel System

"*Victory, Victory*, this is Backstop Leader," Blair said, hoping he didn't sound as tired and discouraged as he felt. "Requesting landing clearance. Over."

"*Roger that, Leader*," Rollins replied. "*Clearance is granted. Good job out there, Colonel. You really showed those cats a thing or two.*"

Blair went through the approach checklist by rote, his mind ranging back to the mission they just completed in support of Flash and Vaquero. By the time he and Hobbes launched, Marshall and Chang had already joined up with the two beleaguered pilots and extricated them from the fight with the Dralthi. But Major Dillon not only insisted that he didn't really need support, he had actually been eager to seek out the larger contact at the edge of their scanning range to try to score a real kill, a cap ship kill. Blair barely arrived in time to keep Maniac from agreeing with the idea. Thereafter, they were dogged by Kilrathi fighters but not pressed particularly hard. The most difficult mission problems were the ones associated with reining in the two majors.

Vaquero's fighter incurred damage during the fighting, and the pilot himself sounded shaky. He was waved off *Victory's* flight deck three times before finally catching the tractors and making a successful touchdown. This

208

worried Blair even more than Dillon or Marshall. Lieutenant Lopez always struck him as steady and reliable, but plainly he took more than just a physical pounding on the line this time.

Blair shook off his doubts and worries, forcing himself to concentrate on the final approach. He was the last man inside, and by the time he clambered down the ladder from the cockpit, the others, except for Hobbes, were heading for the ready room to give their after-action reports.

The Kilrathi pilot looked at him with a very human expression of concern on his alien visage. "Are you well, my friend? You seemed . . . distracted, near the end. By more than just the need to control our more spirited comrades."

"Just tired, Hobbes," Blair told him. "Tired of bucking overeager jocks who still think this is all some kind of big game. And tired of . . . everything."

He wasn't sure Ralgha could understand his mood. They had accounted, among the six of them, for four more Dralthi out there, but in the long run it was just another number to be totaled for the kill board. It wouldn't matter a bit the next time they went into battle. There were always more Kilrathi to replace the ones who died, and Blair was getting sick of having to kill and kill with never a sign that some day the killing might stop.

"It was good, though, to fly a combat mission again," Ralgha said, clearly misunderstanding the attitude behind Blair's bitter words and tone. "To take the battle to the enemy once more. I have missed the chance to test my skills, since we started this mission."

"Yeah," Blair said. Though he didn't share in the sentiment, he understood how the Kilrathi felt. Ralgha might fly with the Terrans, but his emotions and reactions were still those of his predator species. "Yeah, I suppose all this skulking and hiding's been pretty rough on you. Maybe a little dogfighting is good for your soul, at that."

Hobbes caught something of his real feelings that time, and cocked his head to one side as he regarded Blair. "It is strange," he said. "We are very different, you and I, though I would say you are closest to me of all the humans I know. Your kind does not relish conflict, though you have proven very able warriors. But the Kilrathi spirit . . . despite the skill and courage demanded in flying, is never entirely satisfied by combat in space."

"You like it up close and personal," Blair said, mustering a faint smile.

The Kilrathi renegade raised a paw, allowed his sheathed claws to extend for a moment. "We are taught to use these even before we can speak or walk. To your species this seems . . . what is the word? Savage? Primitive? But it is fundamental to who and what we are."

Blair's eyes narrowed. "Then how can Thrakhath order the death of millions with bioweapons? That's about as impersonal a weapon as you can use."

"Thrakhath. . . . That one defines honor in his own way, I fear," Ralgha said slowly. "When he looks at humans, he sees only animals, fit for labor or food or prey in a hunt. It is not an attitude that is held by all my kind, but it is a convenient way to excuse acts that would otherwise defile Kilrathi honor. Does not your kind hide behind any number of similar . . . conveniences? To justify acts you would otherwise condemn?"

Blair shrugged, then nodded reluctantly. "I guess we do. But . . . killing is killing. Hot-blooded or cold. You do it when you have to because you have to . . . to defend yourself, your people, your civilization. Whether it's hand-to-hand fighting, or dogfighting, or bombing a whole damned planet out of existence; it's still killing, though. And I guess we each have to decide whether what we're protecting is worth the death we're being asked to deal out."

"This is not normally a question a Kilrathi needs to ask himself, my friend," Hobbes said slowly. He fixed Blair with a long, penetrating look. "And in all honesty, there are times I wish your kind had not taught me to ask them. There is no comfort in doubting the wisdom of generations."

Captain's Ready Room, TCS Victory Ariel System

Blair and Hobbes were both summoned to the captain's ready room before even exchanging their flight suits for more comfortable clothing. Eisen looked worried as he sat opposite them. He energized the holographic chart display on his desk top.

"I know you just got back from a tough one, but I doubt you'll have much chance to rest up," the captain told them without preamble. "We're on course for the jump point to the Caliban System. It has the closest Confed military facility, although it's a small one, just an outpost. The main advantage as I see it is that it's like this system, inside the nebula, which means we can hope to elude a Kilrathi pursuit quickly even if they should chase us through the jump point. That could be important, if they have any kind of fleet following us at all."

"You anticipate opposition, then," Hobbes said slowly.

"As soon as your pilots engaged out there you can bet the word went out that there were Terrans in the neighborhood," Eisen said grimly. "If I was the cat CO in these parts, I'd do my best to block as many jump points as possible. We'll have to fight our way out." He looked from Hobbes to Blair. "That's another reason to go for Caliban, though. They might not be expecting a withdrawal to such a minor system. Maybe that jump point will have fewer defenders . . . maybe none at all, if their fleet isn't very strong in these parts."

"Don't count on it, sir," Blair said. "I've been going over the incoming survey reports. While we haven't seen much in open space, there were indications of tremendous shuttle traffic over the base on One, and a fair number of ships in orbital docks and so on. You don't think they would leave all that unprotected, do you?"

Eisen pursed his lips. "No, I guess they wouldn't. A big fleet here . . . that sounds bad. For the Admiral's project." He glanced at Ralgha and changed the subject. "All the more reason, though, to hope we can get the hell out of here without running into too much opposition. And if we do . . . we try to shake them as best we can and still make jump."

"Risky," Blair commented. "But, as you say, it's all we can try. Do you have any special orders for us, sir?"

"I'll want you to deploy a reconnaissance in force ahead of us when we approach the jump point, Colonel," Eisen said. "With scanning so limited, I want an idea of what's waiting for us before we blunder into the middle of it. The timing will be tricky. You'll have to stay out long enough to give us our sneak peek at the situation, and maybe to discourage the bad guys from interfering with our approach. But then you'll have to get your fighters aboard fast, before we jump . . . and possibly under fire. Anybody who misses the boat is stuck." His eyes narrowed. "We can't afford another incident like Locanda, for instance. I don't think we'll be in any position to loiter around waiting for stragglers. Can your people do this?"

Blair nodded slowly, but inside his mind was racing to consider all the problems against them. "It'll be tricky, Captain, but I'll see what we can put together to eliminate the problems as much as possible."

"Good. Navigation tells me it'll be eighteen hours before we hit the jump point. So your people will have a little sack time, at least, before they have to launch."

Eisen gave him a look. "Try to get some yourself, too, Colonel. We need you out there fresh and at your best."

"Yes, sir," Blair said, but he knew the planning and preparation time would make things tight. Sleep was a luxury he had to postpone until he knew the wing was ready. He stood up slowly, and Ralgha did the same. "I'll keep you posted on our plans, Captain. Come on, Hobbes. Looks like we burn the midnight electrons again."

Thunderbolt 300
Ariel System

"All right, people, you know the drill," Blair said over the general comm channel. "Do this thing by the numbers, and we'll be past the cats before they know we're even in the neighborhood. But don't get distracted. You stop to look at the scenery and you'll be stuck seeing it for the rest of your life . . . which won't be long if Thrakhath's little playmates have their way. So . . . let's do it!"

It was another magnum launch, with a full contingent of fighters deployed in space around the *Victory* as she cruised slowly through the colorful, swirling gases of the nebula toward the jump point to Caliban. As before, the point defense squadron would be held back to defend the ship against Kilrathi fighters while the rest of the wing mounted Eisen's recon in force ahead of the carrier.

Blair hoped he'd covered all the likely contingencies in formulating his plans for the mission. If he'd left something out, it was too late now to deal with it. They were committed, for good or ill.

"Major Mbuto, you're up," he said. "Good luck . . . but I hope you won't be mad if I don't wish you good hunting!"

Amazon Mbuto chuckled. *"This is one time when we'd*

all be glad for an empty scanner screen, Colonel," she said.

Mbuto's interceptors were on point, as usual, scouting ahead of the others in hopes of locating any enemy ships around the jump point before they realized the Terrans were on their way. She had six Arrows in all, with orders to locate the Kilrathi but, if possible, to avoid engaging. *Victory* would keep a secure laser channel open with her fighter throughout the op so that Rollins could pick up her sensor feed and analyze the tactical situation ahead of time, despite the sensor interference from the nebula.

If she *did* spot enemy ships blocking *Victory*'s chosen escape route, the other squadrons would be called: Berterelli's Longbows to launch bombing strikes on capital ships and Gold Squadron to provide cover for them or to engage Kilrathi fighters. Meanwhile, once the initial scouting was finished, Mbuto would withdraw and land on *Victory*, followed by the bombers as soon as they dumped their loads and, hopefully, disrupted any enemy capital ships in the neighborhood. The Thunderbolts would be the last to return to the carrier, thus reducing the amount of traffic Flight Control would deal with in the critical minutes before the ship attempted to jump.

That was the plan, at least. But Blair couldn't help remembering an ancient military maxim . . . *No battle plan survives contact with the enemy*. Any number of things could go wrong, and there was precious little room for error.

At least a mistake today wouldn't end in the devastation of an entire colony world. But that was cold comfort as far as Blair was concerned. *Victory*'s fate was on the line, and despite his early reaction to the battered little escort carrier, Blair had learned to think of the ship as home and her crew as comrades, even friends. Losing her wouldn't be like losing the *Concordia*, but . . .

He shook himself out of his reverie. If *Victory* didn't

make it, neither would Colonel Christopher Blair. This time he wasn't likely to outlive his carrier by more than a matter of minutes, hours at most.

The time passed slowly as they waited for a report from the scouts. Comm line chatter was subdued and sporadic, and Blair had plenty of time for second and even third thoughts. Periodically he cursed the prolonged inactivity, knowing it would be demoralizing the others as much as himself, but there was nothing to be done. Until the interceptors reported, the other pilots could do nothing more than keep formation, watch their screens, and wait.

"*Victory to Recon Leader,*" Rollins said at last. "*We're getting sensor imagery from Amazon. Captain was right, Colonel. There's a welcoming committee out there. Stand by for coordinate feed.*"

In seconds, his scanner began displaying targets around the Caliban jump point, and Blair studied them intently. There were half a dozen large targets there, probably destroyers escorting a cruiser or a small Kilrathi carrier. A handful of smaller contacts were fighters, probably Darket on escort duty. The enemy force wasn't overwhelming, but it would present a significant challenge nonetheless.

"Okay," he said at length, using a low-power general broadcast channel that would keep his transmission localized and, hopefully, secret from any Kilrathi who might be trying to monitor Terran comm frequencies. As he spoke, his computer relayed additional data as he entered it, projecting courses, targets, and other information. "We've got 'em spotted now. Major Berterelli, you're going to circle the jump point outside their likely sensor range and attack the targets designated Four and Five on the sensor feed. Gold Squadron will cover for you. When you withdraw, go to ecliptic heading one-eight-one by zero-six-four."

"*That's away from* Victory," Berterelli pointed out.

"Got it in one, Major," Blair told him. "I want to hit the cats fast, rile them up, and then draw them away from the jump point. If they think *Victory's* coming from the far side of the point, they'll deploy in that direction and throw out a wide cordon to try and spot her."

"*Leaving the route in wide open,*" Maniac said. "*You know, Maverick, sometimes you're almost as smart as everybody says you think you are!*"

"Thanks for the vote of confidence," Blair said. "Once you break contact with the bad guys, Green Squadron should circle around to rendezvous with the carrier. Gold Squadron will continue to withdraw on the original heading until I give the word. Then I want you to separate into wing teams and head for home. Don't leave your wingman unless absolutely necessary, and remember the timetable. *Victory* will be at the jump point in . . . seventy minutes from now. If you're not back on board by then, you've lost your ride out of here. Any questions?"

There were none. "Good," Blair continued. "Now . . . Hobbes, you and Vagabond are on point. Then the Longbows. The rest of us bring up the rear. You have your orders. Make sure you all come back in one piece. You know how I hate filling out casualty reports."

Hobbes and Vagabond were already accelerating, steering the course Blair indicated. As he waited for the Green Squadron bombers to move out, Blair switched to the tactical channel for his wingman. "This is it, Cobra. Hope there's enough cats out here for you."

"*It'll do,*" she said. "*But I'm still kind of wondering how I ended up on your wing, Colonel.*"

"Not a whole lot of options, Lieutenant," he told her. "With Flint off the roster and Vaquero banged up from that fight yesterday, I'm juggling. Sorry if the arrangements don't suit you."

"*I guess I figured you'd team with Hobbes, is all.*"

"Not this time," Blair told her. "I figured it was about time I let you show me some of those moves of yours."

Actually, it had been a difficult decision to make, pairing up the pilots in Gold Squadron for this mission. He had wanted Hobbes on point, no question; the Kilrathi's instincts and discipline made him the ideal choice to lead them in. But much as he would have relished flying with Ralgha, Blair's place wasn't on the very front line. As wing commander he had to stay out of the action until he was sure of the tactical situation.

But there were sharp limits in how he could deploy the rest of the squadron. He still couldn't trust Buckley to cooperate with Ralgha, and neither Flash nor Maniac was his idea of a good point man to team with the Kilrathi. So Vagabond was with Hobbes. With great reluctance, Blair teamed the two majors together, even though he knew he was asking for trouble. Neither one was very reliable anyway, so it seemed better to have them let each other down instead of breaking up two different teams if and when they let themselves run wild.

So he'd crossed his fingers and put them together, and ordered Cobra to fly on his wing. He hoped neither choice would turn out to be disastrous. But Vaquero, though physically fit after the battle with the Dralthi, was a bundle of nerves and not really ready for duty so soon. And as for Flint . . .

He almost put her back on the roster, but with so much at stake, he wasn't willing to risk a repeat performance. She was on duty in Flight Control again.

Cobra stuck close by him as they trailed the rest of the Terran flight, keeping strict radio silence now. They wouldn't use their comm channels until they engaged the enemy. Blair hoped Amazon Mbuto had followed her orders and headed back for the carrier. He wouldn't know for sure until the operation was nearly over. . . .

On his sensor screen, images began to appear,

seemingly out of nowhere, as he came into range of the enemy force. The blips that represented the Confed fighters and bombers seemed pitifully inadequate to take on the Kilrathi ships, but they were already starting their runs.

Hobbes and Vagabond opened the fight by engaging a trio of Darket close to the nearest of the two targeted capital ships. Berterelli's bombers ignored them and plunged past, hurtling at top speed toward the Kilrathi destroyer. There were more fighters registering beyond that large ship, and they could pose trouble for the Longbows.

"Maniac! Flash!" Blair said sharply. "You see that formation on the other side of the destroyer? Get in there and have some fun with them."

"Yes, sir, *Colonel*, sir," Maniac said. "*Come on, rookie, last one firing is kitty litter!*"

"*What about us, sir?*" Cobra asked.

"We stick with Berterelli, Lieutenant," Blair told her, "in case something crops up he can't handle."

For several minutes they maintained their position behind the bombers, spectators as Berterelli's pilots unleashed a heavy attack against the first destroyer and then broke off to climb away from the deadly warship, dodging defensive fire all the way. One of the Longbows didn't make it out, but the other five did. The attack didn't destroy the Kilrathi ship, but Blair's sensors registered serious damage to shields, armor, and propulsion systems. The cats knew they'd been hit, that much was sure.

The second destroyer was a tougher nut to crack. Forewarned, it laid down a devastating pattern of fire against the incoming Longbows. A series of shots raked across Major Berterelli's bomber, and the Longbow came apart under the force of the barrage . . . but not before the Italian pilot released a full spread of ship-killer missiles. And the other bombers dropped their remaining loads simultaneously. As if avenging the squadron leader, they received the satisfaction of seeing those shots hit home. Explosions rippled down the spine of the destroyer. A few seconds later, a massive fireball consumed it. Some of the chunks were bigger than the Terran Thunderbolts, adding to the confusion that reigned on the Kilrathi perimeter.

"Retreat! Retreat! All fighters retreat!" Blair called. The Terran ships began to disengage, even Maniac and Flash. They turned away now, on their false escape heading, but Blair and Cobra hung back to cover the retreat.

So far, neither had fired a shot.

A pair of Darket gave chase, but Cobra took out one with a well-placed barrage from her tail gun, and Blair used a hard braking maneuver to change vector and let the second one shoot past him. Then he took it out with sustained blaster fire, saving his missiles in case a real threat developed. No other fighters approached them as they continued their retreat.

Just before losing sensor contact with the Kilrathi ships, Blair saw that the destroyers were in motion. He allowed himself a grim smile. As he hoped, they were spreading out to throw up a detection net . . . but they were on the wrong side of the jump point to block *Victory* now.

Bridge, TCS Victory
Ariel System

"Last of the Hellcats is aboard now, sir," Rollins reported from his post at Communications. "And the first Longbows just checked in, looking for clearance. Looks like it's going down smooth."

"Let's hope it stays that way," Eisen growled. "Helm? What's our status?"

"ETA is fifteen minutes, sir," the helmsman reported.

"Blair's cutting it fine," Rollins muttered. "Hope he knows what he's doing out there."

"A little less chatter, Lieutenant, if you please," the captain said. "Navigation, begin plotting for jump. Mr. Rollins, make it 'Jump Stations,' if you—"

"Sir!" The Sensor Officer broke in. "Captain, the jump point . . . it's not there!"

"What?" Rollins spoke before he could stop himself. "It ain't there? What do you mean, it ain't there?"

"Lieutenant!" Eisen snapped. "Explanations, people. I need explanations . . ."

"It's like the cats just managed to . . . to *close off* the jump point, sir," the Sensor Officer said. "I don't know how. But it isn't out there any more."

"And without it, we're stuck," someone else said aloud.

Rollins looked at Eisen. The man's face was darkly impassive, but he could see the expression in the captain's eyes. However the Kilrathi had done it, there was one thing certain. *Victory* was trapped.

• CHAPTER XIX

Thunderbolt 300
Ariel System

"We haven't been able to determine exactly what's going on, Colonel, but it appears that the Kilrathi have somehow managed to close off the jump point to Caliban."

"How the hell can they do that? It ain't poss—"

"Clear the channel, Maniac!" Blair snapped. He understood how Marshall felt, but they couldn't afford to waste precious time in useless hysterics. "Sorry, Captain. Continue the message."

"We're going to have to try for another jump point instead," Eisen went on as if there hadn't been an interruption. "The Delius jump point isn't far . . . if it's still out there. We're downloading the coordinates to you now. Reform your squadron and keep their light stuff off our backs until we get there. And keep your fingers crossed that this door isn't closed, too."

"Understood, Captain," Blair said. He paused. "And if there's a picket at the other jump point, sir? I doubt we can outfox them a second time around . . ."

"Just pray we get lucky, Colonel," Eisen said grimly. "Because luck's about the only thing that'll bail us out at this point."

"Roger that," Blair responded. "Okay, Gold Squadron, you heard the man. Form on me and keep a sharp eye on your sensors. By this time they've probably got more than Darket out there, so be ready."

"*If they can close down one jump point, they can close 'em all,*" Maniac said, still sounding ragged. "*How the hell are we supposed to fight them if they can do that?*"

"Stay frosty, Maniac," Blair told him. "Same for the rest of you. Whatever the cats are doing, we can't let it put us off our stride now. The ship's counting on us."

He adjusted his course to match the vectors *Victory's* computers fed to the fighters and adjusted the sensitivity on his scanners. If the Kilrathi really could shut down a jump point at will, the war was as good as over . . . but Blair refused to allow himself to dwell on the bitter thought. For now, all that mattered was survival.

Command Hall, KIS Hvar'kann
Ariel System

"They are moving again, Lord Prince." Melek gave a deep, formal bow as he approached the throne on its raised dais. "The destroyer *Irrkham* has them at the very edge of his sensor range. Their vector indicates they are probably trying for the Delius jump point. It is the closest to their present location."

Thrakhath studied Melek without speaking, and the retainer grew uncomfortable under his lingering stare. Finally the Prince spoke. "The Mask has performed its function, then?" he asked.

"Yes, Lord Prince," Melek replied. "The Caliban jump point does not register on any sensors. The Terrans must have believed we simply cut it down, like helpless prey."

"The apes should have remained in the trees of their homeworld, and never challenged warriors of the stars," Thrakhath said, showing his fangs. "They are fools."

"Yes, Lord Prince," Melek agreed quietly. Inwardly he wasn't so sure. It was true that the Terrans still lagged behind the Empire in cloaking technology, but they were catching up fast. They would realize, soon enough, that the Kilrathi couldn't actually close down a jump point, but only obscure it with a particularly powerful cloaking field—and even then only where the dust and gas of a nebula made it possible for the cloak to operate effectively over the large distances needed to cover the jump point.

But Thrakhath remained utterly contemptuous of the Terrans. It was an attitude that worried Melek more and more as the climax of the campaign approached. So far events had unfolded much as the Prince planned, excluding the continued interference of the *Victory* after several attempts to cripple the carrier had failed. No doubt the unexpected Kilrathi ability to make jump points seem to vanish would, as Thrakhath intended, cause the humans to choose a different target system when they deployed their new weapon, regardless of the knowledge concerning their adversaries. But, sooner or later, Thrakhath's disdain for the Terrans might well lead him to underestimate them at a critical moment, and that could have disastrous consequences.

Melek began to wish he had never accepted the post as Thrakhath's *chee'dyachee*. As senior vassal and retainer to the Crown Prince, he wielded great power and commanded much influence . . . and was perfectly placed to watch the Imperial family in the interests of his own Clan. But it was a precarious perch at best, given the Prince's temper, and sometimes it was difficult to restrain himself from voicing the doubts he could not put aside.

He became aware that the Crown Prince was still eyeing him with an almost predatory look.

"You seem . . . distracted, Melek," Thrakhath said. "Is there some problem?"

"No, Lord Prince," he replied. "No problem. I was merely . . . awaiting your instructions now that the Terrans have set their new course."

"The plan remains as I outlined it earlier. Now that they have been frightened by our power over the jump points, we will allow them to escape through the Delius point. Order the ships there to drop the Mask and proceed toward the Caliban jump point, as if to reinforce our squadron there after the Terran attack. If they can punish the carrier along the way, they may do so, but remember that the vessel must escape, both to carry word of our new weapon to their leaders and to preserve . . . our other asset. Understood?"

"Yes, Lord Prince." Melek bowed again and withdrew, thankful the audience was over.

Thunderbolt 300
Ariel System

"We've got company, Colonel. Looks like a destroyer, with at least two fighters on escort. Feeding you the coordinates now . . ."

The information scrolled across Blair's monitor before Rollins finished speaking. The Kilrathi ship was ahead and to port of *Victory*, and from its heading was returning from the Delius jump point. The cats were either reinforcing their first squadron or throwing out a net to intercept the Terrans.

In either case, the destroyer could be trouble. There were two fighters flying close by, Vaktoth by the look of their sensor signatures. They could complicate any attempt to deal with the bigger ship.

Blair wished he still had some of the Longbows available, but Gold Squadron was the only fighter force that had not landed on the flight deck and started securing for jump. It was up to the six Thunderbolts to do what they could to protect the carrier.

"Gold Squadron, this is Leader," Blair said. "Tally-ho!" It was the age-old pilot's cry that the enemy was in sight, dating back to the days before spaceflight. "Follow me in, people!"

He kicked in his afterburners and steered the fighter toward the Kilrathi targets, the rest of the squadron trailing him. Blair checked his weapons status and armed blasters and heat-seeking missiles. He and Cobra had engaged in the least amount of fighting at the first jump point, their ships with the least damage and the most reloads available. That made them the best candidates for taking on the destroyer. But it was essential that they get some reliable protection from the enemy fighters.

"Hobbes, Vagabond, you two keep those Vaktoth off our backs," he ordered. "The rest of us are hunting the big cat this time. Understood?"

"*We are complying,*" Hobbes said calmly.

"*Just let me at 'em,*" Maniac said. He sounded a little less nervous now, as if the prospect of a stand-up fight helped steady him after the shock of having the jump point vanish. Blair hoped he would keep his head.

"*Lead the way, Colonel,*" Cobra added a moment later. She sounded professional, but a little grim.

He reduced his speed and allowed Hobbes and Vagabond to accelerate past the rest of the squadron, diving in toward the enemy formation. Hobbes screamed a Kilrathi challenge as the two fighters closed with their opposite numbers, and that seemed to unnerve the Vaktoth pilots. Both enemy fighters circled away, evading rather than offering battle—unusual for the Kilrathi. Perhaps these were inexperienced flyers, Blair told himself. But was it significant that they were running from Hobbes again . . . ?

He forced the thought from his mind and concentrated instead on the destroyer. It loomed ahead, all menacing points and angles, an asymmetrical, four-pronged dagger aimed at *Victory*.

"*Let's rock!*" Maniac called, accelerating suddenly to

full speed and diving toward the destroyer, all guns firing wildly. Flash was right behind him. The destroyer's main batteries opened up, driving bolt after bolt of raw energy at the fast-moving Terran ships. Somehow neither Terran fighter was hit, but their blasters battered the destroyer's shields. There was a ripple of explosions as Flash dumped three missiles in quick succession. None penetrated the shields, but Blair's scanners showed the enemy defenses weakening.

Blair killed his momentum, bringing the fighter practically to a dead stop. It was a risky move so close to a capital ship, but with Maniac and Flash doing such a good job of drawing the enemy's attention it was too good a chance to miss. Now the destroyer was lumbering toward him, a nice, steady target. If he could just get in enough good shots at the weakened section of the shielding . . .

He opened fire with his blasters, squeezing off shot after shot until his power reserves were exhausted and the guns shut down until their generators could recycle and bring them back up to full power. The Kilrathi shields still held. It was only then that he realized that Cobra had emulated his move. Her ship was a bare thirty meters off his wing, and now her blasters focused on the same narrow target area as Blair.

The enemy ship's shields failed, and Blair gave a wolfish grin. His blasters came back on-line, and he started firing again. This time the shots were taking off armor, chipping away ever closer to the vulnerable hull of the destroyer. The enemy captain must have recognized his danger by this time, but Maniac and Flash were still closer, still weaving in and out and raking the big ship with sustained if less concentrated fire. Automatic shipboard defense systems would naturally try to track and destroy the nearer threats first, and crewed guns took time to realign on new targets . . .

Blair's blasters ran down a second time, and he switched to a salvo of missiles. Cobra launched at almost the same moment. "Let's get moving, Lieutenant," Blair said, starting up his engines again. He was just beginning to accelerate to full speed when a blast from one of the destroyer's main guns caught his port-side shield, knocking it down and ripping into the wing armor in one blow. Then he was clear of the danger and turned quickly to place some distance between his Thunderbolt and the Kilrathi ship.

The missiles began to detonate, tearing through the last of the armor and deep into the bowels of the capital ship. It almost seemed to shudder before it finally tore itself apart.

"Ye-es!" That was Maniac, exultant. "*Scratch one great big kitty!*"

"*Good shooting, Colonel,*" Cobra added.

"Good shooting, all," Blair corrected. "That one was a team effort. Now let's see if Hobbes and Vagabond need any help cleaning up their little mess."

One of the Vaktoth was running, the other was heavily engaged with Vagabond's Thunderbolt. By the time the rest of Gold Squadron was in range, Hobbes had already come to the aid of his wingman and sent the heavy fighter off to join the shattered destroyer.

"What's your status, people?" Blair asked, calling up his own combat data. He couldn't afford to take another hit on his port side, and he was down to only a single missile. Another serious fight would probably be too much for his battered Thunderbolt to handle.

"*Damage is minimal, Colonel,*" Cobra reported. "*But I'm out of missiles, and my fuel reserves aren't looking good.*"

"*I, too, am out of missiles,*" Hobbes said. "*And my forward armor is badly damaged.*"

The others made similar reports, with damage ranging

from Cobra's very minor hits up to Flash, who had
suffered serious damage in the fight with the destroyer
and was now running with damaged engines and an
intermittent fault in his sensors. Blair frowned as he
considered the situation. The squadron couldn't do a
whole lot more at this point. But they had no idea what
else the Kilrathi might throw at them.

"*Jump point is on our screens,*" Rollins reported
suddenly. "*Looks like we got lucky this time!*"

"What about enemy activity?" Blair asked, still
frowning. "Anything on your sensors?"

"*Looks like another cat destroyer out there, Colonel,
but at extreme sensor range,*" Rollins reported after a
moment's pause. "*From his current vector, it doesn't look
like he'll be in any position to interfere with us. Captain
says to bring your birds back to the nest, sir. You're clear
to land . . . and . . . you guys sure did a good job holding
off those sons-of-bitches.*"

"Thank God for small favors," Blair muttered. "All
right, Gold Squadron. Let's pack it in. And pray we don't
get any new surprises before we hit the jump point."

Flight Deck, TCS Victory
Ariel System

Blair climbed slowly from his cockpit, tired and stiff
after the long strain of flying. He hadn't realized his
personal toll from the operation until now. With the
mission over, all he wanted to do was take a long shower,
then catch a few hundred hours of sack time.

Unfortunately, that wasn't how it worked. Before seeing
his bunk again, Blair knew there was a load of work to
finish first.

"ALL HANDS, ALL HANDS, JUMP STATIONS. REPEAT, JUMP
STATIONS. INTERSTELLAR TRANSIT IN THREE MINUTES." The
computer announcement blared over the ship's tannoy,

and all around Blair techs hastened to get ready for the jump, like so many ants stirred up by a threat to their hill.

"You sure did bang the old girl up this time, skipper," Rachel Coriolis said from behind him. He turned to see her pointing at the twisted armor and scorched hull plating where the destroyer's gun had pierced his shields. "Better get clear, sir, before the jump."

He nodded, then turned toward the far end of the hangar. Safety precautions called for the hangar deck to be cleared prior to any jump, and already the huge chamber was nearly empty of crewmen. Blair strode rapidly across the deck with Rachel, a few stragglers close behind.

The doors snapped open to reveal a tense scene in the corridor beside the elevator. A number of pilots and technicians were present, but the main focus was on Cobra and Hobbes, standing face to face in the middle of the passageway. Lieutenant Buckley had an angry expression on her face, and her hands were flexing as if she, like the Kilrathi, had claws that could tear at her enemies' throats. In contrast, Ralgha *nar* Hhallas was calm, impassive, a stoic figure facing Cobra's venom.

"Why didn't you warn us that your kind could close jump points?" she demanded, her voice low and menacing.

"I was not aware that they could," Ralgha told her. "This is obviously a recently developed advancement to Kilrathi technology. And a very serious threat. The ability to close down a jump point will give the Empire a great advantage, I fear."

"Come off it, you fur-faced son-of-a-bitch," Cobra snarled. "You mean to tell us you didn't know anything about this? I don't believe you!"

"I have been in Confederation service for over a decade, Lieutenant," the Kilrathi told her, drawing himself up with an air of quiet dignity. "Much has changed during that time, on *both* sides of the border. Perhaps this represents a breakthrough in jump theory."

"More likely in cloaking technology," Rachel said, stepping between them. "I don't think the Kilrathi can actually shut down a jump point at all."

"Hey, I wasn't hallucinating out there," Cobra said, turning her angry glare on the technician. "We *all* saw the first jump point drop right off our screens."

"Look, I've been studying cloaks," Rachel said. "The new Excaliburs are supposed to mount them. In theory, a big enough generator could project a cloak that could mask out something as large as a jump point. But it would only work in a nebula, and it would be damned hard to maintain even then. That's what we were facing. I'd bet hard credits on it."

"Well, whether they can kill it or just hide it, the cats can mess up our jump points," Cobra said, a little less wild but still clearly angry. She stepped past Rachel and jabbed a finger at Hobbes. "And you claim you had no clue they could pull that?"

"No more than you, Lieutenant," Ralgha told her.

"You're a liar."

Blair stepped forward, thrusting himself between the two pilots. "That will be enough, Lieutenant," he said harshly. "Colonel Ralgha's loyalty is *not* to be questioned in this way again. Is that understood?"

"But . . ."

"I will not have a junior officer making wild accusations about one of her seniors. If you gather concrete evidence to back up your claims, then you see me, in private, through proper channels. Otherwise, you keep your mouth shut!"

"Yes, sir," she said at last.

"JUMP SEQUENCE ENGAGED. ONE MINUTE TO JUMP," the loudspeaker announced.

The elevator doors opened, and Cobra pushed through

the semi-circle of onlookers into the car. Neither Blair nor Hobbes chose to follow her.

Bridge, TCS Victory
Ariel System

"And ten seconds . . . nine . . . eight . . ."

Eisen was determined not to betray his mounting tension as the computer ticked off the final seconds of the countdown to jump. What if the Kilrathi really could shut down a jump point? If they cut this one now, *Victory* would be trapped and totally vulnerable to the destroyers that were beginning to close in.

Or . . . what would happen to a ship initiating a jump sequence if the jump point failed? Would it remain in place . . . or end up trapped in hyperspace, unable to complete the transition to its destination?

"Three . . . two . . . and one . . . initiating transit . . . now."

He felt the familiar gut-twisting sensation of transit, and despite the nausea, muscle spasms, and the wrenching disorientation of the jump, Eisen was relieved. At least *Victory* had escaped the cats, whatever happened next . . .

The jump was over in an instant. Eisen had to blink and shake his head a time or two to clear the fog in his brain, but it didn't take long to regain control over his body, though every nerve was still protesting over the unnatural act of being flung across an unimaginable distance through a realm no human was ever supposed to enter.

"Report," he croaked.

Lieutenant Commander Lisa Morgan, *Victory*'s Navigator, managed to sound alert. "Aye, aye, sir," she said, her fingers moving over her controls to call up a computer program that would analyze their surroundings and confirm that they had emerged on target. After a moment she went on. "Stellar type and data match within 99.4 percent. No planets registering. Asteroid belts . . . it checks, Captain. Delius System . . . or its twin."

Eisen nodded slowly. "Very good. Commander Morgan, set course to Delius Station. Mr. Rollins, raise the local defense forces and let them know we're here. Secure from Jump Stations and resume in-system operations." He paused. "I want the ship combat-ready as soon as possible. After that, I want a full after-action analysis by all combat departments. We have to determine what the hell went on back there, before the cats pull it on us again."

His officers responded promptly, and Eisen felt a glow of pride. They'd been close to the breaking point, but somehow they'd kept on going.

In the end, that was the only thing that counted.

• CHAPTER XX

Command Hall, KIS Hvar'kann
Ariel System

"The Terrans have withdrawn, then, Melek?"
Thrakhath was lounging on his throne, feeling satisfied.
A pair of destroyers had been lost along with a few
fighters, and he intended to see to it that whoever
was responsible for the losses paid the supreme penalty.
But overall, everything went exactly as planned. The
apes had been given a warning they would not soon
forget. It would make them cautious for a time, and
even if they realized that the Empire's ability to mask
jump points was limited to nebulas they would surely
shun this system, so the base where the Imperial Fleet
would gather for Thrakhath's grand stroke would
remain secure.

Now it was time to think of the next stage in the plan.

"Yes, Lord Prince," Melek said. "They have withdrawn
into the Delius System. Of course, there is no way of
telling how long they will remain . . ."

"Then we must act quickly, before they move on,"
Thrakhath told him, pounding the arm of his throne to
emphasize the point. "Is it certain that the one called
Blair is still assigned to the carrier?"

"Yes, Lord Prince," Melek acknowledged. "We
monitored his voice on the comm channels during the
fight, a perfect match to our files. He is the wing

commander. According to recent intelligence, the renegade serves as his deputy."

"Excellent," Thrakhath said, showing his fangs for an instant. "Perhaps it is best that the human escaped our earlier attacks. We have the perfect weapon to use against him, and the results will leave these apes demoralized just when our blow is about to fall."

"You think, then, that the challenge will work, on a human? Their sense of honor is not the same as ours, Lord Prince." Melek bowed low, to show that he did not mean to doubt his Lord's judgment.

"Oh, this challenge will work, I think," Thrakhath said quietly. "They do not have honor, Melek, but they do have pride . . . and anger. We will goad this ape into a foolish gesture, and at the same time . . ."

"The Trigger," Melek said.

"The Trigger. And we will have our claws at their throats once and for all." Thrakhath straightened. "Pass the orders, Melek. Assemble the designated task force and be ready to jump within a cycle."

"Yes, Lord Prince." Melek withdrew, bowing again.

Crown Prince Thrakhath contemplated the stars that blazed through the dome above his dais. The stars that would soon belong entirely to the Empire.

Wing Commander's Office, TCS Victory Delius System

"Reporting as ordered, sir."

"Come in, Lieutenant," Blair said, gesturing to the chair in front of his desk. "Sit down."

Flint settled into the seat, her eyes holding a look somewhere between hope and wariness. "Thank you, sir," she said. "Ah . . . those were some good moves you guys put on yesterday, Colonel. Although I couldn't really tell everything that was going on . . . from Flight Control."

He smiled. "You don't need to drop hints, Lieutenant. I know it's been difficult for you, sitting on the sidelines."

"It's just . . . Look, sir, it just isn't the same, flying a console aboard ship. I belong in the cockpit. That's all there is to it. If you can't put me there, then transfer me to a unit where I can get a fresh start."

"You're pretty blunt, Lieutenant," he said. "Let me be the same. If I don't put you back on the flight roster here, it'll be because I have a problem with you flying. So you can be damned sure my report in your file would reflect my doubts. Don't think a transfer is going to get you back in the cockpit just because I'm not your CO any longer."

Her look was bleak, bitter. "I lost it, back at Locanda. I admit it. But I don't think that mistake should hang over me forever, Colonel. Watching those bastards slip past us, knowing they were going to spread their plague on my home—that was more than I could handle. But it isn't likely to come up again." She managed a crooked smile.

"The stakes are less . . . personal, now. Is that it?" He kept his own tone serious.

"I guess so, sir," she said. "I hate to admit it. I mean, when I took my oath it was to the Confederation, not to any one planet. But Locanda was so much more real to me, when it went down. I could see it, in my mind: the places, the people. It made a difference."

"If it didn't, you wouldn't be human," he said. Blair studied her for a moment. She seemed too small, too fragile to be a combat pilot. "The problem is, you made me a promise once before, and you didn't keep it. Do you want to get back in that cockpit bad enough to follow through this time?"

"I can't prove that unless you give me the chance, Colonel," she said. "When I'm out there, with that bird strapped around me and a cat in my sights . . . that's the only time I really feel *alive*."

Blair nodded sadly. He remembered Angel saying something like that once, back on the *Tiger's Claw*. "I knew . . . I know someone who felt the same way. She lived to fight 'the good fight,' as she called it."

"For me, it's the flying," Flint told him. "I love the purity . . . nothing holding me back. Knowing I'm in complete control, for better or worse."

"Yeah," Blair said, nodding again. "Yeah, only a pilot knows that feeling."

"Well, Colonel, if you understand how I feel, then you have to know what I'm going through now. I wasn't designed for cheerleading from the sidelines, or playing traffic director in Flight Control. I'm requesting reassignment to flight status." She paused. "Please . . ."

"I don't usually give third chances, Lieutenant," he said slowly. "But we could have used you out there yesterday. Next time we'll need you even more. You're back on the roster, effective immediately, Flint."

"Thank you, sir . . ."

He held up a hand. "But if you screw up again . . . heaven help you. Because I won't."

"Understood, Colonel." She stood up. "This time you won't regret it."

Flight Wing Rec Room, TCS Victory Delius System

A jagged, irregular chunk of rock eighteen kilometers across dominated the view from the rec room. A few moving lights marked the passage of shuttles and service pods back and forth between carrier and asteroid. In the three hours since *Victory* matched orbits with Delius Station, a thorough inspection of the ship's hull and external fittings had already been completed, and the captain had authorized liberty for the off-duty watch. There weren't as many takers as might be expected—

Delius Station was reputed to be one of the most boring stopovers in the sector—but there was a definite easing of tensions on board at the realization that they really were back in friendly territory at last.

Blair sat alone at a table, sipping his scotch and gazing at the planetoid and the star field beyond. In one corner of the room, Vaquero was softly strumming his old guitar, a quiet, mournful sound. Lieutenant Lopez had been certified fit for flight duty by the ship's Medical Officer the day before, and Blair restored him to the roster. But he still wondered if Lopez was fully recovered from the battering he had taken in the first clash in the nebula.

He heard Maniac Marshall call a greeting as he entered the rec room, and half-turned in his chair to watch the major at the bar. Marshall was his usual self, boisterous, self-assured, wearing a broad smile as he took his drink from Rostov and waved an airy greeting to Flint and Cobra, who were sitting together at a nearby table.

To Blair's surprise, Maniac ambled to his table. "Colonel," he said, giving him a nod.

"Major," Blair replied. He waited a moment before going on. "Something I can do for you?"

Maniac grew visibly uncomfortable, all his cockiness disappearing as he stammered a response. "Er . . . fact is, I wanted to tell you . . . I wanted to say . . . Maverick, that was a damned impressive show back at Ariel. The way you faked that first bunch out of position . . . and the way you kept your cool after the cats pulled their little magic trick." He looked embarrassed. "I know we don't always operate on the same frequency . . . but I thought I should give credit where it's due."

Blair raised an eyebrow. "Well . . ." He wasn't sure how to respond. Maniac Marshall had never before made such an overture. "Thanks for the vote of confidence. It was touch and go there for a while, though."

"Yeah," Marshall agreed. "Tell me about it. When they

made that jump point disappear . . . God, I almost lost it. I never thought I'd feel that way, Maverick. Never."

"You kept your head pretty well, all things considered," Blair told him. "We couldn't have nailed that destroyer without you and Flash."

"We could have taken her out by ourselves, if you and Cobra had let us," Maniac said with a trace of his old spirit. "But . . . yeah, it was a good score all the way around." He looked out the viewport and continued with a sour note in his voice. "You think Chief Coriolis was right about the Kilrathi using a cloak on the jump points, Maverick?"

"That's the official verdict," Blair said. "The analysis the captain ordered turned up sensor traces consistent with the use of cloaking generators. That's the report he ordered dispatched to Sector HQ."

"So we only have to worry about them pulling something like that in a nebula, huh?" Marshall looked solemn. "I guess that's good news, at least."

"It also means we won't be stuck, next time out," Blair said. "It might take longer, but we could use a cloaked jump point providing we already had it thoroughly plotted on our charts."

"Does that mean we're going back? To finish the mission? Or with this weapon everybody's talking about?"

"That'll be up to the brass," Blair told him. "But I doubt it. If we're going to use an experimental weapon under difficult conditions, why borrow even more trouble? Of course, I'm not an admiral. Maybe they could find a good reason, but it seems like a silly risk to me."

"Hope you're right," Maniac said. He studied the view outside in silence for a long moment. "Nebulas and asteroid belts . . . I'll be glad to see the last of them. Give me a stand-up fight, not all this dodging and ducking and worrying about what your sensors aren't showing you."

"Look at the bright side, Maniac," Blair told him.

"There's a bright side?"

"Sure. The bad guys don't like flying through all this space junk any more than we do."

"Maybe not," Maniac said. "But they can take more risks out there than we can. After all, they've got nine lives."

Flight Control, TCS Victory
Delius System

"NOW, GENERAL QUARTERS, GENERAL QUARTERS. ALL HANDS TO BATTLE STATIONS! REPEAT, ALL HANDS TO BATTLE STATIONS!"

Blair turned in his chair to face a monitor and punched up an intercom link to the bridge. "This is Blair. What's going down?"

The screen showed Rollins in the foreground, with the running figures of bridge crewmen hurrying to their posts visible behind him. From somewhere out of the picture the sensor officer was talking. "I'm reading multiple contacts, Captain. Eight . . . no, ten capital ships. Four of them are carriers. Configuration . . . they're Kilrathi, sir. No doubt about it."

Rollins turned to look into the camera. "We've got a mountain of trouble out there, Colonel," he said. "A whole damned cat task force just popped onto our scopes."

The image in the monitor broke up, replaced by Eisen's heavy, scowling features. "I'll take it, Lieutenant," he said crisply. "Colonel Blair, we have four carriers plus escorts incoming. No fighters yet, but you can bet they'll launch a flock of 'em when they've closed the range."

"That's pretty long odds," Blair said slowly. "Delius Station doesn't have much firepower."

"Not enough to make a difference," Eisen agreed. "We're breaking orbit and heading for the nearest jump point. There's no sense in buying it here."

"And our orders? The flight wing?"

"Get ready for a magnum launch, Colonel. Get your birds ready. We may need them to buy the ship enough time to reach the jump point." Eisen's look was grim. "Another bug-out, Colonel. I'm sorry, but it looks like you'll be covering our tails one more time."

"Understood, sir," Blair said.

Eisen had already turned away from the intercom, issuing orders to his bridge crew. "Navigation! Plot course to the nearest jump point. Helm, break orbit. Proceed at full thrust. Gunnery . . . be ready to clear a path if the debris field gets too thick . . ." The intercom went dead.

Blair slapped the red switch that issued the magnum launch alert. A new alarm shrilled, followed by the computer's public address announcement. *"LAUNCH STATIONS! LAUNCH STATIONS! ALL FLIGHT WING PERSONNEL TO LAUNCH STATIONS. MAGNUM LAUNCH!"*

Flight Deck, TCS Victory
Delius System

Blair checked his instruments for what seemed like the hundredth time, knowing that nothing had changed yet feeling compelled to do something. Every one of *Victory's* fighters was crewed and ready, even a pair that the technical staff had downchecked as unreliable. Now they were waiting, and that was an agony worse than any combat situation.

The carrier had opened up a fair lead over the Kilrathi ships, bulling her way through the asteroid field with weapons blazing to clear away any chunk of rock big enough to pose a threat to the ship. The Imperial vessels were more cautious, keeping to a tight formation and lumbering slowly after *Victory* as if reluctant to commit themselves to an attack. Perhaps they had learned to respect the Terrans in earlier clashes . . . or perhaps they simply regarded it as triumph enough to drive the ship away from Delius Station, leaving the Terrans there— including a small contingent of the carrier's crew still on liberty—completely at the mercy of the Kilrathi task force.

Blair was starting to hope they might not have to beat off any genuine attack, but the threat remained. They wouldn't be able to relax their guard until they made the jump to Tamayo, if then.

"Colonel, sensors are reporting a launch in progress from the lead Kilrathi carrier." Rollins gave him a welcome distraction, however grim his news might be. "It's the flagship . . . *Hvar'kann*. Looks like you'll be having a party after all."

"Acknowledged," Blair said. "Flight wing, from Blair. Begin launch sequence on my mark . . ."

At that moment his comm panel went crazy. The visual display broke up in a kaleidoscope of patterns and colors, and the speakers in his helmet squealed and whined. It took several seconds for the noise to fade and the screen to come back on-line. Blair stared at the monitor, as if it might give him some clue to what had just happened.

A glowering Kilrathi face filled the screen, a face Blair had seen many times before.

Thrakhath.

The image jumped and jittered again, then returned. Blair studied it thoughtfully, wondering what was causing the distortion. Ship to ship video transmissions used computers to encode and decode messages, and to provide automatic translations of foreign languages. For the computer to have this much trouble reconstructing whatever message Thrakhath was broadcasting meant the signal content must be massive. Evidently, the Kilrathi were trying to overload *Victory*'s whole comm system and jam every frequency the Terrans might be using.

Thrakhath's image began to speak as the computers processed their translation of the Kilrathi language. "I have heard of your Terran Bible with its predictions that there will be a weeping and gnashing of teeth. These the Imperial Race will soon fulfill. We will tear out your tongues, we will scoop out your brains. You will learn to beg for the release of death."

Blair tried to switch to a different comm channel, but Thrakhath's hissing, taunting image remained on the screen. "You will be prime examples to the other races in the galaxy, you clownish baboons. Your race will suffer a thousand torments and more. And do not think that the presence of the Heart of the Tiger among you can make a difference. Colonel Blair will be reduced to a pile of entrails, his bones will be gnawed by our young."

Hearing himself referred to directly made Blair stiffen. It wasn't often that the Kilrathi chose to grant a name to one of their human adversaries . . . and it inevitably meant that the individual they chose to "honor" had become the prime target of a Kilrathi challenge.

"Heart of the Tiger, you shall pay for the blood of every Kilrathi noble you have dispatched in battle. They shall make songs of your death, of the failure and disgrace you shall know even before your death. Already you have failed, Heart of the Tiger, failed at Locanda Four, failed at Ariel . . . failed your lair-mate, the one known as Devereaux, the Angel."

Blair gasped as the image of Thrakhath on his monitor blacked out, only to be replaced by a new scene. . . .

A scene from hell.

It was a large room, red-lit, dark, with ornate fittings and decorations more suggested than seen among the shadows. A throng of Kilrathi in garb Blair recognized as that of the high nobility were gathered in the middle of the open chamber, bowing low as Thrakhath and an aged Kilrathi, the Emperor himself, entered. As the

Emperor sat on the imposing throne, Blair became aware of movement in the shadows on either side of the two figures. It was difficult to judge exactly what was happening, but when he finally realized what he was witnessing, he wished he had not.

There were Terrans along the wall behind the throne, men and women hanging in chains, their Confed-issue flight suits in rags. Bulky Kilrathi guards carrying nerve-prods moved among them, striking out almost at random, eliciting cries and moans from their victims.

"Once again an enemy threat to our very homeworld has been thwarted," the Emperor intoned solemnly. "This puny contingent of their soldiers was captured aboard a hijacked Imperial transport in orbit around Kilrah itself."

There was a scattering of calls from the assembled nobles—shock, anger, hatred plain in their voices and bearing. The Emperor silenced them with a curt gesture and gave Thrakhath a sign to speak.

"This incursion was an act of desperation," the prince said, showing his fangs. His arms made encompassing gestures toward the victims behind the throne. "Look at these pathetic hairless apes. They have failed their race utterly."

A growling cheer rose from the crowd.

"Do what you will with them," the Emperor said.

Red light glimmered off Thrakhath's fangs. "There will be no interrogation for these pitiful apes . . . and no warrior's death. They are offal, fit only for death." The Prince waved a dismissive hand. "Only one among them is worthy of being treated as a warrior. Their leader . . . the one they call . . . Angel."

Blair wanted to look away as a pair of burly Kilrathi warriors half-pushed, half-dragged a familiar petite figure into the middle of the throne room directly in front of Thrakhath. Like the other Terrans, she had been tortured, her flight suit reduced to tattered ruin, the face that

haunted Blair's dreams bruised. There was dried blood
on her forehead, a livid welt on one cheek, but she wore
her defiance like a shield. Whatever the Kilrathi had
done to her, Jeannette Devereaux's spirit remained as
fiery and determined as ever.

At the sight of the woman, the Kilrathi nobles grew
more agitated. Blair recognized the bloodlust in their
eyes, in the way they bared claws and fangs as they
jeered the captive. Only the sheer force of Thrakhath's
personality held them at bay as he stepped down from
the dais to inspect Angel more closely.

"Still defiant, Colonel Devereaux?" the prince asked.
"You should know by now it is a pathetic and useless
gesture. The hunt has nearly run its course, and your
race is prey beneath our claws."

"You bore me, *monsieur*," she told him, mustering a
faint smile. "I would prefer to join my comrades, rather
than listen to more of your boasting."

"You will not join them, Colonel," Thrakhath said. "Your
fate shall be different."

Angel replied by spitting in his face. There were hisses
and jeers from the crowd, a harsh growl from Thrakhath's
throat. He turned to address his nobles.

"The human cannot appreciate the honor I bestow
upon her. She is not only a great warrior, but her lair-
mate is the one known as the Heart of the Tiger." He
turned back to her; his eyes narrowed in a deadly stare.
The cries of the Kilrathi reached a bloodthirsty crescendo.
"You have slain many fine warriors during your career.
You have earned this honor."

The prince unsheathed his claws. With a single thrust,
he jabbed them deep into her stomach and lifted her
off the ground, high into the air. Blood flowed freely
from the wound. The view on the screen caught her
face in close-up as the life drained from her eyes. Blair
thought he saw a final look of appeal there, as if she

was crying out to him for rescue . . . or for vengeance.

Then the prince released her, and her lifeless body crumpled to the ground.

Thrakhath's image filled the screen again. "Come, Heart of the Tiger," he said. "I am leading my warriors into battle today. If you would live up to the honor your lair-mate earned, come and fight. Or be shown for the pathetic coward you are."

Christopher Blair stared at the screen, his mind a whirl of anger and pain and hate. At that moment, all he wanted to do was kill. . . .

• CHAPTER XXI

Bridge, TCS Victory
Delius System

"Can't you shut the damned thing off, Lieutenant?" Eisen demanded. On his communications screen, Thrakhath's feral features continued to glare hatred and challenge. The message was starting all over again.

"I'm trying, sir," Rollins answered. "But it's not an ordinary transmission. Damn thing's got the whole comm system tied in knots. Hold on a minute . . . I think I can kick in a backup system . . . everybody cross your fingers!"

The communications officer entered a code sequence on his board, and a moment later the Kilrathi message broke up into static. A few seconds later Eisen's screen was back to normal, the green light shining above it indicating the system was ready to use.

"Thank you, Mr. Rollins," Eisen said. "Ensign Dumont, get me an updated sensor reading. What are those bastards doing out there? Oh . . . and Rollins, put me through to Colonel Blair."

"On the line, sir."

Blair's head appeared on the monitor. Even though his flight helmet faceplate hid Blair's features, Eisen thought he looked pale and stricken. There was no mistaking the barely-suppressed snarl in his voice. "Ready to launch, Captain," he said.

"Not so fast, Colonel," Eisen told him. "We're still trying to get a picture of what the cats are doing. The ship's less than fifteen minutes from the jump point, and we might make it yet without having to launch."

"If they've got fighters out, sir, you'll have to put us out there to hold them off," Blair replied. "At least for a little while."

"Look, Colonel . . ." Eisen trailed off. He didn't know what to say to the man, after Thrakhath's message. "Maybe you ought to sit this one out, Blair. Let Hobbes take over."

"No, sir," Blair said curtly.

"Is that the Wing Commander talking . . . or a man who's looking for revenge?"

"Both, sir," Blair answered. He was silent for a moment before going on. "Look, Captain, I won't pretend . . . that bastard got me where I live, using Angel like that. He's trying to goad me into doing something stupid. And I'd be lying if I said I didn't want to oblige him . . . bad. Real bad. But in this case, playing along with his little game is our best option. As long as Thrakhath figures I'm going to take him up on his challenge, the rest of his fighters will hold back. Nobody's going to get into the middle of the Crown Prince's blood feud."

"I don't like it," Eisen said. "I've never thought this Thrakhath was very well-equipped in the honor department, however much the cats make of it. What do you say, Colonel Ralgha? You know more about the Prince than any of us."

Hobbes was slow to answer, and when he did his voice sounded blurred, distant. "I could not . . . say for sure. The message was intended to . . . provoke a response. But the challenge could well be legitimate. If Colonel Blair has been honored with his own warrior's name, then the Prince must consider him to be important somehow."

Blair's voice betrayed a sudden concern. "You all right, buddy? What's wrong?"

"A . . . headache," Hobbes said slowly. "Some of the higher-pitched harmonics in the message were . . . grating." He paused. "And, of course, I mourn for Colonel Devereaux. She was a brave warrior. And a friend."

"That she was," Blair said. "Captain, what about it? Do we get out there and buy you some time?"

"I don't like it, Blair. But I don't have a whole lot of options." Eisen paused as the Sensor Officer displayed new data on the main bridge monitor. "We definitely have a launch in progress from the Kilrathi flagship. So far they're still forming up. No way to tell if they plan to press something, or if they're just threatening. Looks like . . . at least a squadron already. More likely two, if they're still launching."

"Then we'd better get out there," Blair said. He cut the connection without awaiting a reply.

Eisen leaned forward in his chair. "God go with you, Colonel," he said softly.

Flight Deck, KIS Hvar'kann
Delius System

"Lord Prince, surely you do not need to take personal command today. The cockpit of a fighter is no place for the Imperial Heir when the battle is so insignificant."

Thrakhath paused halfway up the ladder to the cockpit of his Bloodfang and turned to glare his contempt down on Melek. "I have issued the challenge. Would you have me hold back now, in front of our warriors?"

"No, Lord Prince . . ." Melek trailed off, looking uncomfortable. "But if something was to happen to you now, with triumph so close under our talons, we would lose everything we have worked to achieve. The personal challenge was a risk you did not need to take. Others would have willingly taken on the Heart of the Tiger for you."

"No! We want to cut this ape out of his troop, and for that he must be goaded beyond all reason. I killed his lair-mate. He will not turn back from the chance to kill me in return. And then . . . we have him."

"He is a skilled pilot, Lord Prince," Melek warned.

"I know it well." Thrakhath showed his fangs. "I am not a fool, Melek. Honor requires me to be present for the challenge, but it doesn't require me to sacrifice myself. My escorts will intervene if the need arises. But the important thing is to eliminate this Colonel Blair now, so that he does not stand in the way of our plans for the Behemoth. Go now. You command in my absence. Let the hunt begin!"

Thunderbolt 300
Delius System

Blair's fighter leapt from the end of the launch tube into the void, building thrust as he steered toward the rest of Gold Squadron assembling beyond the stern of the *Victory*. It required all of his will to stay focused on his instruments, the sensor screen, and the battle ahead. He couldn't afford to let himself dwell on Angel.

"Thunderbolt three-zero-zero, under power," he reported. "Gold Squadron deployed and ready."

"*You sure we shouldn't let Whittaker's boys and girls give you a hand out there, Colonel?*" The duty Flight Control Officer, Lieutenant Rashad, sounded worried.

"Keep them on stand-by, Lieutenant," Blair said. "I'll let you know if we need them."

It was the same problem encountered at Ariel. With the carrier heading for the jump point, too many fighters in space would only complicate their escape. Blair overruled the original call for a magnum launch, preferring to put out the eight fighters of Gold Squadron and hold the others in reserve in case they were needed. But he didn't intend to need them, not today. All the Terrans needed to do at the moment was keep the Kilrathi distracted until the carrier was ready to jump.

So far, the cats were cooperating quite nicely. Their fighters were maintaining a tight formation well out of range of the carrier's guns. None showed any desire to venture close enough to threaten the Terran vessel.

"Eight minutes," Rollins' voice informed them.

"What are they waiting for?" Flash complained.

"Maybe they're scared of you, kid," Maniac responded.

"Cut the chatter, people," Blair growled. He was feeling as impatient as Dillon. If only Thrakhath would put his fighter in Blair's crosshairs . . .

"Does the Heart of the Tiger hide among the other apes?" Thrakhath's mocking voice filled his helmet speakers. *"And under the guns of his ship? The challenge was to meet in personal combat."*

On his screens, he saw a Vaktoth accelerate away from the other Kilrathi ships, but it stayed well clear of *Victory*. For a moment Blair toyed with the idea of ordering the squadron to attack, but he knew the Kilrathi would be on their guard against such a move. The name of the game, for now at least, was to keep from letting a full-scale battle develop for as long as possible.

Thrakhath must have realized the same thing, for a few seconds later a pair of Vaktoth broke formation, followed by two more. These streaked toward the carrier. Gold Squadron lay directly in their path.

"Here they come!" Cobra called. *"Permission to engage?"*

"Let them come to us," Blair ordered. "Wingmen, stick close to your partners."

The first two Vaktoth drove into the center of the Terran formation then rolled outward, opening fire with guns and missiles. Cobra and her wingman, Vaquero, went after the first one, while Maniac and Vagabond engaged the second. Blair watched the second pair of fighters and felt his pulse race. "Hobbes, you and Flash take the one on the left," he said. "Flint and I'll take the other guy."

"*Understood,*" was Ralgha's reply. He still sounded distracted. Flash gave a whoop and kicked in his afterburners, racing to meet the oncoming fighter.

Blair couldn't spend any more time worrying about the others. The fourth Vaktoth was almost on them, concentrating fire against Flint's Thunderbolt. Blair turned sharply and accelerated, opening fire with his blasters, while Flint banked sharply left to try to keep her weakened port-side shields from taking any more damage.

The Vaktoth pilot was good. He maintained his fire on Flint, randomly altering vectors to dodge most of Blair's fire while he kept up the pressure on his original target. Blair gave a curse and locked a heat-seeker on the Vaktoth's tail, then followed the missile with his blasters, pouring out all the power his weapons system could muster. The shield collapsed, and blaster fire tore into the armor until the power cut out, recharging.

His opponent seemed to realize then that Blair represented too great a threat to ignore any longer. He started turning away from Flint to bring his weapons to bear and to cover his exposed rear, but as he turned, Flint took the opening without hesitation. Her blasters continued where Blair's ended, and a moment later the Vaktoth exploded in a thousand whirling fragments.

"Nice shooting, Lieutenant," Blair called. "Good to have you back on my wing."

"*It's where I belong, Colonel,*" she replied.

"*Somebody get this bastard off me! Hobbes! Colonel!*" Flash's voice was hoarse with panic. "*I can't shake him!*"

On his scanner, Blair saw Flash trying to break away from the Vaktoth he challenged, but the enemy pilot was right on his tail. Hobbes was closing in, but slowly, cautiously, as if the Kilrathi renegade was afraid of getting too close to the dogfighting pair. Blair banked the Thunderbolt, increasing his speed, but he knew he wouldn't be able to reach Flash in time to do any good.

Hobbes took up a position behind the enemy fighter and opened fire, but his first shots went wild. The Vaktoth unleashed another attack. This time a deadly hail of energy bolts and missiles rained on Flash's ship as the young pilot tried to turn out of the Vaktoth's line of fire.

He was too late. Blair heard him scream as a fireball consumed his craft.

Once again Hobbes fired, but this time his opponent rolled sideways and accelerated back toward the rest of the Kilrathi formation. More Vaktoth were on their way.

"Five minutes to Jump Sequence start," Rollins announced. *"Captain wants to know if we should launch additional fighters?"*

"Negative," Blair grated. His sensors showed that the other two Vaktoth from the first flight had both been destroyed. The Terran fighters were regrouping again, ready to meet the next threat. "Hobbes, without a wingman you'll be a sitting duck. Retreat to the carrier and land."

"I should remain, my friend."

For a moment Blair considered having the Kilrathi switch positions with one of the other pilots, someone less steady, less reliable. Flint, or Vaquero, or perhaps Maniac. But the way Hobbes had been handling himself today, he was no more reliable than any of them. Even Marshall seemed to have himself under control, but Ralgha was plainly off his game. And Flash had paid the price. "No, Hobbes. Pack it in. That's an order."

"As you command." Ralgha's Thunderbolt broke away

and headed toward the carrier. Now there were only six Terran fighters to face the next wave of Kilrathi.

This time four Imperial craft came at once, holding a tight formation all the way. Blair waited until they were just outside of weapons range before ordering Gold Squadron to turn from the oncoming Vaktoth and go to afterburners. The Kilrathi gave chase.

"Maintain course," Blair said quietly. It was almost a mantra. "Maintain course . . . Break! Break and attack! *Victory*, pour it on!"

The Terran fighters split up, each pair of wingmen peeling off in a different direction and looping back toward the pursuing Kilrathi. At the same time, *Victory*'s defensive batteries opened fire, filling the void with searing bursts of raw energy. A pair of hits took out one of the enemy ships in the blink of an eye, and another suffered heavy damage as it tried to dodge the carrier's beams and pursue Cobra. Vaquero, on her wing, finished the attacker off with a well-placed missile.

Maniac dove straight towards his target, all guns blazing, passing bare meters away from his opponent before the Kilrathi pilot could even react. Slowly, carefully, Vagabond trailed him, and his blasters exploited the weakened shields to burn through the fighter's cockpit and kill the pilot. The Vaktoth plunged on, uncontrolled, until *Victory* destroyed it a few seconds later.

Meanwhile, Flint and Blair split and circled the last Imperial fighter from opposite sides, hammering the hull with blasters as they sped past. As a parting shot, Blair dropped a fire-and-forget missile. It hit the Vaktoth's starboard wing moments later. The explosion didn't destroy the enemy craft, but it was visibly damaged as it turned and ran, trailing debris and leaking atmosphere. Maniac caught the fighter as it tried to flee and finished it with a few well-placed blaster shots.

"*Three minutes*," Rollins said.

Blair studied his scanners. The Kilrathi fighters were still out there, but the countdown was getting close enough that he had to start thinking about getting the rest of the squadron on board. Anyway, the Imperial ships wouldn't be inclined to cut things too fine by staging an attack now. The energy discharge of a carrier going into jump could do terrible damage to fighters close enough to be caught by the creation of the Transition Field.

"Take them in, people," he ordered. "Maniac, Vagabond, you two first. Don't miss the first approach. You might not get another one. Cobra and Vaquero, you go as soon as they're clear. Flint, you're with me."

No one argued, though he thought he heard Maniac muttering a protest. The first two Thunderbolts peeled off and headed back for the carrier; the second two followed, but more slowly, to give Marshall and Chang time to set down and clear the flight deck. Time passed with agonizing slowness, with no further moves from the Kilrathi. But Blair was tense. He was sure Thrakhath wouldn't let them leave without some kind of final shot.

"*Two minutes,*" Rollins announced at length. "*Maniac and Vagabond are aboard. Vaquero's in the beam now.*"

"You're up, Flint," he said. "Take her inside."

"*Don't be slow following me, Colonel,*" she responded. "*I'm getting too used to flying on your wing.*"

She left him, and Blair started a quick checklist for his own approach and landing. It was starting to look like Thrakhath wasn't planning a last push after all . . .

"*Jump Sequence start in ninety seconds,*" Rollins said. "*Better bring her in now, Colonel.*"

As he started to turn, Thrakhath's voice boomed loud in his speakers. "So, I was right, ape. In the end you do run. You did not meet my challenge. . . . Even your lair-mate showed more courage, facing death."

"*Seventy-five seconds, Colonel.*"

Blair tried to shut Thrakhath's words out of his mind, but the Kilrathi's mocking voice went on. *"We misnamed you, perhaps, in calling you the Heart of the Tiger. You are weak . . . a coward . . . a failure. Not worthy of your lair-mate at all."* The Kilrathi's voice took on a harsher edge now. *"I enjoyed the feel of her blood running over my hands, Terran. As I enjoyed the taste of her flesh, in the victory feast."*

The words hammered at him on a level below conscious thought, and blind rage threatened to claim him. The carrier was looming large ahead of his fighter, but Blair hardly saw it through the red haze that clouded his eyes. He wanted to turn around, accept the Kilrathi's challenge, batter through Thrakhath's defenses and silence his taunts once and for all. That *thing*, that *animal*, had killed Angel and served her up at one of the barbaric Kilrathi ritual feasts.

"Almost in the beams, Colonel," Rollins said. *"Keep her steady . . . steady . . . Reduce your speed! If you don't cut your speed you'll overshoot!"*

"For God's sake, skipper, don't let him get to you!" That was Flint's voice. *"If you take his challenge, you're stuck out there! Thrakhath'll wait . . . you'll get another chance at him!"*

The words penetrated his fog, and Blair killed his forward momentum with a hard braking thrust, like a kick from a horse. Almost sobbing, he stabbed at the landing gear controls as the beams took hold. Slowly, gently, the fighter dropped toward the deck and touched down.

He hardly noticed as the fighter was drawn into the hangar area. A pair of spacesuited figures released his cockpit, urging him to get out even before gravity or pressure were restored, and Blair neither helped nor resisted them. They guided him across the open space in long, low-G bounds. Pressure was restored as they reached the door, and one of them—Blair vaguely realized it was Flint, still clad in flight suit and combat helmet—helped him remove his own helmet as they guided him into the corridor. His other helper fumbled with helmet releases and finally freed the bulky headgear. It was Rachel Coriolis.

"JUMP SEQUENCE ENGAGED," the computer announced blandly. "ONE MINUTE TO JUMP."

"You gave us a scare, skipper," Rachel said. "Thought you were gonna pull a bolter and miss the landing."

"I should have," Blair said. "I should have stayed out there and nailed that damned furball."

"That's exactly what he wanted," Flint told him. "If you had let him draw you into a fight, you'd never have made it back before we jumped. I thought you were the one who never let it get to you? Isn't that what you said when you were chewing me out?"

He looked at her and slowly shook his head. "Maybe so. And maybe I was wrong when I said it." Blair looked away. "I guess I'll never know, now."

Blair brushed away their offered help as the elevator doors opened and he stepped into the cab. They followed, but he ignored them both, staring rigidly ahead at the keypad controls, unwilling to talk. Inside he felt drained, empty of everything except the knowledge that he had failed.

The knowledge that Angel remained unavenged.

Flight Deck, KIS Hvar'kann
Delius System

An honor guard greeted Thrakhath as he disembarked from his fighter, but he ignored them all in his anger. He glared as Melek approached, bowing.

"Lord Prince, the Terran carrier has jumped. The captain of the *Toor'vaas* reports that the asteroid base has been breached, and Assault Marines are penetrating the station. There is no sign of further resistance anywhere."

Thrakhath gave him a dismissive gesture. "I expected none," he said, not bothering to hide the angry growl in his voice. "See to it there are no apes left alive once their base has been secured."

"But, Lord Prince, there will be many suitable slaves there." Melek looked shocked. "Surely you would not deny the Clans their right to take back captives—"

"No survivors, I said!" Thrakhath snapped.

Melek stepped back as if physically stricken. "As you wish, Lord Prince," he said, bowing again.

"We have been at war with these apes for more than a generation, Melek. But I still cannot understand them. How could any sentient creature, however lacking in honor, fail to respond to a chance for vengeance?" Thrakhath studied his retainer for a long moment. "You are sure that this Blair was truly lair-mate to the one we killed?"

"Intelligence reports claimed so, Lord Prince. Based on many interrogations of captured human pilots. The knowledge was evidently widely known in their warrior community."

Thrakhath took a moment to chain his anger and speak calmly, as befitted a Prince. "Clearly the animal humans are even less civilized than we thought. They do not even respect their lair-mates enough to fight for them." He paused. "But even if the Heart of the Tiger survives, the rest of the plan shall move forward. He cannot deflect the fate that pursues the Terrans now."

"Yes, Lord Prince."

"Order a carrier to follow the Terran ship, but wait until it has had time to get well clear of the jump point before sending it. *Sar'hrai* would be a good choice. Give his new captain a chance to prove his worth. They are to mount a close surveillance on the enemy carrier, using stealth craft. When our agent makes his move, we must be ready." Thrakhah showed his fangs for a moment. "Our claws are at their throats, Melek. They will not escape the hunt."

• CHAPTER XXII

Flight Deck, TCS Victory
Tamayo System

Once again the flight deck was crowded with officers and crewmen gathered to bid farewell to one of their own. The neat ranks of pilots, technicians, and ship's crew . . . the honor guard with weapons held in a stiff rifle salute . . . the chaplain's service, and the empty coffin waiting by the launch tube—only the names changed, but never the trappings or the emotion.

Christopher Blair slowly stepped forward to the temporary podium. He never relished this duty, but today he hated everything about it.

"Major Jace Dillon was a reluctant warrior in the Confederation's battle against the Empire," Blair said slowly. He raised his eyes to study the front ranks, especially the pilots of Gold Squadron. For a fleeting moment he wondered what Ralgha was thinking. Did the Kilrathi renegade regret letting the young Terran pilot down in that last battle? Hobbes had certainly been withdrawn ever since. It was a feeling Blair understood entirely. "Nevertheless, Flash never turned back when the going got tough. He more than made up for his youth and inexperience by flying with vigor and courage, and he died carrying the fight to the enemy."

As he stepped back to allow the chaplain to advance and carry on with the funeral ceremony, Blair's eyes rested on the lone coffin. He wished he could have said a few words about Angel, but it would have been out of place here. Still, it wasn't Flash he was thinking about as the coffin accelerated out of the hangar deck, or as the honor guard fired their low-powered volleys. And when he bowed his head to offer up a prayer, it was Angel Devereaux who was foremost in his mind.

Flight Wing Rec Room, TCS Victory Tamayo System

Blair sat alone at a table by the viewport, staring down into his empty glass as if it was a crystal ball that might give him a glimpse of another time and place. He was hardly aware of his surroundings, the other pilots and crewmen who talked, laughed, and carried on with their lives, with only an occasional glance at the solitary, withdrawn figure of their wing commander.

A shadow fell across the table, and he looked into the knowing eyes of Rachel Coriolis. She put a bottle down on the table beside him. "You look like you could use a little more anesthetic," she said softly.

He poured a shot and drank, wincing a little at the bite of the cheap liquor in his mouth and throat. Rachel studied him for a moment, as if waiting for him to speak. Instead he refilled the glass and held it, watching the reflections dance in the amber liquid.

"Thrakhath really got to you, didn't he?" Rachel asked. "He knew all the right buttons to push."

Still Blair didn't answer. He took a longer, slower sip, then looked up at Rachel.

"I know how you feel, Colonel," she said, even softer this time. "I know what it's like, losing someone to this damned war." She hesitated a moment. "Do you want company? Or is the bottle enough?"

Those words got through his defenses at last. He looked from Rachel to the bottle, then back at her again. "Company? Yeah." He pushed the bottle away. "Yeah, I guess talking is better than drinking, but it isn't easy."

She settled into the chair across from him. "No, it isn't. But you can't run away from people, and you can't take refuge in getting drunk. Those things just postpone the inevitable."

"I knew, deep down, that she might not be coming back," he said slowly. "I was afraid she was dead. I had nightmares about it. But seeing it like that . . . and having that bastard gloating about it . . ."

"Well, kick in a bulkhead or something. Get it out somehow, okay? Don't wait until you're back in the cockpit again. If you try to take it out on the cats—look, I've been through that already, with somebody I cared about very much. I wouldn't want to go through it again."

He met her eyes. "Somebody you cared about . . . I hope you're not thinking. . . ?"

Rachel looked away. "I know better than to put the moves on somebody who's just had a kick like the one you've had," she said. "Let's just say . . . let's just say you're a man I could care about . . . if there was nothing else holding you. And I wouldn't want to see you throw your life away, no matter what."

"I'm a dangerous man to be around, Rachel," he told her. "My friends, my shipmates . . . Angel . . . they keep leaving on the last flight without me. If you're smart, you'll give me a wide berth."

"Nobody's ever accused me of being smart," she said with a ghost of a smile. "And I think it's better to take your chances than to steer clear of . . . a friend."

Wing Commander's Office, TCS Victory Torgo System

"All right, last item on the list," Blair said, ticking off another point on his personal data display. "Captain says we're due for a visit from some VIPs tomorrow. Thirteen hundred hours. We need to police the flight deck and hangar areas and try to get them somewhere approaching shipshape. Maniac, I'm putting you in charge of that detail."

Marshall looked up. "Me? When did I become the maid around here?"

Whittaker, Mbuto, and Captain Betz, the acting CO of Green Squadron, all chuckled. Ralgha, sitting in the corner of the office away from the others around the desk, studied his claws with an expression resembling boredom.

"Just do it, Maniac. We want to make a good impression. Now that we're back at Sector HQ, we have to pretend we're in the Navy instead of playing at being the pirate scum of the galaxy." Blair looked around the office. "Anybody have anything else to talk about?"

No one spoke, and Blair nodded sharply. "That'll be all, then." He stood up when the others did and watched them file through the door. Hobbes was the last to leave, and Blair intercepted him. "Anything on your mind, buddy? You've been pretty quiet, the last few days."

Ralgha shook his head ponderously. "Nothing of importance," he rumbled.

"Look, if you're upset at getting sent in after Flash bought it . . ."

"I am not," the Kilrathi said. He fixed Blair with a look the human couldn't easily fathom. "We have been friends for many years, you and I. Faced many things together. But just as you have trouble sharing your pain over Angel, I have . . . feelings I find hard to share now."

"Losing her hit you pretty hard, too, didn't it?"

The Kilrathi didn't speak for a long moment. "I fear that humans . . . have rarely been my friends. She was one of the few. I . . . regret her passing. And what it may lead to." He was watching Blair closely.

"If you're worried about me, don't," Blair said. "I had a long talk with myself the other day, after Flash's funeral. Somebody reminded me that I've got responsibilities I can't afford to let go of just because I'm hurting over her. So I won't do anything stupid."

The Kilrathi gave a very human shrug. "Your species is resilient," he said. "But . . . Colonel Devereaux's death may not be the worst thing we will see, before the end."

"I know what you mean, buddy," Blair told him. "Look, you get some rest. I think this whole mess has been about as rough on you as it's been on me." He clapped Hobbes on the shoulder. "If it helps any, I want you to know that I think she'd be proud, knowing you thought of her as a friend."

Before Ralgha could answer, the door buzzed, and Blair opened it. Rollins stood outside, with Cobra behind him. She gave Hobbes a disdainful look as he passed them, then followed Rollins into the office.

"What can I do for you two?" Blair asked, gesturing to the chairs by the desk and resuming his own seat.

"Colonel, we've been talking," Cobra said. "About Thrakhath's broadcast, before the battle at Delius."

Blair frowned. "What about it?"

"We're puzzled, Colonel," Rollins said. "The whole thing was pretty strange, by my way of thinking. All that effort to issue a challenge to you, and then . . . well, not much of a follow-up. I mean, he did his best to sucker you into a dogfight, but think of how poorly they handled the whole op. They gave us plenty of warning they were coming, and let us get all the way to the jump point before they put on much of an attack. Then that signal, and some bluster and threats. It doesn't add up."

"Hmmm . . ." Blair nodded slowly. "You're right. It's almost as if they wanted me, but they didn't care about the ship. If they'd come in with everything blazing while we were still at Delius Station they could've had *Victory* for breakfast . . . and me with it. You think they wanted the ship to get away? Bad enough to let me go despite Thrakhath's challenge?"

"It could be, Colonel," Rollins said.

"The question is, why?"

Cobra leaned forward in her seat. "Colonel, there's something else that could be important here. I don't know what it was for sure, but there was something . . . familiar about that transmission."

"What's that supposed to mean?"

She shrugged. "I can't put it into words, sir. It wasn't anything I heard . . . or saw. I just had a sense of . . . something. Something familiar. It . . . it gave me a headache, when I was watching it."

"Hobbes said something similar," Blair mused. "Rollins, can you shed any light on it?"

"Beats the hell out of me, Colonel," the communications officer said. "I want to run some checks on the recordings we made. That wasn't just an ordinary audio/video signal, you know. It was a broad-spectrum transmission that had damn near every channel blocked. At first I thought they were just trying to jam us so our comm system would crash. But it was like the whole attack. In the end, they just weren't trying very much. Otherwise they would've kept the jamming up during the battle. But I have to say this . . . if all they were trying to do was get you upset with their challenge and . . . all the rest . . . well, it was overkill. Pure and simple."

Cobra bit her lip. "Sir, I know we've had our differences, and I know what you told me about accusations. About wanting proof . . . and I don't have any. But I have to say this anyway, even if you're going to throw me in the brig over it. I think there could have been some kind of hidden signal in all that junk. To a Kilrathi agent."

"You're talking about Hobbes, of course," Blair said, frowning. "Lieutenant . . ."

"I didn't say it was Hobbes, sir," Cobra said. "But we know the cats have agents in the Confederation."

Rollins cleared his throat. "Colonel, I think you should hear her out on this. It would explain a lot, if the cats had an agent aboard."

"Like how they keep throwing us softballs in tight corners," Buckley amplified. "Letting us get away at Delius. Ariel, too, if you think about it. They could make jump points disappear, but the second one stayed open for us. And it wasn't defended, either."

Blair looked from one to the other. "It still isn't proof of anything except the fact that both of you have active imaginations," he said at last. "You know where I stand. I don't like having accusations leveled at Hobbes, and all you've really got here is a conspiracy theory." He looked down at his desk. "It's a very serious charge to make . . ."

"Hell, Colonel, I'm not saying it is Hobbes," Cobra told him. "I mean, he's a Kilrathi, and you know how I feel about him, but I know this doesn't prove anything." She laughed, a short, bitter, humorless sound. "For all I know, Colonel, you're the Kilrathi spy. You love the cats . . . a cat, at least, and you were in command when things went sour at Locanda Four. All I'm saying is that it would explain some pretty strange shit. I think we have to consider it."

"All right, Lieutenant. I'll consider it." Blair leaned back in his chair. "Suppose you two keep looking into the matter, and let me know if you find anything concrete we can use. And keep your suspicions to yourselves. Have you talked with anyone else?"

"No, sir," Rollins said. "I was going to take it to the captain, but Cobra wanted to come to you first."

"I didn't want you to think I was going behind your back with this thing, sir," she amplified.

"Good. For now, let's keep the matter between us. That way nobody gets embarrassed by a lot of gossip. Nobody. You read me on this?"

"Yes, sir," Rollins said.

Cobra met his look with a level stare. "Aye, aye, Colonel," she said.

"All right. Dismissed, then."

They both started for the door, but Blair held up a hand. "Mister Rollins. I have some reports for the captain. Stay a moment while I round them up, if you please."

"Yes, sir," he responded.

Blair waited until the door closed behind Cobra. He gave Rollins a long, hard look. "Forgive me, Lieutenant, but I have to ask this. How much stock do you put in all this?"

"Sir? I think there's a lot to consider here."

"How much of this is your idea?"

Rollins frowned. "Well, Lieutenant Buckley came to me asking what I thought about the battle . . . about how the Kilrathi fought it, I mean. She made some good points . . ." He trailed off, frowning. "But I had some suspicions about the signal content already, sir. She had nothing to do with any of that." He hesitated. "Just what are you trying to get at with all this, Colonel?"

Blair sat down heavily. "Cobra makes a good case, I'll give her that. And if I didn't have complete faith in Ralgha *nar* Hhallas I might be ready to go along with it. But she doesn't know how much we've been through together, Hobbes and I. And all her hate isn't going to make me change my mind about him now."

"She admitted she wasn't pointing any fingers, sir."

"True enough. But ever since I've been on board she's been running Ralgha down. She accused him of everything but mopery and dopery on the spaceways." Blair paused, reluctant to go on, but Rollins was the only one he could talk to, under these circumstances. "There's another possibility I can't help but think about, Lieutenant."

"Sir?"

"Rumor is that Cobra was a Kilrathi slave for ten years. You hear any of that from your sources?"

"Er . . . no, sir. Not really. Some scuttlebutt in the rec room, maybe, but nothing solid."

"I heard it from somebody I trust," Blair told him. Rollins didn't need to know about Rachel Coriolis and her friend from the *Hermes*. "The point is this: if I was in Kilrathi Intelligence, and wanted to plant spies in the Confederation, I don't think I'd use Kilrathi as agents. They'd have a tough time winning acceptance. I'd use humans, slaves who had grown up in a Kilrathi labor camp. The things they can do with personality overlays are pretty wild from what I've heard, and I'll bet you could make sure they got through debriefing so they were 'rescued' and brought back to Terran space."

"You think Cobra's our spy?" Rollins looked incredulous. "Hell, Colonel, she's the one who suggested we look for a spy!"

"As you said, you already had some questions about those Kilrathi signals." Blair frowned. "You thought there might be other signals buried in there somewhere? Maybe there were—orders, for instance. But a clever spy might want to figure out how much we suspected, and steer our suspicions in an acceptable direction."

"Like Hobbes." Rollins was frowning. "It's . . . how did you put it, Colonel? A conspiracy theory? But I don't see any more proof that it's Cobra than I do for Hobbes.

And Cobra . . . she'd have to be one hell of an actress, making believe she hated the cats so much."

"It's pretty thin, isn't it?" Blair gave him a sour smile. "I don't want to believe it, Lieutenant. She's a good pilot, and a good wingman. But Hobbes is one of the best friends I ever had."

"Why are you telling me this, sir?"

"I just want you to . . . keep your eyes open. And your mind, too. You two are going to be looking for proof about a spy on board. I just want to make sure none of that proof winds up somewhere it doesn't belong. Like Ralgha's cabin, for example."

"So you want me to spy on Cobra? Is that it, Colonel?"

"I just want you to put that famous Rollins paranoia to work for our side for a change. If there's a spy on this ship, we have to know about it. Whether it's Hobbes, or Cobra, or somebody else entirely. Just don't make the mistake of letting Cobra steer you the wrong way." He held up his hand. "And I don't just mean because she might be a Kilrathi agent. She could believe everything she's saying, sincerely and totally. But her hate . . . it warps things. I'm counting on you to get past her bias and look at this whole mess objectively."

"I'll . . . do what I can, Colonel," Rollins said. He sounded reluctant. "But I'm not sure I'll like it."

"You think I do? Damn it, I like Cobra, despite the attitude. Despite the bigotry and the hate. Down deep, she's always struck me as somebody to admire for being tough enough to overcome everything she's been through, and for being one hell of a good flyer." He shook his head. "No, Lieutenant, I don't like this any better than you do. But it's something that has to be done."

"Aye, aye, sir," Rollins said quietly.

Flight Deck, TCS Victory
Torgo System

"Ship's company, atten-SHUN!"

Blair straightened at the crisp order from Eisen, feeling a little uncomfortable in his starched dress uniform with the archaic sword hanging at his side. The assembled crewmen were all dressed in their best, though in some cases it was a little difficult to tell. And despite Maniac's best efforts, there was no disguising the run-down appearance of *Victory* herself. He remembered his own first impression of the carrier's shabby, overused fittings, and wondered what the admiral would make of it all.

He found himself wondering when had he come to accept the carrier's faults, to think of the ship as his home?

The crewmen lined up in ranks on either side of a red carpet that was unrolled to the shuttle's door. It looked out of place on the flight deck, gleaming, new, a gaudy bauble cast into a peasant's hovel.

The door opened slowly, and Admiral Tolwyn stepped into view, pausing to survey the deck before descending the ramp. A trio of aides followed him, Kevin Tolwyn conspicuous among them, and a pair of Marine sentries brought up the rear. Geoff Tolwyn was dressed in the plain tunic of a deck officer, the only sign of his rank the cluster of stars pinned to his lapel.

Eisen stepped forward to meet him. "An honor and a privilege to have you aboard, Admiral," he said, snapping off a salute.

Tolwyn returned it. "Pleasure to be here, Captain," he said. His roving eye caught sight of Blair. "Colonel Blair, good to see you."

Blair saluted, saying nothing.

He turned back to Eisen. "This is the beginning of a momentous campaign, Captain. The end of the war is in sight at last." He gestured toward a second shuttle that was just opening up to disgorge the rest of his staff and entourage.

"Let's get to work, gentlemen," Tolwyn announced and he headed for the bridge.

Blair fell in behind the Admiral. Geoff Tolwyn had a reputation as a man who got things done . . . he hoped the man would live up to that reputation now.

• CHAPTER XXIII

Flight Wing Rec Room, TCS Victory Torgo System

"Scotch," Blair told Rostov. "Make it a double."

"Sounds like you're having a bad day, Colonel." That was Flint, coming toward the bar behind him. "Not looking forward to dinner with the Admiral?"

As he took his glass from Rostov and turned to meet her, Blair's look was sour. "Let's just say there are things I like better . . . like being out on the firing line with my missiles gone and my shield generators down."

She smiled. "Must feel like old home week, though. I mean, Maniac, and Hobbes, and now Admiral Tolwyn. And Thrakhath, for that matter. Who's next?"

For a moment he saw Angel in his mind's eye, and it must have shown in his expression. Flint's smile vanished. "Sorry . . ." she said. "That was stupid of me. I should have realized . . ."

"Never mind," Blair said, shaking his head. "It was just force of habit, I guess. I get to thinking about the people I've flown with, and she's right at the top of the list."

"I know," Flint said quietly. "It was that way with Davie, too. One minute, you're fine. The next . . . *Bamm!* The memories just won't let go."

"Yeah." He took a sip. "Look, Flint, I never took the time to thank you for what you did back there at Delius. I was just about ready to circle back and go after

271

Thrakhath. You're the one who got through to me. I won't forget it."

"You did it for me," she said. "And took a lot more risks. I was just looking out for my wingman." Flint hesitated. "Angel—Colonel Devereaux—tell me about her. She was in Covert Ops, wasn't she?"

Blair studied her through narrowed eyes. "I didn't think that was common knowledge," he said slowly. "Are you a mind-reader, or have you been cultivating some of Rollins' sources?"

She laughed. "Neither one. Just . . . a student of history. I try to make it a point to study things and people. For instance, the way I hear it, you and Admiral Tolwyn have crossed paths a time or two before."

"Bumped heads is more like it," Blair told her. "He's a good man, in his own way. I just have a little trouble dealing with his ambition. It puts lives on the line. And he's always been big on rules and regulations."

"I know the type," Flint said. "He knows the rulebook backwards and forwards . . . he just doesn't know anything about the human heart."

"Can't argue with you there, Flint," he said. His mind went back to that time aboard the *Tiger's Claw*, when the admiral made the carrier the flagship of a ramshackle squadron. He took her into action against overwhelming odds to hold off a Kilrathi fleet until Terran relief forces could arrive. At the height of the action he relieved old Captain Thorn, the ship's commanding officer, and filed charges against him for cowardice in the face of the enemy. Thorn had later been reinstated, but no one serving with the old man ever quite forgot the day.

There was a short, awkward silence before Flint spoke again. "I . . . I was serious about wanting to hear about Angel. If it would help to talk about her at all . . . well, I'm a good listener."

Blair hesitated. "I appreciate it, Flint, I really do.

But . . ." He shrugged. "Maybe another time. I'm . . . supposed to meet someone."

At that moment the door opened and Rachel Coriolis came in, greeting him with a cheerful wave. Flint looked from Rachel to Blair.

"I see. I'm sorry . . . I didn't know you moved quite that fast, Colonel." She turned and walked away before he could respond.

Admiral's Quarters, TCS Victory Torgo System

Admiral Tolwyn took over a set of interconnected compartments one deck below the bridge; one of these was converted into a dining room with a table able to seat twelve. Blair was the first to arrive, and Tolwyn greeted him with a hearty smile and a handshake.

"Ah, Colonel," he said expansively. "Let's hope that this is our last cruise together."

Blair felt a flicker of apprehension. The comment could be interpreted several different ways and he wondered if subconsciously Tolwyn was revealing an anxiety about his plan to end the war.

Tolwyn glanced around the room. Though clean and reasonably neat, there was no disguising the fading paintwork, the frayed carpets, or the general air of age and neglect that permeated the entire ship. "I never dreamed that we'd be reduced to pulling ships like this back into the front line. The Battle of Terra put us on the ropes, no matter what the government is now saying about it being a glorious victory. One more victory like that and the human race will be a forgotten footnote in the history of the universe!"

Tolwyn looked away for a moment. "When will this end," he whispered. Blair watched him closely, surprised at the clear evidence of strain.

"She's a good ship, Admiral," Blair said quietly. "And Eisen's a good captain. We haven't had much time for spit and polish lately. The Kilrathi have been keeping us busy."

"Indeed." Tolwyn looked back up, barely regaining his composure. "I've been following your operations with some interest, Colonel. You ran into our old friend Thrakhath, I hear."

"Yes, sir," Blair admitted, trying to keep his voice level. He looked away, thinking about Angel again.

"I was sorry to hear about Colonel Devereaux," Tolwyn went on, almost as if he was reading Blair's mind. "A pity, really. General Taggart made a mistake, committing her to his little project before a final decision was made."

"When did you know she was dead?" Blair demanded.

"The information couldn't be released," Tolwyn said quietly. "I'm sorry Blair, we had to keep our sources safe. It was strictly 'need-to-know' material. You understand."

"What I understand, sir, is that you and General Taggart have been competing over your damned secret projects, and Angel got caught in the middle." Blair gave Tolwyn an angry look. "And now it's our turn. *Victory*'s . . . and mine. I don't much care what happens to me any more, Admiral, but I hope you don't make these other people pay the same kind of price Angel already shelled out, just to prove that your damned gun works the way you said it would."

"Still the same old Chris Blair," Tolwyn said evenly. "Always tilting at windmills. Look, Colonel, I know you don't like my methods, but the fact is that I get things done. I first got involved with the early planning of Project Behemoth nearly ten years ago. I got pulled from my job as head of Terran Defense to bring it on-line and I'm going to see it through to the end. And God help anyone who stands in my way, even a living legend like yourself. Son, I know you don't like some of the implications behind this project, but it is kill or be killed. It's that simple."

"I'm all for ending the war, Admiral," Blair told him. "And if it means giving you the credit—and a shot at being the next Confederation President, no doubt—that's fine by me. But I won't stand by and watch you trample good people in the dirt. Captain Eisen, for instance. What are your plans for him? Are you planning on usurping command of this ship the same way you did on *Tiger's Claw*?"

"I'd be careful regarding my choice of words if I were you, Colonel," Tolwyn said. "Admirals, by definition, do not usurp command. Captain Eisen retains his post . . . but I am in overall command of this mission. Period." He turned away from Blair. "I had hoped that we would finally achieve a measure of respect for one another, after all this time, Colonel. I am the first to admit that I once misjudged you, back at the start of your career, with the *Tiger's Claw* incident. Perhaps now you are misjudging me. Still, you'll obey your orders, like a good soldier, won't you, Blair? No matter where they end up taking you."

Blair studied the slender, elegant back for a long moment in dawning understanding. "All that guff Kevin handed us about warning shots . . . We're headed to Kilrah with that thing, aren't we? No matter what . . ."

The Admiral turned back to him. "What would you aim for if you had the biggest gun in the universe? When are you going to realize, Colonel, that we're playing for keeps here? I would have thought you, if anyone, would approve . . . after what happened to Angel."

He had trouble framing a reply. There was a part of Blair that agreed with Tolwyn. After what happened to Angel, he wanted nothing more than revenge, and if that meant taking apart all of Kilrah . . .

But despite the rage inside him, Blair couldn't see

himself taking part in the destruction of an entire race.

The door buzzed before he could come up with an answer. As Tolwyn admitted Captain Eisen and Commander Gessler, *Victory's* First Officer, Blair found himself wondering if the admiral might be right after all. Perhaps all that really mattered, in the end, was winning.

He was very quiet over dinner that evening.

Captain's Ready Room, TCS Victory Torgo System

The atmosphere in the ready room was tense as Blair entered. It was strange for Eisen to be relegated to a chair at the foot of the table, while Tolwyn presided in the captain's accustomed place. The sight sent a little shiver down Blair's back, making him think of *Tiger's Claw* and Captain Thorn, all those years ago.

Commander Gessler and Colonel Ralgha were also present, as was Kevin Tolwyn and another of the admiral's aides, Commander Fairfax, representing the carrier's intelligence department. They watched the admiral expectantly as he settled into his seat and switched on the map table's holographic projector.

"Gentlemen," he said, smiling with the pride of a father displaying photos of his firstborn. "I give you the Confederation's finest achievement . . . the *Behemoth*."

The image was ugly, an ungainly, bulky, barrel-shaped monstrosity that dwarfed the Confed dreadnought shown alongside it for scale. A few dozen ships the size of *Victory* could have fit in the enormous maw at one end of the barrel. *Behemoth* might well have been the largest spacecraft ever constructed, certainly the largest ship to sail under Confederation colors.

"This device is the product of a decade of research and development by some of the finest scientific minds in the Confederation," Tolwyn continued. "It is the weapon that will bring an end to this war once and for all."

The view changed from an external shot to a computer schematic as Tolwyn continued. Taking up a laser pointer, he used its narrow light beam to highlight features as he spoke. "*Behemoth* is a series of linked superconducting energy amplification conduits, focusing an output of five hundred million gigawatts into one lancing point. A target at the end of that point is destroyed . . . utterly. And the energy released by the impact is enormous; devastating. Even the scientists can't say for sure whether the energy beam itself would destroy an entire planet, but they do agree that the resultant seismic stresses should be enough to tear it apart, particularly a world like Kilrah which is already highly unstable. The upshot, gentlemen, is this. *Behemoth* can destroy worlds, and properly employed it can knock the Kilrathi Empire out of the war in a few short strokes."

Some of the others made suitably impressed noises, but Blair remained silent. He was still thinking over his own distinctly mixed reaction to the weapon's capabilities.

"We would have liked another year or two for testing and development," Tolwyn said. "Unfortunately, circumstances have forced me to order the weapon to be deployed now." He gave Blair a long, hard stare. "We are in danger of suffering attacks similar to the biological devastation on Locanda Four, perhaps against more vital targets."

"Seems a pretty large escalation, Admiral," Blair said.

"The truth is, Colonel, that even without the biological attack, the Confederation is in trouble." Tolwyn looked around the room, speaking more softly now. "This is not for public consumption, of course. It remains classified. But the Kilrathi are winning on just about every front, and if the worst-case scenario were to come true they would be in a position to land troops on Terra herself within another six months. We have to use *Behemoth*, gentlemen. And we have to use it now."

Once that information sank in, he used the pointer again. "Because of the accelerated deployment, the ship's defensive systems are . . . somewhat incomplete. There are a few, shall we say . . . soft spots . . . located here . . . and here . . . where the shields are thin and there's been no time to complete keel mounts or add extra shield generators or defensive laser turrets."

"Those soft spots could spell real trouble, Admiral," Blair commented. "Looks like a couple of well-placed shots could take that monster out."

Tolwyn gave him a stern look. "That is why your flight wing is being assigned the job of protecting *Behemoth*, Colonel," he said. "I expect you to be especially aware of the vulnerable points. Make sure your people know what must be protected, under any circumstances. Make no mistake, Colonel, gentlemen. This weapon is our last hope. Nothing must be permitted to get through to threaten it."

"Protecting the weapon will be a large task, Admiral," Hobbes said slowly. "It makes a . . . very big target."

"Hmmph." Tolwyn looked at Ralgha for a moment, as if trying to decide if he was being sarcastic. "Colonel, full data on the defense of *Behemoth* will be made available to your people for analysis. Major Tolwyn will also assist you in programming a series of simulations so that they can practice before we begin the actual deployment."

"Sir, the wing's pretty short-handed. What's the chance of getting some new blood to bring us up to strength?"

"We're damned short-handed as it is, Blair," the admiral told him. "Two carriers just passed through last week and pretty well cleaned out Torgo's replacement pilot pool. However, I did arrange to rotate your bomber squadron off the ship and replace them with a second point-defense squadron. *Victory* won't be called upon to perform offensive operations this time out, and the additional Hellcats will be used to cover the *Behemoth*."

Blair frowned. Something told him that behind Tolwyn's smooth explanation there were other problems he wasn't willing to discuss. The admiral had more than his share of political enemies within the High Command, and it was likely that he'd found it necessary to tread on a lot of toes to get his Behemoth project approved. Not everyone would share his belief that this overgrown cannon could bring the war to an end, and Blair could see stubborn rivals of Tolwyn's digging in their heels and refusing to give him all of the ships and men he wanted. Very likely he snagged *Victory* because she was widely perceived as the fleet's poor relation.

That raised other questions about the whole affair. Tolwyn was convinced he was on the winning track with *Behemoth*, but what was the High Command really planning, at this juncture? If they didn't agree with Tolwyn's threat assessments, they might be looking for the admiral to fall on his face.

"Now . . . as to operational planning. *Behemoth* is undergoing final power-up tests this afternoon. By eighteen hundred hours standard tomorrow evening, we will leave the Torgo Proving Area and proceed in company with the weapons platform to the Blackmane jump point." He looked at Eisen. "It's plain from your reports that Ariel is a totally unsuitable test site for the weapon. Luckily, Captain Moran and the *Hermes* turned up a much more likely target: Loki Six. There is a jump point to the system from Blackmane, so we will pass directly between jump points in the Blackmane System and then transit to Loki."

Fairfax cleared his throat. "I've reviewed the data downloaded from HQ on the *Hermes* survey mission. Loki Six is a fairly minor Kilrathi outpost. Not likely to be heavily defended. In fact, it's only apparent purpose is to serve as a sort of advanced base for raiders passing through the Ariel System." He looked doubtful. "I'm not sure what kind of a message we'll send the Kilrathi by destroying the outpost. A larger facility would have been better. The Empire may not take the hint if all they lose is a second-rate base."

Tolwyn gave him a stern look. "If Loki doesn't give them the right message, we'll give them something bigger to think about." He shot Blair a glance. "We have to take this one step at a time, gentlemen. But one way or another, *Behemoth* is going to end this war."

On the map table, the schematics of the weapons platform were replaced by a chart of the Loki System. "We will proceed from the jump point to here . . . Loki Eight, a gas giant. *Behemoth* will require fuel, which we can skim from the gas giant's atmosphere. Then we will move to this position, near Loki Six, and begin the firing sequence. Throughout the operation, gentlemen, we will be accompanied by a small escort squadron, three destroyers. They will be used for advanced scouting, and as general support vessels. But *Victory* and her fighters will have the primary responsibility of providing close support to *Behemoth*. I want you to be clear on this. The mission stands or falls on this ship's ability to protect that weapon." Tolwyn's look was challenging. "Any questions?"

There were none, and Tolwyn turned his intense gaze on Hobbes. "Colonel Ralgha, I would like you to work with Commander Fairfax and my staff over the next several days. You're the closest thing we have to a genuine expert on the Kilrathi mind. I'd like you to help us develop some likely models of how the Empire will react. To the destruction of Loki Six, and to other measures we may be forced to take if that doesn't bring them to the peace table."

Hobbes inclined his head. "As you wish, Admiral," he rumbled. "I warn you, though, that I cannot predict the reactions of my . . . former comrades . . . with any degree of certainty. Anything I suggest will necessarily be . . . imperfect at best."

"It will do, Colonel. It will do." Tolwyn glanced around the room again, then nodded crisply. "Very well. That's an overview of the situation. You'll each be receiving detailed orders as needed. In the meantime, you're dismissed."

Blair took a last look at Tolwyn before he left. The admiral was studying the map of the Loki System intently, the expression on his face one of anticipation and undisguised eagerness. He wasn't sure he cared for the look in the man's eyes. It promised victory or death with no middle ground, and no room to adapt to circumstances.

Flight Control, TCS Victory
Torgo System

"Okay," Blair said into the microphone. "That's it. End simulation."

Kevin Tolwyn looked at him from the adjacent console. "Not bad. Not bad at all. Your boys and girls are pretty damned good, Colonel."

"It could've been better," Blair grumbled. He switched on the mike again. "Cobra, Vagabond, if that had been the real thing there would have been a fifty-fifty chance of that Vaktoth slipping past you and getting off a shot at the *Behemoth*. You were lucky the computer called it the way it did, but you're going to have to tighten up next time, okay? The defensive specs are in the tactical

database. Study them. We can't afford to leave those
weak spots uncovered."

"You want us to run through it again?" Vagabond asked.

"Not now," Blair told him. "We'll run another set
tomorrow morning, after the new point-defense squadron
is on board. For now, get some rest. And study that
database. Now . . . dismissed."

"You're starting to sound like my uncle," Tolwyn said
with a grin. "Don't tell me you've become a convert."

"Hardly. Matter of fact, I have a feeling you've been
holding out on me, Kevin. The admiral as much as
admitted he's planning to take that monstrosity to Kilrah,
one way or another. I don't think he'd stop if the Emperor
himself offered to sign peace terms . . . with Thrakhath's
blood for the ink!"

Tolwyn shrugged. "I told you everything I know,
Maverick. But you know the admiral. He wouldn't tell
his left hand what his right hand was doing if he thought
it would get him a tactical advantage."

"Yeah . . ." Blair trailed off. He looked hard into
Tolwyn's eyes. "What do you think, Kevin? Really? Should
we blow Kilrah while we have the chance?"

"I don't know, Maverick, and that's a fact." Tolwyn
looked down. "After what you said the last time, I started
doubting the whole project. At the Academy they taught
us we were serving a higher purpose, and a weapon this
devastating . . . But what if the Intell reports are right?
What if we're on the verge of losing everything? If it's
us or them . . ." He met Blair's eyes again. "Don't tell
me you've changed your mind."

Blair shook his head. "Not . . . changed. But nothing's
as clear as it was before. Angel died out there, and
Thrakhath's the one who killed her. In front of a damned
screaming audience of . . . barbarians. Part of me would
like to wipe them all out, Kevin. But another part of
me says it's wrong." He paused. "I'm glad it's the admiral

who has to pull the trigger on that thing. I'm not sure I could do that. And if I did, I would never know if I did it to save the Confederation, or to even the score over Angel."

Tolwyn nodded slowly. "Yeah. And could you live with yourself afterward, whichever course you took?"

• CHAPTER XXIV

Communication Center, TCS Victory Torgo System

The intruder entered the compartment silently, moving with complete confidence among the consoles and computer banks in the darkened room. Seen through a bulky night vision device, the room glowed with an eerie greenish light. Normally, no one stood a watch in the Communications Center except when the ship was at General Quarters, and the intruder was confident that no one would notice this stealthy foray.

Gauntleted hands fumbled for a moment with the controls on one of the consoles. The panel came to life. On a monitor screen, bright letters glowed as the computer responded to the intruder's commands.

ENTER IDENTIFICATION AND SECURITY CODES.

The intruder tapped the keypad awkwardly. Voice command would have been easier under the circumstances, but it was more difficult to cover one's tracks afterward with a voice record . . .

IDENTITY AND SECURITY CODE ACCEPTED. PLEASE INDICATE DESIRED FUNCTION.

It took a moment to identify the proper selection and key it in. Another console came to life across the room.

TIGHT-BEAM LASER LINK ON-LINE. INPUT LINK COORDINATES.

Consulting a personal data pad for the required information, the intruder entered a short alphanumeric string through the keyboard. A green light glowed beside the monitor as the computer's reply appeared.

COORDINATES ACCEPTED. READY TO TRANSMIT.

The intruder slid a tiny cartridge into the chip receptacle below the monitor, then keyed in another command. The computer responded.

DATA ON-LINE. TRANSMITTING AT 100:1.

The monitor showed a dizzying succession of images, external views and schematics of the *Behemoth* platform. Seconds later, a new message flashed on the screen.

TRANSMISSION COMPLETED. FURTHER INSTRUCTIONS?

The intruder paused a moment, then entered another command. Once again the computer was quick to flash an answering message on the monitor.

WIPING . . . TRANSMISSION RECORDS PURGED.

The screen went blank, and the intruder powered down the console and collected the PDP and the data cartridge, tucking them into a pocket. One last quick sweep using the light intensification headset, and the job was done.

Within moments there was nothing in the compartment to suggest that the intruder had ever been present.

Bridge, KIS Sar'hrai
Torgo System

"Message coming in, my Lord. From the Watcher."

Khantahr Tarros *nar* Poghath turned in his chair to face the communications officer. "On my screen," he ordered.

His monitor lit up with a series of images, transmitted at high speed from the stealth fighter that had penetrated the Terran defenses around Torgo. Tarros watched the fast-changing views thoughtfully. It seemed that Prince Thrakhath's plan was unfolding perfectly. The Kilrathi spy in the Terran fleet had completed the mission and was transmitting the information the Prince required to the waiting fighter, and now the data was being relayed to *Sar'hrai*. Soon the carrier would be on its way to rejoin Thrakhath, and the next phase of the operation could begin.

The transmission ended with charts detailing a star system and the operational plans for a Confederation incursion. Tarros leaned forward in his seat. "Navigator, plot a course to the jump point. Communications Officer, when the Watcher communicates with us again instruct the Watcher to rendezvous with us there. Pilot Officer, best speed." He allowed himself to relax again.

They had done their duty. Prince Thrakhath would reward them well, once the Terrans had fallen into his trap.

Flight Wing Rec Room, TCS Victory Blackmane System

The view from the rec room was impressive; Blair had to admit that much. As he walked in, his eyes were drawn to the massive shape of the *Behemoth* keeping pace with the carrier as they cruised slowly through the Blackmane System. Since leaving orbit around Torgo, their pace had been slow—apparently the weapons platform didn't carry its full allotment of engines, either—but they had made the transit to Blackmane and were on their way to the next jump point, and Loki VI.

He found himself wishing they could make better time. Limping along at this snail's pace only gave them all time to think, too much time. There was a restlessness in the air, a feeling of mingled excitement and tension. It wasn't long before the rumor mill started churning out details about the new Confederation weapon, and for many on board the *Victory* the war was already as good as over.

Vaquero looked up from a table by the door as Blair

stood there and watched the monster shape outside the viewport. "Want to buy a ticket, sir?"

"To what?" Blair looked down at the man's smiling face. He, at least, seemed pleased.

"Opening night party at my cantina," Lopez told him, grinning more broadly. "Once we pull the trigger on that *Behemoth* thing, it'll be *hasta la vista a los gatos*. And I figure on filing for retirement pay about two minutes after that. I've got enough to make the down payment on a nice little place . . ."

"Don't start calculating your profit margins just yet, Lieutenant," Blair said quietly. "Even that monster might not be enough to shut the Kilrathi down overnight."

He turned away, leaving Vaquero to frown over the words. Blair spotted Rollins and Cobra sitting together in a remote corner, well away from the rest of the crowd. He crossed the floor to join them.

"So . . . how's the espionage business today?" he asked flippantly. "Run any Kilrathi agents to ground yet?"

Cobra gave him an unpleasant look. "I know you don't take us seriously, Colonel."

"No, Lieutenant, you're wrong. I take you both very seriously. But you've been on this for . . . how long's it been? Over a week, now, isn't it? I'm just not sure there's anything there for you to find."

Rollins looked up at him. "Don't be so sure, Colonel," he said. "Two nights back, after we broke orbit, there was a two-minute dead space on one of my computer commo logs. And I can't account for it. I think it was sabotage."

"It could also have been a computer glitch," Blair pointed out. "You might have noticed that the systems on this ship are not exactly up to snuff." He paused. "Or, if it wasn't the computer, it might have been something to do with the admiral. He might've ordered a message sent, then had the record wiped."

"Nobody said anything about a transmission . . ."

"Nor would they, Lieutenant, if Admiral Tolwyn told them to keep quiet. You've said it yourself, Lieutenant. The brass don't tell us everything. And the admiral's always been particularly good at playing his hand close to his chest." Blair shrugged. "A little paranoia can be a good thing, but make sure you've discounted the other possibilities before you see sabotage every time the computer hiccups or the admiral decides to keep his laundry list classified."

"Yeah, maybe so," Rollins said. "But I've also been analyzing that original transmission. Some of the harmonics in the message are pretty wild, Colonel." He produced a personal data pad and called up a file on the screen. "Look at this . . . and this."

"I'm no expert in signals analysis, Lieutenant," Blair said. "To me, you've got a bunch of spikes on a graph. You want to tell me what they mean?"

"I'm not sure yet," Rollins admitted. "But I've seen these kinds of signals somewhere before . . . something outside of normal communications use. If I could just figure out where . . ." He trailed off, looking apologetic. "Sorry, Colonel. I guess I still have a ways to go before I can deliver. But it isn't for want of trying, or for a lack of things to look into, either."

Blair looked again at the *Behemoth*, framed in the viewport. "I have to admit, if there was a spy around, he'd surely be interested in that thing. But I'd figure the admiral's staff would be the place to plant an agent."

"Hobbes is working with the staff," Cobra said quietly. "Or hadn't you noticed?"

Rollins stood up, looking uncomfortable. "I've got to be on watch in a little while. I'll catch you both later." He moved away quickly. Blair sat in the chair he'd vacated.

"It never stops with you, does it, Lieutenant?" he asked. "An endless program loop."

"You'd never understand, Colonel," she said, looking weary. "You just don't have a clue."

"Maybe that's because you've never tried to explain it," he said bluntly. "Blind hatred isn't very pretty, or persuasive, either."

"It's the way I'm wired," she said. There was a long silence before she spoke again. "I'm sure you've heard the rumors. Some guys from the *Hermes* spread a lot of stories around. I used to have these . . . nightmares. People talked, you know how it is."

"Rumors don't always tell the whole story," Blair said.

"The stuff I heard was . . . pretty accurate, I guess. Look, they took me when I was ten . . ."

"The Kilrathi?"

She nodded. "I ended up in a slave labor camp. Escaped during a Confed attack ten years later. Most of the camp was destroyed in the fighting. Might have been the Navy's fault, might have been the cats, I don't know. But there were only a few of us who lived through it."

"It must have been—"

"You'll never have any idea of what it 'must have been' like, Colonel. I saw things . . ." She trailed off, shuddering. Her eyes were empty.

"So the Navy pulled you out of there . . . and you signed up?"

"The Psych guys spent a couple of years wringing me out," she said. "First it was debriefing . . . you know, regression therapy, trying to find out everything I'd seen and heard in case there was something worthwhile for Intelligence. Then they started on the therapy." She paused. "But they couldn't wipe it all out, not without giving me a personality overlay. And I wouldn't let them do that. I'm Laurel Buckley, by God, and if the cats couldn't take that away I'm damned if my own kind will!"

"You must have been damned tough, Lieutenant, after something like that . . . to go on to join the fight . . ."

"It was all I ever wanted, Colonel. A chance to kill cats. And that's what I'm still doing today."

He gestured toward the *Behemoth*. "And if that thing puts an end to the war? What then?"

She shrugged. "I don't know. Hating cats is the only way I know to keep myself human." She gave a short, grotesque laugh, an unnerving sound that reminded Blair of jeering Kilrathi. "The fact is, Colonel, there's a little bit of the Kilrathi prowling around inside my skull and I can't get it out. Every day, I can feel it getting a little bit stronger . . . and one day, there won't be any human left inside me any more."

He didn't answer right away. "I think you aren't giving yourself enough credit, Lieutenant. You survived a horror most people could never handle. You'll outlive this, too. I'm sure of it."

Her look was bleak. "I hope you're right, Colonel. I really do. But . . . well, maybe you don't understand it, but I can't let go of the hate."

He thought of Angel, of the raw emotion that had surged through him when Thrakhath's taunts were ringing in his ears. "Maybe I do understand, Cobra. Maybe, in your place, I would have cracked up long ago."

She raised an eyebrow. "Cracked? You? I can't imagine you giving anybody the satisfaction of seeing you crack."

Blair didn't tell her that she was wrong.

Flight Deck, TCS Victory *Blackmane System*

"COUNTDOWN TO JUMP, ONE HOUR, FIFTEEN MINUTES."

Blair glanced up at the digital readout below the Flight Control Room window to confirm the time remaining. Activity was reaching a fever pitch aboard the carrier as they approached the jump point taking them to the Loki System. No one really expected the Kilrathi to have much in the way of defenses at their Loki outpost, but the preparations in hand assumed they would be jumping into a combat zone. With so much riding on the *Behemoth*, nobody wanted to make any mistakes.

Technicians prepped the fighters for launch, working quickly but with a care born of long experience and a respect for the dangers of the flight deck. Red-shirted ordinance handlers busily fit missiles and checked fire-control circuits while engineering techs dressed in blue supervised the topping of fuel tanks. Thrusters were put through their final checks. The huge hangar area was one large scene of frantic activity, and Blair felt like an outsider as he watched the crews go about their jobs.

Rachel Coriolis appeared from behind the tail section of a Hellcat. Her coverall was considerably cleaner than usual . . . and so were her hands and arms. She looked, in fact, almost regulation, a far cry from her usual go-to-blazes sloppiness. Blair smiled at the sight, earning himself an angry glare.

"Don't say a thing," she growled. "Unless you want a number-three sonic probe up your nose."

"Heard you got chewed out by the admiral himself," Blair said. "But I never thought it would actually take."

"Sloppy dress means sloppy work," she said, mimicking Tolwyn's crisp British accent flawlessly. "Well, excuse me, but I don't have time to change my uniform every time I swap out a part, you know?"

Blair shrugged. "He's got a real thing for the regs. But you should wear the reprimand as a badge of honor. I figure it's a wasted week if I don't get at least one chewing-out and a couple of black scowls from him, myself."

"After the war, I'm going to make it my personal mission in life to loosen the screws on all the moving parts on guys like him." She was smiling, but Blair heard the edge in her tone.

"Save a screwdriver for me, okay?" Blair said. "Meanwhile, what's the word on the launch?"

"Pretty good, this time out," she said. "Only three down-checks." Rachel hesitated. "I'm afraid one of them's Hobbes, skipper."

"What's the problem?"

"Power surge fried half his electronics when we went to check his computer. It's about a fifteen hour repair job."

Blair frowned. "Damn, bad timing. But I guess his bird was about due. What about the others?"

"Reese and Calder. One interceptor, one Hellcat. There's an outside chance we can get the Arrow up and running by H-hour, but I wouldn't count on it."

"Do what you can," Blair told her.

"Don't I always?" she said with a grin. As he started to turn away, she caught his sleeve. "Look . . . after the mission . . . what say we get together?"

He looked into her eyes, read the emotion behind them. Everyone who served on the flight deck knew that each mission might be the last one. "I'd . . . like that, Rachel," he said slowly, feeling awkward. "Ever since . . . ever since I found out about Angel, I've felt like you were there for me. It's . . . made a big difference."

Someone called for her, and Rachel turned back to her work without another word. Blair watched her hurrying away. She wasn't anything like Angel Devereaux, but there was a feeling between them that was just as strong, in its own way, as the one he'd shared with Angel. Less passionate, less intense, yet it was a more comfortable and familiar feeling, exactly what he needed to balance the turmoil around and within him.

Bridge, TCS Victory
Blackmane System

"*Coventry* has jumped, sir. *Sheffield* is next up."

Eisen acknowledged the Sensor Officer's report with a curt nod and studied the tactical display with a critical eye. This was the period of greatest danger in any squadron operation, when ships performed their transits in succession and everyone involved hoped and prayed they wouldn't be emerging in the middle of an enemy fleet.

They weren't taking any chances this time. *Coventry* would go through first, ready to engage anything waiting near the other end of the jump point. The destroyer that followed her would jump at the first sign of trouble, to warn off the rest of the Terran force.

That would be tough on *Coventry*. Eisen wondered how Jason Bondarevsky felt about flying point on this mission. He was supposed to be one of Admiral Tolwyn's shining young proteges, but apparently the admiral's patronage didn't extend to protecting a favorite from a dangerous mission.

Eisen glanced uneasily at the admiral. He was dressed to perfection, uniform starched and crisp, every hair in place. But Tolwyn did look nervous, pacing restlessly back and forth behind the Sensor Officer's station. For all the man's air of confidence, it was clear that he had his share of worries.

"*Sheffield* has powered up her jump coils," the Sensor Officer reported. "Jump field forming . . . there she goes!"

Tolwyn glanced at the watch implanted in his wrist. "Start the final countdown, Captain," he ordered.

For an instant, Eisen wanted to bristle. Ever since the admiral came on board he'd interfered in routine ship's operations: barking orders, taking over briefings, dressing down crew members who didn't live up to his image of the ideal Terran warrior. Tolwyn seemed to need to control everything and everyone around him, as if his personal intervention was the only thing that could guarantee the success of the mission.

But perhaps Tolwyn had good reason to be concerned. Eisen leaned forward in his chair and repeated the

Admiral's order. Commander Gessler slapped the switch that started the automated jump sequence.

"NOW, JUMP STATIONS, JUMP STATIONS," the computer announced. "FIVE MINUTES TO JUMP SEQUENCE START."

The seconds ticked away, with no sign of *Sheffield* turning back to warn them away from the jump. Eisen began to relax a little. Maybe this operation would go by the numbers after all. . . .

"Remember, Captain, *Behemoth* will be five minutes behind us all the way," Tolwyn said. "I expect response times to be tight. We can't afford a screw-up. Not now."

"Yes, Admiral," Eisen said. They'd been over it all a dozen times before. He decided Tolwyn was talking just to distract himself from thinking about the ticking clock. In a few more minutes, they'd be committed.

And nothing would ever be the same again.

Flight Deck, TCS Victory
Loki System

"And five . . . and four . . . three . . . two . . . one . . ."
Jumpshock!

Blair's guts twisted and churned as the carrier went through transition. No matter how often he experienced it, he could never get used to the sensation. The physical nausea passed quickly enough, but there was always the disorientation, the essential feeling of wrongness that left him confused, numb.

He blinked and shook his head, trying to get his bearings. Everyone in the wing had gone through this transit strapped into their cockpits, a standard precaution when jumping into hostile space. They had the flight deck to themselves. Force fields and gravity generators sometimes faltered during jump, and technicians stayed clear of the flight deck for fear of a catastrophic failure. So the pilots were alone, lined up at their launch tubes, as ready for action as anyone could be in the aftermath of jumpshock.

Blair's eyes came back into focus, and he checked his readouts and control settings automatically.

A voice crackled in his headphones. "Jump complete," Eisen said. "Welcome to Loki System."

There was a pause before Rollins took over. "According to sensors, the area is clear," the communications officer announced, still sounding a little groggy. "And *Coventry* says the same. Sorry to disappoint you, ladies and gents, but it looks like an all clear."

Blair let out a long sigh, not sure if he was disappointed or relieved. They had cleared the first hurdle, but they weren't finished yet, not by a long shot.

The admiral's voice came over the channel, clipped and precise. "Colonel Blair, you will relieve yourself from launch stations immediately. All flight wing personnel remain on alert status until further notice."

He still disagreed with the admiral's decision to suspend all flight ops from the carrier until they had to deploy to protect the *Behemoth*. *Coventry's* four fighters and the destroyers flying escort would give adequate cover, but Blair didn't like keeping all of his people on standby alert for hours on end without relief. Better to let them fly patrols, get some down-time, and take the risk that the wing might be a few hands short when things hit the fan. But Tolwyn had overruled him.

He started to unstrap himself from the Thunderbolt's cockpit. If all went well, Blair thought hopefully, this interlude would soon end. And then . . . ?

It was difficult to picture what peace would be like, after a lifetime dedicated to the war.

• CHAPTER XXV

Bridge, TCS Victory
Loki System

"God, that sucker sure is thirsty," Rollins commented. "Good thing you don't have to pay for a fill-up when you're skimming hydrogen."

"Eyes on your board, Lieutenant," Eisen growled. "And put the mouth in neutral."

"Yes, sir," Rollins replied quickly. The edge in Eisen's voice made it clear that the captain was dead serious.

The Terran squadron had proceeded from the jump point to their first destination, the gas giant Loki VIII, without encountering any sign of Imperial resistance. *Victory* remained close by while the *Behemoth* moved into a tight, hyperbolic orbit around the huge ball of gas. The cruiser and her consorts stood further off to give warning of any enemy interference, but there was nothing. The weapons platform dipped into the atmosphere long enough to top off the depleted tanks of liquid hydrogen needed as reaction mass to move her ponderous bulk toward the target world.

"Sensors are still reading clear, sir," the Sensor Officer reported. "Looks like we're home free."

A red light flashed on the Communications board, and Rollins called up a computer analysis of the stray signal locking onto his computer. "Captain . . ." he began, hesitating a moment. "Sir, I've got some kind of low-band transmission here. Seems to be coming from one of the gas giant's moons."

"What do you make of it, Mister Rollins?" Admiral Tolwyn cut in before Eisen could respond.

"I'm not sure, sir . . . uh, Admiral. I don't think it's a ship. More like an automated feed . . . from an unmanned relay station or sensor buoy. But powerful. A very strong signal . . ."

"Any idea what it's saying?" Tolwyn asked.

"No, Admiral. It's scrambled. Could be almost anything." Rollins looked up at him, apologetic, but Tolwyn had already turned away.

"Colonel Ralgha? What do you think?"

Hobbes had been scratched from the fighter roster with a down-gripe on his Thunderbolt, so Tolwyn decided he should join other members of the admiral's staff at supernumerary positions on the bridge. The Kilrathi renegade shook his head, a curiously human gesture.

"I am sorry, Admiral. I do not know."

"Well, I do," Tolwyn said. "It means we've been noticed. And the cats will be organizing a welcoming committee for us."

"Any orders, Admiral?" Eisen asked. Rollins had never heard him sound quite so stiff and formal.

"The squadron will continue as before," Tolwyn ordered. "Have *Behemoth* secured from fueling stations and fall into formation. *Coventry* to take station ahead." He paused, almost seeming to strike a heroic pose. "Maintain your vigilance, gentlemen. And be ready for anything."

Audience Hall, KIS Hvar'kann Loki System

"Lord Prince," Melek said, approaching the dais and bowing deeply. "We have a report from one of the sentinel stations near the eighth planet. Terran ships have been detected. Their movements conform to a wilderness refueling operation, and one of the vessels appears to be their *Behemoth* weapon."

Thrakhath leaned forward on his throne, his eyes gleaming in the harsh red light. "Ah . . . so it begins." He showed his fangs. "You see, Melek, how well our agent has performed? Not only the design specifications of the weapons platform, but also the intended Terran movements. Refuel at planet eight, then a crossing to six. Exactly as specified in the report from *Sar'hrai*."

"Yes, Lord Prince," Melek agreed. Behind his mask, he allowed himself a moment's impatience. As the plan unfolded, the Prince was becoming increasingly filled with a sense of his own self-importance. The arrogance of the Imperial Family was one of the major sources of disaffection among the great nobles of the realm, and Melek was finding it difficult to maintain his pose of sycophancy as Thrakhath's posturing grew more blatant. "It seems we will indeed have a battle here, and soon."

Thrakhath's gesture called for silence. "The strength of the Terran force?" he asked.

"Five capital ships, Lord Prince," Melek replied. "Plus the weapons platform itself. Only one carrier . . . *Victory*. The others—a cruiser, and three destroyers. Nothing to challenge our force significantly."

"Excellent. They assumed the outpost here was not worth a larger squadron." Thrakhath paused. "How are our preparations proceeding?"

"Nearly completed, Lord Prince. The Terrans will find their planned firing position difficult to reach. Our own forces will be deployed by the time they realize the threat." Melek paused. "There is still time, Lord Prince, to order more capital ships into the battle zone, to ensure the Terrans are destroyed."

The Prince gestured denial. "No, Melek. Fighters will

have the best chance to penetrate the defenses of the weapons platform. We do not want to scare the enemy away with too great a . . . detectable show of strength. Even if some of their ships escape, we will have the *Behemoth*. And with it . . . the war."

"As you wish, Lord Prince." Melek bowed and retreated, but a part of him wished he could see Thrakhath lose some of that arrogant assurance. Perhaps then the prince would finally come to understand the true nature of the dangerous game he played with the future of the Empire.

Gold Squadron Ready Room, TCS Victory Loki System

It took hours to cross interplanetary distances, and the flight wing settled into a grim routine of waiting, with two squadrons on watch in their ready rooms and the other two snatching downtime while they could. There were only six of them in the Gold Squadron ready room, with Hobbes on the admiral's personal staff, but it seemed unpleasantly cramped after nearly four hours of boredom waiting for an alarm that never came. No one wanted to take up Vagabond's challenge at cards any more, and talk lagged. Most of them sat quietly, enveloped in their own thoughts.

Blair wasn't sure how much longer his staff could wait.

"Man, I'd almost rather the cats would try to stop us," Maniac Marshall said suddenly. "Anything would beat sitting here on our asses with nothing to do."

"Hey, get used to it," Vaquero told him. "If that *Behemoth* thing works, and we get peace, then we're history. No more magnum launches, no more long patrols . . ."

"I'll believe it when I see it," Cobra said. "I figure we'll still have to keep the fleet ready, peace treaty or no. You can't trust the cats to keep to any treaty. Just look at what they did the last time we signed an armistice with them!"

At that moment an alarm siren cut off all talk. "LAUNCH STATIONS, LAUNCH STATIONS," the computer announced. "ALL FIGHTERS UP. MAGNUM LAUNCH."

The Gold Squadron pilots scrambled to their feet, snatching up helmets and gauntlets and heading for the door.

"Thanks a lot, Maniac," Blair said as the two nearly collided at the door. "Looks like you're getting your wish."

Marshall grinned, a wolfish, uncanny smile similar to Paladin's. "What's the matter, Colonel, sir? You'd rather sit here and collect dust than get out on the firing line again?"

He ignored the comment and followed the others down the corridor to the entrance to the hangar area. Just inside he stopped at an intercom station and punched for the bridge. "This is Blair," he said as Rollins appeared on the screen. "What's the scoop, Radio?"

Rollins looked flustered. "Wait one minute, Colonel," he said.

A moment later Admiral Tolwyn's face filled the monitor. "*Coventry*'s hit a mine," the admiral said. "She's falling behind, with heavy damage to her shield generators. Looks like a Kilrathi mine field right across our planned course, and I don't like it one little bit. So I'm putting your boys and girls out there until we see what else the cats might have waiting for us."

"So we don't have anything definite yet . . . except the mines?" Blair wasn't sure if he was relieved or concerned. If this was just a false alarm, it would sap the wing's morale even more. But the *Hermes* survey hadn't reported any mine fields on the approaches to Loki VI. Blair didn't like any coincidence this suspicious. Not here, not now.

"Finding a bunch of mines this close to the planned firing point . . . I don't like it, not one bit." Tolwyn's words echoed Blair's uneasiness. "Your job is simple, Colonel. Cover the *Behemoth* until it's ready to open fire."

"Sounds simple enough, Admiral," Blair replied. "But sometimes the simple jobs are the real killers."

Tolwyn broke the circuit. Blair retrieved his flight gear and turned back to the bustle in the hangar deck. Four of the Thunderbolts were already rolling into place in front of their launch tubes, while four Arrows from Denise Mbuto's squadron were in place on the opposite side. By the time the two ready squadrons launched, preparations were well in hand for the other two: the point-defense fighters. By then their pilots, roused from much-needed rest, would be ready to fly.

Rachel Coriolis hurried to him. "Better get saddled up, Colonel, or you'll miss the party," she said.

He smiled. "They can't do that. Didn't you hear? I'm the Heart of the Tiger. Can't have a party without the Heart of the Tiger, you know."

Her look was serious. "Take care of yourself out there," she said quietly. "I wouldn't like it if . . . someone else I cared about didn't come back."

"I'll be back. Now that I know I have something worth coming back to, they won't get to me again." He turned away and hurried toward his fighter, drawing on his helmet and gauntlets as he strode briskly across the broad metal deck.

Stalker Leader
Loki System

Flight Captain Graldak *nar* Sutaghi studied his sensor screens and wished his pressure gauntlets had room for him to unsheathe his claws in anticipation. The Terrans had discovered the mine field and were beginning to deploy their fighters. It was unfolding just as Prince Thrakhath outlined. With the mines across their intended course occupying all their attention for a critical few minutes, there was a perfect opening for stealth fighters lying in wait to launch a devastating attack.

The huge blip on his screen had to be the weapons platform, the primary target. It had come to a dead stop while the carrier edged closer to the mine field and began to launch its fighters. For the moment, at least, the *Behemoth* was actually closer to the waiting Kilrathi ships than the enemy carrier.

Now was the time to strike.

"Stalker Flight, this is Leader," he said aloud. "Stand by to disengage cloaks and attack on my mark. Three . . . two . . . one . . . mark! Attack! Attack! Attack!" As he spoke, he cut the power to the Strakha's stealth device and brought his shield and weapons power on-line. He rammed his throttles full forward and felt the fighter surge, a predator eager to seek out the prey.

"All fighters, concentrate attack on the weapons platform," Graldak ordered. "Remember the briefings . . . attack the weak points."

"And the enemy fighters?" someone asked.

"Do not let them interfere with you," Graldak said. "But do not be drawn into a dogfight until the primary mission is achieved." Inside his bulky flight helmet, he was showing his fangs. Graldak was eager to get the first phase finalized so his squadron could engage the Terran fighters. In the fighting at Locanda, it had been galling to avoid combat and run under cloaks. This time they would show the apes how warriors fought.

And today there were no limits on engagement, no fighters declared off-limits to attack. Any enemy pilot who wanted to fight, even the Heart of the Tiger or the Kilrathi renegade, was fair prey to the hunters today.

The Kilrathi attack group, four squadrons strong, drove straight toward the daunting bulk of the enemy planetkiller. Graldak's blood sang within his veins.

Thunderbolt 300
Loki System

"Targets! Targets! Targets!"

Blair's eyes shifted instinctively to his sensor screen as Rollins chanted the warning. Suddenly the monitor was crawling with the red-orange dots representing enemy fighters, four distinct swarms of Kilrathi craft arranged in a rough half-globe. But they were close, too close . . . well inside the range of Terran sensors. And on the far side of the *Behemoth* from *Victory*.

Cloaked Strakha, then. They had lain in wait while the Terran squadron passed by, striking only now when the mine field cut off their advance and the *Behemoth* was momentarily uncovered and vulnerable.

The Kilrathi must have known the significance of the weapon and the Terran plan of attack. It was blatantly clear that all the talk about a possible spy giving away secrets to the Empire was more than just speculation.

Blair pushed the thought aside. Time enough to worry about that later. Right now, the Kilrathi were closing fast with the *Behemoth*.

"Red and White Squadrons!" he snapped. "Double back and engage the enemy as quickly as possible." That would send the point defense ships into action directly, but it wouldn't provide much cover to the weapons platform itself. "Blue Squadron, Gold Squadron, follow me!"

He banked sharply, lining up on the *Behemoth*'s looming mass and opening up his throttles to full power. With afterburners blazing, Blair dove straight toward the huge weapon. The others trailed him, only thirteen fighters in all. A part of Blair's mind dwelt idly on the question of whether or not the number of ships was significant. An ill omen, perhaps?

"Skipper . . ." Denise Mbuto roused him from his reverie. *"Don't you think . . . ?"*

"Comm silence!" he snapped. "Follow my lead, damn it!"

And still they dove, until the weapons platform filled the entire forward cockpit view and he could make out individual structures and projections on the hull of the gigantic device. As they swept down toward the metal surface, Blair suddenly pulled up, skimming within fifty meters of the *Behemoth*. He had a maniacal grin on his face as he pictured the reactions in the other fighters behind him.

"*Whooeee! What a ride!*" Marshall shouted, and Blair didn't reprimand him for breaking communications silence. The man's reaction was something he could understand perfectly. He wanted to shout out loud himself.

Instead he forced himself to think about the battle as a whole. "Watchdog, Watchdog, this is Guardian Leader," he said on the command channel. "Come in, Watchdog."

Again it was Tolwyn, and not Rollins, who answered his call. "*Damn it, Blair, get in there!*" he snapped. "*You have to protect the* Behemoth*!*"

"We're on it, Admiral," Blair replied. "But some support from the destroyers would be a good idea. *Coventry*, too, if she's able."

"*Negative on that,*" Tolwyn replied. "*We've just spotted a flotilla of Kilrathi cap ships closing on us. They're at extreme range but coming in fast.* Sheffield *is moving to delay them. And* Ajax *is trying to clear a route through the mine field.*"

"She'll never make it," Blair said. "You know the odds against spotting every mine when you're in something as big as a destroyer."

"*Coventry's launching her fighters, but she's in bad shape. And Bondarevsky's been wounded . . .*" The Admiral was struggling to maintain control. He stopped, visibly gathering his composure before he spoke again. *"Just do your job, Blair. Tolwyn clear."*

The channel went dead, and Blair cursed under his breath. Tolwyn was so concerned with finding a way around or through those mines that he was throwing away valuable assets just when they needed them most.

Blair dismissed the thought. Tolwyn would fight this battle his own way. What mattered now was the flight wing's part in it all.

Still skimming low over the curved body of the *Behemoth*, the Terran fighters flashed past the pressurized section of the hull where the control center and crew's quarters were housed. Beyond lay the battle zone, where the two squadrons of Hellcats were already making their presence known against the Strakha. Blair pulled up sharply as his sensors registered the fighting, climbing steeply away from the weapons platform. His maneuver had placed the two squadrons, Arrows and Thunderbolts, between the Kilrathi and their target. Now all they had to do was make the move count for something . . .

Stalker Leader
Loki System

Graldak let out a Kilrathi oath as he spotted the Terran fighters forming near the hull of the weapons platform. He hadn't expected the apes to fly so recklessly close to the surface of the huge weapons platform. It was a daring move. A warrior's move. He recognized the hand of the one Thrakhath had dubbed the Heart of the Tiger, the same one who had so nearly defeated the attack force off Locanda IV. That was one ape who knew how to fight. . . .

"So, Heart of the Tiger," he said over the comm channel. "You would stand in my way? You will not stand long, I assure you."

The *Behemoth* was the primary target, but that did not preclude swatting aside any resistance that sought to stop his attack run. With all weapons armed, Graldak switched on his targeting computer and drove the Strakha straight toward the Terran fighters.

Thunderbolt 300
Loki System

"Here they come!"

Blair saw the leading Strakha accelerating toward them just as Flint gave her warning cry. The Kilrathi fighters were no longer spread out, but formed a wedge behind their leader. They were keeping tighter formation than usual, probably hoping to bore through the Terran defenses and reach Behemoth through sheer numbers and concentrated firepower. A quick glance at the sensor screen revealed the other Kilrathi ships now thoroughly engaged. The two Hellcat squadrons tied up most of the enemy, while the rest were being pursued by the half-squadron off of *Coventry*. The cruiser itself limped in closer. Apparently Tolwyn was wrong about the situation aboard the capital ship. . . .

"Close up," Blair ordered. These were the only Kilrathi ships in a position to hit *Behemoth* for the moment, but unless the Terrans shifted to meet the unexpected Imperial formation their advantage would be lost. "Form on me."

But the cats were driving in too fast. An Arrow flashed past Blair, blasters firing wildly, but three of the Strakha hit the interceptor with massed fire. Blair tried to catch up to support the Arrow, but he was too late. The Terran fighter's shields went down, and in seconds the Kilrathi blasters chewed through armor and hull, boring into the reactor. The Arrow went up in a blaze of raw energy.

It was only then that Blair realized it was Denise Mbuto's fighter.

Now the leader was almost on top of him, and the rest of the wedge close behind. Blair set his crosshairs on the lead Strakha and opened fire. Several Kilrathi ships began to return his volley, but Cobra and Vaquero appeared from nowhere to engage on their flank, and in their haste to meet the new threat, the Kilrathi did little more than graze Blair's shields.

He maintained fire on the leader, looping to follow as the wedge shot past him. Fingers dancing over the fire controls, Blair called up a pair of dumb-fire missiles. They were simple unguided rockets, without any of the sophisticated homing systems common in other weapons in the Terran arsenal, but in this situation they were exactly what Blair needed. If he fired any of the other types, they were apt to be confused by the sheer number of available targets. And Blair wanted the leader.

He kicked in his afterburners once more, driving right into the enemy wedge. His targeting reticule centered over the lead Strakha and flashed, and Blair's fingers stabbed at the fire controls. The two missiles leapt from their launch rails almost as one, speeding straight toward the Kilrathi ship. His opponent, realizing what was happening at the last possible moment, started to swerve, but it was too late. The missiles detonated, and the Kilrathi shields began to fluctuate wildly.

Blair locked on his blasters and opened fire.

The Kilrathi pilot continued his maneuver even as the armor was being ripped off his stern section. The Strakha was changing course, but no longer in an evasive turn. He was lining up on a vector only slightly different from his previous heading . . . straight toward the *Behemoth*.

With a shock, Blair realized that the pilot's new course had his fighter aimed directly at one of the exposed shield generator housings that Tolwyn had indicated as a weak point in the weapons platform's defenses. The Kilrathi pilot had decided to make his death count. . . .

The Strakha came apart, but hurtling chunks of debris stayed on course, raining on the surface of the *Behemoth*. A ripple of explosions erupted from the huge vessel's hull. A moment later, two nearby Kilrathi ships let loose missile barrages to take advantage of collapsing shields on the weapons' platform. Flint and Maniac accounted for the two cats, but the damage was already done.

Blair could see lifepods and shuttles detaching from the *Behemoth* as the explosions spread and swelled. He pulled up sharply, steering back through a gauntlet of Kilrathi Strakha, knowing he had to put some distance between his fragile fighter and the doomed planetkiller.

The final explosion, when it came, overwhelmed his sensors and external cameras. For a moment he was flying blind, buffeted by spinning bits of metal and stray shots from enemy fighters. Kilrathi jeers and taunts were loud on the comm channel, a demonic cacophony of hate and glee.

Behemoth was gone. . . .

Elsewhere, the Kilrathi fighters were turning away. The Terran resistance had been stiff, and with the destruction of the weapons platform their mission was accomplished. As the Kilrathi began to withdraw in the direction of their capital ships, Blair ordered the flight wing to regroup near *Victory*. No one offered to pursue the retiring foe.

Tolwyn's face appeared on Blair's comm screen. *"I'm ordering the fleet to withdraw,"* he said, shock and pain etched plainly on his face. *"Ajax will stall the enemy fleet as long as possible. Land your fighters, Colonel."* The admiral's shoulders seemed to sag. *"It seems we've lost our last chance . . ."*

• CHAPTER XXVI

Flight Deck, TCS Victory
Blackmane System

The retreat from Loki had cost the flight wing five more pilots, and the destroyer *Ajax* was destroyed while attempting to hold off the enemy so the rest of the squadron could withdraw through the jump point. Still, it might have been considered a victory of sorts, extracting the Terran squadron from the trap at Loki VI . . . if it hadn't been for the loss of *Behemoth*.

The last hope for mankind . . . that was how the *Behemoth* was described. Now it was gone. And it was Christopher Blair who had failed in his duty to protect the weapon from the Kilrathi attack.

The bitter thought gnawed at Blair as he stood on the flight deck, surrounded by other senior ship's officers. The failure had been his . . . but right now, it was Admiral Geoff Tolwyn who was suffering the consequences of that failure. The orders came in two days after the squadron retreated to the Blackmane System. They were conveyed by a fast courier ship that had carried Tolwyn's report to sector HQ and then returned. Tolwyn was relieved of command over the erstwhile Behemoth Project. He was to strike his flag aboard *Victory* and return to Torgo immediately to face an inquiry into his handling of the entire operation.

Victory, meanwhile, was to maintain position and

complete field repairs pending the arrival of a new squadron commander. No one aboard was sure what that portended.

Tolwyn dressed as precisely as ever, but defeat was plain in his carriage as he stepped onto the flight deck, his staff trailing behind him. The admiral did not seem surprised to note that the turnout to see his departure was smaller and less impressive than upon his arrival. His star fell, and he with it. Tolwyn was well aware of the fact. He stopped to return Eisen's crisp salute.

"I relieve you, sir," the captain said quietly.

"I stand relieved," Tolwyn replied. "Permission to leave the ship?"

"Granted, Admiral." Eisen saluted a second time.

"A word of warning," Tolwyn said, again returning the salute. "The cats knew exactly where we were going, and when. They even knew exactly where to strike." He paused, running a sour eye over the assembled officers behind Eisen. His gaze seemed to come to rest on Blair. "I believe you may have a leaky ship, Captain."

"With all due respect, sir," Eisen responded stiffly. "I resent any such suggestion regarding my people. They've served this ship and the Confederation with honor, one and all. There are never any guarantees when it comes to battle, Admiral. And no such thing as certain victory, no matter how awesome your weapon may be."

Tolwyn's expression was bleak. "Victory is certain enough now, Captain, for the Kilrathi. I hope the honor of your crew is enough, in the fighting that lies ahead. It will only get worse from here."

He turned away and stalked toward the shuttle without another word. Climbing the ramp, he turned back to look at the flight deck one last time, and again Blair felt that the admiral's gaze singled him from the rest. Then Tolwyn boarded the craft, and the door swung shut behind him. The assembled officers and men withdrew as the shuttle powered up.

The hangar area was empty by the time the shuttle rolled onto the open deck beyond the force field curtain, rising slowly away from the carrier and into the black void.

Bridge, TCS Victory
Blackmane System

"Captain, we've got a ship coming through the Torgo jump point. Looks like a big one . . ."

"On the main monitor," Eisen ordered, leaning forward in his chair. The viewscreen showed a computer-enhanced view of open space, with no outward sign of the jump point or the disturbance the sensors picked up indicating a ship in transit.

Four days had passed since Tolwyn's departure, and aboard *Victory* and the other ships in the ill-fated Behemoth Squadron, the passage of time was starting to weigh heavily on crew morale. Being driven back with the loss of the weapons platform—not to mention *Ajax*—was bad enough. But to wait here, useless, without a word of the war from other quarters . . . that was even worse.

A ship took form on the viewscreen, slightly larger than *Victory* but similar in configuration. It was one of the latest models of escort carrier, but its sleek, modern lines were marred by battle damage.

"Jesus," someone muttered. "Looks like half the flight deck got cooked."

"Transponder code's on line, Captain," Rollins said a moment later. "She's the *Eagle*. Captain Chalfonte."

"Confirming," the sensor officer added a moment later.

"Message coming in," Rollins reported. "They're sending across a shuttle. No details, sir. Just . . . sending a shuttle.

We're to stand by and await further communication."

Eisen nodded. "Very well. Alert Flight Control we have an incoming shuttle. Mr. Gessler, you have the bridge. I'll be in my ready room if there's anything further."

Flight Control, TCS Victory Blackmane System

"*Victory, Victory*, this is shuttle *Armstrong*. Request landing clearance and approach vector."

"Shuttle *Armstrong*, cleared to land," Blair replied. He was standing a turn as OOD in Flight Control, one more way to keep himself busy so that he wouldn't brood over recent events. He signaled to one of the technicians to activate the carrier's approach beacon.

The shuttle skimmed low over the flight deck and allowed the tractor beams to lock on and pull it in. Blair monitored the landing, and when the stubby little craft was down, he gave curt orders to activate the force fields and revive pressure and gravity inside the hangar area. Behind him, two of the techs were swapping speculations about the shuttle and its reason for paying the ship a visit from *Eagle*, but Blair silenced them with a quick look.

The shuttle doors opened up, and a single stocky figure appeared at the top of the ramp. Blair stared, wide-eyed, as the man glanced around the hangar deck and gave an approving nod of his graying head. Rachel Coriolis appeared at the bottom of the ramp, holding out a PDP so that the shuttle's pilot could log in, but she nearly dropped it as she took in the rank insignia on the man's well-worn flight suit.

It wasn't often that a full general visited the flight deck of a carrier.

Blair wasted no time in getting to the flight deck to join Rachel. By the time he reached the shuttle, General

James Taggart had descended to the deck, taking the data pad from the chief technician's hands. He was smiling as he signed it and thrust it back at her.

"There, now, lassie, 'tis all legal and proper," the general said, his thick Scots accent a welcome reminder of better days. He caught sight of Blair and his grin broadened. "Och, lad, dinna hurry! I'm nae sae old that ye maun rush tae see me before I keel over!"

"Paladin!" Blair said, saluting the man who had been his first squadron leader on the old *Tiger's Claw*. "Er . . . General . . ."

"Paladin I'll always be tae my auld mates, laddie," Taggart told him, returning the salute carelessly and then seizing Blair's hand in a warm handshake. " 'Tis aye good tae see ye again."

"Why didn't someone tell us you were on the shuttle?" Blair demanded. "We would have laid on a proper welcome." He was thinking of the contrast between Taggart's arrival and Tolwyn's just two weeks earlier.

"Och, lad, I cannae be bothered with all the pomp and circumstance. Ye should ken that well enough by now. The business I'm on doesna allow time for all that folderol."

"Business?"

"Aye, lad." Paladin stroked his salt-and-pepper beard and fixed Blair with a steely stare. "The business of putting right the mess Auld Geoff made of things, at Loki. I just hope 'tis nae too late tae salvage this mess." The general gave him another smile. "So, if ye dinna mind, lad, I need tae see Captain Eisen as soon as may be. But I'll be wanting tae talk to ye, as well, soon enough."

General Taggart strode briskly toward the door, leaving Blair behind. Rachel exchanged glances with him.

"That was General Taggart?" she asked as Paladin's broad back disappeared through the doorway.

Blair nodded. "In the flesh."

"Good God," the woman said softly. "I feel sorry for the Kilrathi who gets in his way . . ."

"The last one who tried ended up with a Paladin-sized hole in him," Blair agreed. "I just wonder what the hell he's doing here. . . ?"

Wing Commander's Quarters, TCS Victory *Blackmane System*

The door buzzer made an irritating noise, and Blair swung his feet from his bunk and said "Enter" just to shut it off. He wasn't surprised to see Paladin when the door slid open. "Come in, General," he said formally.

Taggart cocked an eyebrow at him. "General, is it, again? Have ye decided tae go all formal on me, lad?"

Blair shrugged wearily. "It's hard to think of you as Paladin any more, you know. It's been a long time."

"Those were the good days, though, laddie," Paladin told him, crossing the cramped cabin to perch on the only chair. "I wish I was still out on the firing line with you young lads and lasses, instead of flying a bloody desk."

"I wish you were out here, too," Blair told him. "A few more pilots like we had in the old gang and we might've saved *Behemoth* last week."

"That bucket of bolts," Paladin said, making a face. "Auld Geoff really thought that monster of his would work. He always believed that bigger was better."

"You had a better solution, I take it? Kevin said you had some scheme cooked up, over in Covert Ops." Blair couldn't help letting some of his anger show in the comment.

Taggart studied him. "I hear you . . . heard about Angel," he said, answering Blair's tone rather than his question. "In a tangle with Thrakhath, no less."

"Yes, I did, you son of a bitch."

"I'm sorry that ye had tae find out that way."

"How long have you known?" Blair demanded.

Paladin didn't answer right away. "Since . . . since before *Concordia* was lost," he admitted.

Blair felt the anger surging within, his fists clenching with the sudden desire to strike out at the man. "You bastard," he said. "When I asked, you stood there and lied to me."

"Laddie, I had to do it. I was under orders myself. . . ."

"All the missions we flew together—they didn't mean a damn thing, did they?" Blair demanded. "You out there on my wing, protecting me . . ."

"Don't you see that's what I was doing by not telling you?" Paladin said. "Look, laddie . . . look what ye almost did out there, when ye learned of it all. I was protecting you again . . . from yourself."

Blair looked away, at the holo projector sitting beside his bed. He hadn't played the message again since learning she was dead, but he heard it in his dreams all too often. "You know what she meant to me."

"Aye, lad, I do indeed." Taggart paused. "But we're fighting a war, son. We've all lost someone close to us. It doesna make you special."

"Yeah, right," Blair said. "I've heard the whole routine before. It doesn't get better with repetition."

Paladin shrugged. "I suppose not. But the fact is, lad, that we couldna tell anyone about Angel. Not until now. Not without ruining the work she did before she died."

He didn't answer, but he met Taggart's eyes.

"Her last mission was a part of my project, laddie. Not sae grand, perhaps, as Auld Geoff and his *Behemoth*, but a way tae end this war, once and for all. And 'tis up tae you, Chris Blair, tae finish what Angel started."

Captain's Ready Room, TCS Victory
Blackmane System

Like his arrival, the briefing Paladin gave the next morning was a low-key affair. Instead of an audience of aides and ship's officers, the general limited the briefing to Blair and Eisen. He wasted no time on useless preliminaries or self-congratulation.

"We've got a lot to cover, and damned little time to do it in." Blair always noticed that Paladin's accent faded as he focused on important matters, and today was no exception. "Covert Ops lost out to Admiral Tolwyn when it came time for HQ to decide on a response to the Kilrathi biological threat, but like him we've had an operation in train for several years. It's a long shot, I'll grant you, but it can work. It has to."

Blair noticed a look of distaste on Eisen's face. After *Behemoth*, another long shot was the last thing any of them wanted.

"You hae already been briefed on the seismic instability of Kilrah," Paladin went on. "It was central to the whole *Behemoth* project, the notion that even if the weapon wasn't able to bust a planet cold, it could at least shake the place apart when applied against the right target. Our project tackled the same concept from anither angle, one more in keeping with the philosophy of Covert Ops."

He punched a code into the keypad in front of him and the map table came to life, projecting an image of a torpedo-shaped device into the air between the three men. "This is the Temblor Bomb," he said quietly. "It was developed by Doctor Philip Severin, one of the top research men in the Confederation. It's been undergoing tests for some time now . . . nearly a decade, in fact."

The view changed to schematics. It brought back unpleasant thoughts of Tolwyn's *Behemoth* lecture, and Blair shifted uncomfortably in his seat. Eisen's face was a study in bland neutrality as he regarded the holographic image.

"The bomb operates on the principle of seismic resonance," Taggart continued. "Detonated in the right place, at the proper juncture of tectonic fault lines, it will set up a series of quakes which will increase in intensity until Kilrah is quite literally shaken apart." Paladin spread his hands. "Unfortunately, the weapon doesna lend itself to pretty demonstrations on backwater worlds. There's only a handful of planets we know of where the Temblor Bomb could do its work, and Kilrah is at the top of the list. The High Command wanted something they could escalate up to gradually, so they threw their weight behind Admiral Tolwyn and the *Behemoth*."

Blair frowned. "I've said all along that I'm against—"

"Laddie," Taggart said sternly. "I'd like nothing better than to find a solution that didn't involve civilian casualties, but the simple fact is we do not have one at hand." He paused. "Right now we have to stop the Empire cold. Not just a defeat, but a final defeat. The Imperial hierarchy is so centralized, so built around the idea of Kilrah as the core of their entire culture, that the destruction of the planet will bring the rest of the Empire to a halt. Even if there are a few warlords who want to fight, the other Kilrathi worlds will come apart as clans and factions and splinter groups start fighting for a new equilibrium. And that's our only hope of bringing the war to a quick end."

Eisen looked at him. "The brass must have thought a negotiated settlement was possible," he commented. "They wanted Tolwyn to demonstrate *Behemoth* and make the Kilrathi come to the peace table."

"Aye, that was the hope," Paladin admitted slowly. "Though you must know that the admiral had no plans tae stop with Loki. He knew, just as I do, that Thrakhath and his Emperor willna stop fighting as long as they see a hope of winning. And a balance of power, their bioweapons against our *Behemoth*, would have meant the advantage of numbers and strategic position was still with the Empire."

"It sounds to me like there was never any choice at all," Blair said quietly.

"Laddie, there wasn't." Paladin looked grim. "Fact is, even if Auld Geoff had decided tae hold off, I was ready to launch a Temblor Bomb attack on Kilrah on my ain authority."

"What?" Eisen looked shocked. "You'd have been court-martialed six ways from Sunday!"

"Aye, true enough," Paladin said. "But my career doesna mean much set against the end of this damned war. Our hope was that the cats would hear about *Behemoth*'s attack on Loki and assemble the bulk of their reserve fleet tae intercept it. I persuaded Captain Chalfonte tae take *Eagle* into Imperial territory tae launch the Temblor Bomb strike on Kilrah while the cats were chasing *Behemoth*. But they were a step ahead of us, it seems. Thrakhath had a strike force ready at Loki, and never touched the reserves. *Eagle* ran into trouble before we got anywhere near Kilrah. We had tae break off and retreat with heavy damage."

"So it's over, then," Blair said bitterly.

"Not yet, it isn't," Taggart said. "That's why I'm here. Now that *Behemoth* has failed, Sector HQ has authorized the Temblor strike. This time, when we go in, we'll be supported by a fleet. If we can penetrate the defenses that turned *Eagle* back, and get a few fighters through, we can still drop the bomb and destroy the planet."

"That doesn't sound like a long shot," Blair said. "It sounds like no shot at all. A fleet couldn't penetrate all the way to Kilrah, and anything less than a fleet would be carved up before you could say 'here, kitty, kitty!'"

"Dinna be sae sure, laddie," Paladin said with a wolfish grin. "Covert Ops didna gae into this thing blind. Fact is, a squadron of fighters can do what a fleet cannot hope to . . . thanks to Jeannette Devereaux."

"Angel? Where does she come into all this?" Blair was still frowning.

"Her last mission was to Kilrah, laddie, aboard a captured Kilrathi freighter we rigged up with a nice little cargo of goodies." Despite his almost bantering tone, his eyes were dead serious. "You see, we kenned just fine that we couldna bull our way through to Kilrah. So instead we've arranged for a . . . more stealthy approach." He manipulated his keyboard, and a new schematic appeared. Blair recognized it. He had seen Rachel pouring over these same plans once.

"An Excalibur?" he said, raising his eyebrows.

"Aye. *Eagle* carries a squadron of them, the first operational squadron. They have a limited jump capability, and a cloaking device—which means they can penetrate the Kilrah System in secret, carry out the mission, and hopefully get clear again when it's over." Taggart raised his hand to ward off the protests that sprang to Blair lips. "Hear me out, laddie. You'll be wanting to say yon fighter doesna have the range tae make a jump and proceed all the way in to Kilrah. That's true enough. But Angel's mission was to survey a jump point that we didna previously know about, and tae make some stops along the way in to Kilrah." A map appeared over the table, showing the Kilrah System. "Here . . . here . . . and again, here. Asteroids . . . the last of them Kilrah's outer moon, which barely merits the label. And on each one, a hidden supply cache hollowed out by Angel and her crew. Big enough to take in a squadron of ships, but well camouflaged. Each equipped with fuel, missile reloads, the works. And this one—" He indicated Kilrah's tiny second moon. "In this cache, a pair of Temblor Bombs, all set and ready to load."

"You mean they're already out there?" Blair demanded. "But Angel's people were caught. Interrogated. The Kilrathi could have found them all by now, . . ."

Taggart shook his head. "Nae, laddie. These were Covert Ops people, dinna forget. Conditioned not tae remember anything of the mission, once they were caught. Not even Thrakhath's torturers could hae pried anything out of them."

"So the caches are still there," Blair said slowly. "Just . . . waiting."

"Aye. Waiting," Paladin said. "Angel did her job well. Those bombs are aye big, laddie, so big ye couldna carry any other missiles once you mounted one. Planting them here was the best solution. You go into the system fully armed, so you can deal with any patrols you run into along the way. But when you make the bomb run, it'll be from close range. There's less chance of disaster this way. Even if you lose ships going in, the ones that are left can still pick up the bombs and carry out the mission."

"If they're hidden, how do we locate them?" Blair asked. "Transponders?"

Paladin nodded. "Aye. They'll respond on a very high band, and only when you fire a query at them. Believe me, laddie, we've done everything we can tae make this work."

"You're sure Colonel Devereaux got all the way and set up all three depots?" Eisen asked.

"She did," Paladin said quietly. "She managed tae send out a coded signal, before the cats took her ship. A scout ship posted in the Oort Cloud monitored it and brought word tae us." He paused. " 'Twas frae them we learned of the capture . . . and the execution, as well. Then the cats put it out on their propaganda broadcasts. . . ."

"And you really think this plan can work?" Blair said

quietly, changing the subject. He didn't want to think about Angel's death, not now.

"Aye, laddie, it will work. Because it has to."

Officer's Quarters, TCS Victory Blackmane System

"Because it has to." The image on the screen was too small to pick up details, but the voices had been clear enough. It had been a good idea, placing cameras where they might pick up important meetings.

The spy shut off the monitor as the briefing dispersed. It seemed that the threat to Kilrah was not over yet, even with the destruction of *Behemoth*. Thrakhath's instructions didn't cover this eventuality, and there would be no ships lurking nearby to pick up another broadcast.

If the spy was to alert the Prince of this new danger, it would require careful preparation indeed. But it had to be done. . . .

For the glory of Kilrah!

• CHAPTER XXVII

Flight Control, TCS Victory
Blackmane System

"That's the last of 'em, Colonel. Eight Excaliburs, all ready for action."

Blair stared at the flight deck through the transparent wall of Flight Control, studying the lines of the last of the new fighters as it rolled slowly to a halt inside the hangar area. On Paladin's orders, the Excaliburs came from *Eagle* in exchange for Gold Squadron's Thunderbolts. They certainly looked impressive enough. Blair hoped a few days of patrols would give the pilots a chance to get used to them before they went into action in Paladin's crazy scheme to attack Kilrah. "I hope they're all they're cracked up to be," he said quietly.

"Believe me, skipper, they're the hottest birds that ever hauled jets off a carrier deck," Rachel Coriolis said. She wore an expression of sheer joy as she contemplated the new craft. "These beauties are a mechanic's dream. At long last, I get to really show what I can do."

"Oh, I don't know, Chief," Blair said, glancing at her enraptured face and giving her a smile. "I've been pretty impressed right from the start."

"Yeah, but you haven't seen everything, not by a long shot," she said, flashing an answering grin. She moved a little closer to him and lowered her voice. "It might not be proper protocol to make the first move with an officer and all . . . but how 'bout we get together later on and I'll show you the rest? Sooner or later, you and me, we've got to let go of the ghosts. Figure out if the parts'll fit somewhere else . . . if you know what I mean?"

Blair hesitated, looking into her dark eyes. He couldn't now deny being attracted to Rachel, her quiet strength and her irreverent humor. Always before it seemed too much like a betrayal of Angel. . . .

But Angel was gone, and she would have been the first one to want him to pick up the pieces of his life and move on. Rachel had already helped him over the first, most difficult adjustment. It seemed right, somehow, that they travel further down the road she helped him find that led out of the darkness.

"You think our parts might mesh, Chief?" he asked her, his smile broadening.

"You never know until you take a test run," she said. "Tonight, maybe?"

"Tonight," he agreed quietly.

He was almost surprised at the intensity of the emotion behind that one simple word.

Flight Wing Rec Room, TCS Victory Blackmane System

"Got a minute, Colonel? Before I have to go on watch?"

Blair looked up at Lieutenant Rollins and gave him a curt nod. "Sure. Pull up a chair." He hesitated, studying the young communications officer's worried expression. "What's on your mind, Lieutenant?"

Rollins sat down, looking uncomfortable. "I think I've finally turned up something solid, Colonel. In that . . . matter Cobra and I've been looking into."

"And that is?"

"I figured out where I'd seen that harmonic pattern before," Rollins told him. "It's been used a time or two in psychiatric work. Personality overlays . . ." Rollins hesitated. "Sometimes, with a subject, you want to be able to switch from a substitute personality to the original, or back again. They use it in therapy, overlaying a well-adjusted behavior pattern over a personality that's got problems, but the doctors want to be able to retrieve the original identity, locate the root of the problem."

"Yeah, I've heard about it. You think it applies here?"

"If I'm right, the Kilrathi might have used that message from Thrakhath as a carrier for a personality trigger. When it was played, it brought up a different personality in a Kilrathi agent on board." Rollins hesitated. "If Cobra's right, it would have brought back an original personality in Hobbes, something overlaid by the one we've known all along. Or . . ."

"Or what?" Blair demanded.

"I . . . was thinking about what you said. About Cobra. She admitted there was something familiar about the signal, but she didn't say what. But it set me to thinking. What if the signal was supposed to bring up an implanted personality in her . . . something programmed by the Kilrathi to make her work as a spy. Hell, she might not even be aware of it any more, if the work was sophisticated enough."

Blair looked down at his drink. "Once again, there's no real proof," he said slowly. "We can hatch theories until the sun goes nova, but without real evidence . . ."

"I know, sir," Rollins said, biting his lower lip and looking worried. "But . . . hell, I don't know what to think any more or who to trust. I think I've identified another part of Thrakhath's transmission that carries a low-frequency side message, but it seems like it's a pretty old code. It was discontinued a while back, and is no longer in our current files. I'm still trying to reconstruct it. Maybe we'll know more then. But meantime, what do I do? Tell Cobra? If she's the spy . . ."

"Keep it to yourself, Lieutenant," Blair said. His wrist implant chimed a reminder. "Damn. I've got a meeting with Paladin and the Captain." He stood up. "You keep working on that signal, Lieutenant. Crack it fast because we have to find out if there really is a leak—before we start General Taggart's new mission."

Flight Deck, TCS Victory
Blackmane System

Lieutenant Laurel Buckley studied the sleek lines of the Excalibur and gave a low whistle of appreciation. "Man, oh man, that is a thing of beauty," she said softly. Cobra was looking forward to trying the new craft out, even if it was only a routine patrol.

"I'll say," Chief Coriolis said, looking up from where she was kneeling, checking the locking mechanism on the forward landing gear. "This is one nice piece of machinery."

"Where's Ski, Chief?" Cobra asked. Technician First Class Glazowski was her usual plane captain, but he was nowhere in sight.

"Had to put all the Gold Squadron plane captains through a crash course on how to care and feed these beauties," Rachel told her. "I'm the only one who's up on the specs at the moment. Don't worry, he'll be done by the time your patrol gets back." She looked around. "Who's going out with you?"

"Vaquero," Cobra said. "Except he's late, as usual." She moved over to the cockpit ladder. "I swear he'll be late to his own cantina opening."

"I'll have Flight Control put out a call for him," Rachel said. "You need any help strapping on this baby?"

"Nah. Looks like you're overworked as it is."

"I'll say. I'm supposed to have five techs on every bird. Today I've only got three to get both you guys up and flying." The tech looked disgusted. "My watch roster looks thinner every day, seems like."

"Well, I can run through my checklist just fine by myself. Just don't forget to send somebody out here to give me my clearance when it's time to launch!"

Rachel chuckled and turned away. Buckley paused at the bottom of the ladder and cocked her head to one side. Something . . . someone was moving around on the other side of the Excalibur.

She set her helmet and gauntlets down on the wing and ducked under the fuselage to investigate. From what Rachel just said there shouldn't have been any technicians working in that corner of the bay. . . .

Something struck her in the stomach as she straightened, knocking her backward against the hull of the fighter with such force that she banged her head. As she shook it, trying to clear her blurring vision and the ringing in her ears, she became aware of the pain in her abdomen. Her fingers, clutching at the spot, came away sticky with blood.

And then her vision did clear, for a moment, as she slumped to the deck. The bulky figure standing over her might have stepped out of her worst nightmare.

"Hobbes . . ." she gasped. Then blackness took her.

Flight Control, TCS Victory Blackmane System

Rachel Coriolis entered the Flight Control Center and dropped into the nearest vacant seat. "God, I'll be glad to get some sack time," she said. She suppressed a grin as she remembered the plans she'd made with Blair. She doubted either one of them would get much sack time tonight. "They're all yours, Captain. And good riddance."

Lieutenant Ion Radescu, the duty Flight Controller, gave her a grin. "Come on, Rachel, you know you love it. What would your life be without fighters to work over, huh?"

"A hell of a lot cleaner," she said, returning his smile. Since Admiral Tolwyn's departure, she'd gone right back to her old habits of dress.

Radescu chuckled and turned to his console. "Okay, boys and girls, let's get this show started." He thumbed a mike switch. "Prowler Flight, this is Control. Radio check."

"Prowler Two," Vaquero said. "Read you five by five."

There was a moment of silence before Cobra's voice came on the speakers. "Clear signal."

The FCO frowned. "Prowler One, I'm not getting anything on video from you. You got a fault showing?"

Again there was a pause. "Negative."

"Damned thing ought to be working," Rachel said, joining Radescu at the console. "Those birds are so new you can still smell the fresh paint."

"Want to have a look?" Radescu asked.

"It ain't enough to get a down-gripe," Rachel told him. "Long as audio's working, I don't see a problem." She paused. "I'll take a look when they get back in."

"Okay, Chief," the FCO nodded. "Prowler Flight, cleared to launch."

Out on the flight deck below them, the fighters rolled into position in their launch tubes. Green lights flashed on Radescu's board. "Launch when ready," he ordered.

And the two Excaliburs hurtled into space.

Rachel turned away. "I'm gonna grab me a cup of something hot and then check on my students in Ready Room Three," she said over her shoulder. "Yell if you need me—"

The intercom shrilled. "Flight Control, Bay Twelve," a hoarse voice was loud over the speaker. "I just found Cobra down here. She's hurt . . . real bad!"

"Cobra?" Rachel and Radescu spoke at the same moment.

"What the hell . . . ?" the FCO added. "Rachel, get down there and find out what's going on." He was already punching in a combination on the intercom. "Bridge, this is Flight Control. We have a problem . . ."

Captain's Ready Room, TCS Victory Blackmane System

"Our job, then, is tae remain clear of the fighting unless absolutely necessary. Let the rest of the fleet thoroughly engage the bloody moggies and then slip around to the back door, the jump point to Kilrah. Then, laddie, your squadron will launch."

Blair nodded as Paladin finished. "With luck, the Excaliburs will cloak before the cats see us out there, and we can reach the jump point without ever being noticed. Very pretty planning, General."

Taggart grinned. "Another fine product of the Covert Ops planning staff," he said. "Just remember, laddie, that the cloak's nae good at close range. It hides ye from sensors, but it doesna make you invisible."

"I'm still not very happy about sending the fighters through blind." Eisen spoke up for the first time since the briefing had started. "They'll have no support . . . and if they run into trouble before they refuel they won't be able to recharge their jump generators and make it back here safely. If this really is a back door into Kilrah, wouldn't it be better going in with them?"

"We dinna ken how well defended the jump point might be," Paladin said. "The fighters will have to decloak to jump, of course, and they'll be detected as they enter the system. But if they cloak right away, they can evade any reception committees in the neighborhood. Send a carrier in, and we stir up a hornet's nest."

"I appreciate the concern, Captain," Blair added, meeting Eisen's eyes. "Fact is, our chances of getting back aren't that good one way or another. I'm treating this as a one-way mission . . . volunteers only. If we can get back, great. But none of us will be under any illusions."

"Laddie—" Paladin began. He was cut off by the ululation of an alarm siren.

"Flight deck. Emergency." The voice on the tannoy belonged to Rollins, but it was almost unrecognizable, choked with emotion. "We have a problem on the flight deck!"

"Blair, get down there," Eisen rasped, pushing back his chair and getting to his feet. "I'll be on the bridge . . ."

"On my way," Blair said. He was already halfway to the door, but Paladin, despite his age and bulk, was right behind him. They raced to the elevator, all pretense of officer's dignity forgotten.

Rachel met them at the door to the hangar deck. "Bay Twelve," she said, grim-faced. The two men didn't wait for an explanation. They hurried down the row of fighter bays to the empty space that had housed the Excalibur assigned to Lieutenant Buckley.

Cobra was lying near the back of the bay, half hidden by a rack of testing equipment. There was blood on the deck where she'd been dragged to the niche, and a larger pool of blood around her. Someone had tried to staunch her wounds with a makeshift bandage, but it wasn't controlling the flow of blood. Blair knelt beside her and lifted it to examine her injuries. Four deep slashes cut across her stomach, and the sight of those wounds made Blair, hardened veteran that he was, turn his head away.

He had seen that kind of disemboweling cut before, after the ground fighting on Muspelheim a decade ago. The cuts could only have been made by a Kilrathi's claws.

Blair tried to ignore the nausea welling up inside him. Cobra's eyes fluttered open. "Colonel . . ." she gasped.

"Hobbes?" he asked, knowing the answer.

"He . . . hit me. Don't know why . . ."

"I do," Paladin said grimly. He held up a holo-cassette. "He must have dropped this when he dragged her over here."

Taggart pressed a button, and a small holographic image formed in the air above Cobra. It took Blair a moment to recognize the scene. It was a view of Eisen's ready room, shot from a high angle. The three figures there belonged to Eisen, Paladin, and Blair.

"This is the Temblor Bomb," Paladin's image said. "It was developed by Doctor Philip Severin, one of the top research men in the Confederation. It's been undergoing tests for some time now . . . nearly a decade, in fact."

Taggart switched it off. "The briefing . . ."

"All this time," Blair said slowly, shaking his head. "All this time, he's had us bugged. . . ."

Rachel returned, with a team of medics running after her. Paladin moved away to give them room to work, while Blair cradled her head and shoulders in his arms. "We'll get you to sick bay," he told her.

"Too late . . . for me," she gasped out. "Get Hobbes. You still have time . . ."

He could almost feel the life ebbing out of her as the awareness faded from her eyes. One of the medics shook his head. "It's no good, sir," he said. "She's gone."

Blair lowered her head to the deck gently and stood up. "What about Hobbes?" he asked Rachel, voice flat and harsh. "Any idea where he is?"

"He took Cobra's fighter," she said. "Launched with Vaquero a few minutes ago. He must have had a tape of her voice to answer the radio check."

Flint appeared at the mouth of the bay, running. She pulled up short at the sight of Cobra, then fixed her eyes on Blair. "Prowler One just broke off the patrol route," she said, breathing hard. "Fired on Vaquero when he tried to intercept." She paused. "The fighter's heading for the Freya jump point, maximum speed. Vaquero's pursuing."

Blair looked at Paladin. "Even without that holo, Hobbes can tell them about the plan. About the caches . . ."

Taggart nodded. "If he makes it through the jump point, it's all over, lad," he said.

"Not yet, it isn't," Blair said. He looked at Rachel. "Which of the Excaliburs is prepped for Alert Five?"

"Three-oh-four," she said. "Maniac's bird."

"Get it on the line now. And get me a flight suit." He turned to Flint. "You get to Flight Control. Order Vaquero to keep up the chase. Stop that bastard at all costs, or at least slow him down until I get there."

He looked back down at Cobra, and had to blink back tears of grief and rage. "You were right," he said through clenched teeth. "It was Hobbes . . ."

Blair turned away and started toward Maniac's fighter, grim and determined. Hobbes had betrayed them . . . and now the renegade had to be stopped before he destroyed everything.

Excalibur 304
Blackmane System

"Victory, Victory, *I need help out here! He's flying rings around me!*"

Blair muttered a curse under his breath. Even with the Excalibur's superior acceleration, it would take three more minutes to overtake Vaquero and Hobbes. The Latino pilot had managed to engage Ralgha and keep him busy, but it was an uneven match. Hobbes had always been a good pilot, but Blair had never expected to see him matched against one of his own comrades.

On his sensor screen, he saw Hobbes making a long, slow loop, circling back toward Lopez. Vaquero had already taken damage to his engines, and was having trouble matching the Kilrathi's maneuvers.

"He's *coming in again* . . ." Lopez said. "*Firing* . . ."

A smaller blip showed up on the sensors. Vaquero launched a missile. It must have been a fire-and-forget model, judging from the way it bobbed and weaved in pursuit of Ralgha's fighter. Hobbes tried to dodge it, but it caught him across the port-side shield. Lopez let out a whoop and dove. Blair could almost see his blasters pouring on the fire.

"All right!" Lopez shouted. "*That one's for Cobra! Get ready to say good-bye, Hobbes.*"

"*Not today, I'm afraid,*" Ralgha replied evenly. The Kilrathi's fighter released a barrage of missiles. They struck in quick succession.

"*Cristos* . . . *I'm breaking up!*" Vaquero called. "*Adios, amigos* . . ."

And then he was gone.

"God damn you," Blair growled. "God damn you to hell."

"*Is that you* . . . *old friend?*" Hobbes asked. For a moment, he sounded like Blair's old wingman, worried, ready to help. "*It would be wisest if you turned back, Colonel. Before I am forced to deal with you as well.*"

"Deal with this . . . old friend!" Blair shouted. Ralgha's Excalibur was just coming into extreme range, and Blair let loose a volley of blaster fire. But Hobbes anticipated it, and the shots only grazed his shields.

Ralgha turned away, as if to run. Blair's hands clenched on the steering yoke. If Hobbes decided to use his cloak, he might still get away . . .

But a cloak used a lot of power, and that would slow him down. Too much of a delay would give *Victory* time enough to get more fighters into the area, and since Hobbes could only be heading for the Freya jump point to warn the Kilrathi fleet, it wouldn't be that difficult to find him.

Ralgha suddenly rolled up and back, a classic

Immelman maneuver that almost took Blair by surprise. He cursed again as he dodged the Kilrathi's fire. He of all people should have anticipated Ralgha's moves. But he wasn't flying quite the way he usually did. There was something different in his style, more reckless, more aggressive. More like the Kilrathi Blair usually met in battle.

As Hobbes sped past, Blair checked his sensor readouts on the other Excalibur. Vaquero had penetrated the armor, all right. If the port shield went down, Ralgha would be vulnerable, and he was sure to be sensitive to that weakness. Hobbes had used all of his missiles to knock out Lopez, giving Blair a significant advantage.

The Kilrathi started to swing around as Blair turned to follow him. He let Hobbes finish his turn, then suddenly opened up his afterburners for a charge right at the other fighter, a move he was sure Hobbes would never expect from him. Blaster fire raked across his forward shields, but he ignored it, even when the shield generator alarm went off. His shields were going down . . .

Ralgha stopped firing, his weapons on recharge. The Kilrathi swerved sharply away, trying to keep his port side out of Blair's line of fire. The two fighters were close together now, and Blair had to kill his momentum quickly to keep from shooting right past Hobbes.

The Terran allowed himself a grim smile and locked on a pair of heat-seekers. As Ralgha finished his turn and exposed his tail, Blair let the missiles go and opened up with every beam weapon he possessed.

"*Impressive, my friend,*" Hobbes said as the barrage struck home. "*Impressive . . . I fear that you have bested me . . . Now I shall never see Kilrah again.*"

The missiles detonated almost simultaneously as the Excalibur's rear shields went down. The fighter came apart.

Blair thought he heard Hobbes call out his name before the fireball consumed his craft.

"Excalibur three-o-four," he said, his voice sounding dead in his own ears. He couldn't feel anything, either sadness or satisfaction, at the knowledge that Ralgha was gone. "Hobbes . . . is gone. I'm coming in."

• CHAPTER XXVIII

Flight Wing Quarters, TCS Victory Blackmane System

Blair punched in a security code to unlock the door and stepped quickly inside. He was glad there had been no one in the corridor to see him, to ask questions, or to offer comments. He didn't think he could face anyone just now, especially not here, in the quarters that had belonged to Ralgha *nar* Hhallas. The door slid shut behind him and the lights came on automatically. They were set to the dim reddish hue Hobbes favored, a reminder of Kilrah's K6 star.

A reminder of Ralgha's home . . .

Ralgha . . . Hobbes . . . It surprised Blair to realize how deep this wound went, deeper even than Angel's death. He had known Ralgha *nar* Hhallas, flown with him, loved him like a brother over the better part of fifteen long years. When others had raised doubts, he had been firm in his faith in Hobbes, the one being Blair would have trusted to the bitter end . . . and beyond. Yet Hobbes betrayed him, betrayed them all. And the knowledge of that betrayal hurt as nothing Blair had ever felt.

He turned to check the cabin control keypad beside the door, punching for Terra-normal lights and lower heat and humidity than Ralgha had preferred. The changes helped him push away the bitter thoughts of

335

Hobbes, but not far enough for any real peace of mind.

No doubt Paladin would want Ralgha's effects searched with a fine-tooth comb in hopes of finding clues about the Kilrathi's treachery. Blair didn't plan to disturb anything that might interest Covert Ops. But it was one of his duties, as wing commander, to deal with the personal property of any pilot who died while under his command, and much as he wanted to delegate it, this was one duty Blair felt he had to see to himself. He could at least take a quick inventory of Ralgha's property, though he had no idea where it would go when Paladin was through with it. Usually personal effects were returned to the family, but what family did Hobbes leave?

He defected in the company of a retainer named Kirha. Had the retainer been another agent? Or legitimate? Blair wasn't even sure if the other Kilrathi was still alive. The last he'd heard, Kirha had vowed allegiance to a Terran pilot, Ian "Hunter" St. John, but that was years ago. Blair hadn't heard anything of Hunter for a long time.

Well, if nothing else, he could always have Ralgha's property returned to the Empire when the war was over, if it ever was over. Perhaps Hobbes still had family somewhere. He claimed they had all died before his defection, but that could have been yet another lie.

Blair shook his head sadly. He didn't know what the truth was any more, about Hobbes . . . or about anything else.

A slender box lying on the bunk drew his eye, and Blair crossed the room to pick it up. It was a holographic projector, much like the one Angel had sent him. Curious, Blair sat on the edge of the bed and thumbed the switch.

A life-sized image of Hobbes appeared in front of him.

"Colonel Blair," the holographic figure said in Ralgha's familiar tones. "I am returning to my Homeworld, but my admiration for you compels me to provide an explanation for my actions.

"You must understand that the being you knew as Hobbes was a construct, the result of an identity-overlay experiment initiated long ago by Imperial Security at the behest of Prince Thrakhath. You have never met the real Ralgha *nar* Hhallas, nor would you have become his friend, for he was and is dedicated to the service of the Empire. Only the construct-personality could become your comrade and friend. I myself was entirely unaware of my true self until the message broadcast by Prince Thrakhath that day at Delius, the message where you were given your Kilrathi title, the Heart of the Tiger. Embedded in combination with a signal embedded in that transmission, the phrase 'Heart of the Tiger' was the trigger that awakened my true personality, hidden for so many years. There were buried messages within it that gave me my Prince's instructions, which I have carried out since that day. Once Ralgha *nar* Hhallas was restored within me, I had no choice but to act as I did. Thus, my friend, you possess the Heart of the Tiger, but I *am* the Heart of the Tiger."

The Kilrathi paused for a long time. His expression was one Blair had never seen on his stern, solemn features before, the look of someone torn in two by conflicting emotions. "Kilrathi do not surrender, my old friend, and neither do they betray a trust once given. And yet, in being true to my race and obedient to my duty, I have been forced to betray you. For though I am no longer the same being you once named Hobbes and befriended when I was alone among strangers, I retain a full memory of everything that Ralgha thought and did. I remember you, Colonel, for what you were and are, and know that you are an honorable warrior. If I could have performed my duty without betraying you, I would have done so, but that was not possible. And if we meet again . . . we will have no choice but to perform our duties . . . with honor.

"I hope, Colonel Christopher Blair, that we need never meet in battle. But if we do, I will salute you as a warrior . . . and I will mourn you, as a friend lost to me forever."

The holograph flickered and faded out, leaving Blair alone again in the tiny cabin with bitter thoughts as his only companions. He remained there a long time, unmoving, until someone buzzed at the cabin door.

He put the projector down. "Enter," he said harshly.

It was Maniac. "Thought I might find you here. Captain called down to Flight Control asking after the final operations plan for this mission of the General's." Marshall looked around the cabin, plainly curious. "Cleaning out the cat's stuff, huh?"

Blair shook his head. "Not yet," he said. "Just . . . an inventory. Before the captain gets started with the investigation . . ."

"Yeah," Maniac nodded. "Guess they'll have to look into . . . everything, huh? What'd I tell you about trusting a cat, all those years back?"

Blair just stared at him, wordless. There was nothing to say any more.

"Too bad Cobra had to die to get her point across," Marshall said.

Blair surged out of the bunk and caught him by the collar, raising a hand to strike the man. All his anger had came rushing out, and all he wanted to do was knock the mocking smirk off Maniac's face.

"Temper, temper," Marshall said. "You shouldn't start something you can't finish, Colonel, sir. And you know you can't afford to lose any more wingmen. Not now."

Blair dropped his hand and let go of Marshall's collar. The major took a step back, smoothing his wrinkled uniform.

"For once, you're right," Blair said slowly.

"I am?"

"Yeah. Yeah, there's precious few of us left, Major. Two Excaliburs destroyed yesterday, and another one damaged. Only four of us left in Gold Squadron." Blair backed away a few paces, his eyes fixed on Marshall's face. "I'd deck you right now, Maniac, and to hell with the consequences. But I figure I'd rather have you on my wing when we hit Kilrah."

Maniac snorted. "Yeah, right. You never thought I was any good before. So why would you want me this time?"

"Simple," Blair told him. "Odds are none of us are coming back from this one, but I figure you're too arrogant and too stupid to bow down. So maybe I will have the pleasure of seeing you fry before the damned mission's over and done with."

Marshall looked at him doubtfully, as if uncertain how serious Blair was. "You're crazy, man," he said.

Blair didn't answer him. He pulled a PDP out of his pocket and started the inventory, ignoring Marshall until the other man snorted again and left the cabin.

After Maniac left, he took time out to use the intercom to pass a message to Eisen, identifying the computer file that held the work the flight wing staff had put into refining Paladin's attack plan. Then he finished up in Ralgha's cabin and left, locking the door behind him with a security seal to keep out unauthorized visitors.

He still had other unpleasant duties to take care of, however. The next one took him down the corridor from the single rooms assigned to senior wing officers to the block of double cabins assigned to Gold Squadron. He halted in front of the door labeled LT. WINSTON CHANG— LT. MITCHELL LOPEZ and set down the empty cargo module he picked up on his way.

Blair touched the buzzer beside the door and stepped back. It took a few moments before it slid open. Inside, the lights were out, but a figure was sitting on one of the two narrow beds.

"Come in," Vagabond said. There was little of his usual bantering manner about him today. He squinted into the light. "Oh, Colonel. What can I do for you?"

Blair kicked the cargo module through the door and stepped inside, letting the door slide shut behind him. "Sorry to bother you, Lieutenant," he said, feeling awkward. He wished he could have faced this part of the job alone, as he had in Ralgha's quarters. "I just . . . I came to round up Vaquero's stuff. Shuttle's heading back to the *Eagle* later today, and I figured they could take the personal effects back to Torgo when they jump . . ."

"In case we don't make it," Chang finished the thought for him. He raised his voice slightly. "Lights."

The computer brought the light level up. Under the illumination, the lieutenant's expression was bleak.

"Don't borrow trouble, Vagabond," Blair said quietly. "I know how you feel . . . this mess is getting to all of us. But we've all got to get a grip. Bounce back."

"The cliche of the week," Chang said. He pointed to one of the lockers on the far wall. "That one's Vaquero's. Was Vaquero's." The Chinese pilot paused. "He was a good roommate. And a good wingman, for a kid."

Blair nodded and crossed to the locker, opening it with a security magnakey that overrode Vaquero's lock. It was crowded and untidy. Evidently Mitchell Lopez had managed to accumulate a fair number of possessions in the short time he'd been aboard Victory.

"Tell me this much, Colonel," Vagabond said from behind him. "Rumor mill says we've got a shot at the cats after all, even after *Behemoth*. Is it true?"

Blair looked at him, nodded. "Yeah. A shot . . . a pretty damned long one, but a shot."

"Good." Chang gave a curt nod. "Good. 'Cause I want a piece of the bastards."

"Are you sure? You were the one who had doubts about *Behemoth*, as I recall. And the new mission's also designed to knock out Kilrah. No ifs, ands, buts, or maybes . . ."

Vagabond shrugged. "I'm past caring about it now, Colonel. Damn it, the kid didn't have to die like that. He was going to retire, open his cantina. He had it all planned out, and that bastard Hobbes snuffed him out. And Cobra, too. It's one thing to lose your buddies on the firing line, but this . . . it's just wrong."

Blair fixed him with a level stare. "I hear you, Vagabond. I've been there myself, and not just this cruise, either. But you can't let it eat away at you." He pointed to the locker. "Do you know how much I hate this ritual? As his CO, I'm the one who has to send the comm to Vaquero's family . . . you know, the one that's supposed to make them feel proud of their son and the way he died. What am I supposed to tell them? That my best friend turned traitor and killed him in a sneak attack? That I might have stopped it if I hadn't been so convinced that Hobbes was one of the good guys?" He shook his head.

Vagabond shrugged and sighed. "I used to think I could keep myself apart from it, you know? Be the cool professional on duty, and the squadron clown in the rec room. But for the first time, here on *Victory*, I actually felt like I was starting to put down roots. I made friends, real friends . . . Cobra, Vaquero, Beast Jaeger. Now they're gone, and all I want is to see the end of it all . . . one way or another."

Blair didn't reply right away. Vagabond's words struck a familiar chord. "The attack on Kilrah's likely to be a one-way trip, Chang," he said at last. "It's supposed to be an all-volunteer run. I was going to encourage you to opt out of it, since you were pretty well set against bombing civilian targets. Now . . . hell, I don't have enough pilots in Gold Squadron as it is. If you really want in, I'll be glad to have you there. But if you're not sure, speak up now. So I can try to get someone else checked out on the Excalibur from one of the other outfits."

Vagabond shook his head. "Don't bother. I'm in."

"It's nice to know you can count on . . . people." Blair turned back to the locker, saw Vaquero's prized old guitar. He picked it up, ran his fingers over each string. "His family will want this, I suppose . . ." he said softly. Then, with another flash of anger, he went on. "It just isn't fair, Chang. That kid should never have been a pilot."

"But he was," Vagabond told him. "A good one, too. We're all going to miss him, before this thing is over."

Together, they emptied out the locker and packed Vaquero's gear in the cargo module. When it was done, Blair tagged it and left it outside the door for a work detail to pick up later. He fetched a second module from a storeroom nearby and headed for his last stop. He knew this one would be the most difficult of all.

Cobra had shared her quarters with Flint, and the lieutenant opened the door at Blair's signal. She saw the cargo module and nodded. "Cobra's stuff, huh?"

"Yeah." He followed her in. "Er . . . you knew her pretty well, didn't you?"

"As well as anyone, I guess," she said. "Laurel didn't make a lot of friends."

"I guess not." Blair looked away. "Fact is, I'm supposed to send her effects to her family, write a note, the usual routine. But I don't even know if she has a family. Her file was pretty thin."

"We were the only family she had," Flint said softly.

"I didn't treat her very well, for family," Blair said, looking away. "I trusted Hobbes, not her . . ."

"You had your reasons," she replied. "Blaming yourself won't change what happened . . . won't bring Cobra back, or Vaquero, either."

"Maybe you're right. I don't know any more. It seems

like every choice I've made, every turn I've taken since I came on board this ship has been wrong. I'm starting to second-guess myself on everything."

Flint hesitated a moment before responding, her look intent, searching for something in his face. "Everything? Does that mean your romance with your little grease monkey has fallen through?"

"What's that supposed to mean?" he demanded. He was still feeling bad about breaking his date with Rachel the night before, but under the circumstances he hadn't felt like seeing anyone.

She looked away. "I just thought . . . you could do a lot better, you know?"

"No, I don't know," Blair told her. "Rachel's been a good friend to me . . . more than a friend." He studied her. "I know you thought there might be something between you and me. I'm sorry if I gave you the wrong idea about how I felt."

"Just how do you feel?" she demanded.

"You've been a good friend, too, Flint. Hell, I probably owe you my life, after Delius. And under other circumstances, things might have gone further between us."

"Other circumstances . . . ?"

"Don't you get it, Flint? Rachel's not a pilot. You are. And after Angel—I just don't think I could handle getting involved with another pilot. Especially one who might end up flying on my wing." He paused. "Truth is, it isn't fair to either one of you, now. When we hit Kilrah, odds are none of us are coming back. So any romance I get into now is strictly short-term."

"Maybe that's all there is for any of us, now," Flint said quietly. "If this next fight goes against us, there won't be time left for anyone."

Blair nodded. "That's true enough. Look . . . I'm sorry. I didn't want to hurt you ."

"I'm grown up," she told him. "I can handle rejection. But I don't take kindly to losing out to some mechanic who smells like synlubes and uses grease for make-up."

He looked away, feeling helpless. "If it helps any, I doubt she and I are going anywhere, now."

Flint's look was cold. "Do what you like, flyboy," she said. "Doesn't matter to me. And like you said, this next op's probably going to be the last, right? For all of us."

"It's a volunteer mission, Flint. You don't have to fly it. Maybe you'd be better off staying with the ship."

She shook her head. "You've been telling me not to put my feelings ahead of my duty, and that's just what I'm going to do now. I will be in on the kill, all right. Just try and stop me." Flint paused. "But I'll give you a word of warning, Colonel. I may try to keep my personal feelings on a leash, but I don't make any guarantees. And it might not be such a good idea for you to pick a wingman you've just kicked in the teeth. If you take my meaning . . . sir."

Blair had no answer for that. He left Flint to pack up Cobra's gear, and headed back to his office to think.

Sometimes it was easier to face the enemy than it was to deal with the people he cared about most.

Flight Wing Rec Room, TCS Victory Freya System

The carrier made the jump from Blackmane to the Freya System, where the High Command ordered the strike force to assemble for the attack that was supposed to cover the raid on Kilrah. Through the viewport in the rec room, Blair could see a few of the ships of the Terran fleet, some close enough to recognize shapes and configurations, others so far away that they glimmered as moving lights against the starfield.

It was a powerful force, but nowhere near the size of

the fleet that had held the Kilrathi at Terra. Yet this was supposed to be Earth's decisive strike, the knockout punch that would end the war.

Blair watched the other ships, and doubted.

"You look like you could use some company," Rachel Coriolis said from behind him.

Blair turned in his chair. "Rachel . . . I thought you had the duty until seventeen hundred hours."

"This is just a break," she said. "We've still got a lot to get done before the jump to Hyperion tomorrow, so I'm grabbing a bite to eat now and then pulling a double shift." She mustered a weary smile. "So, are you going to invite a girl to sit down, or what?"

"Sure, sure," he said hurriedly. "Please. Sorry . . ."

Rachel laughed. "So, the rough, tough pilot goes to pieces under pressure." She took the seat across from him, her eyes searching his face under a worried frown. "What's the matter? Is it . . . Hobbes?"

He shook his head. "Not that . . . not really. Fact is . . . it's, well, it's us."

"Us? As in you plus me equals us?"

"Yeah. Look, Rachel, I started thinking some things over today, and I realized something. Yesterday I was all set for a nice little seduction scene. Dinner. Music. A quiet talk that could lead to . . . whatever." He looked away. "After what happened . . ."

"Hey, I understood then. I understand now. We'll still have our time together."

"Maybe it was best that we couldn't make it happen," he went on doggedly. "It might be the best thing if we don't try to push it now . . ."

"Are you backing out on me?" Her expression hovered between concern and anger. "I thought . . ."

"Look, Rachel, by this time tomorrow, God only knows where I'll be. Even if we carry out the mission, the deck's stacked against any of us coming back from Kilrah. It isn't fair to start something with you that I might not be able to finish. I wouldn't want you to have to go through what I did . . . with Angel."

"Pilots . . ." She shook her head. "They'd rather crash and burn than make a commitment. Look, Chris, I've been there, remember? I know what it's like. And I also know that if we keep putting our own lives aside because of what might happen tomorrow, eventually we'll run out of tomorrows. We'll never have anything to look back at, anything to remember except the war, just fighting and killing. I want something else to remember . . . whether it's one night, or an eternity. Don't you?"

"Do you really mean that? You want to go ahead, even knowing it might not be more than one night?"

She met his eyes and nodded. "I'd rather we had just one night together. Especially if the alternative is . . . never having any time at all."

"Your shift . . ."

"Ends at midnight. I'll skip the dinner and the music, if you'll be there for me when I come . . ."

"Midnight, then." She stood when he did, and they came together in a long, lingering kiss. "Midnight . . ."

• CHAPTER XXIX

Excalibur 300
Hyperion System

Acceleration pressed Blair into his seat as the Excalibur burst into open space. He cut in his engines and steered hard to port, toward the unseen jump point that would carry him to the enemy homeworld.

To the real Heart of the Tiger, he thought idly.

"Excalibur three-zero-zero, clear and under power," Blair said aloud. "Lancelot Flight, form on me and proceed as planned."

The other three pilots acknowledged, closing around him. Four Excalibur fighters, to attack the Imperial homeworld. It still seemed like sheer madness. But this time it was truly mankind's last chance for victory.

"Lancelot Flight, Lancelot Flight, this is Round Table," Eisen's voice crackled over the comm channel. "Good luck to you all . . . and Godspeed."

Blair didn't reply. Instead he checked his power levels, then spoke to the other pilots. "Go to cloaks . . . now!" he ordered, switching on his own cloaking system. There was no apparent effect, other than the sudden increase in the fighter's power drain. Weapons and shields were useless while the shroud concealed the craft, but detection would be nearly impossible. Already the other Excaliburs had vanished. He was all alone in an endless night.

347

He checked the range to the jump point, and asked the computer for an ETA. Ten minutes. . . .

The timing of this phase of the operation was critical. The Confed's battle fleet had jumped into the Hyperion System from nearby Freya, challenging the local Kilrathi garrison forces with a series of strike attacks by fighters and capital ships. *Victory* had remained in reserve throughout nearly a week of combat ops, keeping to the fringes of the action. The Kilrathi were given every opportunity to commit their forces to the system, and they'd pumped in enough ships to put the Terran fleet at a serious disadvantage. It was all a part of the plan, to encourage the cats to thin out their home defenses and divert attention away from Kilrah. But it had been a costly fight already, and it was likely to get worse.

Today the admiral commanding the fleet had passed the word to General Taggart aboard *Victory*. There was no guarantee that the fleet could maintain the fight for more than a few more hours. Then they would have to break off, or go down fighting. Paladin had given the orders. The attack was on at last.

The carrier edged toward the jump point, seemingly to reinforce the Terran battlegroup built around the *Hermes* and the *Invincible* which had been heavily engaged in the area for several hours. According to intelligence reports, the Kilrathi were unaware of the Terran survey work done around Hyperion, and thus thought the Confederation knew nothing of the Kilrah jump point. But they had to be careful to keep from tipping their hands too soon.

As it was, they nearly ran into trouble when a Kilrathi destroyer escort left the enemy fleet on course for the jump point, but Eisen turned the situation to their advantage by pretending to pursue the enemy ship. That ship had passed through the jump point less than half an hour ago, and that transjump became the main reason for Blair's present preoccupation with the ticking countdown clock.

If the escort withdrew to Kilrah to summon additional reinforcements, the Terrans had to hope nothing else was waiting close to the jump point on the other side. Otherwise they might be blundering into trouble before the mission was even fairly under way.

He checked the ETA again. Three minutes . . .

Audience Hall, KIS Hvar'kann
Kilrah System

"Message from the escort *Ghordax*, Lord Prince. From the fleet at Hyperion."

Thrakhath allowed his throne to swivel past the viewscreen he was contemplating so he could look down on Melek. "What is their report?"

"The battle proceeds well, Lord Prince," Melek said, bowing. "The Terrans cannot last long."

"So there is no further need for reinforcements, then?"

"No, Lord Prince. None."

"Good," Thrakhath said. "I do not wish to further disrupt our buildup. Is there any word from the Logistics Masters on the timetable for launching the Grand Fleet?"

"Six eights of hours, Lord Prince. The bombardment missiles will be fully loaded by then, and the fleet can break orbit any time after that."

"Excellent. Then we will soon be on our way to the Terran homeworld. This time they shall not turn us back." Thrakhath turned his throne again, gesturing to the screen. It showed a view of Kilrah's orbital yards, with capital ships grouped around orbital depots and swarms of smaller craft moving among them, preparing the Grand Fleet for the last great campaign. "Victory, Melek," the prince continued. "It smells sweet, does it not?"

"Yes, Lord Prince," Melek replied dutifully.

"Still, there is one thing missing," Thrakhath went on, almost to himself. "I can only hope for one last chance to meet the Heart of the Tiger in battle. It will make our triumph all the more complete . . ."

Thrakhath continued to study the viewscreen, the light of victory in his eyes.

Excalibur 300
Kilrah System

Jumpshock made Blair sluggish, but he forcing his body to obey his will, he switched power from the transjump drive to the cloaking device. Powering up his engines, he steered the fighter out of the jump point, setting course inward, toward the Kilrathi homeworld.

On his sensor screen, another blip flickered into existence astern, then faded a few moments later. That was Vagabond, acting as wingman on the mission. Maniac and Flint followed in succession, apparently without being noticed. There were no Kilrathi ships in the immediate area, though the escort they had trailed in the Hyperion System was at the very edge of detection range, also on course toward Kilrah. Hopefully, if they spotted anything suspicious at all they wouldn't be able to react until the cloaked Terran ships were well clear of the area.

Blair's comm monitor came alive with an image of Paladin. The old warrior had warned him that the computers aboard all four fighters would trigger periodic briefings as they headed in toward their goal. This tape, for Blair, had been personalized. Taggart smiled out at him. "Laddie, we've covered this ground backwards and forwards waiting for the mission to launch, but I'll give you the straight dope one more time now. Since you're seeing this, you've made the jump successfully, and you're in the Kilrathi System now." The screen changed to show a chart of the Kilrah star system, with navpoints glowing brightly. "Your first job, now that you're through, is tae bring your fighters in tae the first asteroid depot. There you'll find a stock of fuel, spares, and missiles, everything you'll need tae carry you all the way in tae the outer moon of Kilrah." The first depot faded, and another, more distant asteroid was indicated. "Should ye find the first position compromised, laddie, there is a second choice. But remember, if ye canna keep one depot in reserve, there'll nae be enough fuel in your birds tae get you through the jump point after the mission's done. The second depot is supposed to be for the trip back . . . but I ken well you'll do what ye have tae if the mission depends upon it."

Paladin's face appeared on the screen again. "Good luck, laddie. You'll need it."

The screen went blank.

Blair set his course for the nearer depot, knowing that the others would be doing the same. They were maintaining absolute comm silence, hoping to avoid any detection by the Kilrathi. Surprise was their only hope . . . surprise, sheer flying skill, and pure, unadulterated good luck.

He hoped it would be enough.

Excalibur 302
Kilrah System

A warning alarm beeped for attention, and Lieutenant Winston Chang checked his sensor board. There was something ahead, a powered target that glowed amber on his screen as the computer tried to identify it as friend or foe. A moment later, it changed to a reddish orange. An enemy, then . . . no, two enemies, a pair of Darket fighters, evidently making a routine patrol sweep.

Vagabond muttered an old Chinese curse under his breath and cut power to his engines. The two Darket were dead ahead, and only a few hundred kilometers beyond lay the large asteroid where the first depot was established. In order to reach their destination, transmitters aboard the Excaliburs were programmed to send out short-burst signals to activate the locator transponders in the depot. As long as those two Darket were in the neighborhood, the Terrans were stuck. The depot might as well be around Sirius.

Meanwhile, there was another danger. If the Kilrathi got too close, they would spot the Terran ships, cloaked or not.

The two light fighters were making a slow, graceful turn. Vagabond warily watched them, alert for any signs of their detecting the location of one of the Terran fighters. He wondered about the others. Their original tight formation had become tenuous en route to the asteroid, and he was no longer sure where any of his comrades might be.

The Darket were going to pass close to him . . . too close. Vagabond engaged his engines again and started to bank away, but it was too late. Suddenly the two Kilrathi ships were picking up speed, swinging around, pointed directly at him. Cloaked, he had no shields. A few shots would be enough to knock him out.

He cut the cloak, shunting power to the weapons and shield generators and cutting back on his own course with a sharp pull on the steering yoke. Maybe if he disposed of these two fast enough there would be no time for them to summon help.

One of the Darket opened fire just as the green light on his shield status display appeared. Blasters pounded at the shields, but to little effect. He returned fire with blasters and a pair of heat-seekers, closing the range fast. The Darket's shields crumbled beneath the heavy pounding, and a moment later his beams bored through armor and set off the missiles slung under the Kilrathi craft's wings. He was close enough now to actually be caught in the fireball, and the energy release and spinning debris overloaded his own shielding.

In that moment, the second Darket engaged. He didn't have to look at the damage control panel to know that he was losing armor around his reactor. Desperately, Vagabond tried to dodge, but the controls were sluggish.

He broke comm silence. "I can't shake him! I'm going up." And just before the Darket fired again, he managed to add a final plea. "Don't give up, Colonel. You've got to take them down . . . for all of us who didn't make it!"

He slammed the switch to trigger his ejection system, praying he wasn't already too late.

Excalibur 300
Kilrah System

Blair saw Vagabond's Excalibur go up in flames of fury. He let out a cry of rage and grief. The Chinese pilot's last words echoed in his mind, and he made a grim, silent vow that Chang's last effort wouldn't be in vain.

Then Maniac's fighter appeared on his sensors, swooping in from beyond the expanding fireball. Blair spotted the Excalibur a moment later as Maniac opened fire, battering through the Darket's shields. The fighter exploded.

His satisfaction was short-lived, though. Flint broke comm silence a moment later. "We've got trouble, boys," she said. "Heading our way."

Two more Darket appeared from beyond the bulk of the asteroid, moving slowly but gathering speed as they came. Blair's comm monitor picked up a transmission from one of them. They were summoning help.

"Lancelot Flight, break off action," he ordered sharply. "Recloak and head for the backup rendezvous."

It galled him to run, but they didn't have much choice. Though the Excaliburs could deal with these two fighters

easily enough, they couldn't count on being able to refuel
and rearm at this depot before a swarm of additional
Kilrathi ships turned up. A thorough search of the asteroid
would turn up the depot, and if they were caught inside
the result would be disastrous.

He hit his afterburners and punched in the new course.
Paladin's warning ran through his mind. With this depot
compromised and the secondary one depleted, the
Terrans were on a one-way trip to Kilrah.

If they made it that far.

Audience Hall, KIS Hvar'kann
Kilrah System

The Audience Hall was empty except for the Crown
Prince, brooding on his throne. Melek hastened to the
foot of the dais, bowing low. Thrakhath raised his head
at the retainer's approach.

"I left orders that I was not to be disturbed," the Prince
rumbled.

"An urgent message, Lord Prince," Melek told him.
"One of our patrols reported engaging Terran fighters.
Here in our own system . . . and they escaped using cloak
technology."

"Ape ships . . . here?" Thrakhath straightened, eyes
flashing with anger. "Cloaked . . . spies, seeking word
of our fleet, then."

"We cannot say, Lord Prince," Melek said. "But . . .
we intercepted one exchange of messages between them.
And our computers have identified the voice of the
apparent leader." He paused. "It was . . . the one named
Blair. The Heart of the Tiger."

"Him . . ." Thrakhath stood slowly, drawing himself
to his full height. "That one would not come on a mere
spy mission. Could it be . . . could the Terrans be planning
a strike? Perhaps they plan to attack our fleet while it is

still taking on armaments . . . to break up our attack before we can leave orbit."

"It is possible, Lord Prince. But we cannot be sure." Melek hesitated. "The cruiser *Kheerakh* discovered a hidden supply cache in an asteroid near where the encounter took place . . . but I fear the fools destroyed it by bombardment rather than investigating."

"I trust *Kheerakh* has a new captain now?"

"Yes, Lord Prince. One who is . . . less impulsive."

"We must look to our defenses, Melek. I do not believe the Terrans can mount a serious threat, but even a few shipkiller missiles released into the fleet while it is bunched up would be an . . . annoying setback. Order fighter patrols around the orbital yards doubled." Thrakhath paused. "And have my personal ship and squadron readied to launch on short notice. If the Heart of the Tiger has come, I mean to take him myself."

Melek bowed again. "As you order, Lord Prince." He backed away, leaving Thrakhath alone in the empty hall.

It seemed the apes were far more resilient than the Emperor's grandson had ever realized. Melek wondered what other surprises the Terrans might have in store.

Covert Ops Depot #3
Kilrah System

They had come farther than Blair ever dared to hope they would. The three Excaliburs located the backup depot and set down long enough to refuel and replace the missiles Maniac used to destroy the Darket that took out Vagabond. From there, they pushed into the Kilrah System, all the way to the outer moon of the Kilrathi homeworld itself, and the last Terran depot.

Like the first station, this depot was a crude chamber carved out of solid rock with mining lasers. A force field curtain allowed the interior to be pressurized, so Blair and his two pilots worked unencumbered by bulky pressure gear. But the facilities were primitive, and the work was difficult enough even so. The near-weightless conditions didn't help matters much, either. Though the equipment had virtually no weight, it retained its full mass, and none of the three were accustomed to working under such conditions. Care and caution were required at a time when every instinct cried out for them to hurry, to finish the job and get back into space as quickly as possible. It made for frayed nerves.

Nonetheless, they did the work, exchanging the missiles slung under Blair's Excalibur for one of the two massive Temblor Bombs stowed in the depot. He decided against loading the second one onto a different fighter. Originally, he hoped to have two fighters fitted with bombs, each with a fully-armed escort, but Vagabond's death changed his plans. A fighter without missiles wasn't worth much in a dogfight, and one escort couldn't hope to cover two bombers at once. If this run failed—and anyone survived to return to the depot—they could try again later, perhaps. But for now Blair figured two fighters flying cover gave him that much more of a chance to make the bombing run successful.

With the bomb loaded, they topped off their fuel tanks and ran a final test of their on-board systems.

"Do you really think this is going to work?" Flint asked as they were finishing. "Or are we just going through the motions?"

"It'll work," Blair said. "We have to make it work." He was still thinking about Vagabond's last transmission. So many people died to get them here, starting with Angel. Blair was determined to make their sacrifices count.

"I'd be a damned sight happier if Vagabond was still with us," Marshall said. "He wasn't very flashy in the cockpit, but he was steady. And we'll be missing him soon enough, I bet."

"I already miss him," Blair growled. "And not just because he was a good wingman." He caught sight of the sheepish look on Maniac's face. "Look . . . we'll all miss him, the way we miss every single one of the others who bought it. I read somewhere that the darkest times are supposed to bring out the best in people." Blair looked away. "I don't know about that. All I do know is this: we've got to finish the job. Because if we don't, there's nobody else to pick up and carry on after us. So . . . give me everything you've got. That's all I can ask."

He turned away and shoved a chip cartridge into the portable computer they used for their tests. The oversized monitor screen came on, and Paladin looked down at the three with a serious expression.

"This is the final briefing, laddie," Taggart's recorded image told them. "By now you've finished loading the T-Bomb, and you're ready for the final phase of the mission. I pray to God you can carry it out. If you canna do it, I dinna ken who can."

Paladin was replaced by a satellite photo showing part of the surface of Kilrah, a long, jagged canyon in the middle of rocky desert land. "You are looking at your target, a deep natural canyon that goes down nearly a mile. It was formed by one of the most active fault lines on the planet." A computer-generated map replaced the photo image. "If our calculations are correct, this point, here, near the northern end of the canyon, is critical. Three faults come together at this one point, and if the Temblor Bomb is detonated there it should set up a chain reaction of quakes that will devastate Kilrah."

Taggart appeared again. "Lay it in there sweet and easy, laddie. The exact coordinates are already preprogrammed in your flight computers. To make the run, though, you'll have to descend into the atmosphere, into the canyon itself, and drop the bomb on the target. Because you'll need your shields to handle a high-speed atmospheric

insertion, you'll have tae go in the last stretch without
your cloaks. It'll be dangerous . . . but if you move fast
and hit hard, you'll have a chance."

The general paused, and Blair had the feeling his old
eyes were looking right out of the screen at him. "It's
almost over, laddie. You and your people are the best
for the job, and I know you'll do Terra proud. You'll be
in my prayers, all of you. Good luck."

The screen went blank, and Blair turned back to the
others. "All right, time to saddle up. We've got a message
to deliver to the Emperor, and the clock is ticking."

Excalibur 300
Kilrah System

Kilrah was a dirty orange-brown sphere that filled his
field of vision, swelling visibly as the Terran fighters
pressed forward at full thrust. Blair ran his eyes over
his instrument board, checking over all systems one more
time and praying nothing would go wrong now that the
final attack was so near.

His hull temperature gauges were just beginning to
register the friction of the tenuous upper atmosphere.
Soon he would have to switch to shields or drastically
cut his rate of descent. Blair waited until the cockpit
was noticeably hot, until the outer hull was beginning
to glow faintly, before he finally cut the cloak and activated
the shield generators.

Screaming through the thickening atmosphere under
the dull light of Kilrah's red-orange sun, three Terran
fighters plummeted downward toward a final rendezvous
with death.

• CHAPTER XXX

Audience Hall, KIS Hvar'kann
Kilrah System

"Lord Prince, the ground-based defenses have picke up three intruders. Terran fighters matching the descr ption of those engaged yesterday."

Thrakhath rose from his throne and stepped down from the dais. "The ground defenses?" he demanded. "Is every one of my ship captains blind, then?"

"No, Lord Prince," Melek said, voice quavering a little. "But the Terrans . . . are entering the atmosphere. They came out of cloak almost directly below our present orbit, descending at high speed."

"Scramble all available interceptors, Melek," Thrakhath commanded, starting toward the door. "Including my own squadron. We will show them they cannot defile the Homeworld with impunity!"

Excalibur 300
Kilrah

"Eighty kilometers up . . . two hundred ten kilometers to target," Blair said over the comm channel. There was no need for comm silence now. The Kilrathi had surely detected the Terran fighters. "Maniac, you take point. Open me a path. And you watch my tail, Flint. They're going to throw everything they can our way."

"*Affirmative*," Flint replied.

"*You got it*," Marshall chimed in a moment later. His fighter swept past Blair's to take the lead.

He was hardly in position before the first targets appeared ahead. "We got bogies," Blair said. "They look like atmospheric craft—ground-based interceptors."

"*Piece of cake*," Maniac told him. The Excalibur's afterburners cut in, and Marshall surged ahead, his blasters beginning to fire as he closed in on the enemy aircraft.

Conventional atmospheric fighters weren't as well-equipped as space fighters, but they were fast and maneuverable in their own element. Marshall's guns cut a swath through the leading fighters, but the others rolled out and then swung inward from either flank, unleashing a massive bombardment. Caught in a crossfire from four aircraft at once, Maniac rolled left to concentrate on one threat. Blair banked sharply right and opened fire on the remaining pair. His blasters raked across the nearer target, which came apart under the savage force of the beams.

The second fighter looped up, turning away from the battle and accelerating fast. Evidently the pilot had decided against a glorious death today . . .

"*There's more of the bastards up ahead, Colonel*," Marshall reported as he finished off his last opponent and swung back into formation. "*Looks like we're not welcome around here.*"

"As long as they're just conventional aircraft, they shouldn't be much trouble," Blair said. "Stay focused, though. You can bet they'll bring in the big guns soon enough . . ."

"*Targets! Targets! Targets!*" Flint chanted. "*I've got six . . . eight targets on my board. Coming in from orbit!*"

They weren't showing on Blair's sensors yet, so they were still at extreme range. "Watch 'em, Flint," he ordered. A whole squadron of space-based fighters would be a lot harder to handle than the aircraft ahead, but they'd be hard-pressed to close the range as long as the Terrans could keep moving.

The second wave of interceptors closed in from below, eight high-performance jet aircraft in a tight formation. They broke just as Maniac opened fire, scattering, curving in on the Terrans and engaging with missiles and beam weapons. Once again Maniac and Blair had to engage them, and by the time the attackers had been destroyed or forced to flee Blair realized what the enemy strategy was. Each time the Terrans got caught in a dogfight, however short, the orbital fighters closed the range a little more . . .

Excalibur 303
Kilrah

A near miss by a missile buffeted her fighter, and Lieutenant Robin Peters had to fight her steering yoke to maintain control. It had been years since she'd last had to fight a battle in a planetary atmosphere, where all the rules were different from those she was used to in deep space fighting. Shock waves carried . . . and shields were weakened by the energy they absorbed from friction in high-speed maneuvers.

"They're firing," Flint reported. "One Vaktoth . . . and a Bloodfang, both of them in combat range. More Vaktoth coming up fast behind them."

"*Bloodfang . . . Thrakhath's personal fighter.*" Blair's voice was grim. "*Damn it all!*"

She nodded. Intelligence reports on the Prince's personal fighter, code-named Bloodfang by the Confederation, suggested it would be one hell of a tough opponent. "Don't know if I can take the bastard, skipper," she said. "You have any bright ideas?"

"*Go to afterburners,*" Blair ordered. "*Let's see if we can outrun them.*"

She kicked in the extra power, but the Vaktoth matched her . . . continued closing the range. Another missile detonated, even closer this time. "No joy, skipper," she said. "Looks like there's going to be a fight . . ."

Kilrathi blaster fire probed at her rear shields, sapping the power levels with each hit. Cursing, she pulled up in a sharp loop and opened fire on one of her two pursuers with blasters and a spread of four missiles. The two fighters were having as much trouble fighting in atmosphere as she was, and the weakened forward shields of her target went down under the fury of her attack. The Vaktoth exploded in a shower of debris, and Flint let out a whoop of triumph.

It died on her lips as the Bloodfang opened fire. She tried to roll out, but blasters pounded at her shields. They were going down . . . and a pair of heat seekers were already on the way.

"He's got me, skipper!" she called. "Can't . . . evade. Don't forget . . . I could have loved—"

She didn't live to finish the sentence.

Excalibur 300
Kilrah

"Flint!" Blair shouted, but it was too late. The rearmost Excalibur went up in a dazzling fireball, and Robin Peters was gone.

A new voice crackled in his headphones. "*So it shall be with you as well, Heart of the Tiger.*" He recognized the harsh, sibilant voice. Thrakhath . . . "*You are foolhardy, to venture with so few against my Homeworld. Once before you lacked the courage to fight me. This time, you shall not escape. Welcome, Heart of the Tiger, to Kilrah . . . and to your death!*"

"*The canyon's in sight ahead, Colonel,*" Marshall reported. "*I'll drop back and have the next dance. You get in there and do your stuff!*"

Blair hesitated. Thrakhath had challenged him once again . . . and he couldn't stand and fight. It took every bit of his self-control to grit his teeth and acknowledge Marshall's call.

Maniac executed a tight Immelman loop, swinging up and around to head back toward the on-coming Kilrathi fighters. Thrakhath's Bloodfang was still well in the lead, but there were two others closing fast.

Blair saw the canyon ahead, a long, jagged scar on the surface of Kilrah. His target was there, at the far end of the deep trench . . .

"*Watch your tail, Colonel!*" Maniac called suddenly. "*Don't know if I can cover you!*"

His sensor board told the story. Thrakhath had ignored Maniac's Excalibur entirely, refusing to be drawn into a dogfight. Instead he had plunged past Marshall, and the two trailing Vaktoth were all over the Terran pilot now. Blair cursed aloud. Maniac couldn't last long against two heavy fighters . . .

And his underarmed Excalibur was no match for Thrakhath's Bloodfang.

He swung sharply left, away from the canyon, as the Kilrathi prince opened fire. The blaster shots went wide, but the Bloodfang followed his turn, still clinging stubbornly to his tail. All the advantages lay with Thrakhath now.

Blair was only dimly aware of the explosion higher up and off to his right. His monitor told him it was one of the Vaktoth facing Maniac. Somehow Marshall had managed to savage one of his foes, but the other was still pressing hard. For the moment Blair couldn't afford to think about him, though. He cut in full afterburners and tried to climb up and out of range of Thrakhath's fighter. A Kilrathi missile exploded against his rear shields, sending the power levels fluctuating wildly.

And still Thrakhath held on behind him.

"*Heads up, Colonel! Incoming!*" Maniac's call was loud and almost exultant. Marshall had swung away from his second opponent and was diving down on Thrakhath, heedless of the Vaktoth behind him slashing at his shields with bolt after bolt of raw energy.

Marshall released two missiles, then two more, holding steady on his target and refusing to be drawn off by the dire threat behind him.

"*Shields are failing,*" he said as he released the missiles, his voice almost matter of fact now. "*Looks like you're on your own now, Colonel. For what it's worth, I'm proud I flew with you . . .*"

And then his fighter was gone, too, an expanding cloud of flame and smoke and whirling debris. Blair thought he caught a glimpse of the Excalibur's escape pod boosting clear of the explosion, straining to reach orbital velocity, but he wasn't sure. And even if Maniac had somehow managed to survive that blast, he wouldn't be playing any further part in *this* battle.

Blair was alone.

He threw the Excalibur into a tight turn to port and opened fire with his blasters just as Marshall's first two missiles detonated against Thrakhath's shields. The Bloodfang passed close beside Blair's craft, and he maintained his tight turn to stay lined up on the Kilrathi fighter. The other missiles struck the Prince's rear shields, and Blair squeezed the trigger again. Beams tore through the weakened shields, chopping through armor.

"*Curse you, ape!*" Thrakhath snarled. "*You have won today, Heart of the Tiger. But it will not bring back your mate . . . and it will not save your kind from the vengeance of the Empire. This I swear!*"

Explosions tore through the Bloodfang, and it seemed

to stagger in mid-air before plunging downward. Blair watched as Thrakhath fought to maintain control, saw the nose just start to come up as the Prince managed one last masterful maneuver. But it was too late. The Bloodfang ploughed into the red-lit desert floor, erupting in fire and thunder.

There were still several fighters above Blair, but they seemed stunned by the loss of their leader. He turned his fighter back toward the canyon and opened up his throttles. Perhaps there was just time to start his run before the Kilrathi recovered . . .

He dropped down into the steep-sided, twisting gorge. It took all his skill to weave through that narrow gash in the desert. His HUD reeled off the range to the preprogrammed drop coordinates, and Blair's thumb grew tense hovering over the switch that would release the Temblor Bomb from the belly of his fighter.

A part of him recoiled from what he had to do. The destruction of an entire planet, warriors and civilians alike. Once he would never even have considered making this desperate gambler's last throw. What had led to this moment, then? Was it just a thirst for vengeance? Thrakhath's death had left him feeling curiously empty of feeling, as if all his hate after Angel's death had been for nothing. It had been the same with Hobbes. In the end, revenge was a sterile thing. He could slaughter every Kilrathi, here and in the farthest reaches of the Empire, and the killing would never change the facts. Angel and Cobra and Vaquero and all the others would still be dead, and his life would still be empty.

He felt as if they were all there in his mind. Vagabond . . . Flint . . . even Maniac, who in the end had risen above their long rivalry and given his life so that Blair could finish the mission. But in the long run, he knew it was wrong to use that bomb in the name of those who had died.

His range indicator continued to count down . . .

Blair thought of the ones who *hadn't* died. Paladin and Eisen, Admiral Tolwyn and his nephew. Rachel Coriolis, who had accepted the fact that he might never come back and still dared to love him. *They* were the ones who counted. And if the War went on, they would ultimately pay the same price as all the ones who had gone before. He pictured *Victory* broken and shattered as he had last seen *Concordia*, imagined plagues spreading across Terra as they had spread on Locanda Four. It was war to the knife with the Kilrathi.

Kill or be killed. Not for revenge. Not for hate. But for simple survival of the human species.

He gritted his teeth and watched the range tick down. The target was coming up fast. It was now or never . . .

His thumb stabbed down on the release, and as the bomb dropped away he jerked hard back on the steering yoke and cut in his afterburners. The Excalibur climbed fast, the atmosphere screaming past as the fighter accelerated. A Vaktoth had followed him into the canyon and opened fire as Blair pulled up. The Kilrathi pilot followed, but at that moment the Temblor Bomb went off, and the shock wave threw the Imperial craft against the side of the narrow trench. The fireball was lost in the greater blast of the bomb.

He had to wrestle with his own controls as the blast battered at his Excalibur. The rear shields failed, and Blair thought he could feel the impact of bits of debris against the tail section of the fighter. He had no way of telling how much damage he took, but the controls were feeling heavy and sluggish under his hands as he continued his steep climb, clawing for the safety of open space.

Behind and below him, the force of the Temblor Bomb triggered a quake in one of the major fault lines. The effects spread, and spread again, until the entire canyon was trembling with the force of a seismic event of unparalleled ferocity.

Blair didn't see the effects of the bomb. It took time for the first quakes to trigger subsidiary effects, radiating outward through all the interconnected fault lines. The Excalibur had already reached orbit by the time the quakes became planet-wide, collapsing Kilrathi-made buildings and structures within the major quake zones. The Imperial Palace was one of the first to suffer, as the entire massive edifice caved in on itself, crushing the Emperor and his court before they had a chance to react to the violence consuming their world.

The ground was heaving even in regions far from the fault lines now, as the pent-up energy of the entire world's tectonic stresses was all released at once. Dust clouds rose into the atmosphere, huge rents opened up in the crust of the planet. As Blair finally cut his engines and looked down at the planet, it was to see Kilrah disfigured by angry orange gashes spreading across the face of the globe. The Kilrathi homeworld was coming apart before his eyes . . .

And then it happened. Overcome by the awful forces set free by the Temblor Bomb, the planet's core exploded, hurtling huge chunks of the mantle and crust outward. Vast planetoids tore through the orbital yards, smashing the assembled might of the Kilrathi Grand Fleet. Only a few ships, those under power and able to maneuver, escaped the death of the Homeworld.

Blair managed to steer clear of the largest of the debris, but his Excalibur was battered by smaller fragments. As Kilrah came apart, spreading out into a cloud of drifting asteroids, the fighter's engines finally failed. He was drifting free now . . . trapped in the doomed system.

Christopher Blair sagged back in his acceleration couch,

closing his eyes. He was exhausted, drained of anger and fear and hope alike. He knew he would die here, along with the planet and the empire his bomb had brought down.

Barely conscious, Blair didn't see the Kilrathi carrier that edged through the whirling debris toward his drifting fighter. Tractor beams lanced out to seize the Excalibur and pull it down toward the flight deck. He realized, too late, that his death would not be as quick and easy as he had hoped. He would, after all, face the enemy one more time.

Audience Hall, KIS Hvar'kann
Kilrah System

Kilrathi guards in the elaborate harness of the Imperial Guard hauled Blair from the cockpit of his battered Excalibur and used gunbutts and nerve prods to herd him through a maze of dim-lit corridors. Still barely recovered from the beating his ship had taken, staggering with exhaustion, Blair still tried to force himself to remain stiffly upright. He remembered the last images of Angel, the pride she'd conveyed even after torture and imprisonment. The least he could do was to emulate her now.

They brought him into the open expanse of the audience chamber, shoving him forward until he stood before the raised dais that dominated one end. A stocky, massive Kilrathi figure stood beside the throne, regarding him with dark, hooded eyes that gave away nothing.

He was vaguely aware of other Kilrathi warriors in the hall, hidden in the shadows, hissing their hatred, but his full attention was focused on this one dominating figure.

"The Heart of the Tiger," the Kilrathi said in heavily-accented English, sounding like a judge about to deliver a verdict. "I am Melek. Prince Thrakhath was my master."

Blair remained silent, staring into those dark pools that were Melek's eyes.

"In my bones, I wish to kill you . . ." Melek let the words hang in the chamber. From the shadows, there was muttered agreement, sibilant curses.

"Do it, then," Blair said. "Get it over with. It won't bring back your world."

"And what is the Race without the Homeworld?" Melek asked. "Nothing . . . dust in the wind." He paused. "You have defeated us, Heart of the Tiger. Brought down the Empire with one blow. Thrakhath was a fool to discount what you Terrans could achieve, but he and his accursed grandfather have both paid the price for that folly."

Blair squinted up at him, a faint hope stirring within. He hardly dared fan it, for fear it would be false.

"But you Terrans have committed your own folly, this day," Melek went on. "For now the Empire will fall . . . and the enemies who harassed our outer marches will now have nothing to stand between them and your Confederation. They have a power that even Thrakhath was wary of. Do you Terrans, who barely held against us, have the strength to face them when they come?"

Blair found his voice again. "If we're attacked, we'll fight back," he said. "As we did with you."

Melek stepped down from the dais, his face only inches from Blair's. "With the Homeworld gone and the Emperor dead, the rest of the Empire will fall apart. There will be civil war, factions fighting for power, subject races throwing off our rule. Chaos. And enemies waiting to exploit our weakness . . ." He lowered his voice, until Blair had to strain to hear the words. "Perhaps the only hope for either of our races is to face the future together. The Kilrathi Race has become too corrupt, slaves to blood lust and the evils brought by too much power. We have paid a heavy price . . ."

He stepped back and raised his voice again. "Killing the Heart of the Tiger, the one warrior great enough to humble the Empire, will bring me no honor." Melek looked at Blair for a long moment, as if struggling for the will to go on. "Your claws are at our throats. Would your people accept our . . . surrender? The Race cannot be allowed to die, even it means placing our fate in the hands of our enemies."

Blair nodded slowly. "Peace is what we both need now. If you can end this war, I think you'll find we won't demand more than you're willing to give." He paused. "And maybe one day, when the War is over and the hate is past, you and I will be able to meet . . . as friends."

"Friends . . ." Melek seemed to ponder the idea. "Perhaps it is possible. Will you carry our offer to your superiors? To help us put an end to the fighting?"

Blair nodded, the effort almost more than he could manage. As the fear and the adrenaline both ebbed away, he could feel the fatigue sapping his strength. "I'll do it," he said. "*We'll* do it . . ."

Then blackness took him. He never felt himself hit the smooth, unyielding deck below him.

• EPILOGUE

Shuttle Ciudad de Buenos Aires
Terra System

"Our top story is the historic news from the Torgo System, where delegates from the Kilrathi Empire signed a peace treaty to put an end to the war . . ."

On the newspad monitor screen, the view showed the interior of the huge auditorium at Sector HQ. There was a large audience, mostly uniformed members of the Confed Armed Forces, gathered around a raised stage beneath the transparent dome. The ceremony took place at night, and a thousand stars blazed brightly above the delegates.

Blair noted Paladin prominently seated among the Terran representatives, and near him was Admiral Tolwyn. The court of inquiry found the admiral blameless in the loss of the *Behemoth*, and he had returned to active service just in time to be a part of the protracted negotiations. Blair thought it was fitting, somehow, that Tolwyn played a role in the final triumph. Though he never agreed with the man's style or motivations, Admiral Geoff Tolwyn was a central figure in the Confederation resistance throughout the war, and it was only right that he should see it through to the very end. His nephew, Kevin, was also among the host of aides and assistants, and Eisen's dark, craggy features were visible at the table as well. Among the Kilrathi, the only one Blair recognized

371

was Melek, but the ornamentation of the other Imperial delegates made it plain that they represented a cross-section of important surviving nobles and military leaders.

Barbara Miles continued her voice-over report. "Following the incredible raid which led to the destruction of the Imperial homeworld, Kilrah, the Kilrathi decision to sue for peace was greeted with excited celebrations throughout human space. After months of peace talks deliberating a final settlement, the initial cease-fire was finally converted to a lasting peace through the Kilrathi acceptance of the Treaty of Torgo."

The view switched back to a head-and-shoulder shot of Barbara Miles. "TNC attempted to contact the pilot who carried out the Kilrah raid for his reaction to the peace treaty, but Colonel Christopher Blair was unavailable for comment. We will have further details on the signing of the peace treaty later in this Infoburst . . ."

Blair switched off the newspad and glanced out the port beside him. The shuttle began its descent now, crossing the terminator just as the dawning sun lit below the curved blue and white arc of the planet.

Earth . . .

He had dedicated his entire adult life to defending her, and now the long battle was over. And despite Melek's fears of another alien empire beyond the Kilrathi sphere threatening future wars, Blair knew his own days as a warrior were over. After a well-deserved period of leave, he was slated to go on the inactive list so that he could begin a new career, serving with the diplomatic staff that would soon begin work turning the abstract peace treaty with the Empire into solid, working reality. Henceforth Christopher Blair would be a warrior in the cause of peace, fighting a new kind of battle to ensure that all of his fallen comrades—Angel and Flint, Vaquero and Hunter and Iceman, Cobra and Flash and all the rest, even Hobbes—had not died in vain.

It was a daunting challenge, but Blair would not be facing it alone.

She hurried down the aisle as the seatbelt warnings flashed on the forward bulkhead. Blair met her eyes, and they shared a smile.

"What would you like to do first, after we're down?" he asked, strapping her in.

Rachel Coriolis took his hand in hers. "I'd like to take a long walk along the seashore," she said, "with wet sand between my toes . . . and no bulkheads or metal decks or spare parts in sight."

"Sounds good to me," Blair told her, settling into his seat and closing his eyes. The others were all still there, in his mind, but no longer demanding or clamoring. They—and he—had finally discovered peace.

GRAND ADVENTURE
IN GAME-BASED UNIVERSES

With these exciting novels set
in bestselling game universes,
Baen brings you synchronicity at its
best. We believe that familiarity with
either the novel or the game will
intensify enjoyment of the other.
All novels are the only authorized
fiction based on these games and
are published by permission.

THE BARD'S TALE™

Join the Dark Elf Naitachal and his apprentices in bardic
magic as they explore the mysteries of the world of
The Bard's Tale.

Castle of Deception   0-671-72125-9 ♦ $5.99 ☐
Mercedes Lackey & Josepha Sherman

Fortress of Frost and Fire   0-671-72162-3 ♦ $5.99 ☐
Mercedes Lackey & Ru Emerson

Prison of Souls   0-671-72193-3 ♦ $5.99 ☐
Mercedes Lackey & Mark Shepherd

The Chaos Gate   0-671-87597-3 ♦ $5.99 ☐
Josepha Sherman

(continued)

DAVID WEBER

Honor Harrington (cont.):

Field of Dishonor

Honor goes home to Manticore—and fights for her life on a battlefield she never trained for, in a private war that offers just two choices: death—or a "victory" that can end only in dishonor and the loss of all she loves....

Other novels by DAVID WEBER:

Mutineers' Moon

"...a good story...reminds me of 1950s Heinlein..."
—*BMP Bulletin*

Armageddon Inheritance

Sequel to *Mutineers' Moon*.

Path of the Fury

"Excellent...a thinking person's Terminator."
—*Kliatt*

Oath of Swords

An epic fantasy.

with STEVE WHITE:

Insurrection
Crusade

Novels set in the world of the Starfire ™ game system.

And don't miss Steve White's solo novels,
The Disinherited and Legacy!

continued 👉

DAVID WEBER

On Basilisk Station
0-671-72163-1 ✦ $5.99 ☐

Honor of the Queen
0-671-72172-0 ✦ $5.99 ☐

The Short Victorious War
0-671-87596-5 ✦ $5.99 ☐

Field of Dishonor
0-671-87624-4 ✦ $5.99 ☐

Mutineers' Moon
0-671-72085-6 ✦ $5.99 ☐

Armageddon Inheritance
0-671-72197-6 ✦ $4.99 ☐

Path of the Fury
0-671-72147-X ✦ $5.99 ☐

Oath of Swords
0-671-87642-2 ✦ $5.99 ☐

Insurrection
0-671-72024-4 ✦ $5.99 ☐

Crusade
0-671-72111-9 ✦ $4.99 ☐

If not available through your local bookstore fill out this coupon and send a check or money order for the cover price(s) to Baen Books, Dept. BA, P.O. Box 1403, Riverdale, NY 10471. Delivery can take up to ten weeks.

NAME: _____

ADDRESS: _____

_____

I have enclosed a check or money order in the amount of $ _____